TEEN
MAD

01/18/23

Madden, Tobias

Take a bow, Noah Mitchell

TAKE A BOW, NOAH MITCHELL

TAKE A BOW, NOAH MITCHELL

TOBIAS MADDEN

PAGE STREET
PUBLISHING CO.

PAGE STREET
PUBLISHING CO.

First published in 2023 by
Page Street Publishing Co.
27 Congress Street, Suite 1151
Salem, MA 01970
www.pagestreetpublishing.com

Distributed by Macmillan, sales in Canada by The Canadian Manda Group.

27   26   25   24   23   1   2   3   4   5

ISBN-13: 978-1-64567-706-2
ISBN-10: 1-64567-706-0

Library of Congress Control Number: 2022946581

Cover and book design by Kylie Alexander for Page Street Publishing Co.
Cover illustration © Ryan Johnson

Printed and bound in the United States

For my very own "showmance"
My husband, Daniel
I love you

ONE

I'M IN LOVE WITH MagePants69. Which is a huge problem. For so many reasons, including (but definitely not limited to) the following:

1. I've never met him.

2. I have no idea what his real name is or what he looks like.

3. He's possibly a serial killer who uses online gaming platforms (exactly like the one I'm on right now) to groom desperate teenagers (exactly like me), before luring them into the bush and cutting them up into tiny pieces and feeding them to his Persian cat (exactly like Mr. Nibbles, who's currently curled up on my bed, purring like an angel).

But still, despite all of this . . . I'm in love.

It's irrational. It's irresponsible. But it's irrevocable.

A new message pops up in the in-game chat window at the top right of my interface.

MagePants69 <watch those swamp goblins at six o'clock>

I point my cursor at the bottom of the screen and double-click my mouse. My Human avatar leaps through the reeds towards the dirty little swamp goblins and sends five of them flying with a single swing of his axe.

MagePants69 <niiiice>

1

RcticF0x <thanks for the heads-up>

MagePants69 <i live to please>

His avi—a female Half-Elf Bard with a fiery-red plait hanging almost all the way down to the ground—twirls on the spot, finishing in an elaborate curtsy. I type out the command for *</bow>* and my hulking, white-haired Warrior—whose arms are as thick as my torso—sinks into a gracious bow, boots deep in the murky waters of the Southern Quagmire.

RcticF0x <m'lady>

MagePants69 <m'lord>

This is what we call flirting, *Lažov's Keep II: Spire of Dusk* style. Of all the skills in the game, MagePants69 and I are *particularly* proficient in this one.

We're still in the early days of our quest. We've been playing together for over a year, but we only started *Spire of Dusk* a few weeks ago. It's one of those slightly obscure but absurdly well-designed RPGs—Role Playing Games, for the noobs—where the tiniest decision you make at the very start of the campaign can cause an absolute shitstorm of pain later on, when it really counts.

The guys I used to game with think *Spire of Dusk* is too slow and too "early 2010s," but I much prefer it to the shit they're playing these days. All those first-person MMO shooters that make you fork out actual, *real-life* money to learn completely unnecessary dance moves that somehow end up all over social media a month later.

Spire of Dusk has *class*. MagePants69 gets it, even if no one else does.

"Noah?" Mum calls out from somewhere in the house.

Instead of systematically checking the kitchen, the bathroom, and my bedroom—the only three places I'm ever found—Mum prefers to wander around our massive two-story house, singing my name like it's a lyric from some Broadway show tune. Like that one she's always humming about the girl called Sophia. No, Lucia. Marina? It doesn't matter.

I ignore her and keep playing.

MagePants69 casts a low-level Bard spell that sends a spray of colored orbs hurtling towards another gang of swamp goblins, stunning them where they stand. Bards are a cross between mages, thieves, and balladeers. Which means they're spell-casters, pickpockets, and can play a mean tune on the lyre (which is much more useful than it sounds).

With a couple of clicks, my Warrior hurls himself at the little imps and shatters them in a flurry of steel.

RcticF0x <teamwork...>

MagePants69 <...makes the dream work>

I set my avi lumbering north along the path to the town ahead, where we'll be able to regroup, get healing at the temple, and visit the local Tavern for a proper chat.

Every multiplayer game ever created has an in-game chat function, and *Spire of Dusk* obviously has one too, but a visit to the Tav is something else entirely. A visit to the Tav is almost like a real conversation. Your avatars sit opposite each other and say whatever you type out loud. It's kind of like Siri meets FaceTime meets *Game of Thrones*, and I swear it almost feels like you're actually conversing.

Point being, the Tav is where I get to *talk* to MagePants69. Where we spend quality time together. Well, as "quality" as we can get without sharing a single identifying detail about ourselves, as stipulated by his mum's Cardinal Rules of Online Gaming. Which means no physical descriptions, no school names, no friends' names (easy for me), no social handles, no extracurriculars, et cetera, et cetera. The things we *do* know about each other include: We both live in Ballarat (which, given the town has a population of just over 100,000, we figured wouldn't affect our anonymity *too* much); we're both seventeen; we're both gay (score!); and we both think that viral cat videos are the only good things to ever come from social media.

You know, the important stuff.

After dispersing a few more bands of swamp goblins, we finally make it out of the Southern Quagmire. When the next town materializes on my screen, I sit back in my Ergolove Destroyer (yes, I know it sounds like some sort of sex fetish thing, but it's just a fancy gaming chair) and let out a silent *woah*. The town is called Pilar's Crest, and it's this sprawling, feudal village set at the base of a jagged mountain range, stabbing through the earth like a row of shark's teeth.

MagePants69 <cute>

RcticF0x <i've seen cuter> I key in the command for *</point>* and my Warrior lifts his arm to point directly at MagePants69's lithe, flame-haired Bard.

MagePants69 <bahaha thank you, kind sir. you know what's even cuter?>

In unison, we both type: *<the tav>*

Being the responsible "gaymers" we are, we repair all our items at the blacksmith before heading into the center of town to the

Tavern. Once we're inside, MagePants69 orders us a couple of flagons of ale from the non-player character at the bar and we sit our avatars down at a table by the virtual fire. As soon as they take their seats, the camera angle shifts from bird's-eye view to an over-the-shoulder shot, like in a film. I'm now looking at the back of my Warrior's white-blond head as he stares into the piercing green eyes of MagePants69's beautiful Bard. (For the record, I'm not into girls—at all—but knowing it's *him* almost makes me question that for a second.)

"Noahhhh," Mum sings again. Closer this time. Upstairs.

"Well," MagePants69 says, the honeyed tone of his Bard's computerized voice ringing clear in my headphones. *"Pretty sure we nailed that quagmire."*

"That sounds dirty." My Warrior's voice is gruff and sexy, the complete opposite of mine.

"It was dirty," MagePants69 replies. *"It was a swamp."*

I type the </roll eyes> command, but in real life, I laugh out loud. MagePants69 has the perfect sense of humor, somewhere between dad jokes and deadpan.

"Noah?" Mum says from right behind me and I almost jump out of my chair. "I've been calling out for *hours.*"

(Rose Mitchell is a serial exaggerator.)

I slip off my headphones and type a message in the chat window.

RcticF0x <hang on. parental interruption>

"Sorry," I say to Mum, spinning around in my chair. "What do you want?"

"Darling, can we talk for a sec?"

I'm pretty sure I asked her to stop calling me "darling" approximately three years ago, but . . . "Sure. Quickly."

"Can you turn your thingy off?" She flicks her wrists at the widescreen gaming monitor on my desk.

I glance back to MagePants69's Bard, now idly fiddling with her long plait, and type another message.

RcticFOx <brb. mum wants to have a "talk">
MagePants69 <haha all g. i gotta go pee>

I switch the screen off and turn back to Mum, who's now perched on the corner of my bed, legs and arms crossed.

"So . . ." I say.

She brushes a bleached-blonde curl from her face. "Darling, I was thinking . . ."

I resist the urge to say, *That's new*, and say, "And?"

"*And* . . . you know how I've just started re—"

"Rehearsing for the role of Velma Kelly in the Ballarat Musical Theatre Society production of *Chicago*? No, I must've missed that memo somehow, even though it's been the only topic of conversation in the house for the last two weeks."

Mum lets out a Shakespearean sigh. "Darling, do you have to be so sarcastic all the time? It's no wonder . . ."

"No wonder what?" I ask, when she doesn't go on.

"Nothing." She shakes her head. "*Anyway*, as you obviously know, I've just started rehearsing for a *wonderful* production of the Broadway classic, *Chicago*, and David mentioned yesterday at rehearsal—"

"Who's David?"

"Our director. David Dawes."

"You say that like I should know who he is."

"He's a *highly* respected—look, it doesn't matter. The point is, we're short a couple of men in the show, and it's vital to have even numbers in the ensemble for all the partner choreography, so . . . I said I'd ask at home."

I can't help but scoff. "Mum, come *on*. You really think Dad's gonna do an amateur musical with you? He still hasn't forgiven you for making him watch that live musical thing on TV about the girl dancing with the deodorant or whatever when I was in Year Eight."

She pouts her lips and stares back at me, and I'm sure if she hadn't just had a fresh dose of Botox, her eyebrows would be climbing all the way up her forehead right now.

"What?" I crease my brow, making full use of my own facial muscles.

"I'm not asking your father to join the cast . . . ." She tilts her head to one side, blinks a few times, and . . .

"Oh, you mean—" I stifle a laugh. "You want *me* to do the musical with you?"

"You *did* have dance lessons when you were younger, darling, so you're—"

"I had exactly *two* dance lessons, Mum. When I was four. And I cried so much they asked you not to bring me back. Ever."

She clicks her tongue. "Well, it's two more dance lessons than the rest of the men in this town have had, believe me. And I just thought—"

"No, no, no," I interrupt. "Mum, you *know* that's not my scene. It couldn't be *further* from my scene if it tried. It's literally on another planet to my scene. My scene is—" I swivel in my chair and gesture to my computer "—*this*, and only this."

"That's the point, darling," she replies. "You're always in here on that computer. By yourself. All the time."

Okay, so here's some vital information about me: I'm not popular. And by "not popular," I mean I currently have a grand total of *zero* friends. (In the real world, that is.) Unless you count my sister, which, for the sake of this argument, let's not, because that makes me sound even more pathetic. I did *have* friends, once upon a time. But . . . well, let's just say that friends are complicated, and I'd rather spend every second of my spare time killing swamp goblins with the love of my life than dealing with . . . all *that*.

"I'm not *by myself*," I say, turning back to Mum. "I'm playing with other people."

"Who?"

"Why do you suddenly care who I play with?"

"I don't, darling, but they're not real people."

"They *are* real people."

"Have you ever met them?"

I cross my arms, feeling my defenses rising. "No. So?"

"*So,*" she says, "if you died tomorrow, would they come to your funeral?"

"If I *died*?" I reply, searching Mum's face for any remaining signs of rationality. "Mum, what are you talking about?"

"I just *mean*," she says, uncrossing her arms and letting them flop onto her lap, "that they're not real friends, Noah. A *real* friend would be sitting here in the room with you."

My mind flicks to MagePants69's Bard, sitting at our table by the fire in the Tav, waiting for me to return.

"Darling," she continues, in a particularly patronizing tone that she's honed to perfection over the years, "I know how hard it's been since you and Tan—"

"Can we not bring Tan into this?" I snap. "And no, you don't know. For the record."

Mum bites her lip and gazes around my room. "You took all the photos down."

"Um, yeah, like, three years ago. Thanks for noticing."

"Darling—" she shakes her head and turns back to me "—I don't want you to go through Year Twelve alone." (Translation: *I don't want to be the mother of the weird loner kid*.) "You should be going to parties. Hanging out. Having *fun*. Do you remember how to do that?"

It's moments like this when I realize just how little Mum understands me.

"And you think," I reply, trying to keep my cool, "that if I come and play around on stage with you—"

"It's not *playing around*," she cuts in. "I'll have you know that David Dawes is an award-winning actor and director. He even did a season of *Joseph and the Amazing Technicolor Dreamcoat* on the West End. This is serious theatre. A lot of people think David's amateur productions down in Melbourne are equally as impressive as the big pro shows, if not more."

I can't help but roll my eyes. "Who thinks that?"

"*Plenty* of people think that," she replies. "Darling, all I'm saying is that I want you to put yourself out there. You're going to be heading off to uni soon and I don't want you to fall apart when you do."

"Gee, thanks for the vote of confidence, Mum."

"Even Charly struggled when she first moved to Sydney, and you know how popular she was at high school."

"Awesome." I nod. "Because kids just *love* being compared to their perfect, older siblings, Mum."

"Noah," she groans. "I'm serious. This show is very important to me. It's my chance to *finally* show these people what I can do. I need you to do this for me."

And there it is. This isn't about me. At all. It's about *her*.

"Mum," I say, staring back at her. At her impossibly smooth skin. At the hint of grey peeking through at the roots of her golden-blonde hair. At her periwinkle blue eyes that look *exactly* like mine, despite the fact that we are completely different in every other way possible. "I genuinely appreciate your concern, but I will not—I repeat, *will not*—be joining the cast of *Chicago*. In this lifetime or the next. Or the next."

"I just thought it might be ..." She searches my face, as if the right word might be tattooed there somewhere, staring back at her. "You know . . . ?"

"Mum," I reply, my eyes flicking over to my desk, "I'm kind of in the middle of something here."

Her shoulders slump and she lets out a long sigh. "Fine. You can't say I didn't try." She stands up and pats me once on the arm (we're not huggers—well, *she* is, I'm decidedly not) and walks over to the door.

"Mum?"

She stops at the threshold and turns back to me with one hand on the brass doorknob. "Mmm?"

"Please stop calling me 'darling.'"

She opens her mouth to speak, but lets out another little sigh instead. She glances over at my bare white walls, shakes away a thought, and says, "I'm going to bed. Don't stay up too late. It's a school night."

"Okay."

She flicks off the light and Mr. Nibbles darts off my bed into the hallway. The door closes behind her and I just sit here in the dark, feeling suddenly and emphatically alone.

I run a hand through my blond curls, picturing my hypothetical funeral with zero hypothetical guests, then swivel back to my computer. When I switch the monitor back on, the Half-Elf Bard is still at our table in the Tav. There's a new message blinking in the chat window, from four minutes ago.

MagePants69 <you still there? you haven't deserted me, have you?>

A goofy grin spreads across my face as I type my reply.

"Me?" my Warrior says. *"Desert the fairest Bard in the Three Kingdoms? You think so little of me, m'lady."*

The Half-Elf winks. *"You should consider yourself lucky that I think of you at all."*

"Shall we continue our quest?"

"Continue, we shall, m'lord."

And just like that . . . I don't feel so alone anymore.

I don't feel alone at all.

TWO

THE LAST TIME I looked at the chrome clock above the door to the computer lab, it was 9:23 a.m. It's now 9:26 a.m., which means this is officially the slowest Tuesday first period in the history of applied computing.

I glance over at Mr. Conley at his desk, his bald head buried in a pile of paper. On one corner of the desk is his computer—top of the line in every way known to man, because Central Highlands Grammar School would settle for nothing less—and on the *other* corner (in a comically stark contrast) is this ancient, ugly little figurine of a leprechaun sitting on a pot of gold. It has those shifty eyes like the *Mona Lisa* that look like they're following you around the room wherever you go. Conley calls it "Cabbage O'Reilly," and I vaguely remember him saying it's a priceless family heirloom, though I can't imagine it has any real value, other than being able to creep everyone out.

The CHGS computer lab is in the East Wing with the science classrooms. Crisp autumn sunlight is spilling in through the floor-to-ceiling windows, making it kind of hard for me to see the monitor of my computer. We use our laptops in every other class, but we need all the processing speed we can get for applied computing, so communal school PCs it is. I don't usually mind, but you can always tell when the Year Nines have had class just before you, because the mice are greasy and the room smells like lip gloss and ball sweat.

I take a deep breath and rub my eyes, still at least 47 percent asleep. I *may* have stayed up till 3:00 a.m. last night playing *Spire of Dusk* with MagePants69. We didn't plan on staying up *quite* so late, but we were having some great banter at the Tav, and then this random stranger in a spooky, black cloak interrupted and made us follow her into this decrepit old graveyard, and there was this whole thing with these skeletons who'd risen from the dead and *TL;DR* I'm not feeling so great this morning.

"You have a late one, Mitchell?" Simon Zhuang whispers from the row of desks behind me.

I ignore him and open my workbook, looking for a line of code I'd scrawled on a random page last week.

"Up partying all night with your nonexistent mates?" Dylan "Hawk" Hawkins hisses from beside him, and they both laugh.

"Boys," Mr. Conley snaps, looking up from his papers. "Whatever it is, you can save it for recess, thank you."

"Sorry, sir," Hawk says, putting on his Student Leadership Committee voice. "Noah was distracting us. We were just asking him to focus on his own work."

I'd deny it, but it's not worth starting something with Hawk and Simon in front of the whole class on three-and-a-half hours' sleep.

"Eyes on your own computer, Mr. Mitchell," Conley chides, pushing his glasses up the bridge of his nose.

"Sorry, sir," I reply.

Just as Mr. Conley lowers his head back to the stack of papers on his desk, something hits me in the back of the head. I whip around to see a scrunched-up piece of lined paper on the carpet behind my swivel chair. Hawk and Simon are smirking at me from behind their monitors, their eyes flicking down to the makeshift projectile and back up again. I reach down and pick it up, unfurling it as quietly as I can manage. On the wrinkled paper are three words, written in red pen:

HAPPY TUESDAY, SNITCHELL

I roll my eyes and toss the paper in the bin underneath my desk. They've been calling me "Noah Snitchell" for three years now, so it doesn't really have the same effect on me anymore.

My phone buzzes in my pocket and I pull it out under my desk, careful to keep it hidden from Mr. Conley. He has a desk drawer full of confiscated smartphones, and mine is not about to join them. There's a text from Charly on the lock screen:

Hey bub. Heard you're doing the musical with Mum? I kind of love that for you. Flamenco dancer emoji.

I scowl at the message for a second, wondering how "not in this lifetime" could have possibly been misconstrued, then shove my phone back into my pocket.

While I wait for my design project to load on my PC, a *NEW EMAIL* notification pops up at the top corner of the screen. As soon as I click the Mail app, my stomach lurches and my brow practically folds itself in two. I lean forward, squinting at the new email from J. Conley: *URGENT—Please read.*

I glance up at Mr. Conley, who has abandoned his stack of papers and is now staring at his computer. Almost as if . . . as if he's waiting for a reply?

No. Surely not.

He sighs, his eyes flicking up to meet mine for a moment before returning to his screen.

What the actual . . .

I place my hand on my mouse like it could explode at any second and carefully guide the cursor to the email.

URGENT—Please read.

Holding my breath, I double click. Before I know it, my entire monitor is filled with the kind of video you definitely do *not* want playing on a school computer. Or any computer, for that matter, except your own. In your bedroom. *In private . . .*

"Oh my god," Zoe Peterson shouts from the back row. "Noah's watching *porn!*"

It's not like she needed to announce it, since the utterly unmistakable sound of two men having incredibly aerobic sex is resounding off the brick walls of the computer lab around us.

I frantically click my mouse, trying to kill the video, but it just keeps playing. My cheeks prickle with heat, and my eyes sting with tears of embarrassment as the entire class breaks out into hysterical laughter. I press *Ctrl+Alt+Del* about a thousand times in the span of three seconds, but the video keeps playing and playing and playing. I somehow have the mental capacity to reach out and switch the monitor off, but the disembodied moans and groans keep blaring through the speakers.

"Mr. Mitchell!" Conley growls from beside me. "What on *earth* is going on here? Turn that off *right now!*"

"I'm trying, sir," I choke out, just as he leans across me to hold down the power button on my computer. There's a loud beep and the audio cuts out abruptly, replaced by a palpable, deafening silence.

"Take yourself to the vice principal's office," Mr. Conley says quietly, his face flushed, his temper simmering dangerously close to the surface. "*Now.*"

"Yes, sir."

As I stand up to grab my books, I catch Hawk's eye in the row behind me. A smirk tugs at the corner of his mouth and he winks. It was *him*. Simon bites his bottom lip to stifle a smile and the two of them hide their sniggers behind their monitors.

"Mr. Conley," I start, "someone sent—"

But he cuts me off. "What part of 'now' do you not understand, Noah? *Go.*"

I huff in frustration, and he points a stern finger towards the door, eyebrows raised, as if he's challenging me to protest.

"*Fine*," I say, even though every single word I say at this point will probably earn me an extra week in detention.

I shoot Hawk and Simon a *Seriously? Fuck you* glare before stomping out of the computer lab, my classmates' whispers like knives in my back. As soon as I shut the door behind me, Conley says, "All right, everyone, let's pull ourselves together, shall we?" and raucous laughter erupts inside the classroom once more.

How do you know it was them? Charly messages while I'm waiting to meet my fate.

I'm sitting in a very uncomfortable chair outside Mrs. Jamison's office, which I'm certain she chose deliberately in order to weaken her victims before eviscerating them. Our vice principal is known for many things, but compassion is not one of them. Let's just say that if Medusa had immigrated to Australia, married the richest man in Ballarat, and had a daughter, that daughter would be Irene Jamison.

Because, I write back to Charly, **it's ALWAYS them.**

But how could they send the virus thing from your teacher's email address?

Charly has zero tech skills that don't involve finding the perfect Instagram filter.

Easy, I reply. **They would've just made a fake account and used his name. Anyone can do it. It's like all those phishing emails you get from Microsoft that are definitely not from Microsoft.**

WTF is phishing?

Irrelevant. I shake my head at my phone. **Charly, it was MORTIFYING. I'm talking hardcore gay porn. Full screen. Full volume. IN FRONT OF MY WHOLE CLASS. I don't know how I can possibly come back from that.**

She replies with a GIF of one of the Kardashians that says *I would rather die.*

Cool. Thanks Char. Super helpful.

Just tell Mrs. Jamison it was Hawk and Simon. Surely a prank is a much more likely explanation than you actually watching porn in class?

I rub my fingers over a brand-new crop of pimples on my chin. Charly is right. I should just tell Mrs. Jamison the truth. Not that the truth and I have the best history.

Wait . . . I write. **Was that some HELPFUL sisterly advice?**

I'm a new woman, Noah. Sassy-girl emoji. **Sydney is doing me wonders. MEANWHILE. You ignored my other message. You're doing the musical with Mum?**

I scoff out loud. **NO. Biggest no in the 4.6 billion-year history of the world.**

Oh. She said you were doing it. She seemed super excited.

When did she tell you this?

This morning.

I squint down at the screen. **Why would she tell you that after I already said no? Did she ask you to say something?**

Three dots . . . then Charly asks: **Why don't you want to do it?**

I'll send you my 10,000-word essay on the subject this evening.

Please don't.

I chuckle, then remember I'm about to get torn to pieces for alleged public masturbation.

Look, I write. **Mum only wants me to do the stupid show because they need more male cast members and she wants to be the one to save the day. It's nothing to do with me.**

You never know, Charly replies. Shrugging-girl emoji. **Maybe she's sad you're leaving soon and wants some mother-son bonding time?**

No, Char. Incorrect. It's a classic Rose Mitchell guilt trip. This show is her "big break." She just wants everything about it to be perfect, even if it means humiliating her only son in front of a crowd of thousands. All for the sake of not having a gap in the back row of the chorus. It's so not happening. I'm too old for her games.

Crying-with-laughter emoji from Charly. **Jeez, bub. Sounds like you've gotten a little dramatic in my absence. Maybe you've inherited Mum's acting genes after all.**

"Mr. Mitchell," a soft voice says from beside me. I look up to see Mrs. Jamison's mousy assistant, Mr. Urquhart, staring down at me over the top of his tortoiseshell glasses. He's such a cliché that I sometimes wonder if he's actually an investigative journalist in a terribly obvious disguise. "Mrs. Jamison is ready for you now."

Gotta go, I write to Charly. **Pray for me.**

JUST TELL HER THE TRUTH.

I click the lock button and slip the phone back into my pocket, before extracting myself from Mrs. Jamison's torture device. Mr. Urquhart ushers me into the office, then shuts the door with an ominous *clunk*, leaving the two of us alone.

"Noah Mitchell," Mrs. Jamison sighs, like it's the name of her arch-nemesis. "I can't say I'm surprised to see you." She motions to the chair opposite her and I sit, wiping my clammy palms on my shorts.

Her office is exactly how I imagine a stuffy old Ivy League dean's office would look. Framed PhD on the wall. Ornate clock sitting on an antique sideboard. Abstract paperweights (that are probably more expensive than most people's engagement rings) scattered around the room.

"So," she begins. My eyes are glued to the burgundy carpet at my feet. I'm trying to avoid direct eye contact (on account of the Daughter of Medusa thing) but I feel a strange compulsion to return her gaze, like she has me under some kind of Gorgon spell. My eyes flick up to meet hers, and she tents her fingers in front of her thin, pinched lips. "Am I to understand that—as a minor, and a student at one of the state's most prestigious secondary institutions—you genuinely believed watching pornography was an appropriate use of time in your Unit 3 applied computing class?"

I manage to tear my eyes away before her glare burns straight through my retinas, casting them back down at my polished black school shoes. "Uh . . ." I crack my knuckles under the desk.

What I *should* say is that it was Hawk and Simon who sent me the porn bomb. That they still blame me for what happened in Year Nine. That they spend their days trying to make my high school existence as frustrating as possible in every single way. That they won't rest until I meet the same fate as Tan.

"Or," she says knowingly, "is there a more . . . *logical* explanation?"

Now, Mrs. Jamison is no fool. She's also one of the only people in the world who knows the truth about what happened between me and Tan, so I'm sure she suspects my ex-friends' involvement in the gradual decline of my student record, but . . . I can't *prove* the boys have done anything wrong. Not today, and not on any of the other occasions when their pranks have landed me in this very office. It would be my word against theirs, and I'm not playing that game. Not after what happened last time.

Besides, if Hawk and Simon found out that I tried to get them in trouble, they'd just plan an even bigger prank in retaliation. Something even more public. Even *more* humiliating. Which—let's face it—I probably deserve, but would rather avoid, nonetheless. Because the only thing worse than putting up with Hawk and Simon would be getting expelled and having to transfer to North. With Tan.

"Mr. Mitchell?"

I look back up, feeling my face grow hot with shame.

My vice principal arches a razor-sharp eyebrow. "Is there anything we need to discuss?"

Charly's voice pops into my head, shouting in all-caps: *JUST TELL HER THE TRUTH.*

But I can't.

The truth is not my friend.

THREE

WHEN I GET HOME from school, there's an email waiting from MagePants69. I'm still an anxious mess from this morning's applied computing debacle, so the email sends me tumbling into an undeniable pit of despair:

Dungeon Shenanigans

From: MagePants69 <magepants69@gmail.com>
To: Arctic Fox <rcticf0x@outlook.com>
On: Tuesday, 17 March at 3:32 p.m.

M'lord,

Gonna be a bit late tonight, sorry!

I know we said we'd try to smash out the rest of the dungeon levels, but I completely forgot it was Tuesday and I've got a thing after dinner.

See you at 10:15 p.m.?

I promise I'll make it up to you. Haven't figured out how yet, but please email your suggestions to my assistant at: idontactuallyhaveanassistant@fakeassistants.com.au

Yours,

M

My first thought when I read the words *I've got a thing after dinner* is that he's going on a *date*. But then, he signed off *Yours like always*, and I don't think Tuesday night dates are a thing, especially when you're still in school. Let's be honest, though, as someone who's never been asked out on a date, I can't say I'm overly familiar with the protocol.

Regardless, I spend the majority of the night just sitting on the couch, stewing over the mental image of MagePants69 out on a date with some guy with naturally straight teeth, clear skin, and a nice set of pecs. I know I shouldn't be jealous—given we can never meet IRL—but I am. Because I'm one hundred percent sure MagePants69 and I are destined to be together. Which probably sounds absurd, but even a so-called "loser" like me can tell when someone has feelings for him. Like when Hannah Forbes was in love with me in Year Eight and I had to write her a strongly worded letter asking her to leave me alone because I was "not looking for a relationship." ("Not looking for a relationship" was my secret code for "not looking for a relationship unless you're a dude who's devoted to D&D," though even *I* couldn't crack that code at the time.)

What started out last year as a faint curiosity to see what the *real* MagePants69 was like has evolved over time into a desperate, burning desire to meet him. To *know* him. But no matter how close we get in the virtual world, it's never going to happen, thanks to his absurdly overprotective helicopter mum and her rules. MagePants69 said she almost banned him from gaming altogether a couple of years ago when the police in Melbourne exposed this massive child pornography syndicate being run through a new multiplayer game platform. Realistically,

I'm lucky we're allowed to play online together at all, let alone go and get unsupervised milkshakes (or whatever it is kids do these days).

At 10:13 p.m.—and yes, if you must know, I've been perched anxiously on my Ergolove Destroyer awaiting MagePant69's arrival since 9:31 p.m.—Mum knocks on my bedroom door to let me know she's home from rehearsal.

"We ran a bit overtime," she says, "but it was worth every second. There was *such* a great energy in the room tonight."

I successfully get out of having to reply—or worse, explain what happened in Conley's class—by pointing to the towering pile of textbooks strategically positioned on my desk and refusing to take off my headphones.

"Okay, just . . . don't stay up too late," she says, which is her go-to when she can't think of anything more suitably parental to say. "I'm going to have a glass of wine."

I nod and wave her out of the room. She shuts the door behind her with a sigh.

I look back to my monitor just as the time clicks over to 10:15 p.m. . . . but MagePants69 doesn't appear.

10:16 p.m. ticks by.

10:17 p.m. . . .

By 10:18 p.m., I'm having full-on heart palpitations, because he's clearly a) still at his "thing" with Mr. Perfect Pecs, or b) a missing person, and I honestly don't know which one is worse.

But then, at 10:19 p.m. . . .

MagePants69 <yo. sorry i'm late>

I send my reply immediately.

RcticF0x <all g. how was your night?>

I clasp my hands together against my chest, awaiting his response.

MagePants69 <good. draining, but super productive>

A wave of sweet, sweet relief washes over me. Unless his date involved manual labour or some serious Marie Kondo-ing, I don't think it was a date, after all.

The skeleton mage hurls a fireball across the dungeon at Mage-Pants69's avi, who somehow cartwheels out of the way without getting so much as a singed ponytail. Looks like all those ability points he puts in Dexterity are finally paying off.

We picked up where we left off, slashing our way through the dank, rat-infested catacombs below the graveyard, searching for signs of who's been raising the dead and wreaking havoc on Pilar's Crest. Turns out the undead aren't *super* happy about our little visit to their dungeon, but I honestly couldn't ask for a better distraction from the day I've had than obliterating reanimated skeletons with the boy I'm hopelessly in love with.

RcticF0x <nice little rhythmic gymnastics routine you've got going on over there>

MagePants69 <you should see my ball skills>

Ooft. Swoon.

RcticF0x <shall we take care of the homicidal skeleton before we start discussing your balls?>

MagePants69 <sigh. if we must>

At 11:58 p.m., with only a few drops left in each of our health globes, we finally vanquish the skeleton mage. We're not done with our quest in the dungeon yet—we still have no idea who started raising the dead in the first place—but whatever waits for us on the levels below is sure to be ten times as powerful, and ten times as angry. Which means we need a virtual drink.

Once we're safe and snuggly in the Pilar's Crest Tav, our chat moves swiftly away from quests and skeletons and onto what I like to call our Daily Debrief.

"How was school?" MagePants69 asks.

"Next subject," I reply.

His Bard—looking particularly pretty in a new emerald green tunic—laughs across the table from my Warrior. *"What? Another prank?"*

I keep him regularly updated on all of Hawk's and Simon's pranks, but I obviously don't tell him who's committing them, or why they're targeting me. That's the very last thing I want MagePants69—or anyone, for that matter—to know about me.

"Yup." My Warrior nods. *"Super fun one, too."*

"Public pantsing at assembly?"

"Worse." I type in the command for </grimace>.

"What could possibly be worse than your schlong being put on show for the whole school?"

I tell him about the porn bomb, and Mrs. Jamison, and my complete inability to defend myself, like it's the punchline of some awkward and entirely not funny joke.

"Dude," MagePants69 replies eventually, *"that is rough!"* His Bard facepalms herself. I didn't know there was a command for that.

"To be honest," I say, *"I'm lucky I didn't get suspended. If my dad hadn't made another donation to the school library last*

week, I probably would've been straight out the door."

"Okay, humblebrag."

I chuckle out loud, a grin pulling at the corners of my mouth. *"Can you just make me feel better by telling me your extended family walked in on you jerking off this afternoon or something?"*

"Firstly," MagePants69 says, *"how dare you wish that type of masturbatory horror upon me!"*

I'm not surprised that one mention of masturbation is all it takes to get things moving downstairs. I adjust myself in my jocks and thank my lucky stars that Mum and Dad aren't the kind of parents who make me use the family computer in the living room.

"Secondly," his Bard goes on, absently twirling the end of her red plait, *"my day was fine. School was school. Dinner was yum. Rehearsal was good, even though it ran a bit late. Can't complain, really."*

I gasp so loudly at the word "rehearsal" that I'm surprised Mum and Dad don't think I'm being attacked. Because *rehearsal?* I don't want to jump to conclusions, but . . .

1. Mum had rehearsal for *Chicago* tonight.

2. She said they ran overtime, and she got home approximately six minutes before MagePants69 logged onto *Spire of Dusk*.

3. MagePants69's "thing" was draining and productive, much like I imagine a long rehearsal would be.

It seems almost too serendipitous to be true, but . . . it couldn't possibly be a coincidence, could it?

I think . . . I think MagePants69 might be in the cast of *Chicago* with my mother.

I try to play it cool and let the comment pass by, even though I'm literally sweating now. MagePants69 is always super careful about not mentioning *anything* that could potentially identify him in the real world, no matter how ridiculous it might seem. To the point where *I* now have a weird complex about it too. A couple of weeks ago, I accidentally said something about getting my braces tightened, and I thought I was going to get abducted by a serial killer on the spot. Like being a seventeen-year-old guy with braces makes me super distinguishable in a crowd.

Point being, I'm certain MagePants69 has no idea what he just said.

"Cool," my Warrior replies in his uber-manly voice. *"Better than my day, at least."*

"Well," his Bard replies with a wink, *"marginally."*

Even though I'm dying to press for more information before he notices his little slip-up, the last thing I want to do is make a big deal about it, because then . . . well, because then I wouldn't be able to do what I'm about to do.

I quickly type a message in the chat window, breathing out a steady stream of air to slow my racing pulse.

RcticF0x <I probs should get to bed, actually. need to be on my bestest behavior at school tomorrow>

I type *</yawn>* and my Warrior lifts his meaty hand to his mouth.

MagePants69 <all g. we can portal straight back to the dungeon tomorrow night>

RcticF0x <perfect>

MagePants69 <gnite, m'lord>

RcticF0x <nite, m'lady>

And with that, I'm up and out of my chair, striding downstairs to the living room. Mum is sitting up with a glass of red wine, watching one of those tacky American renovation shows she's so obsessed with, despite having an immaculate lakefront home that her neurosurgeon husband bought her.

"Mum," I say, leaning on the arm of the couch.

"Mmm," she replies, without taking her eyes off the screen.

"I want to do the show with you."

She whips around with such force that she nearly spills her wine on the rug. "What?"

"I've decided to do *Chicago* with you. I want to join the cast."

"Seriously?" She sits up, tucking her legs underneath herself, and places her glass down on the coffee table. Her eyes are almost scarily wide. "Wait—you're trolling me, aren't you?"

"No, I am not trolling you."

My heart is pounding. This could end up being the worst decision I've ever made. This might ruin the one thing I truly care about in my life. But all I can think about is being in the same room as MagePants69. Seeing him. Hearing his voice. Finding out—once and for all—if the love I feel through my computer screen is actually *real*.

"But," Mum says, sweeping her hair off her face, "you said you'd rather die than do the show with me."

"That's completely inaccurate."

"Did Charly say something?"

"No," I reply, even though I *knew* my sister was up to something yesterday when she messaged me. "I just . . . You were right. I need to—"

"I'm sorry, what?" Mum interrupts, placing a hand to her

chest in pantomime shock. "Did you just say I was *right?*"

I grit my teeth. "So it seems."

"Darling, I . . . I don't understand. I'm thrilled, obviously, but I mean, why did you change your mind?"

Because my curiosity is killing me? Because I'm reckless and ridiculous? Because I'm suddenly one step closer to meeting the love of my life?

I shrug. "Just did."

FOUR

WHEN I WAKE UP the next morning, I can't help but feel like I've made a horrible mistake. The kind of mistake that makes all my previous horrible mistakes feel like Nobel Prize-winning decisions. I've been lying in bed—wide awake—since 5:30 a.m., making a mental list of everything that could possibly go wrong. And let me tell you, it's a very long list.

My phone buzzes on my bedside table.

Charly: **Wait, so you ARE doing the musical with Mum?** Shocked cat emoji.

It appears so, I reply, sitting up and rubbing sleep from my eyes. **Although I'm seriously considering reneging on my offer now that I've realized it will involve me appearing on an actual stage in front of actual human beings, most likely wearing a bedazzled, glittery, sequinned vest.** (This is an educated guess based on the history of Mum's other amateur music theatre performances I've been forced to attend.)

Nawww, Charly writes. **But it'll be so cute!**

Char, what could POSSIBLY be cute about me klutzing around on stage and making a total dick of myself in front of a thousand people?

You klutzing around on stage and making a total dick of yourself in front of a thousand people, she replies. **Obviously.**

Eye-roll emoji.

Relax, bub. It'll be fine. Live a little.

"Noah?" Mum calls from the hallway. "Are you up?"

I click my phone shut and toss it to the end of my bed. "Yeah."

My door swings open and Mum enters in head-to-toe luxury activewear. "I'm just back from sunrise yoga with the girls."

When Mum says "the girls," she could actually be referring to any number of women (or a couple of middle-aged gay men) she socializes with. There are the yoga girls, the theatre girls, the coffee girls, the pilates girls, the nothing-in-common-with-each-other-aside-from-being-filthy-rich girls—the list goes on and on. Mum is a *people person*. One of the many things we do not have in common.

"I just wanted to let you know," she starts, sitting on the end of my bed, collarbones glistening with designer sweat, "that there's no *Chicago* rehearsal this Thursday because David—he's the director, remember?"

I nod.

"Well, David has a corporate gig down at Crown Casino in Melbourne this week. So, your first rehearsal will be on Sunday afternoon."

"Uh . . . okay."

"And I have to say," she adds, like she's sharing some salacious piece of gossip, "the cast are all *so* excited for me to have my very own son in the ensemble. As if playing the lead role isn't already enough! And you'll *love* everyone. I promise."

My stomach clenches at the word "love." Love is the

reason I'm putting myself in this ridiculous situation in the first place.

"Lots of them are around your age, actually," she goes on, nodding. "The boy playing Billy Flynn is in Year Twelve at St. Peter's. He's *gorgeous*. And gay. Alex Di Mario." She rolls the "r," making his name sound suave and alluring. "Do you know him?"

I shake my head. Ballarat is small, but not that small, and Mum seems to be forgetting that I avoid socializing at all costs. But . . . a gay guy *my age* in the cast? I try not to get ahead of myself.

"He looks like a young Marlon Brando," Mum goes on. "And he's *very* young to be playing Billy—I mean, it's the male lead, after all—but honestly, his talent speaks for itself. You'll see what I mean on Sunday." She pauses, then adds with a wink, "And it doesn't hurt that he's absolutely *swoon-worthy*."

I ignore the fact that Mum just referred to a Year Twelve boy as "swoon-worthy" and mentally move on to more important things. Like picturing MagePants69 sitting at his computer at home, pecs bursting out of a tight white singlet, à la Marlon Brando in *A Streetcar Named Desire*. (We had to watch the film in Year Ten English, and even though it was from the 1950s, Brando was absurdly hot. Like, "special dream" hot.)

"I need to shower," Mum says, jumping to her feet. "Remind me to take you shopping for jazz shoes and rehearsal clothes before Sunday. Oh, and you'll need a dance support, too!"

She claps her hands, beaming down at me. I force a smile in reply, taking a wild guess that a "dance support" is probably not something you want to shop for with your mother, and return my thoughts to MagePants69 in a white singlet and high-waisted trousers. "Can't wait."

Suddenly, it's Sunday afternoon and I'm standing outside an old Lutheran church across town, doubt weighing down on me with spine-crushing force.

The red-brick building looks like a normal church, except for the fact that an ugly weatherboard extension has attached itself to one side, like a boxy, cream-colored parasite. There's a concrete ramp running along one side of the church, leading up to a glass door in the weatherboard annex. A massive sign above the door is emblazoned with the words BALLARAT MUSICAL THEATRE SOCIETY, with the expectedly cliché comedy and tragedy masks in the background, their ribbons looping in and out of the black serif text.

It looks like the kind of place people's hopes and dreams go to die a horribly overacted death.

Mum lets out a squeal of excitement as she trots up behind me on the footpath in a pair of stilettos. "Darling, this is *it*. This is where the magic happens!"

I stifle the urge to groan. "We're ten minutes early," I say, glancing down at my watch. "We should wait out here, right?"

"No, no, no," Mum says, looping her arm through mine. "Everyone gets here early. I need to introduce you to the VIPs!"

Without another word, she drags me up the concrete ramp, shoves me through the glass door, and ushers me into what would have been the nave of the church when it was used for praising Jesus instead of staging *Jesus Christ Superstar*. (The only reason I know that's a musical is because Mum was in a local production of it when I was seven. She played "Leper #1," which I'm now certain was a title she bestowed upon herself.)

The church still *feels* churchy, even though the stained-glass windows have been replaced with regular frosted glass and the altar has been removed. There's a small raised stage in the apse, which seems to be where the cast leave their bags and belongings. One whole wall is covered in mirrors, and the others are adorned not with the Stations of the Cross, but with posters of old musicals and newspaper cuttings of BMTS alumni success stories—the ones who've "made it," according to Mum. It smells like dust and sweat and desperation. The lights are the harshest type of fluorescent, the ones that make you feel like you've been beamed up to an extraterrestrial spacecraft. Or maybe that's more to do with the fact that I feel like a complete alien here—a lone introvert drowning in a sea of toothy grins and over-the-top gestures.

I can't see anyone in the hall who a) looks like Marlon Brando, or b) looks even remotely like a gaymer. There are some high-school girls in lycra stretching in one corner (I honestly didn't know legs could bend that way); a group of straight-looking guys standing in a tight huddle; some older stragglers wandering around the room making the same ridiculous noises Mum makes when she's "warming up her voice"; and a probably-mid-forties Black woman with long pink braids sitting on a chair by the wall, holding court with some of the younger cast members, all of whom are literally crying with laughter over something she just said.

They're all so … I don't know. Big? Loud? *On?*

I keep scanning the room for a single person who doesn't

look like they've walked straight off the set of *Glee* (I'll admit, I've seen a *couple* of episodes, but only because Darren Criss is undeniably hot) and spot two guys around my age chatting in the middle of the hall. One of them is tall and blond, with pretty blue eyes and horse teeth (in an attractive way), and the other is olive-skinned, black-haired, and stocky. He's wearing one of those meme T-shirts with the list of names, but this one says *Hamilton & Jefferson & Madison & Washington & Burr*, and I have no idea who they are. Which means he's not MagePants69, because if he *were*, I'd definitely be able to understand his T-shirt.

I glance past the boys to the upright piano in the far corner of the room. There's a mousy-looking girl sitting there, running her fingers over the keys without actually playing anything. Every now and then, she glances up from the ivories, meets someone's gaze, and then quickly averts her eyes. She's clearly the only other nerd in the room, which—wait . . .

Oh, no. Please, please, *please* don't tell me *she* is MagePants69. I cannot have committed to doing this show only to find out that the boy I'm in love with is not even a *boy*.

"Who's that girl at the piano?" I ask Mum, feeling a little nauseated.

"Oh, that's just Jane, the répétiteur." She flicks her hands through the air. "We have more important people to meet, darling. Come, I'll introduce you to David."

She yanks me across the room towards a tall Black man with his back to us. He's deep in conversation with a withered old white lady who looks like my great-grandma, both of them poring over a skein of bright pink silk.

"David," Mum coos, "this is my son, Noah."

It's the first time I've heard her say the word "son" like it's a compliment since . . . I don't know, maybe ever. Usually it sounds more like an apology. Like she's preparing them for how incredibly awkward I'm about to be.

David whips around, and my first thought is that he's . . . well . . . *hot*. For an old guy.

"Noah!" he says, reaching out to clasp my hand in both of his. "We are thrilled you could join us. *Thrilled*." He squeezes my hand on the word *thrilled*, then lets go. "You and Raf have honestly saved the day. When Juan and Phillip pulled out and we had to bump Eli up to Fred Casely, I didn't think we'd be able to make up the numbers in the male ensemble! And how on earth could we do 'Roxie' justice without her bevy of *boys*?"

He may as well be speaking German (and I do not speak German), because I have no idea if those names belong to people or characters or songs or god-knows-what. I just nod politely, my lips pressed into a very unconvincing smile.

"So, *thank you*," he says, far too earnest for my liking.

"Happy to help," I lie.

My eyes flick to the door of the nave, completely out of my control, when an absolute *god* of a boy walks into the church.

"Alex!" someone calls out from across the room.

I have to give it to Mum, "swoon-worthy" is definitely the most apt adjective for Alex Di Mario, and the young Marlon Brando reference is so accurate it hurts. He smiles a Hollywood smile and jogs over to Horse Teeth and Meme T-shirt. They take turns hugging hello, then both boys laugh at something Alex says, in that overenthusiastic way you laugh when someone infinitely more popular deigns to talk to you.

Staring over at Alex, basking in his tanned, athletic glory, my stomach sinks into my feet. He has to be the *least* likely online RPG player I have ever laid eyes upon. He's the sort of guy who's into sunbaking and selfies, not Dungeons and Dragons. Besides, it's a scientific fact that Hot People don't lock themselves inside their dark bedrooms all day where no one can see how attractive they are. That's *not* how the world works.

So . . . if not Alex Di Mario, which cast member is MagePants69? Horse Teeth looks like a typical Drama Gay, but I guess Meme T-shirt is giving off a bit of a nerdy vibe. And then there's Jane the pianist, of course, who is clearly nerdy enough to play computer games, but that would be some seriously intense karma for me trying to secretly stalk my online crush.

Unless . . . Could I have been way off with this? Maybe MagePants69 isn't here at all? Realistically, he could be rehearsing for a million things that aren't *Chicago*. Maybe I've sent myself on an undercover mission as a chorus member of an amateur musical—with my *mother* playing the lead role, no less—for *absolutely no reason*.

No. He's going to be here.

He has to be here.

I know it.

"Noah," Mum snaps from beside me and I turn back to her. "David asked you a question."

"Oh," I reply. "Sorry, sir."

He laughs, loud and expansive. "'Sir?' We'll have none of that private school nonsense in my rehearsal room, thanks, Noah."

"Uh, sorry," I say again.

"I asked if you're ready for the challenge?" He says it like it's a dare. "You've certainly got some catching up to do. Luckily, your mother is one of the most talented women I've worked with in many years."

"David, *stop*," she says, slapping him on the arm. "You'll embarrass me."

Un-fucking-likely.

"I'm sure you've got some of that 'Rose Mitchell sparkle' inside you somewhere," David says, clamping a hand on my shoulder.

Ugh. Theatre people are so *touchy*.

"Somewhere very deep down," I reply. "Buried under all the layers of sparkle-repellent teen angst."

Mum laughs possibly the fakest laugh I've ever heard (which is saying something for her). "Didn't I tell you he was *funny*?"

David chuckles. "Welcome to the cast, Noah." He steps aside, claps his hands twice, and the room falls silent. "Chairs around the piano, people. Let's revise what we've learned so far."

"Grab a chair, darling," Mum orders, pointing to the wall. "Find somewhere to sit."

Suddenly fending for myself, I fall in step with the rest of the cast as they form a semicircle around the piano. As we shuffle around the room, I continue searching for signs of MagePants69's existence. Not that I know what I'm looking for. Something that screams *I love online D&D games and Noah Mitchell is my soulmate* would be preferable.

"Are you a bari?" Horse Teeth asks from beside me, taking a seat on his plastic chair.

"A what, sorry?"

"A baritone."

"Uhh . . ."

He raises an eyebrow. "Is this baby's first show?"

"Is it that obvious?"

"I mean, you do have a bit of a deer-in-the-headlights vibe about you," he replies with a smirk, and all I can think is, *Are you MagePants69? Are you smirking at me because you know who I am and you're in love with me?*

"Is your singing voice low or high?" he asks.

I can't say that I've ever tested it out, given I'm hardly the type of guy who belts along to Beyoncé in the shower. Having said that, my speaking pitch *did* drop considerably when my voice broke, so . . .

"Low?" I reply with a shrug. "Low-ish?"

"Sit with us, girl," he replies, pointing his thumb at Meme T-shirt beside him. "We're the baritones. The fun ones, anyway. You'll catch up quickly. The harmonies are so easy."

As I take my seat next to Horse Teeth, I realize that's probably the longest conversation I've had with anyone not in my immediate family since Year Nine. This tiny voice in the back of my head (that happens to sound a lot like Charly) says, *See, it's not so bad.*

"I'm Keegan, by the way," Horse Teeth says. "And this is Chris."

"Noah," I say, forcing a smile for Meme T-shirt, who is grinning at me almost fanatically.

"Nice to meet you, Noah," he replies.

"Nice to meet you t—"

But before I can finish, someone shouts from the door, "Sorry I'm late, David! I missed the bus!"

"It's fine, Eli," David replies, and I turn to see a young guy wearing a green knitted jumper and black jeans jogging into the room. "Take a seat," David goes on. "We're just about to start on 'All That Jazz.'"

I keep my eyes on the boy as he crosses the hall, dumps his backpack, grabs a chair, and jogs back over to our huddle around the piano. The guys directly in front of me shuffle apart so he can squeeze in between them.

My heart is suddenly beating triple-time. Because this boy—*Eli*—with his quaffed, flame-red hair and angular Elven features, looks *exactly* like a certain Half-Elf Bard avatar I know all too well . . . .

He glances over his shoulder and his sparkly, emerald green eyes meet mine. He gives me the briefest smile and my heart stops dead.

Because it's him. I'd bet my life on it.

MagePants69.

FIVE

"LET'S PICK IT UP again from Fred's line," the musical director, Pania—a Māori woman with a soccer-mum-who-takes-no-shit attitude—calls out over the chatter. "We'll take it all the way through to the end this time. I'll read Roxie's lines for now. She won't be joining us till after the break."

We've been singing the same song over and over and *over* for the past hour and a half. And by "we," I mean every single cast member *but* me. I've been sitting here in my uncomfortable plastic chair, staring at the back of Eli's beautiful ginger head, trying to plan the perfect introductory greeting. Something that sounds confident and flirty and like I frequently meet new people, but not like I've scripted it and rehearsed it in my head a million times. (The best thing I've come up with so far is "Hey," so it's safe to say it's not going well.)

Pania counts Jane in with a flourish of her hand, and the mousy girl stabs out the lead-in to the underscore—a word I didn't realize had any connotations outside coding and computers until now.

"Listen," Eli—who's playing Fred Casely—says over the piano in a pretty convincing American accent, "your husband ain't home, is he?"

"No," Mum says from across the room, in her—I hate to admit—even more convincing accent, "her husband is *not* at home."

The piano swells and the full cast joins in for the chorus of "All That Jazz." The singing is loud and boisterous and I couldn't feel more like a fish out of water if I tried. I desperately want to go back to my quiet little tank (read: my bedroom), and if it weren't for the boy sitting in front of me, I'd have been straight out the door an hour ago. Correction—I never would've walked through the door in the first place.

Keegan has a deep, booming voice, and I find myself wondering if it would be rude to bring earplugs next time. He said I could share his sheet music—which is just a jumble of shapes and lines to me—and pushed his chair right up against mine. I'm a big fan of personal space, so I edged as far away from him on my chair as I possibly could, to the point where my right ass cheek is now hanging in midair. The left one is almost completely numb.

I can't pick out Eli's voice from the crowd, mainly because Keegan's bellowing is drowning out the entire world, but I'm sure it's as beautiful as the rest of him. Every now and then, he'll turn his head to the side while he's singing and I'll catch a glimpse of his profile. It's actually mind-blowing how much he looks like his *Spire of Dusk* avi. His features are striking and angular but with this delicate femininity about them. His flame-red hair is the perfect kind of floopy that I'm certain wouldn't require hours of wrangling in the morning. It falls across his head in short, easy waves, strands of blond glinting under the fluorescent light amongst the sea of fiery red.

He's not what you'd call "typically beautiful" or "classically handsome" like Alex Di Mario—whose attractiveness struts into the room beside him and smacks you across the face—but he's still *way* out of my league. Honestly, the only thing wrong with Eli is that he's *too* perfect. I foolishly assumed his interest in gaming meant he'd be a major geek like me—not only in terms of his personality, but his appearance, too. Staring at his glorious marshmallow lips right now, I can't help but feel like this battle was lost before I even arrived.

"Not bad," Pania announces when we reach the end of the song. (Again, by "we," I do not, in any way, mean *me*.) "The harmonies still need a bit of work—altos, I think you've made up your own line—but we're getting there. And Rose—" she looks to Mum, who's sitting in the front row at the opposite side of the semicircle, a pencil behind her ear, hands perched on the music stand in front of her "—you're sounding *fantastic*."

I've spent my whole life listening to Mum sing—and I don't mean humming around the house or embarrassingly singing along to the radio in the car like most people's parents, I mean literal concerts in the lounge room—so I've never thought of her voice as anything out of the ordinary, and certainly not as "fantastic." She can obviously sing, but she's . . . you know . . . *Mum.*

Everyone gives her a little clap and she attempts (and fails) to feign humility.

"Let's take ten," Pania says, glancing down at her watch, "and then we'll run 'We Both Reached for the Gun.'"

The church hall explodes with activity as people dash off to the bathrooms, while some start stretching—do these people ever *stop* stretching?—and others form chatty cliques around the room.

"How'd you go, hun?" Keegan asks from beside me, his paper-white teeth gleaming.

"Uh . . . fine?" He clearly didn't notice I chose not to sing a single note.

Suddenly, Eli swivels around on his chair in front of us, crossing his legs and draping his arms over the backrest like the world's most beautiful sloth. "So," he says with an impish grin, "who's the new guy?"

There's something so unmistakably attractive about his confidence. He just seems so . . . comfortable. In his clothes, in his environment, in his own skin. It's something I've never experienced myself.

"This is Noah," Keegan replies, doing jazz hands next to my face like I'm a brand-new blender on a tacky infomercial. "He's our baby baritone."

"I'm Eli." He locks eyes with me—multifaceted emerald green—and I melt into a puddle of love-struck clichés.

"Noah," I reply, my voice cracking on the "o" like I'm a hormonal fourteen-year-old.

He chuckles, but not unkindly. "Yeah, I got that. You're one of the ring-ins, right?"

I nod.

Keegan adds, "And it's his first show."

"Fresh meat," Eli says, and I feel myself blushing. The corner of his mouth curls up at the side. "What school do you go to?"

"CHGS."

"Ooh, fancy," Keegan coos in a British accent.

"Why, where do you guys go?"

"Me and Chris go to St. Peter's with Alex."

"And I go to good old East High," Eli says with a cheesy thumbs-up.

I don't know much about St. Peter's, other than that it's an all-boys school (my idea of personal hell), and I've heard some fairly unsavory rumours about East. Nothing as intense as North Secondary, with its daily punch-ons and underground drug trade, but it sounds a bit . . . rowdy.

"Do you know someone in the show?" Chris asks, poking his head around Keegan. His dark eyebrows remind me of fluffy little caterpillars.

"Uh, yeah, my mum. She asked me to help out because they—*you*—needed more boys."

"Beth?" Keegan says, glancing over at a stick-thin blonde woman leaning on the piano chatting with Pania. I'll give it to him, there's definitely some family resemblance. "An illegitimate love-child from a previous hetero relationship?"

"No, not her." I look around the room to find Mum so I can point her out to them, but she's nowhere to be seen. "Her name is Rose. She's playing Vel—"

Eli gasps. "Rose Mitchell is your *mother*?"

"Are you serious?" Chris asks.

"Very serious," I reply, not sure what I'm admitting to.

"Holy shit," Eli says, his eyes glued to mine. I've never met anyone who makes eye contact like this. It's slightly disconcerting but also weirdly hot. "What was it like growing up with a *goddess* for a mum?"

"A what, sorry?"

Keegan laughs. "Your mum is like royalty around here."

"Excuse me?"

"Oh, please," Eli scoffs. "You don't have to play Humble Harry with us, Son of Rose Mitchell."

"I . . . don't understand."

"What do you *mean* you don't understand?" Keegan says. "Rose Mitchell is the real deal. It's a crime against humanity that she was stuck in the BMTS ensemble for so long. Everyone knows that."

"Politics," Eli and Chris say in unison, rolling their eyes.

"But David has no time for that shit," Keegan adds. "This is the first time he's directed a show in Ballarat, and he's finally given Rose the chance she deserves."

I honestly feel like they're talking about someone else. Some Hollywood star. Someone to be adored. Revered, even. Not the woman whose greatest ambition in life is to become a Real Housewife of Ballarat. (Please, lord, don't ever let them make that show.)

"Yeah," I reply slowly, hoping my face isn't betraying my complete bafflement, "it's . . . so great for her."

"*Noah?*" a girl says from behind me, and Eli lifts his gaze. The rest of us—Chris, Keegan, and me—all turn around.

Standing behind the empty row of plastic chairs is a tall, devastatingly pretty South Asian girl, wearing a black crop top and matching leggings. Her black hair is slicked back and tied into a high ponytail, her eyelashes thick with mascara, her lips painted blood red.

"*Prisha?*" I say, feeling like I've been winded.

She folds her arms and glares down at me. She looks so much

like Tan when she's mad. "What the hell are you doing here?"

"I . . . I'm . . ."

"He just joined the cast," Eli says cheerily, when I fail to form words. "He's Rose Mitchell's son."

"Yeah, I know who he is," Prisha replies, her voice dripping with disdain.

"I thought you were m-meant to be in Melbourne?" I stammer. "You've finished uni in Perth, right?"

Prisha lifts one eyebrow. "Not that it's any of your business, Noah, but I have a very important project coming up later in the year, so I figured I'd come home and chill with the fam while I wait. Then David asked me to play Roxie, and I mean, who's gonna turn down a role like that?"

"Oh . . ." I nod. "Cool. Well, I hope—"

"No, no," Prisha interrupts, shaking her head. "We're not doing that, Noah. We're not pretending to be friends."

"Jeez, Prish," Eli says. "Chill."

"Don't tell me to chill," she snaps. "This is *my* goddamn show, and I need to be able to trust the people I'm working with."

No one replies. The silence is long and painful. Heat rises in my cheeks.

"Keep an eye on this one, boys," Prisha warns. "He's not as harmless as he looks."

She turns on her heel and struts off across the room. She finds Alex Di Mario and plants a kiss on his cheek, smiling and laughing, suddenly a completely different girl than the one who just tore me to pieces.

"What was *that* about?" Eli asks, and I turn back around. I meet his eyes again, but I'm so thrown by Prisha's warning that

I can't summon a reply. He searches my face for a moment, the sparkle gone from his eyes, then says, "I gotta go fill up my water. It was . . . nice to meet you, Noah." He jumps out of his seat and darts out of the church hall.

"Wow," Chris breathes. "Prisha is so hot when she's mean."

Keegan groans, and slaps his friend on the shoulder.

Prisha Kandiyar is a lot of things, but "forgiving" is apparently not one of them.

SIX

"DARLING, YOU JUST NEED to relax," Mum says in the car on the way home. "You looked so tense in there. I know we can't all be classically trained vocalists—" *cringe* "—but it's not that hard, really. It's just like talking. But louder. And on pitch."

Her character, Velma, wasn't in the songs we rehearsed after the break, so she took it upon herself to spy on me while I sat there decidedly not singing. I was too busy stewing over the look on Eli's face. More accurately, the two *different* looks on Eli's face:

1. When he smiled at me and it felt like I was going to float straight up through the vaulted ceiling and into the clouds.

2. After Prisha's little interruption, when he looked at me like I was a homeless person asking for money and he'd said, "Sorry, I don't have any change," even though he had a wallet full of gold coins. That weird mix of pity and dismissal and guilt.

"It was fine," I say to Mum, staring out the passenger window. "It's just … going to take a while to get used to, I guess."

I desperately wanted to pull Eli aside after rehearsal to explain Prisha's warning, to defend myself, to assure him I'm a completely benign person in every way, but he was up and out of the church hall as soon as David dismissed us. It's probably for the best, though, because what would I have said to him if he'd stayed? How on earth would I have explained why Prisha and her brother hate me so much without telling him *everything*?

"I know you don't *love* being around people," Mum says as we pull up to a traffic light around the corner from home, "but this will be good for you." She looks in the rear-view mirror and wipes a tiny smudge of lipstick from the corner of her mouth. "And David was *thrilled* that I singlehandedly saved the show by bringing you along."

I puff air into my cheeks to stop myself from groaning out loud. I grab my phone while Mum starts prattling on about something to do with the tempo of her song and how Jane should follow *her*, not the other way around, and type out an email.

Re: Dungeon Shenanigans
From: Arctic Fox <rcticf0x@outlook.com>
To: MagePants69 <magepants69@gmail.com>
On: Sunday, 22 March at 5:17 p.m.

M'lady,

We still on for some good times in the dungeon tonight? Had a bit of a shitty day, so I'm desperate to shatter some skeletons. Wow. Sorry. That's morbid/creepy AF. (But seriously, can we go shatter some skeletons?)

Yours,

RcticF0x

"—and it's not my fault Beth couldn't handle the pressure at the auditions, you know? Don't take your frustration out on *me*. She can't expect special treatment just because she's married to the musical director."

Mum keeps rambling after I hit send, so I throw in an "exactly" and an "I know" so she doesn't think I'm completely ignoring her.

My phone pings as we pull into the driveway.

Re: Dungeon Shenanigans
From: MagePants69 <magepants69@gmail.com>
To: Arctic Fox <rcticf0x@outlook.com>
On: Sunday, 22 March at 5:20 p.m.

SHATTER SOME SKELETONS WE SHALL
(See you at . . . 6 pm? I need pre-skeleton-shattering sustenance.)
Yours,
M

I quickly send an all-caps YES in reply and jump out of the car.

Our house is directly opposite Lake Wendouree—Ballarat's sparkling centrepiece—a block or so down from St. Margaret's girls' school. Dad has been saying for years that he wants to buy a house that backs onto the Ballarat golf course, but Mum refuses to sacrifice our "lakeside living" status. I mean, how would she ever show her face at her absurdly overpriced yoga studio again?

Dad is in his natural post-work habitat when we walk

through the door: on the couch, in the front lounge room with a glass of red wine in hand, a personal cheese platter on his lap, and golf playing on mute on the TV.

"Well, *what* an afternoon that was!" Mum says, walking over to kiss Dad on the forehead.

"Mmm," he replies, without looking away from the TV.

"Beth was up to her usual tricks," Mum says, heading down the hall into the kitchen, raising her voice to shouting-point so we can still hear her, "but David said he's really happy with my character development so far, and you know he doesn't dish out praise for no reason."

"How was work?" I say to Dad.

"Fine."

"Just *fine*? No gross brain stories?"

"Believe it or not," he huffs, eyes still on golf, "I don't feel the need to relive every minute of my day for an audience. Unlike your mother."

"Fair enough," I reply, feeling like we've probably hit our quota of father-son bonding for the day. "Well . . . I'm going to shower."

"Mmm."

I head upstairs and rinse off the awkwardness of the day, then dress in my pajamas and power up my computer. The soft whirr of the processor's cooling fan is instantly comforting.

I log on to *Spire of Dusk* at exactly 6:00 p.m. and MagePants69 is already waiting. Our avatars spawn deep in the dungeon under the graveyard, right where we left off.

More than anything, I want to write <ARE YOU ELI?> but refrain, for obvious reasons.

MagePants69 <you ready for some skeleton shattering?>

RcticFOx <actually . . . how do you feel about a quick visit to the tav first?>

I'm not exactly sure what I intend to do once I get MagePants69 to the Tav, but sending us into battle right now—when all I can think about is Eli, with his legs crossed and his arms draped over that plastic chair and his green eyes twinkling at me—is a one-way ticket to our *Spire of Dusk* demise.

MagePants69 <but the skeletons are patiently awaiting their obliteration . . .>

RcticFOx <drink first, obliteration later? pretty please? cherry on top etc?>

The Half-Elf lets out a long sigh, and then . . .

MagePants69 <fine. i guess the skeletons won't mind waiting a few more minutes . . . >

It's not until our avatars are sitting opposite each other in the Pilar's Crest Tav that I realize I *really* don't know what to say to MagePants69. There's legitimately no way to confirm that he is who I think he is without admitting I'm a creepy stalker. I bite my lip, fingers hovering over the keys. But then . . .

"I have some news," his avi announces in her sweet, computer-generated voice.

Staring at the Bard on my screen, all I can see is Eli's face. The pointed nose, the green eyes, the high cheekbones, the auburn eyebrows. It *has* to be him.

"News?" my Warrior asks. *"Do go on."*

"Well," the Bard says, twirling her red plait as always, *"I met a boy today."*

My heart skips a beat. Or maybe it skips five. Or maybe I'm dead.

"Oh?" my Warrior says, because I can't manage to type anything else.

"I can't give too much away, obviously, but he was . . . kind of cute. I think."

If it's actually *me* he's talking about, *kind of cute* is quite literally the biggest compliment I've ever received.

"Kind of cute?" my Warrior asks, which sounds ridiculous in his deep, gravelly voice. *"Please elaborate."*

"I can't tell you more, can I? The rules . . ."

"You could go into a bit of detail, right?" I don't know if this is pushing it, but I have to try. *"Telling me what some random boy looks like is not technically breaking any of your mum's rules."*

"Hmm . . ." The Bard raises her flagon of ale and takes a sip. It's an automated action that happens when you're in the Tav, but it adds a surprisingly accurate layer of awkward realism to the conversation.

"So," I press, because I have to be sure, *"tell me!"*

"Okay, fine," MagePants69 replies. *"He's blond."* Tick. *"And super shy."* Tick. *"And lanky, but in a weirdly adorable way."* I've never thought of being stick-thin with limbs too long for my body as anything close to adorable, but I'll take that as a tick. *"He's not my usual type—"*

Welp.

"—but he has these beautiful blue eyes. And they're not your run-of-the-mill blue, they're like . . . um . . ."

My heart thuds along with the rhythm of my fingers on the keyboard. *"Periwinkle blue?"*

"Please excuse me while I google that."

I sit back in my chair and take a moment to wipe my sweaty palms on my T-shirt, letting out a long, slow breath. This feels dangerous. It feels like I'm about to jump on a runaway train heading straight for its own destruction.

"Yes! Periwinkle!" the Bard replies after a minute. *"How the hell did you guess that? That's so random."*

Holy shit. It *is* me. And he *is* him.

AND HE THINKS I'M KIND OF CUTE!

"Lucky guess?" my Warrior replies, his voice different enough from my own to make it feel like I'm not responsible for the words he's saying.

The flame-haired Half-Elf sighs from across the table. *"Alas . . ."*

Oh, no. Here it comes. *"Alas what, m'lady?"*

"My friend knows him."

"And?"

"And I'm not sure what their deal is, but she was pretty, um, hostile."

"Hostile how?"

A shrug from the Bard. *"She said to 'keep an eye on him' and that he's 'not as harmless as he looks.' Whatever that means."*

Damn you, Prisha Kandiyar.

"How do you know she's telling the truth?" my Warrior asks.

"Why wouldn't she be?"

"I don't know," I reply. *"Who knows what their history is. And

you just met this guy, right? Shouldn't you give him the benefit of the doubt?"

Am I really doing this? Defending myself in third person? If Eli ever found out . . .

But here's the thing, there's no way he's going to fall for someone like me without a little . . . *assistance.* Especially with Prisha meddling from the sidelines. So, as far as I'm concerned, this is my only option. The *only* logical path.

I have to do this.

"I think," my Warrior goes on, *"you should get to know him before you jump to conclusions."*

After a moment, MagePants69's Bard says, *"You know what . . . you're probably right. As usual. I shall give the boy a chance. One chance. And just because you're so sure."*

But there's only one thing I'm truly sure of right now . . .

I need to make a *plan.*

"To the dungeon?" MagePants69's Bard asks, after several more flagons of virtual ale.

"Do you mind if we have a quick snack break first?"

The Half-Elf rolls her eyes at my Warrior. *"Already? Didn't you eat before we started?"*

"Yeah, but . . . growing boy and all that."

"Okay, whatever," the Bard replies. *"I don't want to be held responsible for you fainting at your desk. You've got five minutes. Those skeletons have been awaiting obliteration for far too long."*

I type the *</laugh>* command. *"See you in five."*

I hit pause and reach across my desk to grab some yellow sticky notes and a black pen. I stare down at the pad, my mind completely blank. Eventually, I blow out a breath and write:

THE PLAN

But that's all I've got.

Yes, I confirmed Eli's identity. Yes, I confirmed that my feelings for him are real. But what did I think was going to happen after that? Immediate marriage proposal?

I glance up at the clock on my computer. Only two minutes of snack-time left.

I let out a sigh and put pen to paper once more . . .

THE PLAN
STEP 1: Get Eli to fall in love with me, with the assistance of RcticF0x. (confirmed by him saying "I LOVE YOU" directly to me (Noah Mitchell) in person)
STEP 2: Tell him the truth about my identity. (by which point he'll be so in love with me that he couldn't possibly be angry at me for lying)

I know it's far from an elaborate plan—okay, it barely even constitutes using the word "plan"—but the crucial elements are there.

Get Eli to fall in love with me.

Then—and only then—*Tell him the truth.*

It's definitely risky. I could lose my best and only friend in the process. But, when it comes down to it, *Spire of Dusk* isn't going to last forever. How long can the two of us keep playing anonymous computer games? We'd both have to move on at some point. Once Eli and I are friends or—dare I even think it—boyfriends in real life, we won't need *Spire of Dusk* anymore. RcticF0x will disappear into the recesses of the internet from whence he came.

Because Eli and I will have each other.

I stick the note to the top corner of my monitor and stare up at it, cracking my knuckles, until MagePants69 reappears.

MagePants69 <miss me, m'lord?>

More than you'll ever know.

RcticF0x <shut up and get slashing>

SEVEN

SO . . . AT THE RISK of sounding highly dramatic . . .

I type a message to Charly on my way from applied computing to physics on Monday morning. It's quite chilly today, even in the science wing corridor, so I'm wearing my burgundy knitted jumper under my CHGS blazer. The cold always seems to get to me more than everyone else. I guess I don't have much insulation.

There might be a boy, I write. Awkward grin emoji. **A cute boy.**

Charly's reply is almost instant. **I'M SORRY WHAT?**

Don't get your hopes up. I only just met him. (If you don't count the staggering amount of hours we've spent slaying dragons together online, which, obviously, I do.) **But I have intel that would suggest he might potentially think I'm cute too.**

Intel? Who are you? Spy emoji. **But YAY.**

Thanks, Char.

So where did this mystery boy come from? WAIT. Is he in Mum's show with you?

Technically, it's OUR show now. But yes.

TELL. ME. EVERYTHING.

For The Plan to work, no one can know about it. Not even Charly. So, even though I *want* to tell her everything . . . **I don't really know what there is to tell,** I reply. Shrugging-guy emoji.

What's his IG handle? Imma stalk him.

I don't know.

Okay, Jane Eyre. What century are you living in? How did you not get his IG handle?

I reply with a single eye-roll emoji. Charly knows I don't have Instagram. Because why would I? Which of my zero friends would follow me?

Fine, she writes. **At least tell me his name.**

Eli.

It's only one word. Three letters. But telling Charly makes the whole thing feel so real. Which is terrifying. But also . . . kind of nice?

Eli who?

Huh. **I actually don't know.**

Omg bub. You are so shit at this.

I chuckle to myself. **I'M AWARE.**

When I arrive at our physics classroom, Mrs. Nkosi is nowhere to be seen. She's probably held up in her Year Eleven psychology class on the other side of the campus. (Do I know my teachers' timetables? Maybe.)

I head to my usual seat up at the front of the class, but stop dead in my tracks (no pun intended), because sitting in my chair, with a striped CHGS tie around his neck, is none other than "Bonesy," the science wing's life-size replica of a human skeleton.

I feel my entire body flush as everyone's gaze shifts towards me, eagerly awaiting my reaction.

Hawk and Simon—sitting at their table in the middle row—are the only ones in the room *not* snickering. Instead, they're simply staring up at me, blank-faced, as if to say, *What? You think we had something to do with this?*

As calmly as I can manage, I walk over to the desk, dump my textbooks, and reach down to grab Bonesy by the ribcage.

"Oh, *sorry*, Noah!" Hawk calls out above the hubbub of anticipation. "We thought that was *you*."

Simon adds, "You never told us you had a twin brother!"

One of the Orc-ish rower boys in the back row lets out a guffaw that sets off the rest of the class. To the soundtrack of thirty students practically wetting themselves with laughter, I hoist Bonesy out of my chair and carry him towards the supply cupboard beside the whiteboard.

"Wait, wait, wait," Hawk says, jumping out of his seat and dashing around the tables to intercept me. "Don't you want to introduce us?"

"Very funny," I reply dryly. "I look like a skeleton. Now just . . . get out of my way, please."

Simon sidles up beside him, barely unable to control his glee. "But we want to say hello to your twin." He reaches out to shake Bonesy's hand. "How do you do, Snitchell the Second?"

From the back corner, Lisa Kenway cries out, "Maybe they're *boyfriends*?" and then Felix Simms, another one of the rower boys, scoffs and says, "Nah, even Bonesy's got better taste than that!"

The hysterical laughter in the classroom reaches fever pitch. My face is on fire. My eyes are stinging. I try to push past Hawk and Simon but they block my path to the closet, snatching Bonesy from my grip.

"Just let me put him away before Mrs. Nkosi gets here," I whisper, trying to contain my chagrin.

Simon smirks. "But that would ruin all the fun."

The next three seconds tick by in extreme slow motion, like I've hit replay on an epic KO in an old-school arcade fighting game. I grab Bonesy by the arm—well, the humerus—and try to pull him away from Hawk. But Hawk pulls back just as Simon shoves me in the chest. I start to topple backwards but yank myself forward using Bonesy's arm, overcompensating and tripping over my own feet. Hawk lets go and I fall flat on my face, Bonesy's entire body between me and the cold, hard tiles. There's an awful crunching sound as his ribcage shatters and bone fragments skid across the floor of the science lab. A few girls squeal. Some boys in the back make a noise that sounds like they just watched someone get tackled in a football game. Then there is complete silence.

I just lie there on the floor, utterly defeated, until . . .

"What is *this*?" a woman shrieks from the doorway.

I turn my head, wincing as something pinches in my shoulder, and wincing again when I see it's Mrs. Jamison at the door. Of course. The Daughter of Medusa has arrived just in time to witness my humiliation. But not—much to my anguish—Simon's and Hawk's involvement. The boys are perched safely at their bench in the second row, ghosts of smiles on their lips.

"I came to tell you all that Mrs. Nkosi is dealing with an accident over in the humanities wing, and *this* is what I find? Destruction of school property?"

I push myself up off the floor, feeling like parts of my own skeleton might be broken too.

"Noah Mitchell," Mrs. Jamison drawls, shaking her head. "Why am I not surprised."

"Mrs. Jamison, I *swear* this wasn't—"

"Spare me, Mr. Mitchell," she snaps, holding a hand aloft. "My office. *Now.*"

I grab my books and trudge out the door, leaving whatever was left of my self-esteem buried under a pile of Bonesy's pulverised ribs.

I sit through Tuesday morning's applied computing class bracing for another prank from Hawk and Simon, but it never comes. I have maths methods with them straight after, but still nothing. My free period is spent the same way I spend all my free periods: sitting in the library, studying. Alone.

At lunchtime, my phone pings.

Re: Dungeon Shenanigans

From: MagePants69 <magepants69@gmail.com>

To: Arctic Fox <rcticf0x@outlook.com>

On: Tuesday, 24 March at 1:34 p.m.

Hey heyyy,

So, I'll be home late again tonight. Sorry! Actually, I'll be home late every Tuesday and Thursday for a while . . .

Is 10:15 p.m. too late for you on the reg? Totally get it if you need your beauty sleep or whatever, we'll just have to make up for lost time on the weekend. Those skeletons won't exterminate themselves!

 Yours,

 M

If I didn't already know the reason MagePants69 was going to be home late every Tuesday and Thursday night, that email would've sent me into a doom spiral of epic proportions.

Re: Dungeon Shenanigans

From: Arctic Fox <rcticf0x@outlook.com>

To: MagePants69 <magepants69@gmail.com>

On: Tuesday, 24 March at 1:39 p.m.

M'lady,

 I shall be completely lost every Tuesday and Thursday between the hours of 3:30 p.m. and 10:15 p.m. HOW WILL I POSSIBLY COPE?

 (Kidding, I'll be totally fine. I just hope whatever you're up to on Tuesday and Thursday involves the Kind of Cute Boy . . .)

 Yours,

 RcticF0x

(Yes, I still feel weird talking about myself as if I'm some random stranger, but desperate times.)

Re: Dungeon Shenanigans

From: MagePants69 <magepants69@gmail.com>

To: Arctic Fox <rcticf0x@outlook.com>

On: Tuesday, 24 March at 1:41 p.m.

YOU'LL BE TOTALLY FINE?! How VERY dare you. And yes, Tuesdays and Thursdays MAY involve the Kind of Cute Boy, but probably not in the way you're thinking, unless that's me and the Kind of Cute Boy having hot gay sex. Kidding, stop picturing me naked. Kidding, you don't have to stop. KIDDING, you couldn't picture me naked even if you wanted to because you have no idea what I look like! *insert evil villain laugh* okay, I'm gonna go now.

Yours,

M

When the bell rings for last period, I head to the Year Twelve lockers to grab my books for media studies. Right-Wing Barbie (AKA Maddison Whitely, who's been in love with Hawk since the dawn of time, and whose locker happens to be right next to mine) sidles up beside me and gives me her typical scowl.

"Destroyed any school property today?" she asks, spinning the dial on her combination lock.

"Attended any straight pride rallies today?" I reply, fumbling my own combination and having to start again.

Maddison scoffs and pulls her phone out of her locker.

I carefully turn the dial on my lock until it clicks open, then sift through the piles of loose-leaf paper in my locker, feeling Maddison's eyes on my back the whole time.

"Can I help you?" I snap, but she just slams her locker closed, clicks her lock, and turns away.

"Obviously not," I say to myself, as she prowls off down the corridor, her white-blonde hair swishing annoyingly across her shoulders as she walks.

The final period of the day drags on and on, but then it's home to scoff an early dinner and off to *Chicago* rehearsal with Mum.

There's a sentence I never thought I'd say.

My nerves about the rehearsals themselves have now been surpassed by the stress of having to win the heart of my dream boyfriend. Not only do I have to convince him I'm chill and fun and sexy (okay, I'll never be "sexy" but I'll settle for an upgrade from "kind of cute" to just plain "cute"), but I now have to do it while fending off Prisha's attempts at character assassination. It would be easily achievable for someone like Alex Di Mario, but for the geeky, skinny, pimply, braces-wearing, painfully uncoordinated, socially awkward, overly self-deprecating Noah Mitchells of the world, a situation like this presents *quite* the challenge.

When Eli walks into the church hall, I'm standing with Keegan and Chris, listening to them rank the all-time best per-formances of a song called "No Good Deed" from some musical I've never heard of. Eli dumps his backpack on the stage with the rest of the bags, then I watch him as *he* watches Alex saunter into the room. Suddenly, all I can think about is how much I look like Bonesy in this exercise ensemble Mum forced me to wear. Clothes always look so boxy and baggy on me, my limbs protruding from the fabric like twigs, whereas Alex's outfit—

a burgundy gym singlet and tapered black tracksuit pants—fits as it would the in-store mannequins, with their huge pecs and thighs and weirdly erotic Ken-doll bulges.

Eventually, Eli strolls over to us in the middle of the hall and says, "How are we, girls?"

"Good, bro," Chris replies. I've already gathered (in the very short amount of time I've spent with him) that Chris feels the need to remind everyone of his straightness whenever he's around Eli and Alex and Keegan. Not in a bad way, just in a way that says, *I'm totally into musicals and I'm one hundred percent cool with dudes who like dudes, but I just want to make it clear that, personally, I'm all about the ladies.*

On second thought, maybe that is bad. Maybe I should be offended. I don't know. I've only been around a handful of other gay guys in my life—they're a bit of a rarity in Ballarat—so the whole thing is slightly foreign to me. MagePants69 and I both came out to each other at the start of last year (and everyone at school found out about me when Hawk and Simon hacked my email account) but the only gay guys I've actually met are:

1. Greg Carpenter (a Year Seven at CHGS who rose to social media fame when someone live-streamed him telling Mrs. Livingstone that she looked like one of the drag queens from *Ru Paul's Drag Race* and that she shouldn't be mad at him for saying that because he'd obviously meant it as a compliment)

2. Phil McNamara (who is at least sixty, and one of Mum's "yoga girls")

3. Dinh McNamara (who is Phil's husband, and about thirty years his junior)

And now suddenly 4, 5 and 6—Keegan, Alex, and Eli (and

probably half the cast of *Chicago*, let's be honest).

I laugh out loud at the thought.

"What's so funny?" Eli asks.

"Nothing," I reply. "I was just . . . thinking about this ridiculous YouTube video."

"I'm quite partial to a ridiculous YouTube video."

I know I shouldn't do this, but . . . "Have you seen the one with the cat and the snow and—"

"And the succulent?" Eli says, placing his hand on his chest. "I *love* that video."

I know he loves it, because I'm the one who sent it to him a few weeks ago.

"It's the second-best cat video of all time," I reply, trying to remain chill.

"What's the first-best?"

"I'll have to show you sometime." I honestly can't believe these words are coming out of my mouth. I feel like someone else. Someone who's good at talking out loud—at *flirting* out loud. I think it's because talking to Eli feels exactly the same as messaging MagePants69, an art in which I am very well-versed. "My perfect afternoon consists of cat videos and double-coat Tim Tams."

"Double-coat Tim Tams," Eli says, his voice all sultry and syrupy. "My favourite food group. Correction, the *only* food group. Like, I would eat them for breakfast, lunch, and dinner if I could."

"Don't forget elevenses!"

"Oh," Eli chuckles, "I am *always* here for a *Lord of the Rings* reference."

Keegan laughs, short and sharp. "Uh, should we leave?" He motions to Chris. "We're like, totally crashing this date right now."

"I feel dirty," Chris adds flatly.

Eli smirks, seemingly able to shrug their comments off, while I just stand here spontaneously combusting.

EIGHT

"AND A FIVE, SIX, seven, eight!" David shouts from the front of the room.

Turns out, if I thought I was out of my depth in the vocal rehearsals, I'm currently stranded at the bottom of the Mariana Trench in this "choreography call." We're rehearsing "We Both Reached for the Gun," one of Alex's big numbers in the show. He plays a cheesy ventriloquist who's puppeteering Prisha's character, Roxie Hart. She sits on his lap for the whole song with his hand up the back of her dress (which I'm sure she's not mad about, and I probably wouldn't be either) mouthing the words he's singing. I hate to admit it, but the song is pretty clever. The whole show is, actually. It reminds me of *Cabaret*—which I also had to study in Year Ten English thanks to Mrs. Weiss, our theatre-obsessed English/drama teacher—where the songs are all metaphors. *Chicago* is dark like *Cabaret*, too. It's like *How to Get Away with Murder* but with jazz hands.

This particular number doesn't involve a whole lot of *dancing*-dancing—thank god, because I'd die if I was subjected to that level of humiliation in front of Eli this early on in our real-world relationship—but it still takes a certain level of coordination that I most certainly do not have.

We all play reporters at Roxie's press conference, and we basically just have to stand up and sit down on specific counts in the music, like a bunch of marionettes on speed. The problem is, there doesn't seem to be any real sequence to who stands up when, or at least not one I can decipher. Every time I'm supposed to stand up, I'm always a second late. The other new guy—Raf, a middle-aged man never seen *not* wearing a burgundy beret— seems to have picked up the choreography perfectly, which makes me look like an even bigger fool every time I fumble the steps.

"Stop!" David says, clapping so loudly it's like his hands are amplified. "Noah, you're still late on all your counts. Do we need to go over them? Again?"

Given this is my second rehearsal, I think David is being *slightly* dramatic, but I'm sensing that's a bit of a theme with these people.

Every single cast member in the church hall is now looking directly at me, awaiting my reply. Eli is smiling supportively, his eyes glinting with the slightest hint of pity, like he wishes there was a way for him to save me from this awkwardness. Alex is staring at me absently, like he's wondering what he's having for dinner. Prisha—who is still sitting on Alex's lap—leans back in a perfect arch to gain a better angle for glaring. (I tell you what, she's giving Mrs. Jamison a run for her money in the gaze-that-could-turn-someone-to-stone department.)

"No," I reply, cheeks burning. "I'll get it. I'm just . . . not . . . I'll get it."

"Don't worry, David," Mum calls out. She's not in this number, so she's "supporting" me from a chair in front of the mirrors. At least, that's what she told the cast, because she knows that's what an Encouraging Mother would say—she's always playing a different role, Rose Mitchell. "Noah and I will work on it at home." She smiles at me, saccharine sweet. "Won't we, darling?"

Calling me "darling" in the privacy of our own home is patronizing enough, but here, in front of all these people, in front of Eli . . . .

I crack my knuckles. "Yes, we will."

"Fine," David says. "Let's just run it again. Alex, Prisha, we'll pick it up from the same place."

"Sure," they say in unison, the perfect team.

Eli, who is in the row of reporters on the opposite side of the room, serves me another adorable grin. My stomach flips. He mouths the words *You got this* and, for some reason, I almost want to cry. He doesn't even know me (well, he *thinks* he doesn't know me) and he's going completely out of his way to be nice. I return his smile, though I know it's not convincing, because he laughs, shaking his head as he turns back to face the front.

This time when we run the number, Mum decides to perform every count of my reporter choreography up at the front of the room, miming along with full performance energy. How she knows all of my steps on top of her own is completely baffling, but I know she's not doing any of this to help me. She's doing it to look good in front of David and the cast. If she actually wanted to *help*, she'd know to do it privately, where her presence isn't just compounding my embarrassment and anxiety, making me even *more* terrible at what I'm supposed to be doing, which is literally just standing up and sitting down, so I really should be able to handle it because it's a basic human function, but I can't and I want to stop and run away and I just—

"*Shit*!" I miss my count for the nine-millionth time and slump down into my chair, burying my head in my hands while the others barrel on through the song.

Why am I doing this? Why am I here? How could I have possibly thought this would be a good way to impress a boy?

"Stop, stop, stop," David calls out over the music. Jane's fingers trickle on the keys and the piano dies out.

"Seriously?" Prisha snaps from up front. "If we have to stop every time Noah fails to control his own limbs, we are *never* going to make it through the number."

David purses his lips. "Ensemble, take fifteen. This is not a break, I want you to all go over your counts while I work with Alex and Prisha for a bit."

Everyone breaks off into groups but I stay in my seat, seething, until I sense someone standing over me.

"Hey."

I look up and it's Eli, smiling with his lips pressed together.

"Hi," I reply, unable to look him in the eye. I feel so small right now.

"I don't know about you, but I feel like I've been on a seesaw for three hours." He spins a chair around and sits down, facing me, arms folded over the backrest. "How are you going with it all?"

I let out a wry laugh. "Well, it's been publicly confirmed that I'm the least coordinated human on the planet, so not great, really."

"Don't stress," he says. "We've already had—"

"Darling." Mum appears out of nowhere beside us. "I know this is not easy for you," she says, a terse smile plastered on her face, "but I will *not* have you behaving like a child during rehearsal, it's . . . not a good look. For either of us."

I don't want to snap at her in front of Eli, so I swallow my words (which were going to be mostly profane) and say, "I know. Eli's going to help me out."

She glances at Eli, as if she only just noticed him sitting there. "I'd help Noah myself," she says politely, "but I have my own work to worry about, you know?"

"Of course," Eli replies, nodding. "I'm happy to help."

Mum looks from me to Eli and back again, and I know there's something else she wants to say. But she just clicks her tongue and walks away, finding David by the piano and most likely telling him I'm adopted and that she has *no* idea where my temper comes from.

"Thank you," I say to Eli, feeling like a little kid who just got told off in front of his kindergarten friends.

"All good." He shrugs. "Like I said, I'm happy to help."

"You don't have to, though," I reply. "I only said that to get Mum to leave me alone. I'm not your responsibility. I should be able to figure out how to coordinate my own limbs. It's not rocket science."

He laughs. "I mean, limbs can be difficult sometimes."

"Apparently."

"What's something you're really good at?" he asks.

"What?"

"Tell me something you're great at."

"Rocket science."

He laughs again, this time tipping his head back to the ceiling, and I get a swirling feeling in my chest.

"I meant physics," I clarify. "And it was a joke. I'm . . . not actually that great at it."

"Okay, well, I promise I'm worse. I am *woeful* at physics. And maths. And also biology. Which does not bode well for my end of year exams."

I'm not exactly sure what he's trying to say. "So . . .?"

"So, we're not all great at everything."

"So, you're saying I *am* terrible at dancing?"

"No," he chuckles. "Or, I dunno, maybe you are. Or maybe you'll be amazing when you've had a chance to catch up. But you're here. You showed up. Just like I show up to physics and maths and biology. That's the important part."

"This is a very strange pep talk," I say, trying to stop myself from smiling.

"Sorry," he replies. He lets his head drop onto his arms, still flopped over the backrest.

"But seriously," I say, "you really don't have to help me. You're off the hook."

"Don't be ridiculous," he replies, looking up, his brow adorably crinkled. "I want to be on the hook. I'm like, fully willing to be hooked."

I feel my ears blush.

"Besides, us baritones gotta stick together, right?" he adds when I don't reply.

"Is that a thing?" I ask. "Baritone solidarity?"

He shrugs one shoulder and locks his twinkly green eyes on mine. "We can make it a thing."

If I was Alex Di Mario, I'd smile my Hollywood smile and say, *Can we make* us *a thing?* and Eli would be forever under my spell.

But I'm not Alex Di Mario. I'm Noah Mitchell. So, I just chuckle awkwardly and let the moment pass me by.

NINE

WHO WOULD'VE THOUGHT I'D ever look forward to anything other than locking myself in my room and playing computer games. Since Sunday—which honestly feels like a month ago—the days when I don't have *Chicago* rehearsals seem like filler, even the ones where I get to play *Spire of Dusk* with MagePants69. Because being around the real Eli, even with the constant pressure of the rehearsals themselves, is infinitely better than chatting online with his alter ego. Don't get me wrong, I still love our chats in the Tav, and it's definitely a useful way to decipher Eli's thoughts about me, but nothing can compare to when he smiles at me across the church hall and my heart explodes into a million pieces of pink, love-heart-shaped confetti.

Now that Mum and I are both out two nights a week (and all afternoon on Sunday), Dad has started making constant passive-aggressive comments about having to cook for himself. Mum's response: "Haven't you heard of Uber Eats, Roger?"

Wednesday is a Hawk and Simon-free day at school, but I have physics with them on Thursday morning, and applied computing last period. I sit through both classes feeling super wound up, bracing for another prank, but—thankfully—it never comes. I've been completely on edge at school since the Bonesy debacle. The whole thing was made even more humiliating when it became public knowledge that Dad had to purchase three *more* Bonesies for the CHGS science wing to keep me from getting suspended.

You see, five generations of Mitchells have attended Central Highlands Grammar School (or whatever it was called in the 1900s when it was run by a bunch of nuns) and Dad is clearly not going to let me be the one to destroy the family legacy.

By the time Thursday evening rolls around, I'm bursting at the seams to see Eli. Last night on *Spire of Dusk* he said, and I quote, "the Kind of Cute Boy also has great banter, and great taste in snacks," which obviously replaced "kind of cute" as the biggest compliment I've ever received. Plus, as far as I can gather, snacks are the basis of any great relationship, so I'm taking it as a massive win.

"I can tell you're nervous, darling," Mum says, as we hop out of the car outside the church hall. "Nerves will just make it even harder to pick up the choreography, trust me. You're better off without them."

Yes, because it's that simple, Rose.

But I say, "I'm not nervous," which is partly true, because I'm not nervous about what she *thinks* I'm nervous about. "I just . . . had too much coffee today."

As we walk up the ramp to the glass doors of the BMTS building, I notice Prisha standing outside on the phone, speaking in Tamil. I used to love listening to her and Tan talking to their aunties back in India and Singapore in their family's first language. I only ever managed to pick up a handful of words, and what I *did* learn was basic: vaṇakkam (*hello*), appuram parkalam (*see you later*), nān̲ velvēn̲ (*I win*, which I didn't get to say very often when Tan was around, if I'm honest).

Prisha sees us coming, says a quick goodbye in English, and hangs up the phone.

"Hi, beautiful," Mum says, as we walk past.

"Hey, Rose," Prisha replies, before cutting her eyes to me. "Have you learned to count to eight yet, Noah?"

Mum laughs. "He'll get there. Won't you, darling?"

"Let's hope so," Prisha says, smiling for Mum's sake.

"I'll see you in there," Mum says absently to both of us before leaving me alone with Prisha.

"I don't know what the fuck you think you're doing here, Noah," she says, not even bothering to lower her voice, "but whatever it is, you need to get your shit together. This show might be a joke to you, but it's not to me. And it's sure as hell not a joke to Rose. So whatever bullshit agenda you have, you'd better not wreck this for the rest of us."

My throat practically closes over. "I don't have an agenda," I lie. "Mum asked me to do the show as a favor, and . . . here I am."

Prisha scoffs. "Look, whatever. But just so we're clear, if you ruin this for me, I will make sure everyone in this show knows *exactly* the kind of person you are. Okay?"

Before I can reply, she flips her sleek ponytail over her shoulder and marches inside. I let out a long breath, turning my face to the cloudy sky above. If Prisha didn't know the truth about what happened in Year Nine, her threats would be completely hollow. But, as it stands, she could easily turn Eli and everyone else in the cast against me if she wanted to. I'm powerless here, just like I am at school with Hawk and Simon.

I need to toe the line. Do whatever I can to keep Prisha happy. Which probably includes learning how to dance, so you may as well kill me right now.

I push open the glass door and head straight for the bathrooms down the hall. I feel the sudden need to splash water on my face like people do in the movies when they need to snap out of whatever doom-spiraling they're doing. There's a sign on the door that says ALL GENDERS BATHROOM, which is surely a first for Ballarat, where being openly gay is still considered edgy, let alone being trans or non-binary or genderqueer (let's be honest, half of the country probably doesn't even know what those words mean). I smile at the sign for a second, then push open the door. Standing at the sink, leaning over the bench, is Alex Di Mario, staring determinedly at his expression in the mirror and muttering something I can't quite catch.

I freeze just inside the door, feeling like I've interrupted a very private moment.

Alex flinches, and turns to face me, his brow heavy. After a second, he rolls his shoulders back and relaxes his expression. "Oh, hey," he says, as nonchalant as can be. (Side note: I would *kill* to know what it feels like to be nonchalant, just for like, one minute.)

"Uh, hi," I say, still standing in the doorway. It's the first time I've actually spoken to Alex. "Sorry if I . . . I didn't mean to—"

"It's fine." He turns on the tap to wash his hands. "I was just running some lines. We're doing the 'Razzle Dazzle' scene later and the dialogue is all underscored, so I was just working on the timing."

Unless the dialogue in "Razzle Dazzle" involves some super intense staring (which I'd hazard a guess it doesn't, given the title), I have a feeling Alex is not being entirely truthful with me.

"Oh, cool," I say, heading into one of the cubicles, mainly to save myself from having to think of anything else to say.

I wait until I hear the bathroom door open and close again, then head straight into the church hall to find Eli. I spot him in the middle of the room, chatting and stretching with Keegan, Chris, and Luana, who's playing Go-to-Hell Kitty (a role that suits her a little too well).

"Hey," I say, and they all say hello back in harmony. "So, I just bumped into Alex in the toilet—"

"This sounds familiar," Luana cuts in, arching an eyebrow.

"Very," Keegan says, elbowing Eli.

"Stop," he says. "This is not the time."

Keegan and Luana both giggle, but don't say another word.

"*Anyway*," Eli says. "You bumped into Alex . . . ."

But suddenly it feels wrong to tell them what I saw, if I saw anything in the first place, which I might not have. I could have imagined the pained expression on Alex's face, his sharp whispering to no one.

"You know what," I reply, "it doesn't matter."

Eli narrows his eyes at me. "*Okay.*"

Keegan raises his eyebrows and Chris looks at the floor. Luana bites back a smile. It's obvious there's a conversation bubbling under the surface between them, some unspoken dialogue I'm not privy to. I glance over my shoulder at Alex, who's now standing by the piano with Prisha and Jane.

"Can we go over 'We Both Reached for the Gun' before we

start?" I ask the group, eager to change the subject.

"Please," Chris says. "I could definitely do with a refresher on the counts at the end."

"Like it's hard," Keegan scoffs, then adds to me, "No offense."

"None taken." I chuckle, though if I'm honest, there is some taken.

"I gotta go pee," Eli says, turning his back on us.

"But Alex is in *here* now," Luana replies, deadpan.

"Not funny," Eli snaps over his shoulder, already jogging towards the door.

The others exchange a look that skims straight past me.

"Is he okay today?" I ask. "He seems a bit . . . disgruntled."

"He's fine," Keegan sighs. "He just—"

"Has a weird thing about Alex," Luana finishes, which is possibly the most loaded comment I've ever heard.

"Why does he have a weird thing about Alex?" I ask, feeling like I've started reading a book halfway through and missed all the exposition and character development.

Keegan rolls his eyes. "I'm bored of this conversation."

"Can we go over the counts already?" Chris asks. "David's got the shits tonight and I don't feel like being yelled at."

We all know *I'm* the only one who has a chance of getting yelled at, which is the only reason I'm prepared to let this conversation go.

For now . . .

TEN

WE PLAY *Spire of Dusk* that night, but—as always—there's no rational way for me to bring up what happened at rehearsal without completely outing myself to MagePants69. Besides that, we don't have time for a trip to the Tav, since we're buried up to our necks in quests bestowed upon us by Leora, the High Priestess of the Church of the Lightseekers.

It turned out that the person responsible for raising the dead in the dungeon was this sexy vampire dude called Queran, who had a distinctly non-Cullen demeanour and who tried *very* hard to kill us. Luckily, High Priestess Leora swooped in to save the day, just as Queran was about to hand us our asses on a non-silver platter. But then he started ranting about how Leora and the Lightseekers were the *real* bad guys and how we should pledge our allegiance to him and the Vampires of the Vale instead, so we can rid the Three Kingdoms of its true plague—blah, blah, blah—and I've played enough games like this to know that once we'd chosen a path, there'd be no going back.

But, when forced to choose between Queran and Leora (or, as MagePants69 likes to call them, "the bloodsucker with the eight pack" and "Cate Blanchett from *Lord of the Rings*"), the decision seemed like an absolute no-brainer . . . .

MagePants69 <what do we do, m'lord???>

RcticF0x <i mean . . . wouldn't you feel a little bit weird siding with the psychopath who's been trying to kill us for the past half an hour? we should go with the good guys, right?>

MagePants69 <is that your final answer?>

RcticF0x <yep. lock it in>

MagePants69 <cate blanchett it is>

Anyway, *TL;DR*, it turns out you don't get to align yourself with the Church of the Lightseekers without first proving your allegiance a million times over. Hence, our complete lack of time for hangs in the Tav.

Thankfully, Eli is his usual adorable self at rehearsal on Sunday afternoon. He also looks cuter than ever, thanks to a fresh haircut and a green T-shirt that brings out the color of his eyes so much that it looks like someone's bumping up the saturation in real time.

Today we're working on the choreography for "All That Jazz," which is one of Mum's "star turns" in the show. She already warned me in the car how important this rehearsal is for her, so I'm to be "as switched on as possible." The problem is, I still don't know the words to "All That Jazz" and the movements are set to the lyrics, not the counts, so it's going to be an epic struggle no matter how "switched on" I am.

The thing that's really not helping is that Alex and Prisha are sitting at the front of the room with Sierra, our Mama Morton, watching the whole rehearsal. Prisha has her arms crossed and one eyebrow raised, unabashedly glaring at me in disgust, and Alex is just sitting there like some marble statue, all handsome and muscly and incredibly distracting. (Tight grey tracksuit pants should be illegal, in my opinion.) If it weren't for the occasional encouraging smile from Eli, I'd probably shrivel up and die right here in the church hall.

"Right," David says, weaving through the cast spread out around the room. "We're getting there. Slowly."

Eli catches my eye and gives me a thumbs-up-thumbs-down, as if to say, *You good? Not good?* I shrug in reply, giving him a noncommittal thumb-lying-on-its-side. He laughs silently, returning his attention to David.

"Rose," David says, sidling up to Mum. "Fabulous. Really great. I just want you to sink into your hips a bit more on 'aspirin' and through that whole line. I want you to feel grounded. Strong. Just show me quickly." She moves into a slight lunge, bending at the knees and arching her back. David places his hands on her hips, guiding her a little lower. "Just a bit further."

There's something about the way his hands slide across the fabric of her tights—almost like he's caressing her—that makes me feel weirdly protective all of a sudden, like I want to shout out, *Hands off, mate, she's married!*

"Perfect," he says. "That line is gorgeous."

Mum straightens up, looking slightly flushed. "Thank you, David," she says, brushing her hips with her hands, almost like she's trying to wipe away his touch.

I look around the room, seething internally, but no one else seems to think this is anything out of the ordinary.

"Let's run what we've got so far!" David announces. "Then we'll take a quick drink break and go on."

We reset to the start of the number and David counts Jane in. "And a five, six—*make it a good one, everyone!*"

Much to my surprise, I remember approximately 60 percent of the steps this time (a new record, though I'm sure I still look terrible doing 99 percent of that 60 percent) and I only run into two people (another record). One of those people happens to be Yvette, one of Prisha's little disciples, who hisses, "Get some fucking spatial awareness!" in between counts of choreography. I fail to come up with a witty comeback on the fly, which is probably for the best, since it's definitely not worth aggravating Prisha by proxy.

"Good, good, good," David says when we finish. "Ladies, you're doing so well. Men—" he huffs out a breath "—we've got a bit of work to do. Eli, Keegan, you boys are giving me exactly what I need, so if anyone needs help over the holidays, they're your guys, all right? Next time I see this, I want it to be *slick*. You've got two weeks off, so do *not* come back in here after the break not knowing your shit. We clear?"

The cast murmurs and claps half-heartedly. I completely forgot it was almost school holidays. It's usually my favorite time—no Hawk, no Simon, no pranks—but I can't imagine not seeing Eli for two whole weeks.

"Rose," David says over the top of the noise, "a word?"

He ushers Mum outside into the annex of the church and my instinct is to follow, to check she's okay. David may have his youthful good looks, and he may be an award-winning director, but . . . something is wrong here. I know it.

Just as I'm about to sneak over to the door, Eli materializes before me, his forehead glistening with sweat.

"So," he says, flapping the front of his green T-shirt to get some airflow underneath. Suddenly, I'm praying he'll just take it off right here in front of me. "I was thinking . . . if you need some help with any of the choreography, maybe I could give you a hand sometime over the holidays?"

I blink back at him, my mind now picturing a one-on-one shirtless choreography tutorial. (Just to be clear, *I'm* not shirtless in the fantasy, just Eli. Because no one needs to see this skeletal frame in the flesh.)

"Not that I think you're struggling," he says quickly. "I just thought it would help to catch you up a bit. Drill some things."

Drill some things? Uh, yes, please . . . .

"I think that's a great idea," I reply, hyper conscious of the heat in my cheeks. "Anything to spare me from another monologue from Mum in the car about how I need to 'get into my body,' whatever that means, considering there's nowhere else I could physically *be*."

"We'll get you into your body." Eli smirks, and my ears start to burn too.

"You, uh—" I crack my knuckles "—sure you don't mind helping me out?"

"Nah, it'll be fun," he replies with a very casual but very sexy shrug. "Plus, it'll give us a chance to hang. If your taste in snacks and YouTube videos is anything to go by, I think we could possibly be soulmates." He laughs, and even though I know he's joking, it's true. We *are* soulmates.

It takes all my self-control not to tell him who I really am, right here, right now.

"Well," I say, "I'm happy to provide double-coat Tim Tams for the occasion."

"Now we're talking," Eli smiles, and I smile back at him, and

I wish more than anything that this moment never had to end. "Okay, cool," he says. "I'm working a fair bit in the holidays, but you could meet me at my work one day when I finish? There's plenty of space to dance there."

"Sounds great."

"I'll text you the address et cetera," Eli says. "Gimme your phone."

"My what?"

He knits his brow. "Your phone. You know, that thing you use to message your friends?"

"Oh," I say, picturing the nonexistent friends I'm messaging all the time. "Why do you need my phone?"

"Uh, so I can give you my number?"

I fish my phone out of my pocket and hand it to him. I'm so overwhelmed by the fact that a boy wants to give me his number—and not just any boy, *the* boy—that I completely forget what's waiting for him on my lock screen.

"Aww, cute photo," Eli says, pouting down at my phone. "Is that your dog?"

My stomach drops and my heart leaps into my throat.

No. It is not my dog. I don't have a dog. It's a photo of an *arctic fox*. As in, *RcticF0x*. As in, a dead fucking giveaway.

"It's . . . my . . . cousin's puppy," I reply, which is possibly the worst lie in history, since I don't have any cousins, and because arctic foxes are solitary creatures and definitely not domesticated-animal material. "They . . . live in Alaska."

"Adorable," Eli replies, and I just stare back at him, waiting for the penny to drop. "Oh, it's locked." He holds the phone up to my face to unlock it, then taps away at the screen. "Done!" He hands it back to me. "Just message me so I've got your number."

"Of course," I say, still waiting for him to realize that my cousin's puppy is, in fact, a wild animal and the screen name of his online bestie, who happens to be standing *right in front of him.*

But he just grins and says, "See you soon," looking unashamedly chuffed with himself. "Enjoy your first few days of freedom, mister."

"You too," I reply, feeling my heart slowly return to its usual place in my chest.

Then, without warning, Eli leans in and kisses me on the cheek.

I freeze. The whole room freezes. The Earth itself stops turning.

"Bye," he says, before walking off across the hall, grabbing his backpack, and making his way to the door. He pauses on the threshold and grins at me across the church. I smile back at him, my heart aching, my stomach aching, my crotch aching, my feet still glued to the floor. Then suddenly he's gone.

Mum calls my name from by the piano, and we leave the BMTS hall together, Mum clip-clopping loudly down the concrete ramp, me floating all the way to the car on a cloud of pure, unadulterated elation.

ELEVEN

MagePants69 <dude, watch your back. vamps at three o'clock>

I reach over to my venetian blinds and yank on the cord to snap them closed. We don't often play at this hour, and the morning sun is making it hard to see my screen, especially in a location as dank and dark as the Dock of Lost Souls.

RcticF0x <on it>

My avi draws his brand-new weapon—a rare broadsword imbued with life-leeching, poison damage, and a killer strength buff—and decapitates three hungry vampires in one click of the mouse.

RcticF0x <your turn. seven o'clock>

MagePants69 <already there>

His Bard slings her gilded lyre off her back and strums a heavenly chord. The vampires dragging themselves across the dock flare with azure light, then crumble into little piles of grey ash on the rotting wooden pier.

RcticF0x <loving your new bardsong>

MagePants69 <loving your new sword>

RcticF0x <LOVING US>

To be honest, there's nothing *not* to love about *Spire of Dusk* at the moment. We're absolutely smashing our vampire-vanquishing duties for Leora, our avatars are decked out in the finest equipment that Lightseeker reward coin can buy, and our awesomeness as a pair has reached supreme new heights. It's like our minds are tethered by some invisible thread, allowing us to act as one in every single situation. We've barely taken a hit all week, which could be explained by the simple fact that we're both great at this game, or it *could* be because of all the bonding we're doing off-screen. Ever since I messaged Eli on Sunday night, there's been a constant stream of messages, GIFs, memes, video recommendations, and what I'm interpreting as appropriately geeky sexual innuendo. Obviously, Eli doesn't know it's RcticF0x that he's chatting to, but being in a mood this good can only be beneficial for gameplay.

On screen, the rickety pier splinters at my Warrior's feet and a horde of vampires leap straight out of the grimy dock water below. I double click on the enemy in the middle of the pack and my Warrior swirls across the pier, a literal sword tornado—a swordnado, if you will—eviscerating the vampires where they stand.

The experience bar at the bottom of my interface fills with yellow liquid and the words *LEVEL UP* flash in the middle of my screen in glorious golden light.

RcticF0x <woot. lvl up>

MagePants69 <samesies! teamwork . . .>

RcticF0x <. . . makes the effing dream work>

As I start looting the vampire corpses, my phone buzzes on my desk.

Hey.

It's Eli. It still gives me a nervous thrill having him on my computer screen and my phone at the same time.

Just about to head to work. I finish at 6 pm. Meet me at the front door. You still got the address?

Yep, I reply. **See you later! Get ready to be astounded by my new moves.**

Let's work on the old moves first, shall we?

I send back a straight-mouth-narrow-eyes emoji (which really should have a clearer name, now that I think about it).

Don't worry, Eli writes back, **I've got some new moves for you when you're ready.** Winky-tongue-out emoji.

Pretty much every time Eli messages me, I end up with an erection, and this is no exception.

My moves are in your hands, sensei. See you later!

On screen, a message pops up.

MagePants69 <gtg, m'lord. boring real-world commitments await>

RcticF0x <have fun at work!>

I've hit send on the message before I realize Eli might have just told *me* he was going to work, but MagePants69 certainly didn't tell RcticF0x.

MagePants69 <huh?>

Shit.

RcticF0x <what?>

MagePants69 <how'd you know i was going to work?>

Uhhh . . .

RcticF0x <lol what else could a boring real-world commitment be?>

MagePants69 <um watching paint dry?>

RcticF0x <then have fun watching paint dry, m'lady>

There's an agonizing pause while I wait for the penny to drop, but then ...

MagePants69 <haha thanks. i shall report back on said paint's progress. stay tuned>

He logs off and I lean back in my Ergolove Destroyer, glancing up at my yellow sticky note. I hiss out a long breath through tight lips.

For The Plan to work, I'm going to need to be a hell of a lot more careful. That's two incredibly-near misses in the span of five days, both of which would've ended in disaster if Eli wasn't the sweetest and apparently most gullible boy in Ballarat.

"You sure you got the address right?" Dad huffs from the driver's seat of his Range Rover. Mum was out at pilates or yogalates or one of her many social obligations, so I had to ask Dad to drive me to Eli's work. There was much indignant grumbling, most of which was drowned out by the anxious voices in my head. (At least they're good for something.)

"Pretty sure," I reply, staring out the passenger window at the sprawling red-brick building beside us.

We're parked next to the river that snakes its way through this part of town, lined all the way with gum trees and the occasional stormwater drain. The building by the river looks like some kind of ye olde factory building with a big, empty car park out the front. Just inside the wrought-iron perimeter fence is a massive, cylindrical, brick chimney, reaching up towards the cloudy grey sky. There's a giant sign hanging above the main building's burgundy front door that proclaims: WELCOME TO SUNNYSIDE MILL – EST. 1878.

"What did you say this kid does for work?" Dad asks, squinting at the sign.

"I didn't," I reply. "I don't actually know."

"Well . . ." Dad sighs, glancing down at his watch. "I better get to the golf course."

"Can you just wait five minutes while I go inside and check if it's the right place?"

He exhales loudly through his nose, which is Dad code for *You're really pushing it, Noah.*

"You know what, don't worry," I say as I open the door and slide out of my seat, "I'll just get the bus home if I have to."

"Wait," he says, and I turn back to him. "Is your mother home for dinner tonight?"

I resist the urge to roll my eyes. "Ask her yourself," I say, before slamming the door a little harder than I mean to.

As Dad pulls away, the gravel crunching loudly under his tires, I stare up at the Sunnyside Mill. A small part of me is legitimately worried that I've wandered into one of Hawk and Simon's more elaborate pranks.

I steel myself and walk through the gate, running a hand along the monolithic brick chimney as I pass. There's a wooden door set into the side facing away from the road, bolted shut with a massive brass padlock. I pause for a second, wondering if there's a troll or a witch or family of talking rats living inside the chimney, then traipse across the car park, up the stone steps, and plant myself in front of the burgundy door, heart thumping.

What do I do? Knock? Or do I need some sort of code word like Gandalf at the Doors of Durin?

I pull out my phone to message Eli, and the big door suddenly creaks open, just enough for a ginger head to poke through.

"You made it," Eli says, his grin like pure sunshine.

"What *is* this place?"

"You've never been to Sunnyside?"

"I've never been to a derelict old mill on the other side of town? No. Can't say that I have."

Eli laughs, still just a floating ginger head. "I mean, it's hardly *derelict*. Come in."

"Just so you know, this feels exactly like the opening scene of a horror movie."

"Do you like horror movies?"

"Love them."

He raises one eyebrow. "Then you've got nothing to worry about."

I don't know what I expected to find inside the old mill, but it's certainly not *this*. Eli walks me along an expansive corridor, dotted with skylights and braced with exposed steel beams that are presumably holding the whole place together. On both sides of the hallway are countless burgundy doors opening up into cavernous, warehouse-type spaces. Some of the rooms are empty, while some are filled with shipping crates of god-knows-what, and some contain literal tennis courts and cricket nets. One room even has a floor covered in sand and six "beach" volleyball courts.

"This place is kind of epic," I say as we pass by a room brimming with photography equipment, its walls lined with backdrops in every color of the rainbow.

"The mill has been here for years," he replies, glancing over his shoulder, two steps ahead of me. "About a hundred and fifty years, actually. They repurposed it in the eighties, then it closed down for a while, and then they restored it to its former glory a few years ago. It's awesome. And it's *packed* on the weekends. I'm genuinely shocked that you've never been here with your fancy CHGS mates."

This is another one of those conversations where the fact that I have no friends starts bubbling dangerously close to the surface.

"Well," I reply, jogging a few steps to catch up, "I'm not really the fake beach volleyball type, believe it or not."

"Fair enough." Eli laughs. "This way, sir."

He leads me past another vast room ("This is where they build all the BMTS sets. They'll probably start working on the *Chicago* one soon!") and around the corner into a corridor filled with a hazy pink glow. Down the end of the hallway is a neon sign that I have to squint to read.

SUNNYSIDE ROLLER DISCO

"Wait," I say, staring up at the words when we arrive beneath the sign, "*this* is where you work? A roller disco?"

"Sure is." Eli grins, ushering me through the open archway before us.

Over the threshold lies an enormous, forest-green roller-skating rink, rimmed with a waist-high perspex barrier. A silver disco ball as big as a small car hangs from the ceiling, directly above a yellow ring painted on the floor at the center of the rink. The room walls painted in the same dark green as the rink. Opposite the rink itself is a candy bar, overflowing with chips and chocolates and drinks and treats of every variety, and next to that is a wide booth with a sign that says SKATE HIRE, with rows and rows of wooden pigeon holes lining its walls.

"Okay, wow," I say, finding it difficult to believe that a place like this could have existed in Ballarat for *years* without me having the slightest inkling. I guess you miss a few things when you're confined to your bedroom and no one invites you anywhere on the weekend. "This is . . . pretty amazing."

"Fun, right?" Eli canters off towards the gate leading into the rink, and I follow close behind. "I work in the candy bar, which isn't as glamorous as it sounds."

"Who said it sounded glamorous?" I deadpan.

Eli shoots me a withering look, then breaks out into a smile. "You're right, it's not. And the lighting doesn't do my cheek-bones a shred of justice. *But* I do get an unlimited supply of Frozen Coke, and I also get to skate for free. So—" he shrugs "—it has its perks."

"You had me at Frozen Coke."

"Sugary delights later, young Padawan," Eli says. "We have work to do."

TWELVE

ELI TAKES ME OUT onto the rink and makes me stand in the yellow circle.

"Told you I had enough space for us to dance," he says with a smirk.

"Slight understatement."

"Well, I didn't want to brag." He holds up one finger. "Wait right there."

He dashes off across the rink and I watch him go, head tilting slightly to one side. I won't lie, those jeans are doing things to me, and his "hideous work polo shirt"—as he described it—is far from hideous. The sapphire blue makes his hair look even more fiery, and even though the shirt is too big for him, it's giving him an unmistakable *Stranger Things* vibe, which I am definitely here for.

He returns with two white bentwood chairs in hand, plonking them down behind me.

"All right," he says, as he slips his phone out of his pocket and taps at the screen. The intro to "We Both Reached for the Gun" starts blaring from the concert-style loudspeakers hanging at each corner of the rink.

"How'd you do that?"

"My phone's connected to the sound system. The wonders of Wi-Fi."

"Clever," I say, giving him a little round of applause.

"There's no time for flattery, Noah. Let's do this."

After just twenty minutes of going through my reporter choreography, it seems absurd that I ever had trouble with it in the first place. As soon as Eli explained the pattern of the group— rather than my counts in isolation—the thing just clicked into place. Plus, without the combined pressure of being judged by David, embarrassed by my mum, and humiliated by Prisha, my pick-up skills improved dramatically.

"Yes!" Eli says, high-fiving me when I nail every single one of my moves in succession for the first time. "Perfect score!"

I throw my hands in the air and run a victory lap of the chairs.

"Okay, calm down, Billy Elliot," Eli says, folding his arms. "We're not done yet. We still need to do 'All That Jazz' *and* 'Razzle Dazzle.'"

I slump down onto one of the bentwoods. "It feels like snack time, if you ask me. Surely it's halftime."

"It's called 'interval' in the theatre," Eli says, rolling his eyes. "And you're the worst. Get up."

We start going over my choreography for "All That Jazz," which does nothing but highlight each and every one of my weaknesses. I may now be capable of standing up and sitting down on cue, but this Fosse choreography (he's very famous, google him—I had to) makes me look like a Level One Magikarp, splashing around uselessly on the shore.

"Just bend your knees a little more," Eli says, demonstrating opposite me, like my far more talented (and far more attractive) mirror image.

"They don't bend any more than that."

"And relax your shoulders."

"They *are* relaxed. You should see them when they're not."

Eli chuckles. "All right, let's just try it from 'show her where to park her girdle.'"

"Incidentally, what does that even mean?"

He narrows his eyes. "Pretty sure it's a sex metaphor."

"Oh." I shrug, aiming for some Di Mario nonchalance. "I knew that."

He stifles a smile then presses play on his phone. As we move through the choreography together, I start lagging behind and fumbling steps until my legs eventually twist themselves into a knot and I stumble directly into one of the wooden chairs.

"That was the chair's fault," I moan, bending down to rub my shin.

"Obviously."

"Dancing is a severe OH&S issue."

"Wait a sec," Eli says, stopping the music. "I have an idea."

He runs off the rink again, leaving me leaning on the back of the chair, panting. Apparently, locking yourself in your bedroom and playing computer games all day doesn't do a lot for your cardiovascular fitness. Who would've thought?

When Eli returns, my first instinct is to run straight out the door. Because in his hands are two pairs of bright-pink roller skates.

"I got you a size ten," he says, holding them aloft. "My secret power is guessing people's shoe size."

The size is definitely right, but there is no way I'm donning a pair of *roller skates* in front of the boy I like. The one and only time I ever tried skating was when Charly and I both got rollerblades for Christmas one year when we were little. The day ended with Charly twirling down the driveway and me with gravel-rash on my left ass cheek.

"No, no, no," I say, sitting down and crossing my arms. "If you think my dancing is bad, you do *not* want to see me flailing around in those things."

"That's kind of the point," he replies, handing me a set of skates and taking a seat on the bentwood next to me. "Skating is *great* for balance, and way harder to coordinate than any of the steps in 'All That Jazz.' So, if we can get you skating, the choreography will feel like an absolute breeze by comparison."

I hum in protest. "That logic seems flawed to me."

"C'mon," he replies with an adorably encouraging smile. "What've you got to lose?"

"Uh, my dignity? My kneecaps?"

"Who needs dignity?" He shrugs. "And haven't you heard of a double knee reconstruction?"

"Again," I say, "that is some seriously flawed logic."

"Come *on*," he replies, literally fluttering his eyelids.

My goal of convincing him that I'm "chill and fun and sexy" is being severely put to the test right now. If I agree to roller-skate in front of him, "sexy" will be banished to the depths of hell forevermore, but I *will* gain some points in the "chill and fun" departments. Let's face it, I don't have a chance of appearing anything even close to sexy until I'm well clear of puberty—no braces, no pimples, no patchy stubble, no awkward boners, can you even *imagine?*—so I can probably just let that dream go. For now, anyway.

"Fine," I say with a huff, squeezing my foot into one of the pink skates.

"Tie them nice and tight," Eli says, finishing the bow on his laces with a flourish. "Helps with balance."

"Well, I'll need all the help I can get," I reply. "You don't happen to have an anti-gravity machine, do you?"

Once my skates are on—triple-knotted and tighter than a Victorian corset—Eli reaches out to help me up. The only thought in my head is: *Will this count as us holding hands?*

"Up we get," he says. "I'll take you over to the wall. It's easiest when you have something to hold onto."

I place my hands in his, my stupid heart skipping a beat when our palms make contact.

"You good?" he asks.

I bite my lip to keep from grinning like a fool. "Yep."

Slowly, he rolls me over to the perspex wall, me looking like a wax figure of the Quintessential Nerd, him gliding backwards with ease. When we reach the wall, he lets go and I grab onto it for dear life. Without a word, he zooms off around the rink, his pink skates painting effortless patterns on the forest-green floor. Within seconds, he's completed a full lap, coming to a graceful stop beside me using the rubber stopper on the front of his skate.

"Show off," I say.

"Oh, please, I work here," he replies, pulling his phone back out of his pocket. "I've had tons of practice."

With a sharp clang and a faint buzz, the rink is plunged into total darkness. I can't help but let out a little involuntary squeal.

"I thought you said you liked horror movies," Eli chuckles in the pitch black.

"Not funny," I say, gripping the wall even tighter.

"Hang on . . . ."

A couple of seconds later, the rink is filled with thousands of glittering stars.

I look up to see spotlights rigged in a circle on the ceiling, all pointing directly at the giant disco ball above us.

"Um, okay, *wow.*"

"My boss is an ex-lighting designer," Eli says, smiling proudly in the dancing starlight, "and I'm a bit of a tech whiz, so we do some pretty great stuff here. Now all we need is . . ." He taps at his phone a few more times and music starts to play again. This time, though, it's not the *Chicago* soundtrack. It's—

"The Spice Girls?" I say. "Really?"

Eli laughs. "Don't judge. Nothing gets you in the mood for roller-skating like classic nineties pop."

"I'll have to take your word for it."

"That you will."

He holds out his hand again, and even though I know it's just so I won't fall and split my head open on the floor, it still feels gentlemanly and romantic. I grab hold—not as casually as I'd planned—and we start to skate around the perimeter of the rink. The Spice Girls tell us to stop right now, which is the kind of irony you really can't plan.

After four painfully slow laps, Eli says, "Okay, now try on your own."

But I refuse to let go of his hand. "Nope."

"You'll be *fine*."

"I won't be fine. I'll never be fine again. I'm going to die on this rink."

He laughs, tipping his head back to the glittering ceiling. "I'm here. I got you." He pries my hand away from his, then darts out in front of me, skating backwards, his green eyes beckoning me forward. "Just follow me."

I sigh in defeat. "*Fine*. But I won't be held responsible for any injuries sustained by either of us."

"Deal."

We skate around the edge of the rink, no longer touching, but connected all the same. The giant disco ball glimmers overhead, casting constellations on the walls and the floor and across the planes of Eli's angular face. The Backstreet Boys ask us to show them the meaning of being lonely—which is something I could certainly teach them a thing or two about—and Britney Spears apologizes for doing it again. Eli artfully skates backwards the whole time, and with his eyes on mine, nothing else seems to matter. For a second, I forget that I'm skating at all. I'm gliding through the stratosphere.

Eli smiles. "You're doing it!"

Just as he says it, the light from the disco ball flickers across my face, blinding me momentarily. When the bright-green spots in my vision fade, it's no longer Eli skating ahead of me, it's the fiery-haired Bard. She twirls her plait with one hand, raises an auburn eyebrow, and holds out her other hand.

"Take it," she says, in her sweet but slightly robotic voice.

The second I look away from her too-green eyes, it's all over. My left foot collects my right and I topple forward, a tangle of bony limbs on the floor, my sacrum pounding, my elbow stinging.

"Baby's first fall," Eli says, skidding to a stop beside me. "Are you okay? You looked kinda spooked for a second there."

I groan, pushing myself up to sitting. "I'm okay," I say, rubbing my elbow, expecting to find a gaping wound but only feeling a tiny scratch. "Sorry."

"Don't be sorry. Everyone falls over the first time."

"You're just saying that."

"First times aren't meant to be perfect."

The way he's staring into my eyes right now makes me think he's talking about an entirely different kind of first time. And now, all I can think about is whether he's already had his first time, which he probably has, especially if he's giving me advice about them, but I'm also wondering if he can tell I *haven't* had my first time yet, and whether he'd mind that I haven't or if he'd be happy to be my first, and then I'm thinking about how gay guys technically get *two* first times, and now I'm just flat-out picturing us having sex, and—

"Noah?" Eli frowns down at me.

Then again, maybe he's just talking about roller-skating . . . .

"Here," he says, grabbing me by the forearms and pulling me up to my feet. "Back on the horse."

"Trust me, you're never getting me on a horse."

"Shame," he says, clicking his tongue. "I was just about to bring out the Clydesdale."

I half-laugh-half-groan in reply.

"You know what," he says, "why don't we take a break."

He starts to drag me slowly towards the wooden chairs, but

my legs instantly turn to jelly, collapsing beneath me.

"Whoopsidaisy," he says, catching me under the arms, and suddenly we're in this weird lopsided hug, our faces only an inch apart.

My breath catches in my chest and I just hang there, limp, in Eli's arms. He gazes down at me, his eyes flicking from one of mine to the other, and I'm frozen, hypnotized, mesmerized. His lips part ever so slightly and my heart starts thumping against my ribs in time with "Lollipop (Candyman)" by Aqua, which is the least romantic song in history, but still, here I am, about to kiss the boy of my dreams . . . .

But then I blink, and it's not Eli's nose grazing mine, it's the Half-Elf Bard's. It's MagePants69. It's—

"Wait," I say, and Eli flinches. "Sorry, I just . . ."

He clears his throat and pulls away, before hoisting me up and setting me back onto my skates.

"Sorry," he says, blushing a little under the dim lights. "I just thought—I mean, I assumed you were—"

"No, no, I am," I reply. "I'm gay. It's just . . . I'm . . ."

A desperate urge to tell Eli the truth blooms in my chest. We can't have our first kiss under false pretenses, can we? We can't build the foundation of an actual relationship on a lie. Can we?

I honestly didn't expect kissing to be involved this soon (although I guess I should have had an inkling when the disco ball started spinning).

But if I tell Eli the truth—right now, in this moment—we might not even *get* our first kiss. He might not ever want to speak to me again.

I need to stick to The Plan:

Get Eli to fall in love with me.

Then—and only then—*Tell him the truth.*

Otherwise, this whole ridiculous thing will have been for nothing.

"You're what?" Eli asks. He lets go of my arms and I immediately lose my balance. He catches me again and silently guides me back to the bentwood chairs in the middle of the rink. We sit down and he pauses the music. The disco ball keeps spinning, sending stars silently dancing all around us.

"I . . . I'm . . ." I clear my throat, force a grin, and say, "I'm really freaking hungry."

"You dick!" He slaps me on the arm. "I thought you were going to tell me something awful!"

"Sorry," I reply, shielding myself from a barrage of playful punches. "I'm just . . . practicing my acting."

"Well, practice on someone else," he replies, the corner of his mouth curling up. He pulls off his skates, and I do the same, happy if I literally never have to wear them again. "Come on." He gives my leg a pat, before reaching down to slip his shoes back on. "You must be about to die of snack deprivation by now. Lucky for you, we have a whole candy bar at our disposal."

"We can't eat those snacks," I protest, tying the laces on my Cons. "They belong to the rink."

"I don't think the rink will mind, given it's an inanimate object." He holds out his hand, smirking. "Live a little, Noah Mitchell."

"Wait," I say as he pulls me up to my feet, "I don't even know your last name."

Eli scoffs. "So?"

"So, I mean . . . I really shouldn't have followed you into a deserted building without knowing your last name, and I sure as hell shouldn't be stealing snacks with you if you won't tell me what it is. What if you kidnap me and I need to call the police?"

Eli's lips twitch up into a smirk. "I have a feeling the police would be on my side, to tell you the truth."

"What is that supposed to mean?"

"It's Callaghan," he laughs. "Elijah Callaghan. And you're very dramatic."

I shrug. "I guess there must be some of those Rose Mitchell genes lurking around inside me somewhere, after all."

His fingers brush mine, and a jolt of nerves shoots up my spine. "You two have the same eyes, you know. Periwinkle blue."

I bite my lip. Is he going to try to kiss me again?

"Your eyes are green," I reply, then silently beg the rink to swallow me whole for having about as much game as an unwashed potato.

Eli chuckles. "How poetic."

"Well, Mr. Callaghan," I say, desperate to change the subject, "I believe I was promised a Frozen Coke."

He performs an elaborate curtsy, not unlike the one his Bard does on *Spire of Dusk*. My stomach does a guilty backflip at the thought. "And a Frozen Coke you shall have."

I smile and follow him to the candy bar, trying to push all thoughts of Bards and Warriors and MagePants69 and RcticF0x out of my mind. Right now, I want us to be Noah Mitchell and Elijah Callaghan and nothing more. Just two real-life boys, a couple of Frozen Cokes, and a first kiss still waiting to happen.

THIRTEEN

I'VE BEEN SPRAWLED ACROSS the couch in the upstairs lounge room all morning watching *Avatar: The Last Airbender* with Mr. Nibbles curled up between my legs. I've seen the whole series a million times, so I'm not really *watching* it, more just letting the episodes breeze over me in a comforting wave of sound and color.

I tried so hard to stop myself from googling "Elijah Callaghan" (which was why I put *Avatar* on in the first place, and also why I hid my phone underneath the couch cushion, a deterrent that lasted approximately three minutes) but the desire to learn more about the boy who almost kissed me last night was far too compelling.

The search brings up the usual things: his Facebook (private); his Instagram (*not* private, and filled with a combination of adorable selfies, pics of his Cavoodle, way too many photos in ridiculous theatre costumes, and a handful of shirtless beach shots that I mentally bookmark for entirely non-suspicious reasons); an old Tumblr full of random videos of girls belting out music theatre songs; and an IMDb page for a D-grade American actor with the same name. I have to admit, it's slightly disappointing to not find anything more out of the ordinary (a childhood act of heroism, a Pulitzer Prize), but it's also a relief to learn that Eli hasn't committed any newsworthy crimes.

I swipe out of the browser and tap into my messages, holding the phone directly over my face so it blocks out the glare from the light above.

So . . . I write to Charly. **Hypothetically . . . If I ALMOST kissed Eli last night but accidentally ruined the moment and wanted to send him a cute message this morning to let him know that I do, in fact, definitely want to kiss him . . . what should I say??? Hypothetically . . .**

Two seconds later, my phone starts buzzing.

"Hi, Char."

"Okay," she replies (no greeting necessary), "what is this 'hypothetical' bullshit? Did you *actually* almost kiss this boy? Because I've been waiting for this moment for a very long time, Noah, and if you are messing with me . . ."

"Relax," I laugh. "Wait, where are you? There's a weird humming noise on your end."

"I'm hiding in the stock fridge at work."

In a surprising turn of events, Charly has started working at a café in Sydney. She refuses to let Dad pay her rent, which means she has to work every hour of the week that she's not in class to afford her tiny room in Randwick. Her and Dad have never exactly been *close*, but their tolerance for one another seems to have diminished considerably since Charly started uni. I guess a neurosurgeon and a fine arts student see the world in *slightly* different ways . . . .

"Talk quickly," she says, "it's freezing in here."

"It would be *freezing* if you were in the *freezer*. But you're in the fridge, so it's ac—"

"*Noah.*"

"Fine," I say, sitting up on the couch. "I will save my jokes for someone who appreciates them."

"No one appreciates them."

"*Anyway*, what do I say? To Eli? I completely blew my opportunity last night because . . . well, because I'm horrifically awkward. And I don't want him to think I'm—"

"Friend-zoning him?" Charly interrupts. "Been there, bub. But in reverse. Several times. I'm your gal."

"Okay, so . . ." I tuck my legs underneath myself and mute the TV.

"You just need to send him something—anything, really—that is the total opposite of something you'd send to your friends." Charly knows I don't message anyone but her, and she must sense my eye-roll on the other end of the line, because she adds, "I mean, send him something that makes it very clear you want to be *more* than friends."

"Are you telling me to send him nudes? Because that is not a conversation I can have with my sister."

"No," Charly giggles, and I wish more than anything she was here on the couch with me. Sydney feels so damn far away sometimes. "Though, to be fair, my gay friends all go straight for the dick pic—"

"Char, *please.*"

"—but you're obviously too young for that. And you're a classy guy. You're smart. And adorable. So just send him the Noah Mitchell version."

"The Noah Mitchell version of a *dick pic?*" I reply. "What could that possibly even mean?"

My phone buzzes in my hand and I take it away from my ear to check the notification. It's a message from Eli. I put Charly on speaker immediately.

"Wait. Char, he just messaged me."

"Who?"

"Eli."

"Saying what?"

I click into the message and read it out loud. "*Hey. Last night was fun. Is it weird that I'm hoping you still need help with the choreography so we can do it again sometime?*"

"Um, adorable," Charly replies.

"Wait, wait, wait. He's typing more."

Five seconds later, another message pops up. "*Also,*" I read out to Charly, "*you promised me double-coat Tim Tams, which I have yet to receive.*"

"Oh my god," Charly breathes. "Noah, he's *so* into you."

"No, he's not."

"Uh, yes he *is*. How can you not see that?"

"That's another ten-thousand-word essay I'm happy to provide."

"I'm good."

"Regardless, this still doesn't solve the 'what do I actually write back' problem."

I stare down at Eli's messages while Charly starts brainstorming out loud. A new email notification pops up on the screen and I click into my mailbox. When I see who it's from, I get a sharp twinge of nerves right behind my sternum.

Brb . . . off to Siberia

From: MagePants69 <magepants69@gmail.com>
To: Arctic Fox <rcticf0x@outlook.com>
On: Friday, 3 April at 11:54 a.m.

M'lord. Don't hate me. I'm being shipped off to my grand-parents' place in Siberia (otherwise known as Frankston, commonly referred to as Franga) for a week. They don't have wi-fi (I KNOW) so I won't be able to play Spire of Dusk. . . . Feel free to email me though. That's about all my crappy phone data can cope with. The worst.

Actually, the WORST was how I hung out with the Kind of Cute Boy last night and I went for the big cinematic kiss moment and got rejected. He said it was because he was hungry but, let me tell you, the Kind of Cute Boy does NOT have a poker face. We kept hanging out afterwards but all I could think about was what my friend said about him. (In case you needed me to jog your memory, she said: He's not as harmless as he looks.) So, now I'm like, is he harmless? I don't know. Is this really someone I can trust? I DON'T KNOW.

Anyway, my mum was so furious that I didn't tell her we were hanging out that I'm now being sent into exile. Which will totally NOT be worth it if the Kind of Cute Boy ends up friend-zoning me . . .

Send advice (and chocolates).

Yours from the Dark Ages,

M

I was right. Eli thinks I don't want to kiss him. And not only that, he now believes what Prisha said about me.

Is this really someone I can trust?

I wipe a thin film of stress-sweat from my forehead.

"Noah, are you even listening?" Charly's voice blares from the phone in my lap.

"Sorry," I reply absently, eyes skimming over the email again. "What did you say?"

"I *said*," Charly groans, "why don't you just ask him out again? You know he's keen to see you, so there's no risk of rejection. Just ask him to hang out. But in a very non-friends way. Like, actually use the word 'date' so he knows it's not a friendly catch-up."

I cringe at the thought. "Isn't that too forward? It feels . . . awkward."

"Bub, in the grown-up world, people *like* forward."

"What 'grown-up world'? Char, you've been at uni for approximately twelve minutes. You're not a grown-up yet."

"All I'm saying is that people like to know where they stand."

I hear high-heeled footsteps on the wooden stairs outside the lounge. A couple of seconds later, Mum pokes her head in through the door.

"Darling," she says, as I take Charly off speaker and hold the phone back up to my ear.

"Hang on one sec, Char." I press the mute button. "Yes?"

"I need to talk to you," Mum replies solemnly, perching herself on the armrest of the couch.

"Yeah?"

"Can you hang up the phone?"

"It's Charly. She's on mute."

"Oh, can you tell her to reply to my messages about Ballarat?" Mum's tone would suggest *I'm* the one ignoring her texts.

"Tell her yourself."

She lifts both eyebrows and tilts her head to the side with an implied *Noah* . . .

"Fine," I say, tapping the un-mute button. "Char, Mum said to reply to her messages about Ballarat. Whatever that means."

"Ugh, just tell her I'm going to be busy on my uni break and I'm not going to be able to come home."

"Tell her yours—"

"Just tell her, bub. Please."

"Bye, Char. Love you." I hang up the phone. "She's going to message you later," I tell Mum.

Mum pouts her lips and rolls her eyes, an expression that should be reserved exclusively for people under the age of eighteen. "I don't know why she won't just let your father pay for her flights back. Why wouldn't she want to come home?"

"To see *us*? When she could be hanging out with all her super cool art school friends in Sydney? I have no idea . . . ."

"You know I don't like your sarcasm, darling."

I don't reply.

"So, can we talk?"

"We already *are* talking."

She inhales sharply, then lets out a slow, ostensibly calming exhale. Something she learned at yoga, no doubt. "I'm worried about you getting involved with Eli."

"I'm sorry, what?" I get a weird sinking feeling in my chest.

"I'm happy you're making friends in the cast," Mum says, keeping her voice pleasantly neutral, "but I don't think it's a good idea for you to hang out with Eli outside rehearsals."

"You said it was a good idea for him to help me with the choreography."

"Yes, well, that's a little different than hanging out at the Sunnyside Mill after dark, isn't it?"

"We were rehearsing."

"Is that *all* you were doing?"

"Oh my god, Mum, does it really matter?"

"It *does* matter," she snaps. "Because there is nothing that can ruin a show and tear a cast apart like a showmance gone wrong."

"Sorry, a *what* gone wrong?"

"A *showmance*. A show romance."

"Okay, well, Eli and I don't have any kind of 'mance.' Show or bro or otherwise. He's just helping me learn the choreography."

Mum scoffs. "Of *course* he is. That's how it starts, darling. You're not the first boy Eli has dated in one of our shows, you know."

I try to ignore the rush of burning jealousy that floods my stomach.

"And let me tell you," she goes on, "his last showmance did *not* end well. I refuse to allow that kind of drama to jeopardize *my* big moment."

"Mum," I reply, "you seem to have forgotten that you *begged* me to do this show. You *told* me to make friends. And now that I am, you're telling me I'm making them with the wrong people and that I'm ruining your show?"

"I see the way you look at him, darling," she says, ignoring my protests. "You want to be much more than Eli's friend."

As annoying as it is that Mum can tell I'm hopelessly in

love with Eli, it also makes me wonder why he can't see that for himself . . . .

"You should be happy for me, Mum. You should be supporting me. Isn't that what parents are supposed to do?"

"Aren't children supposed to be supportive of their parents, too?"

"*What*?" It's honestly like talking to a child sometimes. "Mum, it's not a competition."

She folds her arms, and I fold mine in retaliation, locked in a sudden stalemate at opposite ends of the couch.

When I can't bear the silence any longer, I say, "I have to call Charly back. Can we resume this discussion later?"

She twists her glossy lips from one side to the other. "*Fine. But we're not done here.*"

"Fine."

As soon as Mum leaves, I unlock my phone and type a reply to Eli. I obviously can't make it seem like I—*Noah*—know he's been shipped away, but I need to make my intentions clear regardless.

Don't worry, I write back, **I suspect I'll need a LOT more help with the choreography. We still have seven hundred more songs to learn, remember? Meanwhile, what are you doing today? Can I take you on a coffee date to thank you for last night?**

Typing the word "date" makes me feel a little queasy, even though I know Eli can't say yes.

That sounds lovely! he replies. **But I'm down in Melbourne for a week.** Sad-face emoji. **But let's do something as soon as I get back?**

Definitely! Winky-face emoji.

118

The wink is probably a bit much, but hopefully the sentiment is clear.

I click back into my emails and reply to MagePants69.

Brb … off to Siberia

From: Arctic Fox <rcticf0x@outlook.com>
To: MagePants69 <magepants69@gmail.com>
On: Friday, 3 April at 12:04 p.m.

Sorry to hear about your exile in so-called Franga. Maybe having no wi-fi will provide some—wait, sorry, I can't even pretend to be positive for your sake. That really is the worst.

ALSO, my wealth of kissing experience tells me there are MANY reasons someone might lie to get out of kissing you. Sometimes it means they don't want to kiss you, in which case, definitely leave them alone. But SOMETIMES it's because they want to kiss you so badly that when it finally becomes a legitimate option, it's so unbelievably overwhelming that they freak out and ruin the moment.

My advice: Try again. But tell the Kind of Cute Boy how you feel first. People like to know where they stand.

Yours,

RcticF0x

FOURTEEN

IT'S BEEN APPROXIMATELY TWO hundred and ten hours since I've seen Eli. I've been asleep for around seventy-two of those hours, which leaves a grand total of one hundred and thirty-eight waking hours that I've *not* been looking into Eli's emerald eyes, that our fingers *haven't* been brushing against each other's, that he's *not* been making me smile like a giddy fool.

Point being, it's been one of the longest weeks of my life. Now that I've spent quality time with Eli in the real world, I find myself constantly craving the sound of his voice, the melody of his laugh. I need to be in the same room as him. Not even *doing* anything, just . . . inhabiting the same space. I can't really explain it. Maybe that's what love feels like? (Or is that obsession? Eeek.)

When Saturday rolls around again—with only two days left of the April holidays—I wake up to the most glorious text message I've ever received:

Guess who's back in Ballarat? Flamenco dancer emoji. **Do you want to come over? I have to unpack etc but I want to see you. I know that's not quite a DATE but Mum said it's okay so long as we don't leave the house. She'll be back in a couple of**

**hours but we'll have the place to ourselves for a bit. And then
you can meet her!**

I write my reply with a dopey grin plastered on my face.

Sounds great!

But it's so much better than great. It's me finally being invited
into MagePants69's world.

It's almost too incredible to fathom.

He sends me his address and I'm out the door with a quick
"Going to a friend's place!" to Dad, who replies with a mumbled
"Okay" without taking his eyes off the golf on TV. Mum is out,
thank god, so I don't have to deal with her protestations about
me hanging out with Eli. We never ended up finishing that
conversation, which is probably for the best, because I would've
yelled and she would've cried, and that's exactly the kind of
drama I don't need in my life right now.

Eli's house is in a cramped estate just out of town, where the
wide, tree-lined residential streets give way to brown paddocks
full of cookie-cutter houses. I'd be lying if I said I didn't get
lost in a maze of cul-de-sacs when I first got off the bus, but,
eventually, I find 9 Athena Court. It's a grey brick house with
a manicured lawn, a garden bed filled with white stones, and a
complete absence of plants and flowers. Depending on how you
look at it, it could be described as either "minimal" or "prison-
esque," and I guess we'll find out which one it is when I meet
Eli's mum.

I ring the doorbell, which is a plain old *ding dong*, rather than a novelty musical one like I was expecting. A dog barks from inside the house and I hear Eli say, "No barking, Glinda. It's just Noah."

I brush a piece of lint off my woollen jumper and quickly check my breath. The door swings open and a sandy-haired Cavoodle bounds out onto the welcome mat, wiggling like its life depends on it. It makes Mr. Nibbles look like a dismissive little jerk, which I guess he is, most of the time.

"Sorry," Eli says, bending down to pick up the dog. "She has literally no chill. Glinda, meet Noah."

"She's so cute," I say, reaching out to pat Glinda on her perfect fluffy head. She's possibly the most adorable thing I've ever seen, aside from Eli himself.

"Don't be fooled," Eli scoffs. "She's a demon wearing a dog costume. Just ask my socks."

I laugh.

"Also, hi!" Eli leans in and kisses me on the cheek, and Glinda kisses me on the other one.

"What a welcome," I say, chuckling and wiping my face.

"Come in, come in!"

With Glinda trotting along at my heels, I follow Eli into the kitchen, which is just as grey and plain as the exterior. Eli gives me a tour of the house (it's a relatively short tour) and I realize he—with his fiery orange hair, his baggy pink T-shirt and navy-blue sweats—is the only bit of color in the whole place.

We pause in the lounge room and he points over to a wooden desk in the corner with a chunky grey PC sitting on top.

"My prized possession," he says.

"Your computer?"

He cringes. "Don't judge me but . . . I'm a total gaymer. Like, completely obsessed."

"I didn't know you could be a theatre nerd and a computer nerd at the same time," I reply. "But there you go. You've done it. You're double the nerd."

"Do you play?" he asks, ushering me into the hallway leading towards the far end of the house.

"No," I reply, possibly a little too firmly. "Not really my thing."

He clicks his tongue. "You're totally missing out. You should play with me sometime. I reckon I could get you hooked."

"We'll see," I say with a nervous cough. "Let's just tackle the singing and dancing first."

We stop outside the grey door at the end of the short grey hallway. "This—" he pushes the door open "—is where the magic happens."

His bedroom is an explosion of color and fun. The walls are strung with multicolored fairy lights, and almost completely covered with posters, photos, pieces of sequinned fabric, sticky notes, cork boards, newspaper clippings, hanging plants, and everything else you can imagine that can feasibly be stuck to a wall.

"And, uh, what magic would that be, specifically?" I ask.

Eli shrugs and shoots me his trademark smirk. "Oh, you know. Solving climate change. Penning a bestseller. Hosting gay orgies. The usual."

I lift an eyebrow, a skill I've almost perfected since starting *Chicago*.

"Okay, fine," Eli admits. "Sleeping. That is all that happens in here."

"How come your computer's not in here?" I ask.

"Mum's one of those 'whatever you're doing on there, you should be able to do it in front of your mother' type parents."

I laugh, though I guess I should have seen that coming, given MagePants69's mum's Cardinal Rules of Online Gaming.

"Safe to say I keep it strictly PG on there," he chuckles. "Nerdy computer games and not a thing more."

I can't help but wonder . . . If I told Eli right now that he's been playing said nerdy computer games with *me*—and that I've known for over a month now—what would actually happen? Would we both laugh it off and make out on his bed? Or would he ask me to leave and never come back?

"You okay?" he asks, and I snap out of my mini daydream. "You zoned out for a sec."

"Yeah, sorry," I reply with a smile. "Your room is amazing. I'm not allowed to put stuff on my walls."

"Really?"

"Except photos. But I . . . never got around to putting any up." Which is obviously not true, but it's much easier than telling him why I tore down all the photos of the boys three years ago. "Mum has a 'design vision' for the house, and I'm strictly forbidden from doing anything that interferes with that."

"That's . . . intense."

I snort. "That's one way to put it."

"It's so weird seeing Rose from your perspective. Like, as a mum, and not just as a theatre goddess."

The last thing I want to talk about right now is my mother.

"You, uh, said you had unpacking to do?"

"'Tis true. You wanna chill while I put my clothes away? Or is that super unsexy and boring?"

I didn't realize "sexy" was on the table . . . .

"Sure, go for it," I reply, trying (as usual) to emulate a hint of Alex Di Mario's chill.

Eli motions to his bed and I awkwardly perch myself on one edge.

"Make yourself at home," he laughs. "This could take a while."

We debrief Eli's time in Frankston with his grandparents—"as dull as dull can be"—and my week here at home—"even duller than *that*"—then move on to more important topics (read: general banter).

As the minutes tick by, I start to feel more and more comfortable in Eli's space, like I could soon become an important fixture here, a part of the colorful tapestry that makes up his room and his life. The thought makes me feel all warm and anxious and excited and terrified.

When Eli has finished unpacking his giant suitcase—which seems like far too much clothing for one week—he swings a leg up onto the bed beside me.

"Scooch over," he says, wiggling his bum onto the mattress. I move over, but there isn't far to go, so now we're squished on the bed with one whole side of our bodies touching.

"Cozy," I say, my heart suddenly pounding.

We sit in silence for a few seconds, my mind buzzing with a million things I could say, none of which are remotely cool or sexy or appropriate. Honestly, why is there no instruction manual for this? Like a walkthrough for an RPG?

"It's . . . nice having you here," Eli says, placing his hand gently on my thigh.

I'm instantly hard, but I don't think it's obvious in my jeans, thank *god*. I glance down at Eli's crotch and then wish I didn't, because his trackies leave *nothing* to the imagination and there is a *lot* going on down there.

"Sa-" I start, but my voice catches. I clear my throat and try again. "Same."

Smooth, Noah. *Smooth.*

"You look really handsome," he says, and my stomach does a flip.

No one has ever called me handsome. Seriously. Never. Not even Mum. Frankly, it almost feels like Eli's making a joke, because—objectively speaking—I'm *not* handsome. I mean, I don't hate my hair—even though my curls are unmanageable— and I guess I like my eyes, but apart from that, I'm a jumble of too-long limbs and awkward, mismatched features. But still, even if Eli doesn't really mean it, it's nice to hear.

"You too," I reply.

"So, I, um . . ." He starts drawing little circles on my leg with his thumb. "I wanted to tell you—"

Oh my god, it's happening. *It's actually happening.*

"—that I—"

Just outside the bedroom door, Glinda starts barking her head off.

Eli jumps up from the bed like it's an electric fence. "That'll be Mum," he says with his back to me, and I swear he's doing the "waistband tuck." (If you know, you know.)

"Oh," I say, climbing off the bed and quickly doing the same, "cool. I'm excited to meet her."

He leads me back out into the kitchen, where a tall, broad, red-haired woman stands, wearing a light-blue shirt and navy pants. She looks like a Viking warrior who's been sent to the future and shoved into modern-day clothing.

"You must be Noah," she says, smiling but stony-eyed. "This one won't shut up about you."

"*Mum . . .*"

I swallow nervously. "All good things, I hope?"

"Trust me," she replies, "you wouldn't be here if it wasn't."

It's only now that I notice striped epaulets on her shoulders. The Victoria Police badge on the kitchen bench . . .

Holy shit. Eli's mum isn't just super strict, she's a super strict *police officer*. So, when he used to joke about her locking him up if he broke any of her rules, he was being literal. She could actually incarcerate him. And me. Which seems a likely course of action when she finds out I've tricked her son into dating me and *oh my fucking god* I need to get out of here right now.

"We get it, Mum," Eli moans. "We promise not to commit any felonies."

"No crimes at *all* would be preferable," she replies, adding to me, "I'm Mrs. Callaghan."

"I gathered that," I say, then immediately regret the hint of sarcasm in my voice. (I can't help it, it's just how I talk.)

Eli's mum tips her head and draws her lips into a line. "Or Senior Constable Callaghan if you prefer?"

"And plain old Mother Dearest to me," Eli says in a clear attempt to evaporate the tension flooding the kitchen. "Mum's only kidding. You can call her Sharon. Can't he, Mum?"

She blinks once, making it clear I will *not* be calling her by her first name.

"Mrs. Callaghan is fine," I say, nervously cracking my knuckles. "I'm so happy to meet you."

"Treat my Eli right and I'm sure I'll be happy to have met you, too."

"Of course," I say, with a slightly hysterical laugh.

Mrs. Callaghan gives Eli an imperious look and starts down the hall. "I need to shower. There's leftover pasta in the fridge if you boys are hungry."

Eli waits a moment until we hear the bathroom door shut and then says, "I am *so* sorry. She's just overprotective."

"It's fine. I'm just used to my parents not even noticing I'm there."

"She deals with a lot of domestic abuse cases at work," Eli says, walking over to the skinny fridge. "Kids getting beaten up by their parents and stuff. It's pretty heavy."

"Holy shit," I reply, leaning on the kitchen bench. "That's intense."

"Yeah, and heaps of other messed-up stuff, too." He pulls a plastic container of pasta out of the fridge. "Do you remember that big child pornography ring the cops exposed in Melbourne a few years ago?"

I do. Vividly. Along with the cringe-worthy cyber safety seminars that followed at CHGS.

"Yeah," I reply, my throat closing over a little bit, "I remember."

"Well, one of the kids who was . . . *involved* was from Ballarat." His eyes are wide. "Mum was the one who had to go and tell the kid's parents about it and deal with the paperwork and stuff.

She said the whole thing was just *so* traumatic. For everyone. Herself included. She almost burned my PC and banned me from playing games for all eternity."

I suddenly feel like I can't breathe. Like I'm going to cry or vomit or pass out from the guilt that's clamping down on my chest. Because here I am, in Eli's house, breaking his mum's rules with flagrant disregard, when she *clearly* put them in place to protect him. And not only that, I'm forcing *him* to break them, too, without him even knowing.

I pull my phone out of my pocket and pretend to see some kind of concerning message. Eli glances over as he spoons some pasta into two enormous bowls. I make sure my phone's not on silent and type out a message to Charly.

Ignore this. Just testing something.

"Everything okay?" Eli asks when he hears the little *woop* sound of the message being sent.

"Um, not really," I reply, slipping my phone back into my jeans. "I actually have to go. I'm so sorry. Family stuff."

"Oh." His expression drops.

"We can hang out again soon, I just . . ."

He shakes his head. "It's fine. Honestly. Do what you gotta do."

"Message me?"

"Of course."

I smile awkwardly and head for the door, ruffling Glinda's fur on the way past to make it look like I'm not trying to get the hell out of here as fast as I possibly can.

As soon as I shut the front door behind me, my phone buzzes.

Eli: **I hope my mum didn't scare you off. She can be a bit intense x**

I write back, **Not at all x** and head straight for the bus stop.

As I make my way out of the estate, all I can think about is what happened with Tan and the boys in Year Nine . . . .

I lost everything back then because I told the truth. Please, *please*, don't let me lose Eli now because of a lie.

FIFTEEN

MY FINAL TWO DAYS of freedom are dominated by the following things:

1. Slaying vampires on *Spire of Dusk* with MagePants69 (which feels a little different now that I can picture Eli sitting at his computer in the lounge, a police woman with extensive experience in online crime peering over his shoulder).

2. Messaging Eli (which primarily consists of me trying to convince him I'm not afraid of his mum without letting slip why I definitely *am* afraid of his mum).

3. Telling myself not to freak out.

4. Freaking out anyway.

In the end, despite my brain's best efforts to completely ruin my life, I manage to convince both Eli and myself that everything is going to be okay. Because neither Senior Constable Callaghan nor her son will ever find out that Noah Mitchell and RcticF0x are the same person. I realize now that I can never let that happen. My plan to reveal everything to Eli once we were madly in love was naïve and, quite frankly, moronic. It needs to stay a secret. Forever. I shall take this lie to my grave.

And it may be a lie—though it's technically more of an *omission*, because nobody has actually asked me if RcticF0x and

I are one and the same—but it's not malicious. I'm not hurting anyone. If anything, I'm *helping* people. Myself included, but Eli benefits from the lie too, even if he doesn't know it. We wouldn't have made it past our very first encounter with Prisha if it weren't for RcticF0x defending me via *Spire of Dusk*. We wouldn't have even *met* if it weren't for the lie.

And I know I said I could happily let my alter ego disappear into oblivion as soon as Eli and I were on the right track, but what if things *don't* work out between us in real life?

I'll be left with nothing. Again.

So, as guilty as I feel about it, I need to keep things ticking along on *Spire of Dusk*. It'll be like playing an RPG as a multiclass character—two separate skill sets, two roles within the party, all combined in a single avatar. But instead of being, for example, a Warrior/Mage, I'll be an Online Best Friend/Real Life Boyfriend.

Simple.

Not that I'm Eli's boyfriend.

(Yet.)

The first day back at school is not nearly as hideous as I expect it to be. Everyone ignores me when I walk into first-period applied computing—which is actually preferable—and my physics and studio art classes are almost pleasant. I have a last-period spare, so I hole up in the library and google *Spire of Dusk* strategies. We've recently found ourselves in a bit of a pickle in our campaign, and by "pickle" I mean a completely impossible quest involving a vampiric dragon. Because that's a thing that exists, apparently.

Tuesday starts like a dream: a good-morning text from Eli, along with a just-woken-up shirtless selfie in bed. It's the first time I've seen his bare torso, and there's something so hot about how casually he slipped the photo into the thread of our messages. Just like, *Oh, hey, by the way, here is my bare chest and my skin and my nipples*, as if he's totally comfortable with how he looks and didn't go through nine hundred different poses to get the perfect angle. He's definitely not muscular like Alex, but he's not stick-thin and lanky like me, either. I guess he's what you'd call "average." A bit of muscle and tone, but still soft around the edges. It's a body that doesn't quite know whether it belongs to a kid or a man. But honestly? To me, it's perfect.

After the selfie, however, the day takes a dramatic downward turn . . . .

One thing about going to a fancy private school like CHGS is that the teachers have this implicit trust that the students will do the right thing by default. It's lovely—and you have to appreciate their faith in the student body—but it's completely misguided. So, when Mr. Conley leaves the computer lab to fetch his notebook from the staffroom, my fellow students immediately break out into chatter. The primary subject of discussion this morning is who hooked up with whom at some party I obviously wasn't invited to on Saturday night, so I pull out my phone and send a message to Charly.

Okay, two things: 1) I almost kissed Eli on the weekend. Again. Almost. 2) I met his mum and she is . . . terrifying.

After a couple of minutes, I get two GIFs in reply. The first one is David from *Schitt's Creek* with a caption saying *Excuse me?*, and the second is Angelina Jolie as Maleficent with a background of iridescent green flame.

Very helpful, Char, I reply. But before I can type anything else, the room falls silent. I look up to see Mr. Conley entering the lab, notebook in hand. I slip my phone back into my pocket and type some gibberish on my keyboard so I look like I've been working the whole time.

"All right," Conley says sternly. "Who has him?"

I poke my head around my monitor to see him standing behind his desk. Arms folded. Brow furrowed.

"Who has what, sir?" Hawk asks in his usual, overly polite tone from behind me.

"Cabbage O'Reilly," Conley replies. "Who took him?"

Sure enough, the corner of his desk is unmistakably empty. No ugly figurine in sight.

"He was here a minute ago," Conley says, planting his hands on his desk and leaning forward to glare around the room. He's right. Cabbage was definitely there when we came in this morning—that little leprechaun is impossible to miss. "Where is he?"

No one replies. I glance around the lab only to see everyone else doing the same. There's something a bit off about the sheepish *where could it possibly be?* looks on all their faces, though. Something put on, almost pantomime. I turn to risk a peek at Hawk and Simon, who both look completely unfazed.

Simon meets my eye for a second, then shoots his hand straight into the air.

"Sir," he says, pushing his glasses up the bridge of his nose, his hand still raised.

"Yes, Mr. Zhuang?"

"I just thought you should know that Mr. Snitchell—sorry, Mr. *Mitchell*—made a peculiar comment the other day about Cabbage O'Reilly."

I turn back around to face Mr. Conley, eyes wide.

"What comment?" Mr. Conley asks Simon, before cutting his gaze to me.

"I can't remember, exactly," Simon goes on, "and I don't want to cast aspersions, but I thought it was worth noting."

"I didn't say—"

"It's true, sir," Hawk cuts me off. "I remember it, too. Noah seemed *very* interested in Cabbage O'Reilly."

I haven't said two words to anyone in applied computing all year, and if I did, it wouldn't have been about a fucking leprechaun.

Mr. Conley strides over to my desk, looking supremely frazzled. "Did you take Cabbage O'Reilly, Mr. Mitchell?"

"No."

"If you give him back, I won't escalate the matter to Mrs. Jamison."

"I didn't take it," I stress, hearing how hysterical I sound. "I was sitting right here the whole time you were gone. I was messaging my sister." (It's worth having my phone confiscated to prove I didn't steal the teacher's most precious possession.)

Conley ignores me and addresses the room, his pale cheeks flushed tomato-red. "Cabbage O'Reilly is a Conley family heirloom. He has been passed down through *four generations* of teachers in my family. He is *priceless*."

I want to say, *Then why the hell do you keep it on your desk?* but now is not the time.

"Did anyone *see* Mr. Mitchell take Cabbage O'Reilly?"

There is a half-hearted shaking of heads around the lab and a few noncommittal murmurs.

Conley sighs, turning back to me. "Do you *swear* you didn't take him?"

"I swear."

He lowers his voice, so that only I can hear. "Lord help me, Noah Mitchell, if I find out you're lying about this, you'll be out of CHGS before you can say 'petty theft.'"

I swallow. I know Dad's well-timed donations have kept me at CHGS so far, but I'm sure Mrs. Jamison draws the line at pornography-watching, heirloom-stealing delinquents. And if I throw thirteen years of extortionate private-school tuition fees down the drain, Dad will likely never speak to me again.

"I'm telling the truth," I reply, as earnestly as I can manage.

Hawk scoffs from behind me. "That'd be right."

"Okay," Mr. Conley announces to the class, "enough of this. Back to work, everyone."

He retreats to his desk and starts tapping out a furious email, no doubt to Mrs. Jamison, requesting an FBI-style interrogation of our entire applied computing class. I turn to glare at Hawk and Simon, and they both smile politely back at me. I shake my head, willing them both to burst into flames in their seats. (Honestly, where's a skeleton mage when you need one?)

Hawk just grins back at me and reaches under his desk. A moment later, a little green top hat appears above the edge of the table, followed by two bright green eyes and a ruddy, bulbous nose.

My jaw drops and I whip around to see if Mr. Conley has noticed, but he's still frantically typing at his desk.

By the time I turn back to Hawk and Simon, they're both quietly working again and Cabbage O'Reilly has vanished from sight. For a split second, I contemplate marching straight up to Conley and urging him to search the boys, but I know better. They'd surely find some way to make the whole thing *my* fault, as usual. So, I just grit my teeth and turn back to my computer, the injustice of the whole situation almost too much to bear.

SIXTEEN

"JUST PUT ME—*SHIT*—NO—UP A bit—*ow!*"

Prisha squeals as my shoulder buckles beneath the weight of her body. She topples off, landing gracefully on two feet, barely making a sound on the wooden floor of the church hall. It's almost 9:00 p.m. on Tuesday night and I am *exhausted*. We've been rehearsing "Roxie"—her character's big number—for the last two hours. After the theft of Cabbage O'Reilly this morning, the last thing I feel like doing right now is being screamed at by Prisha Kandiyar.

Aside from Prisha, there are only eight of us in this particular number. The "men" of the ensemble, as David calls us. We play Roxie's adoring fans in her fantasy of fame, and we basically have to pass Prisha around in mid-air while we sing, performing lift after lift after lift, fawning over her all the while. Some of the boys, including this inseparable trio of straight guys in their late twenties who could *easily* pass as Barbarians from *Spire of Dusk*—Shaun, Shawn, and Steve—can lift Prisha over their heads like she's made of polystyrene. I, on the other hand, struggle to lift her off the ground at all. Chris isn't having the best time, either. He's a head and shoulders shorter than Prisha, and far from athletic. But it's still *me* who's already dropped Prisha about twelve times in a row.

"Jesus, Noah," she snaps, pulling the material of her pink tights up around her slender hips. She glares at me from under thick false eyelashes, and I reflexively glance over at Mum, who's sitting at the front by the mirrors, as usual. Honestly, if looks could kill, either one of them would have sent me six feet under by now.

"Let's . . . try it again," David calls out from beside Mum, his hand resting on the back of her chair.

I shake my hands and bend my fingers back to stretch my wrists. My forearms are burning.

"You good?" Steve—the most Barbarian-ish of the straight trio—asks. He's my partner for this particular lift, so it's more of a *Get your shit together, mate* than an *Are you okay, Noah?*

"Yeah, I think she's slipping off my shirt or something."

Prisha scoffs, her derision cutting through the cool church air.

David puffs out his cheeks. "Okay, let's pick it up from the same place. No music this time, thanks, Jane."

At the piano, Jane nods curtly, not looking up.

"You got this, Noah," Eli calls out from behind us. I can't bring myself to look at him, not when I'm this embarrassed.

"Thank you, Eli," David drawls, before turning his attention back to Prisha, Steve, and me. "All right. I'll count you in . . . a five, six, seven, prepare . . ."

As Steve and I lift Prisha off the ground, there's one whole second where I think I've finally nailed it. But we've done this lift so many times in a row that my biceps are aching and my legs are trembling and my spine is straining. I grit my teeth and hold on tight, using every ounce of energy I have left in me, but then my muscles give way and my body crumples like cardboard. Prisha tumbles off my shoulder, landing with a thud on the hardwood floor.

"Fucking hell, Noah," she cries, immediately springing back up to standing. She turns to our director, massaging her knee. "He's going to kill me, David. Can't we just cut him from the number? I refuse to do this show in a neck brace."

"We need an even number of men," David replies with an exasperated shrug. "This is a two-person lift and the other boys all have choreography at this point." He looks from me to Mum, who purses her lips and shakes her head, as if me being *this* physically useless is somehow news to her.

"Sorry," I whisper to Steve, who exhales loudly, pinching the bridge of his nose. "Sorry, Prisha."

"Whatever," she replies, flipping her long ponytail over her shoulder before storming out of the room.

"Let's take fifteen, shall we?" David calls out to the cast. "We'll pick up with 'All I Care About.' Has anyone seen Alex?"

Defeated, I cast my eyes down at the floor, massaging my throbbing forearms. This *sucks*. Performing in a musical so I can earn the affection of the love of my life is one thing, but I certainly did *not* sign up for weight lifting. I mean, *Bonesy* would have a better chance of nailing this lift than me.

"Noah," Eli says softly from behind me. I go to turn, but he places his hands on my shoulders and leans in to whisper in my ear. "Meet me in the costume room in five minutes. There's something I need to ask you. Two things, actually . . ." His lips brush the tip of my earlobe so gently that I swear I must have imagined it, and a chill runs through my entire being. "See you there in five."

He lets go of me and saunters across the hall, stopping at the door to turn and wink at me over his shoulder. I wait ten seconds—I count them in my head—then half-walk-half-run across the hall.

"Darling!" Mum cries as I speed past her. "I need to ta—"

"Back in a minute," I blurt out without looking at her.

I head straight out into the hallway, past the bathrooms, the kitchen, the cluttered little office, the cleaning cupboard, and the mysterious door that possibly leads to an ancient crypt of some kind, all the way to the end of the corridor. The wooden door before me has a sign in the shape of a gold star that says COSTUME. As I push it open and step into the room, I'm hit by a wall of cool, musty air. It's almost pitch-black inside the costume room, and I fumble around on the wall until I find a set of light switches. I flick them all on at once and the fluorescents overhead stutter to life, illuminating row upon row of overstuffed costume racks.

"Woah," I can't help but say as I take in the sheer volume of clothing before me.

While I wait for Eli to appear, I stroll down the center aisle, running my hands along the costumes on either side of me. There are ball gowns, tuxedos, cowboy costumes, cow*girl* costumes, sequinned skirts, glittering mermaid tails, hats of every conceivable shape and size, an entire section of Dorothy-from-*The-Wizard-of-Oz* dresses, and every type of jacket ever designed in the history of the human race.

I can't say I'm overly fond of dressing up, but when I stumble upon a purple velvet wizard's cloak, complete with an ornate gilded clasp and sleeves, embroidered with Tolkien-style Elven symbols, I'm left with no choice but to slip it off its hanger and try it on.

I swish around in it, loving the way it feels as it trails through the air. Just as I'm about to mumble the incantation for a spell from *Spire of Dusk*, the door creaks open behind me. I whip around to catch a fleeting glimpse of Alex Di Mario slipping into the room. I pull the hood of the cloak over my head, and press back into the rack as if I'm just another costume. I don't exactly know why my first instinct is to hide—it's not like I was doing anything untoward in here (yet)—but once I'm concealed amongst the other fantasy costumes, there's no going back.

"Come on, Di Mario," Alex whispers to himself. "Get it together."

My heart starts thudding in my chest. Even though I was here first, I get the feeling I'm intruding on a very private moment . . . .

"It's just a song," he says from the aisle across from me, closer now. "It's just a fucking *song*. Not even a hard one. Just sing the notes. You've got this. You've absolutely *got this*." He takes an enormous breath and huffs it out, like he's preparing for a boxing match. "There's nothing to be nervous about," he goes on, directly beside me on the other side of the rack. Surely, he can see me here, squished in between the fairy wings and the fake chain mail armor? "You've been doing this since you were five years old. Just sing the fucking song."

I wait for Alex's footsteps to travel slightly farther down the aisle, then—as quietly as I can manage—extricate myself from the overflowing rack. Just as I start tiptoeing towards the door, Alex calls out, "Is someone there?"

I freeze on the spot, still wearing the wizard costume. (With any luck, it's actually a cloak of invisibility.)

"Hello?" Alex says, a moment before his head pokes straight through the rack beside me. "*Noah?* What are you—" His eyes travel the length of my body, taking in every inch of the purple velvet robes.

"Um . . . hi," I reply, still frozen. "I was—"

"I don't wanna know," he interrupts, narrowing his eyes. "Did you, uh . . . Did you hear all that?"

"Well, yes, but—"

His head disappears, then his whole body reappears down the end of the aisle by the door.

"I know what that would've sounded like," he says, reaching one hand up to scratch the back of his head, "but I'm . . ."

I wait for him to go on, but he just stares at me. Smoldering (unintentionally, I'm sure) like the young Marlon Brando that he is.

"You know what," I say, slipping the cloak off and shoving it unceremoniously into the rack, "it doesn't even matter. Pretend I was never here."

"It's just like . . . it's a lot of pressure," he says, his brow folded in two. "That's all. This is a big role. Huge. Bigger than any role I've ever played. And I'm obviously up to the challenge, but it's . . . a lot."

Given this is only the second time we've ever spoken, and

that I didn't actually *ask*, I'm not sure why Alex is telling me any of this.

He shrugs one shoulder. "You know what I mean?"

"I can't say that I do," I reply, with a self-deprecating smile. "Musicals aren't really my thing."

"Clearly," he replies, and I can't help but laugh. "Sorry." He squeezes his eyes shut and shakes his head. "I didn't mean it like that. I know I can come across as a bit of a dick sometimes. Sorry."

"It's okay. I don't think you're a dick."

Unapproachable? Yes. Untouchable? Yes. Barely even real? Most definitely. But a dick? Not at all.

He turns to the cowboy costumes beside him and pulls out the sleeve of a baby-blue shirt. "This was mine from last year. *Oklahoma!* Billy Flynn is a big step up from Ike Skidmore, I can tell you now."

I don't have a clue what that means, but now's clearly not the time for a lesson in theatre history.

"Are you . . . okay?" I ask, feeling like it's not really my place to ask questions, but asking one anyway.

"Yeah, I'm fine," he replies. "Honestly. It's just a weird thing I've got going on at the moment."

"The same thing you had going on in the bathroom that time I walked in on you 'going over your lines'?"

He lets out a wry chuckle. "That's the one."

"For what it's worth—which is probably not a lot, coming from me—you don't need to be nervous. You're . . . well, you're Alex Di Mario."

"And what exactly does that mean?" he asks, his expression

torn between a frown and a smirk.

"It means you have literally nothing to worry about. Trust me."

He smiles weakly. "Thanks, dude. I think."

"Anytime."

"And you're, uh, not going to tell anyone about this, are you? About . . . me?"

Standing here in the harsh fluorescent lights of the costume room, he suddenly looks so young. So small. In this moment, this six-foot-three, carved-out-of-marble, immaculately beautiful young man looks like just another kid, desperate for approval.

"Of course not. And you're doing an awesome job in there." I flick my head in the direction of the church hall. "You're kind of amazing. In my completely inexpert opinion."

Alex's brow crinkles and one corner of his mouth curls up at the side. "Honestly, I think people assume I don't need to hear that anymore, but . . . thank you. Seriously. Thank you."

"No problem. If—"

The door swings open and Eli bursts over the threshold. He pauses for a second, looking from me to Alex and back again. "What the hell?"

"Don't worry, Callaghan," Alex says, dropping his smile, "I was just leaving." He strides past Eli, then turns to thank me one more time before heading out into the hallway. The door whines closed behind him.

Eli folds his arms across his chest. "Well?"

"Well what?"

"*Well* . . . what was that?"

"Nothing."

"What was Alex thanking you for?"

"I don't know. Nothing. We were just . . . talking."

"You just paused," Eli says, his eyes narrow.

"I'm sorry?"

"You said, 'We were just—*pause*—talking.' Which means you're lying. You were doing something else."

"I did not *pause*."

I'm not sure what's going on right now, but it feels like Eli is trying to catch me out for doing something I definitely wasn't doing with Alex.

And I don't know why he's making such a big deal about this, but it's making me nervous and when I'm nervous I look guilty, which is clearly not ideal. "Or maybe I did pause, but it wasn't like, a *purposeful* pause."

Eli rolls his eyes, turns his back, and wrenches the door open.

"Eli, wait!" I say, following him out into the hallway.

"Something wrong, boys?" Prisha asks from up ahead, because of *course* she's standing outside the bathroom on her phone.

"I dunno," Eli snaps, striding past her towards the hall. "Ask Alex Di Mario."

"Eli, relax," I groan. "Just wait a sec!"

Prisha smiles, saccharine sweet. "What mess have you caused this time, Noah Mitchell?"

I ignore her as I brush past her, jogging to catch up with Eli. I follow him to the pile of bags on the little stage, but just as I'm about to start trying to defend myself, David claps loudly and says, "All right, people. Top of 'All I Care About.' You good, Alex?'

Alex, who is standing in the middle of the hall, nods and says, "Sure." His eyes flick over to meet mine and he grins broadly. "Let's do this."

"*Yeah*," Eli scoffs quietly from beside me. "Nothing happened at *all*."

SEVEN-
TEEN

ELI WON'T SO MUCH as look at me for the rest of the rehearsal. He sits at the opposite end of the church hall while we watch Alex and the ladies' ensemble rehearse "All I Care About" (which is all feather fans and general swooning). Looking at Alex now, it's almost impossible to believe there's anything remotely insecure hiding under his gleaming exterior. I guess there really is more to everyone than meets the eye, even when what meets the eye is legitimately flawless.

I try not to watch Alex too much, because the last thing I need is Eli catching me staring and thinking it means something. Which it definitely doesn't. Of course I'm *attracted* to Alex, but it's no different to the way I feel about the ripped (and headless) models on the underwear packets at Target: They're obviously wonderful to look at, but the attraction is purely physical. Aesthetic. Like . . . appreciating a work of art. A work of art who will never appreciate you back.

My attraction to Eli is *real*. It's visceral. Intellectual. Emotional. It makes my heart flutter and the blood drain from my brain and travel to . . . other parts. *That*'s the kind of attraction I'm here for.

"Well," Mum says in the car on the way home, "that was more than a little embarrassing, wasn't it?"

At first, I think she's referring to what happened with Eli— word travels fast in a cast full of drama queens—but then she adds, "You're lucky Prisha didn't get hurt."

"Embarrassing for *me*?" I ask, staring out the passenger window. "Or for *you*?"

"Oh, don't start," she replies, clicking her tongue. "Darling, you know as well as I do that you need to try harder at rehearsals."

"Try harder to be a completely different person?"

"We've talked about the sarcasm, Noah," she chides. "I just need you to focus on the show. Like I already said, this *thing* with Eli—"

"Has nothing to do with me not being able to lift, Mum. Which is actually because I have none of the skills required to be in a musical and I'm only doing the show as a favor to my mother, who is acting like I'm a complete disgrace to the family name simply for existing."

"Look," she snaps, "you know how important this is to me, and if you're going to be like that, maybe you should just . . ."

"Just *what*, Mum? Quit?"

She lets out a long *Why is my son like this?* sigh. "Just pretend I never said anything." She takes one hand off the wheel and smooths down her eyebrows with the tips of her fingers. "I'm only trying to help, darling."

I roll my eyes. "Yeah, and how's that going?"

Another sigh.

But I don't need Mum's help. She's never offered to help me before—not when my mistakes didn't affect her personally. And as much as I almost *want* to be terrible at this just to spite her, if I mess up the show for Prisha, she'll tell Eli what I did to Tan, and the whole thing will be Game Over.

Besides, I refuse to give Rose Mitchell the satisfaction of seeing me fail at this. I may be terrible. I may humiliate myself even further. But there's no getting rid of me now.

"Oh, and for the hundredth time," I say, turning to glare at Mum, "stop calling me 'darling.'"

When I log onto *Spire of Dusk*, I let out an enormous sigh of relief. MagePants69 is already waiting for me in the Andar Valley town square. The village is wedged between two intersecting mountain ranges, one of which houses Lightdrinker's Lair—an enormous granite cavern, inlaid with gleaming veins of onyx, home to Lightdrinker, *Spire of Dusk*'s apparently unvanquishable vampiric dragon. The giant, blood-drinking lizard has become a major roadblock in our campaign. No matter what we try, we cannot kill this damn dragon.

It's no surprise, then, that the first thing MagePants69 types when my Warrior spawns next to his Bard is:

MagePants69 <tav?>

RcticF0x <Y E S>

As soon as our avatars take their seats at the bar, flagons of ale in hand, MagePants69's Bard says, *"Okay, I hate to do this, but I need more advice."*

"Oh?" my white-haired Warrior replies, lifting his drink to his mouth.

"I think the Kind of Cute Boy might have a crush on my ex."

Time stops for a second while the words "my ex" reverberate in my skull . . . .

I sit back in my chair and interlace my fingers behind my head, elbows pressing together. The dark room closes in around me as I realize three vitally important things at the exact same time:

1. Eli has an ex-boyfriend.

2. Eli's ex-boyfriend is *Alex Di Mario*.

3. Eli thinks I have a crush on his ex-boyfriend, who happens to be Alex Fucking Di Mario.

"And I mean," the Bard continues before I have a chance to tame my thoughts enough to formulate a coherent response, *"we were never official, so he's not technically my ex, but we were . . . together. If you know what I mean."*

I *do* know what he means, and I'm suddenly overcome by a strange mix of utter despair and intense arousal at the idea that Eli and Alex have had literal, IRL, guy-on-guy, probably-mind-blowing sex. Which poses the question: What the hell could Eli possibly see in *me*—the real-life Bonesy with added acne and braces—when he's slept with a living, breathing Adonis? I'm like a poor man's knock-off Picasso next to the Michelangelo masterpiece that is Alex Di Mario. I mean, *seriously*. WTAF?

Mr. Nibbles meows loudly from the foot of my bed and I'm shocked back into the moment. I need to calm down. Because I'm not Noah Mitchell right now.

I'm RcticF0x.

I take a deep breath and place my hands back on the keyboard.

"So why exactly do you think the Kind of Cute Boy has a crush on your ex?" I can't help but cringe again at the word "ex," even in my avatar's uber-manly voice. *"Your 'Not-Ex,' I should say."*

"I caught them together tonight," the Bard replies, in her sweet, honeyed tone. *"In private."*

"Were they doing anything?" my Warrior asks, even though I already know the answer to that question.

"Well, no, but I got a vibe."

"What kind of vibe?"

"It's hard to explain." The Bard flicks her ponytail over her shoulder and downs her ale in three gulps. *"It's like . . . If you'd seen the Not-Ex, you'd understand. He's ridiculously beautiful. Everyone is obsessed with him."*

I have to physically stop my own hands from typing *Not me! I'm obsessed with you!*

"We were only together one time," the Half-Elf goes on, *"but it was my first time, and I kind of fell for him. Hard."*

Thank god we're not having this conversation in real life, because I am sweating bullets all of a sudden.

"Why have you never told me this story before?"

The Bard shrugs. *"I was embarrassed."*

"Why? We've told each other far more embarrassing things than this. Remember when I had to go to the doctor because I jerked off using my sister's moisturiser and my penis swelled up like a sea cucumber?"

"No." MagePants69's avi laughs, holding a hand to her mouth. *"You might need to tell me that one again."*

"*Stop. I'm serious. You should have told me. Losing your virginity is kind of a big deal.*"

"*It's just sex,*" the Bard replies. "*The first time doesn't have to be some big, special moment.*"

"I'm sorry, what?" I say out loud in my room.

Eli doesn't think losing his virginity is a big deal? Even when it's with Alex Di Mario?

"*Then, what happened with the guy?*" my Warrior asks. "*Afterwards.*"

"*Nothing,*" the Bard replies. "*Nada. Zip. Zilch.*"

"*What do you mean?*"

"*We slept together. Once. And then he ghosted me. For months and months. We've been doing this . . . thing together for a few weeks now, but tonight was the first time he's said a word to me, and it was basically to tell me to fuck off.*"

I crack my knuckles (my actual knuckles, not my avatar's), thinking back to when I walked in on Alex in the toilet. Keegan and Luana's reactions when I told them. The look on Eli's face. The subtext fizzing beneath the surface.

And how Mum told me Eli had a "showmance" during their last production that didn't end well.

And those times at rehearsal I've caught Eli watching Alex out of the corner of his eye.

I feel faint. I feel sick. I . . . I cannot believe how much I did *not* see this coming.

But as wholly freaked out as I am about Eli having *slept* with Alex Di Mario (*Was it good? Is Alex big? Who did what to whom?*), I need to focus on The Plan.

"*Do you want my honest opinion?*" my Warrior asks.

The fiery-haired Bard narrows her eyes. *"Not if it's something I don't want to hear."*

"I am nine million percent certain that whatever you think happened between the Kind of Cute Boy and the Not-Ex is purely in your head. If you didn't see them doing anything, then they were most likely—drum roll please—not doing anything. There are endless reasons why they might have been talking in private. Including that it could have been an accident. A coincidence."

I want to go on, to make myself perfectly clear, but I'm worried I already sound like I was there in the costume room with them. (Which I was. Obviously.)

"Maybe," the Bard replies, shaking her head. *"I don't know. I guess it's plausible that I'm overreacting."*

"Plausible? More like probable. Guaranteed, actually."

"It's just that I had something important to ask the Kind of Cute Boy, so when I saw him with the Not-Ex, I . . . I don't know, I guess I just freaked out."

Something important?

"Talk to the Kind of Cute Boy," my Warrior says, with a sharp nod. *"It's your only option."*

The Bard rolls her eyes in reply. *"I'm awful at conversations like that. And I really don't want him to be intimidated by the fact that I was with this other guy."*

That ship of self-loathing has well and truly sailed, Eli.

"Just talk to him," my avatar repeats, before draining every last drop of ale from his flagon. *"Now, shall we go get ourselves slain a few hundred times trying to vanquish this damn dragon?"*

EIGHTEEN

ONCE AGAIN, WE DECIDEDLY do *not* slay Lightdrinker.

The next day, I try not to doom-spiral about the fact that Eli and Alex have slept together but, honestly, it's slightly beyond my willpower. The only benefit of picturing the love of my life having earth-shattering sex with the prettiest boy on the planet is that it makes Wednesday and Thursday at school pass by like some kind of weirdly erotic fever dream.

When I step out of Mum's car in front of the BMTS building on Thursday night, my stomach starts doing sickening backflips at the thought of seeing Eli.

Will he bring up what happened with Alex? Will *I* have to be the one to do it? Or will we both pretend it never even happened?

The answer comes almost instantly. "Hey."

I flinch, and turn to see Eli, flushed bright red and sweating, as if he's just run a marathon.

"Oh," I reply. "Hey. How, um . . . are you?"

"I missed my bus," he pants, wiping his brow with the back of his hand. "I had to speed-walk like, twenty blocks to get here in time."

"Noah," Mum cuts in, placing a hand on my shoulder, her false nails digging into my T-shirt. "Sorry to interrupt—" (she's definitely not sorry) "—but shouldn't you be heading inside to practice your lifts?"

"I asked my lifts to kindly practice themselves in my absence," I reply, with a grin so fake it could be an Instagram filter.

"Just . . . don't be late," Mum replies in a disturbingly cheery voice, before giving Eli a simpering smile and clip-clopping up the concrete ramp.

"Sorry," I say to him. "She's not coping very well with the entire Ballarat theatre community knowing her son is a complete choreography dunce."

Eli laughs. "You won't be a dunce when I'm done with you."

I grin and say, "Do you want to—" but he says, "Hey, can we—" and we both stop.

I crack my knuckles and Eli bites back a smile.

After a moment, he says, "Can we talk for a second?"

"Sure." I shrug, trying to look like I wasn't the one who told him to ask me that in the first place. He grabs me gently by the hand and walks me into the shade of an ancient oak tree in the park next to the church.

"I wanted to apologize for being a little dramatic—okay, a *lot* dramatic—about you and Alex." He stares down at the brownish grass and acorns at our feet. "We—Alex and me—have some . . . history. And I'm just super self-conscious around him."

Yes, because of the sex. I'm aware.

"I get it," I say, reminding myself not to repeat anything we discussed on *Spire of Dusk* on Tuesday night. (Honestly, it's getting hard to keep track of what *Noah* knows and what *RcticF0x* knows. I need to start keeping some sort of ledger.) "Who *isn't* self-conscious around Alex."

"It's just that . . ." Eli trails off.

"What?"

"No, nothing." He shakes his head but then carries on anyway. "It's just that the last time you spoke to him, you were like, hiding in the bathroom together, and then this time, you were in the costume room, when you were supposed to be waiting for *me* in there, so . . . I know it's silly, but it just seemed kind of suss."

I can't help but laugh. "Do you really think Alex Di Mario would want to do anything 'suss' with *me*?"

"Oh, come on." Eli smirks. "I'm sure plenty of people want to get suss with you."

Aside from Hannah Forbes—whom you may recall from the "strongly worded letter" incident of Year Eight—no one has ever shown any interest in doing anything even remotely "suss" with me. (For the record, I *did* kiss Hannah Forbes at a shopping center after school one day in Year Eight, but I don't count it as my First Kiss, because a) she's a girl and I felt literally *nothing* for her before, during, or after the kiss, and b) I mainly did it to shut Tan and the boys up so we could go home and play *Darkest Dungeon*. No offense, Hannah.)

"That's lovely of you," I reply, feeling heat rush to my cheeks. "But also highly inaccurate."

"It's completely accurate," Eli says, taking a tentative step closer and interlacing his fingers through mine. "Do I need to prove it to you?"

"Prove it?" I almost choke on the words. "How do you propose you'd do that?"

He hums in pretend thought. "I don't know. I mean, I could . . . kiss you?"

My heart clenches in my chest. "That . . . sounds like a suitable way to disprove my theory."

Eli laughs, then leans in and kisses me softly. He lets his marshmallow lips linger on mine for a moment, then slowly pulls away.

"Did that do the trick?" he asks, his brow adorably crinkled.

I shake my head. "Not quite. I think—"

Then he's kissing me again. At first, it's gentle, but then he opens his mouth and his tongue finds mine. A jolt of anxiety runs through me—What if he's never kissed someone with braces before? What if it turns him off?—but then he lets go of my hands and puts his arms around my waist, pulling me in closer, *tighter*, and I forget that braces even exist.

I try to keep an ounce of restraint, because I don't want to come across desperate or full-on, but how can I?

It's happening.

It's finally happening.

I'm kissing the boy of my dreams. The boy I've been secretly in love with for a year and a half.

The thought makes me kiss him back with the cumulative fire of every tiny spark of passion that's been flickering inside me since the day we first chatted online. Eli must notice the change in my energy, because his hands grasp the fabric of my T-shirt and he inhales deeply through his nose. I loop my arms around the back of his neck and press my hips into his, hyper aware of what's currently happening inside my underwear, and what is *clearly* happening inside his.

He lets out a small moan and pulls away slightly, so that only the tips of our noses are touching. My eyes are closed, but I can tell he's smiling. Maybe because I am, too.

"Noah!" someone cries from somewhere and I open my eyes, reflexively holding my hands over my crotch. I turn and see Mum, standing just outside the door to the BMTS building, hands sternly on her hips. "Hurry up! We've already started!"

"We'd better go," Eli whispers over my shoulder.

"Wait," I say, turning back to him, still able to feel Mum's eyes boring into my back. "When you told me to meet you in the costume room on Tuesday, wasn't there . . . something you wanted to ask me?"

"Noah!" Mum shouts again, shrill and impatient. "*Now.*"

"There was," Eli replies quietly. "But I think I'll save it for slightly cuter circumstances."

And even though it almost kills me, I say, "I'll allow it."

He takes my hand in his and, together, we walk up the concrete ramp, past my glaring mother, and into the rehearsal room. As we take our places amongst the rest of the ensemble, ready to run through "Razzle Dazzle," I feel like a star. As in, a literal star. One that's about to burst into a supernova at any second.

Because we finally got it right. Noah Mitchell and Elijah Callaghan. Two real-life boys, and a first kiss that actually happened.

NINETEEN

This just in . . .
From: MagePants69 <magepants69@gmail.com>
To: Arctic Fox <rcticf0x@outlook.com>
On: Thursday, 16 April at 10:13 p.m.

WE DID IT.

Well, not IT. But we kissed. Me and the Kind of Cute Boy.

And let me just say, he's more than a kind-of-good kisser.

Yours,

M

Receiving an email like that is the stuff dreams are made of. (Not *those* kind of dreams. Actually, yes, those kind of dreams.) But it's now been three days since The Kiss, and Eli *still* hasn't asked me his important question. I know he said he was waiting for "cuter circumstances" but I'm beginning to wonder if he's decided not to ask it. Whatever *it* is.

I spend the whole morning on Sunday working on my choreography in the lounge room. The last thing I need is for Mum to make my life any more stressful than it already is, and I figure the best way to avoid that is by perfecting my *Chicago* routines. I'm hoping a bit of extra rehearsal will also minimize the risk of more mid-rehearsal rebukes from Prisha, but we'll see how that goes. I might be able to go over the choreography nine hundred times in the comfort of my own home, but I can't miraculously grow a set of biceps overnight.

Regardless, I walk into the church hall that afternoon feeling reasonably confident, despite Mum's not-so-subtle comments in the car about how it'll take more than a couple of hours' work to get me anywhere near the David Dawes Standard. But as soon as we're all gathered in the room, David claps his hands and says, "Okay, cast, we're pausing on 'Me and My Baby' today . . ."

Murmurs circulate the room.

". . . as we have a *dear* friend of mine here to get your costumes fitted!"

Prisha, Luana, and Yvette squeal behind me, and Keegan lets out an emphatic, "Fun!"

A nervous lump builds in my throat. I'm not a hundred percent sure what costume fittings entail, but nothing remotely changeroom-related has ever been fun for me.

"They are one of Melbourne's most exciting up-and-coming costume designers, and we are *beyond* lucky they have agreed to help us out with our little show. Please give your warmest Ballarat welcome to—" he gestures to the door "—Sam Hargraves!"

"Oh my god," Eli whispers from beside me, "no way! They're *incredible.*"

Everyone looks to the door as a tall, elegant, East Asian person swans into the room, wearing loose black pants with an angular half-skirt attached to one side, a tight black long-sleeved top, and a pair of stark white high heels. Their blonde hair is tied into a topknot, and a long, acid-green earring dangles from one ear. They give a cheery wave on the way in, calling out, "Hi, folks!" to the group.

David gives Sam a warm hug, kissing them on both cheeks, before turning back to us. "Sam is the *real deal*," David says, with one arm around their shoulder. "Not that the BMTS costume crew isn't *also* the real deal," he adds, tipping his head to the stout woman standing by the door. "Your costumes are delightful, Mary."

Mary, who is looking Sam up and down with a territorial glare, gives David an ingratiating smile.

"This will probably take all afternoon," David goes on, "so we ask for your utmost patience. These are not the finished products yet, and some of you missed out on having your measurements taken earlier in the year, so it's going to be a bit of a process. Okay?"

Everyone nods, and a few people reply with an enthusiastic, "Okay!"

"Let's do it!" Sam announces, and with that, the BMTS costume crew—made up primarily of people who could be my grandparents—start wheeling rack upon rack of costumes into the hall.

"Wait," I say to Eli, my pulse quickening, "we're doing it in here?"

"Of course." He shrugs. "There's no way we'd all fit in the costume room."

"We're not doing it in groups? Like, guys and girls separately?"

Eli laughs. "This is the theatre, *dahling*," he says in a posh British accent, as if that explains everything. He winks and trots off to one of the glittery racks.

And so begins my first costume fitting.

The whole thing is chaotic and overwhelming. Mary and her team—under Sam's watchful eye—start fitting dresses and shirts and shoes and hats on the cast, all of whom seem completely unfazed about stripping down to their skivvies in front of everyone in the middle of the church hall.

When it's my turn to try on a pair of black pants, I retreat to the back corner.

"Not my idea of a fun afternoon either," someone says from beside me, and I turn to see Chris with his pair of "All That Jazz" pants in hand. "This—" he pats himself on the belly "—is not for public viewing."

I chuckle awkwardly and turn to gaze around the hall. Girls are standing around chatting in their bras and undies. The trio of straight Barbarians (Shawn, Shaun, and Steve) are joking around with their tops off like they're in a football locker room. Alex Di Mario is strutting about in nothing but his tighty-whities, which leave very little to the imagination.

Heat flashes in my face. Eli has had sex with *that*.

My eyes must linger on Alex for a second too long, because Chris says, "It's not fair, is it? He's like a walking slayer of self-esteem."

I turn back to face the wall and slip off my trackies, immediately pulling on the "All That Jazz" pants before anyone has the chance to see my spindly, hairy legs, and complete absence of ass.

"Okay, this is *not* gonna work," Chris says, struggling to button up his pants.

"Me neither," I say, having to hold my own pair up at the waist so they don't fall straight to the floor.

Chris scoffs. "Wish I had your problem."

I leave him by the wall and make my way over to Mary, who has a tape measure draped around her neck and a giant pin cushion strapped to her belt like a bumbag. She already looks more than a little frazzled.

"Goodness me," she says, slipping her hand under the waistband of my pants. "We'll need to take these in quite a bit. You're very thin, love."

She says it like she's the first person to ever tell me that. Like I've gone through the last seventeen years of my life without realizing I weigh half as much as the other guys my age.

"Sorry," I reply.

"Take your T-shirt off and pop this on, will you?" She holds out a black button-up shirt with sequins dotted all over the fabric. I take it and turn to head back to the corner.

"We don't have time for that, love," Mary snaps. "Just put it on."

I glance over my shoulder. Prisha and Luana and Keegan are standing only a couple of meters behind me, but they seem absorbed in some kind of salacious gossip, as usual. I find Eli on the other side of the hall with Yvette, sliding into a perfectly fitted pair of black pants. My eyes flick to Alex (still half naked) on the opposite side of the room, where Sam is slipping a black tuxedo jacket onto him from behind. Mum is right beside them in a black, bedazzled leotard. I watch as David runs a hand along the lycra stretched tight over her hip. As much as I want to storm over there and remind him that Rose has a husband at home (AKA my *father*), I have more pressing issues right now.

While the coast is relatively clear, I yank my T-shirt over my head—having to stand in a half-squat so my pants don't fall down—drop it onto the floor, and reach out to take the shirt from Mary.

"Oh, wait a sec," she says with a furrowed brow, before turning to the rack beside her, "this one already has Steve's name on it. Let me just . . ."

She starts riffling through the rack of black shirts, while I just stand here with my top off in the middle of the hall. The fluorescent lights beat down from above, accentuating every rib, every bone, every sharp angle of my body. I feel my cheeks flush instantly and I bite down on my lip. I desperately want to pick up my T-shirt and slip it back on, but I don't want to draw any extra attention to myself and the fact that I'm completely dying inside.

"Sorry, love," Mary says, face still buried in the rack. "Just gimme one minute."

I choke out a "No worries," and fold one arm across my stomach, the other hand still gripping the waistband of my pants.

"Oh my *god*," a girl says from behind me, and I can't help but turn. It's Yvette, eyebrows raised. "Noah, you're so *skinny*."

I want to make a sarcastic reply—like I would without missing a beat when Mum says things like that—but I suddenly have no words.

"I mean," Luana adds, "thirteen-year-old girls would kill for that body."

Keegan stifles a laugh, and Prisha says, "I think you need to go eat a steak or two, Mitchell. No wonder you can't lift me."

Tears build behind my eyes, and I don't waste a single second to see if Eli has noticed any of this. I turn away, snatch up my T-shirt, and dash out of the hall. Mary calls my name, but I'm already gone. I pull my T-shirt on, burst through the front door, and head down the ramp, not stopping until I'm underneath the oak tree where Eli kissed me the other day.

I lean my head against the rough bark, breathing in and out, trying to steady my racing pulse.

You're very thin, love.

Thirteen-year-old girls would kill for that body.

No wonder you can't lift me.

You're so skinny.

Go eat a steak or two.

The words bounce around in my brain, landing crippling blows on what very little self-esteem I have left.

I try to shake the thoughts away, telling myself it doesn't matter what they think, that Eli is the one person who won't care how skinny I am. That he likes me anyway. Even though he's been with—

"Noah?" a deep voice calls from the ramp up to the building. "You good?"

Alex. The *exact* person I want to see right now. He jogs down to the tree, barefoot, wearing a tuxedo jacket over his bare chest, and a pair of black pants. As he gets closer, I see there are still pins sticking out of the shoulders and lapels of the jacket.

"You okay, dude?" he asks, frowning.

"Yeah," I reply, aiming for casual, achieving awkward. "Why?"

Alex pulls his mouth to one side. "I saw what went down in there. I just wanted to see if you were all right."

"You don't owe me anything," I snap, desperate for Alex "Vision of Perfection" Di Mario *not* to be the one to console me about my body image issues. "I'm not going to tell anyone what happened in the costume room. So . . . you don't have to pretend to have my back or whatever."

Alex sighs, then says, "Have you ever seen any old photos of me?"

I narrow my eyes. "Believe it or not, I'm not a member of the official Alex Di Mario fan club."

"Okay, ouch." Alex clutches at his chest. "Here, just . . ." He pulls his phone out of his pocket and taps at the screen. "Look."

He shows me a photo of a stick-thin boy with a heavy mop of black hair. He's wearing a blue singlet that looks about ten sizes too big, grinning with a mouth full of metal.

"Yeah," I say, "and?"

Alex lifts his eyebrows and nods to the phone.

"Wait," I say, leaning in. "That's *you*?"

He clicks his tongue and smiles.

"No, it's not," I scoff. "That's your little cousin or something. You're just messing with me."

"I am not messing with you," he laughs. "That's me. In Year Ten. Two years ago. So, if anyone knows what it feels like to be skinny and self-conscious, it's me."

I stare down at the photo, and then up at Alex. It's almost impossible to believe I'm looking at the same person, only two years apart. "Yeah, but it's not the same. Look at you now. You're . . . you know. And I'm . . . not."

"I worked really fucking hard on my body for years," Alex replies, shaking his head. "I still do. It's a constant thing. It's basically a part-time job."

"Are you trying to tell me that working out will solve all my problems? That I'll be a new man if I just lift some weights? Because that's a) incredibly superficial, and b) not really my thing, Alex. All those—" I swat my hands through the air "—meatheads and bodybuilders."

"Gyms aren't just for meatheads and bodybuilders, dude. You have no idea what you're talking about. Have you ever even *been* to a gym?"

"Do I *look* like I've been to a gym?"

"Come with me," Alex says, matter-of-factly.

"Where?"

"To the gym."

"What? *No*."

"Just come," he urges. "The manager is a mate of mine. I can get you in for free."

Money isn't the issue. The gym itself is the issue.

"No," I repeat. "I can't . . . I . . ."

"Why not?" Alex shrugs. "It's *fun*. And it will help with your lifts in the show."

I fold my arms.

"I promise I'm not trying to turn you into a meathead," he goes on, "or solve all your problems with a few sets of sit-ups. It just helps with confidence and stuff. Trust me. You'll be surprised. It feels good. Endorphins and all that."

"I'm aware of the science," I reply. "But that doesn't mean I want to do it."

"I go every day before school. Seven-thirty. Lakeside Fitness. Meet me there tomorrow morning and I'll prove you wrong."

I shake my head. "You don't need to do this, Alex. I'm not your little pity project."

"I don't pity you."

"Then there's literally no reason for you to help me."

"Maybe I just *want* to help you." He smiles. "Look, I gotta go back inside. Sam is high-key stressed about getting this jacket perfect, and I don't want to keep them waiting."

With that, Alex heads back up the ramp, shouting out, "Seven-thirty!" before he disappears inside.

I slump back against the tree and gaze up at the canopy of green above me, one hand still holding up my pants.

I can't go to the gym with Alex Di Mario. I simply *cannot.* That is a one-way ticket to a small town called Self Hatred, population: me.

Lightdrinker lets out an earth-shattering roar, which is near deafening in my noise-cancelling headphones. The granite cavern on the screen shudders, shards of rock raining down on our avatars.

MagePants69 <grrrrr. take THIS, you filthy lizard>

But before the Bard has time to cast another spell, the dragon engulfs its entire lair with shadow-flame and my screen flashes blood red.

YOU HAVE BEEN SLAIN

Awesome.

When our avatars respawn in the Andar Valley town square, I'm about to march my Warrior straight to the Tav when my phone buzzes.

Eli: **You got a minute to chat?**

It's 9:00 p.m. on a Sunday night, so I've got nothing but minutes to chat.

Yep, I reply. **Gimme one sec.**

I go to type a message to MagePants69 on *Spire of Dusk*, but he beats me to it.

MagePants69 <can we take a break for a bit? i've got some stuff I need to take care of>

RcticF0x <sure. i should prob do some homework anyway>

MagePants69 <you're not going to do any homework>

RcticF0x <haha you know me too well>

I quickly sign out of *Spire of Dusk* and text Eli: **Ready!** I also add a waving emoji, which I instantly regret.

My phone buzzes in my hand.

"Hello?" I answer, as if I don't already know who's calling.

"Hey," Eli replies. "How's it going?"

"Meh. Standard Sunday. You?"

"Yeah, good. Just been playing a game with a friend. A computer game, I mean. Not like, hide-and-seek."

"Fun," I reply with a chuckle, imagining me and Eli playing an updated version of hide-and-seek where you get to make out when you find the other person.

"So . . ." Eli says, almost singing the word. "There's something I wanted to ask you."

Finally.

"And you can totally say no," he goes on. "There is *zero*

pressure. I know it's probably not your vibe, but I just thought it would be really cute, and—"

"Eli," I interrupt, "you might want to tell me what it is before you talk me out of it."

He laughs awkwardly on the other end of the line. "Yeah, fair point. *Well* . . . my friend Siobhan was meant to come with me but she has this big Irish dancing competition up on the Gold Coast, so I thought I'd ask if you wanted to join me for my birthday trip to Melbourne in a few weeks?"

I'm silent for a second while I process the gravity of Eli's invitation. Then I clear my throat and say, "Yes! Of course! That sounds fun. I haven't been to Melbourne in ages."

"Yay!" Eli's smile is practically audible. "So, the plan is to get the train down on the Saturday morning—which is my actual birthday, the twenty-third of May—then we have tickets to see *CATS* that night, and then we've got a room at a hotel—just a cheap one down near Docklands, nothing fancy—and then we can mooch around on Sunday morning and get the train back in the afternoon for rehearsal. Does that sound okay?"

I'm trying to keep up with Eli's plans, but my mind completely stalled at the part about the hotel room.

"Noah?"

"Yeah, sorry," I stammer, my voice suddenly dry. "That sounds awesome. And your mum is cool with all that? The, um . . . hotel, et cetera."

Eli clicks his tongue. "I haven't actually told her that Siobhan can't come, and I'm not sure if she'd be super keen on me taking a boy, so, if anyone asks, you are a seventeen-year-old competitive

Irish dancer with a fondness for geography and giant pretzels. We might just need to get you a wig."

A clandestine trip to a Melbourne hotel room seems like a one-way ticket to juvenile detention, courtesy of Senior Constable Callaghan, but as if I could say no to two days (and one *night*) alone with Eli.

"Well," I reply, "I've definitely got geography and giant pretzels covered, and I'm sure Mum would have a wig I could borrow, but the Irish dancing will be my undoing. Although, I'm pretty sure I'm one-eighth Irish, so you never know, it might be in my blood."

"That's the spirit," Eli laughs. "I gotta go, but we can talk details later, yeah?"

"Yeah, okay. Cool."

"I, um . . . can't wait to have you all to myself in Melbourne." I swallow. "You too."

We say our goodbyes and I flop back onto my bed. I should be rejoicing, because a weekend trip with Eli is legitimately the stuff dreams are made of, but . . .

A hotel room.

A bed.

A boy who's not a virgin.

My stomach twists into a giant pretzel at the thought.

TWENTY

SO . . . I'M GOING TO the gym with Alex Di Mario.

I know I said I wouldn't, but here I am. Shivering my ass off outside the front of Lakeside Fitness, wondering—not for the first time in recent history—WTAF I'm doing with my life. I've somehow gone from the loner kid who's spent basically the last three years locked inside his bedroom living a safe and purely virtual life, to some guy who's a) in a musical, b) semi-romantically involved with the world's most adorable gaymer/music theatre nerd, and c) about to *work out* with objectively the hottest guy in town.

Like I said: WTAF.

Now, there is no part of me that wants to work out with Alex Di Mario, but . . .

Thirteen-year-old girls would kill for that body.

Go eat a steak or two.

How can I ever expect to get naked in a hotel room with Eli if I can't even take my top off in front of an old lady and a few bitchy kids at rehearsal?

My saving grace is that I know Alex won't tell anyone I'm here with him (on account of the costume room incident) and he seems surprisingly chill about the whole thing. I don't sense even the slightest bit of judgement or agenda. And here I thought he was just another pretty-boy jock, but he actually seems . . . nice.

Lakeside Fitness is situated a convenient six-minute walk from my house, nestled between a few of the private school rowing sheds on the banks of Lake Wendouree. It looks more like a day spa than a gym to me, which probably goes to show how much I know about gyms. Or day spas. The best part about it being so close is that I don't have to ask Mum or Dad to drive me. Which is perfect, because it means I don't even have to tell them I'm going.

"Hey," Alex calls out as he jogs across the road. "I didn't think you'd come."

"Yes, well, neither did I," I reply. "But here we are."

Alex laughs. "Come in, I'll introduce you to the manager."

We walk inside and meet Sarah, the gym manager, who is a very buff and very *orange* woman in her probably-mid-thirties. She must notice me staring at the patchy fake tan on her hands because she says, "I just had a competition. I promise I don't usually look like a Charmander."

A Pokémon reference? Ten points to you, Sarah.

She gives us a quick tour of the gym—which is all floor-to-ceiling windows and gleaming silver gym equipment—concluding at the men's locker room.

"I'll let you boys get to it!" she says, clapping her fist into her other palm. "Have fun, Noah. You're in good hands." She winks at Alex and walks back to the front desk.

"We can chuck our bags in the lockers," Alex says, holding the door to the change room open. "You brought your school stuff, yeah? We can shower after the workout."

My stomach plummets into my feet. Please, for the love of all that's holy, do *not* let it be an open shower. "Sounds good."

After we stash our bags, Alex walks me over to one corner of the gym, filled with equipment that could easily be mistaken for torture devices.

"You wanna start with a quick HIIT warm-up and then do some weights?" he asks.

"Hit what?"

"No," he chuckles, "HIIT. As in, H-I-I-T. High-intensity interval training. You've never heard of it?"

"Alex, my general knowledge does not extend to anything that goes on in this building. Just so we're clear."

He laughs. "Oh, this is gonna be *fun*."

After fifteen minutes of jumping and jogging and bouncing and squatting, I'm about ready to pass out. If this is just the *warm-up*, I'm going to need to call an ambulance to deliver my corpse to school when we're done. Alex, on the other hand, has barely worked up a sweat. His olive skin is faintly glowing.

"How do you feel about chest and triceps?" he asks, running a hand across his brow.

Alex has a mind-blowing chest, and the kind of triceps that I thought only existed in Marvel films.

"I . . . like them?" I reply.

"No," Alex says, stifling yet another laugh. "I mean how do you feel about *doing* chest and triceps. For our workout."

I shrug. It's going to be humiliating regardless, so it's all the same to me. "Sure."

We head over to a machine by the window overlooking the

lake. The morning sun is casting a fiery glow across the gently rippling water. A huge part of me wants to jump straight through the glass and swim to safety, but I start repeating the words *Melbourne hotel room* in my head over and over to remind me why I'm here.

"I'll go first so you can watch," Alex says, taking a seat on a machine labeled BENCH PRESS.

He adjusts the yellow pin in the stack of weights, lies back, grips the handles, and starts to press upwards.

"This is just a standard bench press." He continues to lift and lower the weights while he talks, veins bulging in his arms, his chest ballooning inside his tank top. "It works your pecs, and your shoulders assist a bit. Try to isolate the chest muscles, though, as that's what we're targeting."

I nod, highly aware that I'm already blushing. Alex is overwhelmingly hot at the best of times, but there's something about him in this exact moment that is attractive on a whole other level. Maybe it's a pheromone thing. Or maybe the air is full of testosterone and I'm a seventeen-year-old gay virgin and even a slight breeze can turn me on.

Alex finishes his set and I take his place on the bench. As he reaches across my body to decrease the weight, I have to force myself not to actively smell him. He's wearing an earthy, woody cologne that sends my mind reeling.

"Have a go," he says. "Just grip nice and hard, and press up as fast as you can. Hold for a second at the top, then lower the weights down, nice and controlled. We'll go for eight reps."

I take in a deep breath and push with all my might against the handles, straining so much that I almost grunt like my *Spire of Dusk* avi when he makes a critical hit. I push and push and push . . .

. . . but nothing happens.

"Uh, okay," Alex says, reaching back across to the weights. "Let's just take it down a bit more."

Kill. Me. Now.

"Go again."

Thankfully, I can actually move the handles this time, but it takes every ounce of strength within me—which is clearly only several ounces—and my neck and head feel like they're about to explode. I avoid looking at myself in the mirror when I finish the set, because I *really* don't want to know how red and sweaty I am right now, compared to the glistening Italian demigod beside me.

"Good job, dude!" The demigod holds his fist out and I bump it with mine, in what is undoubtedly the most pathetic fist bump in history. "Let's try some tricep extensions."

Alex takes me through a long series of nausea-inducing exercises, each one more impossible than the last. I vomit in my mouth on two separate occasions, but I have no choice but to swallow it straight back down so I don't look like a wimp in front of Coach Di Mario.

Soon, my arms physically cannot lift another thing. When I almost drop a dumbbell on Alex's foot—if he wasn't so nimble, there would be broken bones—he says we should probably wrap it up for the day.

We head into the locker room, and Alex starts taking his clothes off, showing no signs of self-consciousness whatsoever. He tosses his sweat-soaked singlet on the bench in front of him—now that I'm up close and personal, I can confirm that his chest and abs are, in fact, made of marble—then peels off his exercise shorts. He grabs a towel from his locker and drapes it over his shoulders, and just when I think he's about to walk off to the showers . . .

He slips out of his jocks.

Now, it's not like I've never seen a naked guy before. I've watched basically every gay porn video in existence (no judgement, please—it's not as if guys are lining up to get naked with me in real life). But seeing Alex's . . . *stuff* right here in the locker room, less than a meter away, is simultaneously:

1. Unfathomably hot.

2. Legitimately terrifying.

3. Disconcertingly normal.

Alex is so casual about his body that his nudity feels weirdly non-sexual. This doesn't mean I'm not turned on, but it also feels . . . comfortable? Like it's perfectly acceptable for friends to be naked in front of one another. Like there's nothing to be ashamed of or self-conscious about.

Then again, if I looked like *that* (and had a package that impressive—seriously, Eli is taking a big step down with me in *all* departments), I'd probably be naked a lot more often, too.

He disappears into the showers and I just stand here, fully clothed, dripping with sweat, semi-aroused, feeling like I could faint from low blood sugar at any second. I go to take my T-shirt off but my arms seem to have stopped functioning. After about five attempts, I have to bend forward and fold myself in half to pull the sticky T-shirt over my head. I slide out of my drenched tracksuit pants and stand there for a moment in nothing but my jocks.

I can take them off.

I can walk to the shower naked.

I can strut around in the nude like Alex Di Mario.

I can—

I turn and catch a glimpse of myself in the mirrors above the sinks. In the harsh downlighting of the locker room, I really do look like Bonesy incarnate. Lanky and gaunt, with too-long limbs and an angular face. My blond curls are sweaty and gross, my pimply cheeks red and shiny. As usual, the only part of myself that I don't detest entirely is my periwinkle blue eyes, which happen to be staring back at me with a kind of glassy sadness.

I reach over to grab my towel from my locker just as Alex emerges from the showers, his towel wrapped dangerously low around his waist, looking like he's stepped straight off the set of some queer arthouse film.

"You good?" he asks, heading to his locker.

"Yep," I reply, employing my towel as a full-body shield. I duck around the corner, out of sight, and call out, "Sorry, just give me one minute. I'll be quick."

I stand under the scalding water for much longer than one minute, my mind replaying a hypothetical moment over and over in my mind, with an endless stream of humiliating endings:

Eli and me in a hotel room. I take off my clothes. His expression drops.

Eli and me in a hotel room. I take off my clothes. He tries not to laugh.

Eli and me in a hotel room. I take off my clothes. He says, "Actually, I'm a bit tired. Should we just go to sleep?"

"Hey, Noah?" Alex calls out over the sound of the water. "I gotta get to school. I'll see you again tomorrow morning, yeah? You did good today."

Even though I might vomit again at any second, and even though I don't think I'll be able to bend my elbows tomorrow, and *even though* working out with Alex has been one of the most mortifying experiences of my life, I reply with a shaky, "See you tomorrow . . . ."

TWENTY-ONE

THE NEXT FOUR WEEKS are the busiest of my life.

I go to the gym with Alex every morning before school, which induces a level of exhaustion that I didn't know was possible. For the whole first week, I vomited in the shower after every workout. Luckily, I'm a silent spewer—unlike Charly, who sounds like she's being attacked by bears—so I don't think Alex noticed. *Now*, however, instead of needing to throw up, I actually feel quite energized after we work out. It's a great feeling while it lasts, but I keep majorly crashing by the time I get to second period. I fell asleep in physics the other day, which Mrs. Nkosi interpreted as a direct reflection of my interest in the kinetic energy of emitted photoelectrons. Which sounds about right, to be honest.

Mr. Conley escalated the theft of Cabbage O'Reilly to Mrs. Jamison, as promised, and is waiting for her to decide what steps to take next. I wish I could just march up to her office and tell her it was Hawk and Simon who took the figurine but—as usual—I have zero proof, and the risk grossly outweighs the reward. Or, at least, that's what I tell myself whenever I feel the all-too-familiar pangs of guilt associated with anything remotely Tan related.

Mid-year exams are coming up, which do require *some* amount of study and commitment on my behalf. I've never had to try very hard to be good at school, which is great because it means I can spend all my time playing computer games instead of studying, but the teachers have really started putting the pressure on.

As for Mum, it's almost as if she's wearing a pair of magical blinkers at the moment, where she can't perceive anything that doesn't have to do with *Chicago*. I summon the courage to ask her one night in the car if she thinks David is being unnecessarily touchy with her, which she laughs off and says, "Darling, please. I've told you before, theatre people are *very* physically open. David is a consummate professional, you don't need to worry about him." I ask Charly about it, too, and she rattles something off about the power imbalance between directors and actors, which doesn't exactly make me less worried.

Charly ended up refusing to come home for her first set of uni holidays, which Mum took as a personal attack. Dad thinks Charly's ridiculous to not spend his money on flights, but she maintains that she is determined not to be an "entitled Gen Z-er" and to pave her own way in the world. I wanted to say, *Well, can you pave your way down to Ballarat for a few days to see your little brother?* because I really want to tell her the whole Eli story in person, but she's not the kind of girl to change her mind once it's been made up. I envy her for that quality a lot. I'm so ambivalent it hurts.

I messaged her about the secret birthday getaway, an exchange that went something like this:

Me: **So . . . I'm going on a weekend trip to Melbourne with Eli.**

Charly: **OMG, what?! Where are you staying?**

Me: **A hotel.**

Charly: **Please tell me that even though you're a super nerd, you still know about safe sex, right?**

Me: **We're done here.**

Rehearsals—dare I say it—are actually bearable. I've been practicing with Eli on the weekends at the Sunnyside Roller Rink (and yes, we *do* rehearse a bit amidst all the making out), which means I at least *know* the choreography, even if I can't execute it as stylishly as the David Dawes Standard requires. My workouts with Alex have also helped immeasurably with the lifts in the "Roxie" number, as promised. Prisha almost gave me a compliment the other day when I finally nailed the shoulder-sit lift, then literally bit her tongue, rolled her eyes and said, "About time, Mitchell. It's not like it's *hard*."

It might sound ridiculous, but I can't help but feel like I'm leveling up, like a real-life *Spire of Dusk* avi. Not only from my workouts with Alex, but—as much as I hate to admit it—from all the singing and dancing, too. It's like I'm throwing Ability Points into Strength and Dexterity and Charisma every morning and night, day in, day out. I'm stronger, I'm more confident, I'm (slightly) more comfortable at rehearsals. I don't *look* different yet, which is more than a little frustrating, but I figure if I feel this good already, I'll have bulging pecs and washboard abs in no time.

(Probably not, but a boy can dream.)

The only area of my life that I seem to be epically failing at is *Spire of Dusk*. If you can believe it, MagePants69 and I are *still* trying to get past Lightdrinker (the "Unvanquishable Bloodsucking Lizard," as we've started calling him). At this point, we have tried *everything* in our arsenal to bring the dragon down. Every spell, every weapon type, every bard song, every NPC sidekick we can find.

We. Cannot. Kill. Him.

To make ourselves feel less pathetic, we complete all the optional side-quests in Andar Valley and its neighboring towns. There are several nights when I'm so wiped out from gym and school and rehearsals that I have to bail on playing altogether. And then I get this email one night as I'm sliding into bed, my eyes as heavy as lead.

Defeated by a big lizard?
From: MagePants69 <magepants69@gmail.com>
To: Arctic Fox <rcticf0x@outlook.com>
On: Tuesday, 19 May at 10:39 p.m.

M'lord. I don't want to be dramatic, but have we been defeated by that fucking dragon? I feel like you're not really into the game lately, which is fine, I mean, whatever, it's not the only thing that exists in the world. But I don't want to be the Stage-Five Clinger Half-Elf Bard who awkwardly refuses to let something go when it's clearly already dead . . . so . . . let me know.

Yours,

M

PS I just read that email back and yes, I'm being dramatic, but that's just how I roll, so deal with it.

Re: Defeated by a big lizard?
From: Arctic Fox <rcticf0x@outlook.com>
To: MagePants69 <magepants69@gmail.com>
On: Tuesday, 19 May at 10:43 p.m.

The answer to your (dramatic) question is simply: NO. We will not be defeated. Ever. We're MagePants69 and RcticF0x. Till death do us part, or something less romantic/morbid than that, but you get the point.

We will slay that dragon if it's the last thing we do. I promise.

Yours in faithful perpetuity,

RcticF0x

All good for the weekend? Eli messages on Thursday after school—T-minus 41 hours to our Melbourne trip.

Yes! I reply. **Can't wait.**

In reality, I feel completely unprepared. Least of all, physically.

I couldn't help noticing at the gym that Alex is, shall we say, "well groomed" in the pubic region. Not to a porn-star degree or anything, but he clearly looks after himself. I've never done any kind of tidying *down there*, and it's not like I'm a gorilla, but . . . are gay guys expected to "manscape"? If so, how much hair is too much? How much is too *little*? And is it just the front I should be concerned about or, you know, the *back*, too?

As usual, with highly awkward subjects like this, there is no one to ask and no handy manual to consult. I know porn is *not* a good indication of what anything is like in real life, which means my only option is to try to replicate Alex's grooming, especially given Eli clearly approved of his manscaping enough to sleep with him, which—after all—is my goal, too. With Eli, I mean. Not with Alex. Obviously.

I swing by Target on the way home from school on Friday afternoon, then lock myself in the bathroom with literal armfuls of men's grooming paraphernalia. From my locker room reconnaissance—otherwise known as furtive glances at Alex's junk—I have gleaned that he most likely uses a body hair trimmer to tidy up the majority of the area, then possibly waxes his balls. The thought of accidentally waxing off an entire layer of ball-skin is not super appealing, so I decide to do my best with the trimmer before I resort to more drastic measures.

Thirty minutes—and only a couple of minor mishaps later—I gently place the trimmer down on the bathroom bench, cross both sets of fingers by my thighs, and look up into the mirror. For a split second, I don't entirely hate what I see. I straighten my spine, puff out my chest, and place my feet a little wider on the bath mat. And then a vision of Alex Di Mario parading around the locker room naked, his rippling muscles artfully dripping with sweat, quickly dispels my tiny glimmer of positivity.

I let my shoulders slump, eyes still on the gangly boy in the mirror staring back at me.

Tomorrow—if everything goes to plan—Eli is going to see me naked. And no amount of sit-ups or manscaping or praying to the gay gods is going to improve my appearance at this point. This is all I've got. And whether Eli likes it or not . . . it's going to have to do.

I reach down and scratch my freshly groomed crotch. I didn't realize it'd be so itchy.

TWENTY-TWO

"THE ROOM SHOULD BE under Callaghan?" Eli says to the cute Filipino guy behind the check-in desk of the Docklands Holiday Stay Hotel.

I feel like I'm still half asleep. Eli and I got the 7:04 a.m. train down to Melbourne, which is an incredibly early start for a Saturday. I don't usually see daylight until after 10:00 a.m., and even then it's only for a minute while I grab breakfast before retreating back to the relative darkness of my room with Mr. Nibbles.

Having said that, the train ride down was actually rather pleasant. We spent the first half hour nervously chatting, taking tangent after tangent, a palpable sense of anticipation in the air between us. There was only a brief lull in our conversation after we stopped at Ballan Station, and that was all it took for Eli to pass out. I must have followed suit soon after, because the next thing I remember is Eli gently shaking me awake, the carriage already empty, our train stopped underneath the wavy metallic roof of Southern Cross Station. We pulled our bags off the rack above our heads—my modest overnight bag and Eli's *two* suitcases—and dozily strolled the few blocks down Collins Street to our hotel in Docklands.

"Hmmm," the concierge—Danilo, according to his gilded name badge—says, clacking away at his keyboard. "There's a booking for a *Sharon* Callaghan?"

"That's my mum," Eli says, nodding.

(For the record, I did tell Mum about our trip, and while she clearly wasn't happy about it, she couldn't think of a valid reason to stop me from going—not for her lack of trying.)

"But she's not coming," Eli goes on. "It's just us. Is that okay?"

More keyboard clacking.

"The guests listed are Elijah Callaghan and Siobhan Lynch," Danilo says, his eyes flicking up to meet mine. "You don't look like a Siobhan to me."

"I'm, uh, Noah," I reply, feeling like I'm being interrogated. "Siobhan couldn't make it, so I . . . I'm here instead."

Danilo turns his inquisitorial gaze back to Eli. "Do you have any ID, Elijah?"

Eli fishes his East High student card out of his brown leather wallet and hands it to the concierge.

While Danilo examines the ID, Eli leans over and whispers in my ear, "I knew we should've gotten you that wig," and I chuckle out loud.

After we pass the concierge's string of tests—you'd honestly think we were applying for a home loan or something—he hands us both our room keys.

"Level five," he calls out as we shuffle into the elevator with our luggage.

When we eventually find the door to Room 501, after doing a full lap of the floor by mistake, Eli stops and turns to me.

"Thank you for coming," he says, smiling and frowning at the same time, like I'm doing him some enormous favor by being here.

"Are you kidding?" I reply. "Thank you for *inviting* me. I haven't—" But I stop myself. I was almost about to say, *I haven't been invited anywhere since my ex-best friends ostracised me from the entire CHGS school community*, but instead say, "I've been looking forward to this trip so much."

Eli's smile broadens as he turns back to Room 501. He swipes his white hotel key card and the electronic lock clicks loudly. As soon as he pushes open the door and steps inside, he says, "Oh my god. *What?* No . . ."

"What is it?" I ask, peering over his shoulder.

I follow him inside, trying to figure out what he could possibly be so disappointed about. The room is small, with two neat single beds, but super clean and almost elegant in an under-stated way. It's the complete opposite of the lavish suites Mum books when we go on holiday, but I honestly think I prefer this. It's not trying too hard to be fancy.

"I'm so sorry," he says, rolling his suitcases over to one of the beds. "Siobhan and I originally booked a twin room, and they obviously didn't get the memo about swapping us to a double."

"Oh," I say, "that's okay, we—"

Eli lifts his brows, his eyes cutting from one narrow bed to the other. "You know how there's that scene in every cheesy rom-com where the guy and the girl who can't stand each other have to share a hotel room for no particular reason and there's only one king-sized bed covered in rose petals and they're *forced* to sleep together?"

My stomach swoops at the words "sleep together." I crack my knuckles and force a laugh. "Yeah?"

"Well, this is the exact opposite of that." He sighs, slumping onto one of the beds in defeat. "Our room is literally cock-blocking us." He must catch the terror on my face, because he adds, "Sorry, I didn't mean to say that last part out loud."

"Don't be sorry. We'll . . . make it work."

"But I *am* sorry. I was super clear when I talked to the lady on the phone the other day." He shakes his head. "I don't know, maybe the concierge thought it was a mistake when you and I turned up, instead of me and Siobhan."

"I doubt it. It's Melbourne. I'm sure they have tons of gay couples stay here. Not that we're a *couple*-couple. I just meant . . . never mind."

Eli smiles, his lips pressed together. "Thank you for being the voice of reason."

"Anytime." I shrug. "And I—"

But Eli is suddenly standing right in front of me, his arms around my waist, his lips pressed to mine.

When he finally pulls away, I can't seem to think of a single thing to say, other than a breathless, "Happy birthday."

He laughs, planting another kiss on my cheek. "Happy birthday, indeed."

After making out for a while longer, we change into jeans and T-shirts—I retreat to the bathroom, because I'm not quite ready for Eli to see *all* of me yet—and head out into the crisp Melbourne morning. It's always slightly warmer down here than in Ballarat, so we don't need the bulky jackets we're forced to wear at home every day from April till September. Eli is wearing tight black jeans and a white T-shirt that makes his toned chest look stare-inducingly good. I'm in blue skinny jeans and a baggy black T-shirt that hopefully hides my complete *lack* of chest.

My heart gives a little shudder when I realize there'll be no baggy shirts to hide behind when we're back in the room tonight. It's a strange feeling, because I'm definitely *hoping* we have sex—I'm definitely ready—and I know we need to be naked to do that properly, but I'm still dreading Eli's reaction when he sees me sans clothing. It's this weird mix of excitement and apprehension and arousal that my brain doesn't know how to compute.

Eli takes me to a cute laneway cafe for brunch—coffee and pastries—and a restaurant by the river for lunch—juice and burgers and more coffee. I pay for both meals on Dad's credit card, to which Eli ardently objects, but I just say, "It's your *birthday*," and tap away.

We spend most of the day wandering in and out of shops and alleys and streets and gardens, jumping on trams and trains and into one rather expensive Uber when we miss our stop at Chapel St because we're debating who would win in a fight out of Superman and Wonder Woman. (For the record, it's Wonder Woman. You don't want to mess with a woman with fierce hair and an enchanted lasso.)

In the afternoon, we find a beautiful patch of grass in the Royal Botanical Gardens and just lie there beside each other, staring up at the cloudless sky, our fingers twining in and out of one another's until time crawls to a complete stop.

After I'm-not-sure-how-long, I ask, "Are you having a good birthday?" and the clock starts ticking once more.

Eli lets out an expansive, contented sigh. "I am." He turns his head to face mine, smooshing his cheek into the grass. "Are you?"

I chuckle. "It's not *my* birthday."

He slaps me on the shoulder. "But you're having a good day?"

"The best."

He grins, his eyes a little sleepy, and a tingly warmth spreads across my chest.

"If you could have one thing for your birthday," I ask, "what would it be?"

"Hmmm . . ." Eli looks up to the endless blue above us and back down to me, smirking. "Would it be super tacky to say that all I want is you here with me?"

"Yes." I snort. "That's highly unoriginal and plagiarized straight out of some B-grade rom-com."

"Fine," he chuckles, before humming in thought again. "If I could have *anything*?"

"Anything."

After a long moment, he says, "I mean, there is *one* thing that would be pretty cool, but it's like, super corny, too."

"Let's hear it," I reply. "If it's too corny, I'll just make you pick again."

"Okay. Well . . . this is probably going to sound ridiculous, but there's this guy—just a friend, don't worry—who I've been gaming with for ages . . ."

The warmth in my chest is swept away by a cold wave of dread.

". . . and I'm not allowed to meet him, even though he's like, probably my best friend in the world." Eli wrinkles his nose, looking up at the sky. "God, that makes me sound like *such* a loser. I do have actual friends, I swear. But it's different with him. He's the first person I came out to. He helps me with all my drama with like, zero judgement. He's the person who knows more about me than anyone else in the world. Aside from who I *am*."

I've spent so many hours talking to MagePants69 about myself—as in, real life Noah Mitchell—but it never occurred to me to ask *Eli* how he feels towards *RcticF0x*. We haven't spoken much about Eli's gaming habits, mainly because I avoid the subject entirely so I don't risk giving myself away, but hearing him talking about my online alias like this is . . . I don't know. Overwhelming? Weirdly sad? Meta in the worst possible way?

"So," Eli goes on, thoughtfully, "if I could have *anything* for my birthday, it'd be a party that he's invited to. So we can hang in real life."

"That's—" I clear my throat "—really sweet."

"Shut up," he replies, letting his cheek drop back onto the ground. "You're lying. It's pathetic, I know."

"It's not pathetic." I shake my head, blades of grass tickling my ear. "And . . . you're not allowed to meet him because of all that stuff with your mum?"

"Correct. What Constable Callaghan says, goes. No argument. No debate. No compromise. Which means I can never meet this guy. Like, *ever*. I can't even know his name. It's totally unfair."

Should I tell him?

I should tell him.

I can't tell him.

Can I?

No. Not now. Not ever.

"Sorry," Eli says, sitting up. "That was kind of grim. And I don't want you to think I'm like, obsessing over some other guy when you're lying right beside me, because it's not like that with him."

"It's fine," I say, pushing myself up onto my elbows. "I get it."

If only Eli knew just how much I do *get it*.

"It's funny," Eli says, narrowing his eyes slightly, "you actually remind me of him a bit."

My stomach leaps out of my throat and flies off across the park, down the hill and dives headfirst into a muddy pond. "Oh?"

"Yeah." He gives me a playful push on the shoulder. "Must be a nerd thing."

I try to force a laugh, but all I can manage is a strangled, "Yeah. Must be."

We head back to the hotel to change for dinner, then make our way to this amazing Vietnamese restaurant tucked down one of the city's innumerable graffitied laneways.

I do my best to forget what Eli told me in the park. I know it's silly, but I'm *slightly* offended he's only ever thought of RcticF0x as a friend (meanwhile, I've been pining over MagePants69 the whole time and have gone to extreme lengths to meet him IRL), but I shove that thought way down into the depths of my mind, burying it under thousands of counts of *Chicago* choreography and my extensive but entirely useless knowledge of Greek mythology.

We pass by a crêpe stand on the way to the theatre, and both agree that dessert is essential to our survival. Honestly, since I started working out, my appetite has tripled. I've always eaten a lot—contrary to what my body would have you believe—but now it's getting silly. Mum hasn't really noticed (on account of her Rose Mitchell-colored glasses) but Dad got disproportionately angry the other day when he went to make a cheese sandwich only to find I'd eaten the whole block in two days.

After crêpes, it's time for the show. Melbourne's Her Majesty's Theatre is like a bigger, fancier version of the theatre of the same name in Ballarat where Mum does all her shows, and where I'll be performing with BMTS in a couple of months (now, *there's* a scary thought).

The foyer is buzzing with soon-to-be audience members when we arrive, the cool air flooded with countless clashing perfumes. Some of the theatregoers are dressed in cocktail dresses and suits, while some are in jeans and hoodies. There are a couple of kids in full cat costumes, and a hell of a lot of cat ears being worn by people who are definitely too old to be wearing cat ears. The walls are strung with massive black *CATS* posters, with glowing yellow eyes glaring down at us from all angles. We file into the auditorium like lemmings, take our seats, and wait for the lights to dim.

"Oh my god, here we go!" Eli whispers in my ear when the '80s synth overture starts.

The first act goes for what feels like four hours, and I honestly couldn't tell you what the show is about. As far as I can gather, there are a bunch of cats (read: grown adults in lycra) living in a trash heap, and there's this really pretty cat with a tattered fur coat who they hate (for being too pretty?—honestly, who knows), and they decide to host a ball and sing a bunch of songs about each other.

"Isn't it just the *best*?" Eli asks when the lights come back on at interval. It's as if he's been transformed into a five-year-old boy. His eyes are twinkling and his smile is wider than I've ever seen it.

"So good," I lie, because it's his birthday and I don't want to be a buzzkill.

"What's your favourite song so far?"

"Uh . . ." I scrunch up my face, trying to remember if there were any moments in the show that I didn't actively despise. "I liked the bit where the cockroaches did the tap dance?" (And yes, it was as irrelevant to the plot as it sounds.)

"*Yes!*" Eli says with a clap. "'Gumbie Cat' is one of my favorite songs! And their Jennyanydots is *fantastic*."

I smile and nod, because I have no idea what he's saying, but it's obvious how much this means to him. He's so giddy that I'm concerned he might literally burst in his seat.

The second half of the show is equally—if not more—confusing. The pretty cat either dies or gets killed by the other cats or gets abducted by a UFO . . . I'm not really sure. But the other cats seem happy she's finally gone, so I guess that counts as a resolution.

Eli is on cloud nine when we spill out of the theatre onto Exhibition Street. He says he wants to walk the whole way back to Docklands so we can "take in the glorious night." My legs are already cramping from walking around all day, but Eli is twirling off down the footpath before I have a chance to protest.

Half an hour later we're standing outside the door to Room 501, holding hands, slightly out of breath from our twelve-city-block walk. We both just stand there in the hallway for what must be an entire minute—sixty *looong* seconds—staring at the door, even though we both have swipe cards for the room and could open whenever we want.

The thing is, we both know what's going to happen when we cross that threshold. The tension has been bubbling under the surface since this morning. A building desire. An unspoken agreement. And it's exciting. But it's also daunting.

Suddenly, I feel like there are a million eyes on my back. Whispers in the corridor, writing on the walls, a sign on the door to Room 501, all of them saying:

NOAH MITCHELL, YOU'RE ABOUT TO HAVE SEX.

TWENTY-THREE

UNABLE TO BEAR THE tension a second longer, I pull my room key out of my jeans and unlock the door.

"Thanks," Eli says, before heading inside the room, kicking off his shoes, and flopping down onto his back on one of the single beds.

Is this it? Am I supposed to just . . . climb on and get started? Or is that too presumptuous? Should I lie down on the other bed, a chasm of grey geometric hotel carpet between us?

"That was an epic day," Eli says through a sigh that sounds one part exhausted, two parts elated.

I take a seat on the other bed so I can unlace my shoes. "It really was."

"And you're sure you didn't hate the show?" Eli asks, sitting up and crossing his legs. He pats the comforter in front of him. An invitation?

I place my shoes at the foot of my bed and bravely cross the carpet chasm. "I didn't hate the show," I reply, perching on the end of his mattress. I can't cross my legs in these jeans, so I have to sit in an awkward side-saddle position instead. I'm suddenly hyper conscious of what to do with my hands. "I couldn't tell you what was going on," I admit, "but some of those guys didn't look too bad in lycra."

Eli lifts an auburn eyebrow. "Right?" He leans in conspiratorially. "Do you think they stuff their dance supports with socks or something? Because, I mean, some of those guys looked . . . huge."

Sweat pricks on my palms. Should we be talking about penises? Penises that don't belong to either of us? Right before we sleep together? Is that weird? Is this a sign that we're *not* going to sleep together?

Seriously—where is the damn manual?

"Did you know cats actually have barbed penises?" I say, then feel all of my internal organs cringe in unison.

"What?"

"Yeah," my mouth goes on, without permission from my brain, "they're barbed on the end, like an arrowhead. It's so the female can't run away after the male has penetrated them."

Oh my *god*. Why am I like this?

Eli pulls a face. "That's . . . super intense."

"I know, right?" I wipe my clammy hands on my jeans. "My penis is completely barb-free, though, I promise."

STOP. TALKING. RIGHT. THIS. SECOND.

Eli snort laughs, burying his head in his hands.

I groan. "I'm so sorry."

"It's fine." He looks up, a goofy grin on his face. "It's funny."

I shake my head. "No, I am *awful* at this."

"At what?"

"I don't know." I rub my eyes with my knuckles. "Flirting? Being sexy?"

"Noah, you don't need to be sexy."

I scoff. "So, you're saying I'm *not* sexy?"

Eli laughs. "No, I mean you don't have to *try* to be sexy. You don't need to like, impress me or anything. I'm already here." Then he adds with a smirk, "You already know I'm keen to get suss with you."

I bite back a smile. "Okay, well, I apologize in advance for any and all awkward things I say for the remainder of the evening. I'm just nervous."

"Oh, please," Eli says, scooching over to join me on the edge of the bed. He places one arm behind me, not hugging me, but gently supporting my back. Like a lovely little scaffold. "You have nothing to be nervous about. We don't need to do anything you don't want t—"

I lean in and kiss him mid-sentence, which surprises me as much as it does him. After a moment of shock, he kisses me back, hard. He reaches his other arm across me and places it on the side of my body. I hope he can't feel my ribs too much through my T-shirt.

"Did I ever tell you that you're an amazing kisser?" he asks when we swap angles.

"Maybe," I reply, my words muffled by the press of his lips on mine. "But you can say it again if you want."

He chuckles, then dives in for more.

I've kissed Eli plenty of times, but this feels different. A kiss can be just a *kiss*, or it can be a kiss that leads to something more, something bigger, something new. This is one of *those* kisses.

He gently pushes me back onto the bed so that he's lying half on top, half beside me. He slides his leg up and down mine, his knee edging dangerously close to the ever-growing bulge in my pants. My right arm is trapped underneath his neck, but I run my free hand through his ginger hair, along his neck, down his back, over the back pocket of his jeans.

"This is fun," he says, pulling away just enough to look me in the eye. I have a flashback to when I first met him in the church hall and how he held my gaze, how it was both disconcerting and extremely hot. Staring into his emerald eyes now, it's not at all disconcerting. Only hot. So very, very hot.

Things move a lot faster than they have in any of our other make-out sessions. Probably because we're finally alone. In a bed. Horizontal. There are limbs everywhere, zips being unzipped, buttons unbuttoned, fingers slipping under waistbands.

I accidentally let out a little gasp when Eli first takes me in his hand, and he pauses.

"You okay?"

I nod.

"Is this okay?" His stare is intense.

"Yes," I say. "It's . . . more than okay."

And so we continue. Four hands exploring, caressing, roving, stroking, grasping. Who knew there were so many ways to use your hands. I feel like my body is made of electricity, or static. Like I'm buzzing personified.

At some point, we make an unspoken, unanimous decision to take off our clothes. Skinny jeans are notoriously difficult to get out of in a hurry (even when you're as thin as me) so we both spend thirty seconds hopping around on the spot doing the "jeans dance." Eli laughs, and I laugh, too. I didn't think laughing was allowed in this context, but it honestly makes the whole thing so much sexier.

Once I've eventually extricated myself from my jeans, I flick on the small lamp beside the bed. Eli darts across to the door to turn off the overhead lights—thank god, because downlighting is a skinny boy's worst enemy.

We meet each other's eyes for a second, then slide our jocks off in unison, almost as if it's been choreographed. Suddenly, we're both just standing here in the middle of the hotel room. Naked. It's the first time Eli has seen me without my shirt on, let alone nude and . . . uh . . . fully at attention. I feel my entire body blush.

Please don't let him be disappointed.

"Hi," he says softly, a dark gleam in his emerald eyes.

"Um, hi?"

It's only now that I allow myself to lower my gaze to the rest of him. As soon as I do, a burning hunger blooms in my chest and floods down to my stomach and my balls. I close the distance between us in two steps, shocking him again with my boldness. I press my body—my *whole* body—against his, and kiss him like my life depends on it.

Before I know it, the room tips off its axis and we're on the bed again. This time, it's not just hands exploring, it's mouths too. And *holy shit*. Mouths are a whole other level of incredible.

After a long while—or maybe it's not long at all—we pause to come up for air.

Eli slides his head onto the pillow next to mine. "Do you want to . . ."

"Yes," I reply in a heartbeat.

"Are you sure?"

"I'm sure." I nod my head as best I can against the fluffy pillow. "Like you said, it doesn't have to be some big, special moment."

Eli's brow folds in two. "What?"

"Huh?"

"Did I say that?"

Shit. Eli *did* say that, but not to me. He said it to RcticF0x. My pulse instantly skyrockets. "Ummm . . ."

"When did I say that?" He inches his head back across the pillow.

"Uh . . ." I reach up to loop my fingers through his hair so he can't retreat any further. "Sorry, I must be thinking of someone else."

His eyebrows fly up.

"Not that there's anyone else," I add, panic creeping into my voice.

"What are y—"

"It was probably Charly. My sister. Not that we should be talking about my sister when we're naked. And not that—shit. Sorry. I'm ruining this."

"You're being weird."

"I'm not being weird," I say, desperate to find a way to gloss over this moment. "I promise. I'm just—I told you I'd say awkward things, didn't I? I apologized in advance. Let's . . . let's just rewind like, two minutes."

Eli stares back at me for a second. I run my thumb along the sharp edge of his jaw.

"Please?" I ask, willing my heart to slow down.

After an excruciating moment, he relaxes into my touch. "Of course. Sorry. I didn't mean . . ."

"I know. It's my fault. I'm sorry."

He kisses me lightly on the lips, and I feel sweet relief coursing through my veins.

That was close. *Way* too close. And not only that, there couldn't be a less appropriate time for me to have to explain The Plan to Eli than when we're lying naked and hard on a bed together.

"And you're definitely sure you want to do this?" he asks, as if we really did just rewind the night to *before* I almost destroyed it. I honestly don't deserve this boy.

"I am one million percent sure," I reply.

"Do you have . . .?" He gestures with his chin to the space between us.

"Condoms?" I ask, before realizing there's probably a much less blunt way to phrase that. "Yeah."

"And do you want to . . .?"

I don't know if Eli has a preference, and I honestly don't know if I do either. I don't want to make any assumptions though, so I say, "Can I, um . . . top? If that's okay?"

The word "top" feels almost like a swear word, even though it's most definitely not. Probably because sex ed only covered penises and vaginas and baby-making, so it's always felt oddly taboo to say gay things out loud.

Eli shrugs one shoulder forward. "Fine by me. I douched before dinner, just in case."

The next five minutes of my life are intensely awkward for

the following three reasons (not including any of the horrifically cringey remarks that fly out of my mouth during those
five minutes, including "oopsies," which I have never said in my
entire life):

1. It takes me way too long to open the condom wrapper.

2. I put it on inside out, then have to take it off and start all
over again.

3. By the time I get the second one open, I'm as soft as a
feather duster.

"It's fine," Eli assures me, pushing himself up onto his knees
and planting a commiserative kiss on my cheek.

"It's not," I reply, feeling utterly useless. "I'm sorry. I just—"

"Noah, stop. Don't worry. It's seriously fine."

"Let's just try the other way," I say, taking him in my hand.
"You're still clearly good to go."

Eli lifts his eyebrows. "Are you sure? It's . . . The first time can
be . . . I mean, it's a *lot*."

"Yes, let's just try. I don't want to ruin the whole night."

"You haven't ru—"

"Quick." I lie down on my back and wave Eli forward, like
I'm an air traffic controller.

And we try. And try. Which is possibly the only thing more
awkward than what has already transpired in this room tonight.
I don't know if some guys are just not built for . . . receiving,
but no matter the configuration, no matter the angle, we cannot
seem to make it work. And let me tell you: It hurts like hell.

"Jesus, Mary, and Joseph," I exclaim at one point, which is
probably the pinnacle of blasphemy, given our current bodily
configuration.

Eli lets out a chuckle. "It's honestly not even in yet."

"Please don't laugh," I groan, covering my face with my arms. "This is the worst night of my life. And yours. I've completely ruined your eighteenth birthday."

"It's absolutely *not* the worst night of my life, and you haven't ruined anything." Eli plonks himself down on the bed beside me. He places one hand on my chest and starts tracing delicate circles on my skin. "Maybe you're just not ready?"

"I *am*," I protest, sounding like a toddler. "Or I want to be. I don't know. I'm so *into you*. I really thought—"

But what *did* I think? That if we had sex, everything would be perfect? That Eli would automatically ask me to be his boyfriend and tell me he loves me? That I could put an end to this whole charade?

"Thank you for trying," Eli whispers in my ear. "I'm . . . honored."

I let out a noise somewhere between a groan and a laugh.

"I'm serious," he says. "I don't mean to be patronizing or whatever, but it's awesome that you wanted to try with me."

Ugh. Why is he so totally, completely perfect?

"Now," he says, patting me twice on the chest, like he's beating a little drum. "Are you hungry? Because I know we already had dinner and dessert and theatre snacks, but I am *famished*. And I don't know about you, but I've always wanted to order a ridiculous amount of room service so I could ride the empty trolley down the hall. Just saying."

I laugh properly this time, then lean over to kiss Eli on his marshmallow lips.

"Sounds great," I say. "But we'll have to order *two* of

everything on the menu so we get *two* room service carts. We can't race each other down the hall if we only have one."

Eli narrows his eyes at me, his mouth perking up at the side. "I knew there was a reason I brought you on this trip, Noah Mitchell."

TWENTY-FOUR

I FLOAT INTO THE BMTS church hall on Sunday afternoon on a bright, fluffy cloud of contentment.

The second half of last night—after what will henceforth be known as our Abandoned Attempts at Intercourse—was like something straight out of a '90s family movie. The endless spread of room service food. The hallway antics. The getting yelled at by hotel security. The subsequent fits of uncontrollable giggling. And, finally, the single-bed snuggling.

In the midst of our midnight shenanigans, I completely forgot to give Eli his birthday present. It wasn't until we were halfway home on the V/Line train that I fished it out of the bottom of my overnight bag for him. Seeing his face light up when he realized it was a vintage *Chicago* Playbill—fully signed by the original Broadway cast—was *well* worth the hours and hours of hunting on eBay.

"This must have cost you a *fortune*," he exclaimed breathlessly as he turned the booklet over in his hands.

"Nah," I said, "it was a total bargain." (If you call three hundred and forty-eight dollars plus postage a "bargain" for a musty old program.)

Mum is already there when we arrive, looking supremely flustered. We're doing our first full run-through of the show this afternoon, and it appears she's treating the day with a typical Rose Mitchell amount of melodrama. She gives me a stiff wave and a tight-lipped smile before turning to her bag and fishing around for something that is apparently *much* more important than hearing about her son's weekend away.

I immediately bristle, then calmly instruct myself to take a breath and shake off the annoyance. Nothing is going to kill my good mood today. Not even *her*.

"I'm gonna go stretch," Eli says from beside me, before kissing me on the cheek and dashing to the back of the room where Keegan, Luana, and some of the other girls are spread out on the floor, contorting themselves like ancient yogis.

I head to the bag area on the stage to dump my stuff. Alex is standing in the middle of everyone's belongings, fingers pressed to his cheeks, blowing air through his lips like a horse. He pauses when he sees me approaching and smiles.

"Hey, dude," he says. "How was the big weekend?"

Alex is the only person in the cast who knows about the Melbourne trip, aside from Mum. I told him in between sets of an excruciating deadlift exercise at the gym last week, before realizing he might not necessarily want to hear about me going on an overnight date with his not-ex.

"It was . . . great," I reply, with a sheepish shrug.

"And how was *CATS*?" he asks, licking a "paw" and brushing

it against his temple.

I hesitate, not wanting to offend him if he's a fan like Eli, but then he says, "It's kind of weird, right?"

"*So* weird," I laugh. "Like, completely incomprehensible."

"Yeah, it's definitely an acquired taste." He lifts his fingers back to his cheeks and carries on with his vocal warm-up.

"How are you feeling about the run-through?" I ask.

He shrugs, still making his horse-slash-siren noises.

"You're not nervous?"

He shakes his head.

"Are you sure?"

He drops his hands, leans towards me and whispers, "Dude, of *course* I'm nervous. I'm *shitting* myself. I'm just pretending everything is fine because I need to nail this run." His eyes are a little wild. "David has been on my back about my characterization, saying I'm not 'carrying the weight of the role.' And I'm like, yeah, probably because it's meant to be played by a forty-year-old man, David."

"You'll be fine," I reply. "If I can survive a month's worth of pyramid sets and plyometrics with Alex Di Mario, you can make it through the next two hours."

"Look at you and your gym terminology." He shoves me playfully on the shoulder and I stumble back a step, happening to glance over my shoulder as I do. Eli is staring in our direction from the other side of the room, clearly trying to conceal a spark of jealousy. I smile at him, doing my best not to look guilty—which I'm not—and he gives me a quick smile before turning back to Keegan.

David taps out a loud rhythm on the wooden lid of the

piano, calling us to attention. We huddle around in a semicircle and the chatter dies down. Pania, our musical director, gives us a long list of vocal notes to keep in mind during the run-through—meanwhile, I'm still trying to remember to sing in the first place—and then David gives us a speech that everyone else seems to think is super inspirational but that, in my opinion, is completely condescending.

And then . . . we begin.

The whole run-through is a total blur. Half my mind is still firmly in Melbourne with Eli, reveling in the glorious moments and agonizing over the awkward ones. The other half of my brain is here, in the church hall, trying to remember an endless string of counts and spacing and harmonies and on-stage "traffic." I mess up a bunch of things here and there—including almost (but thankfully *not*) dropping Prisha on her head during a lift in "Roxie"—but simply *surviving* feels like a victory.

At the end of the show, there's a song called "Nowadays/Hot Honey Rag" (don't ask me why it's called that), which is the big song and dance finale for Roxie and Velma. Mum and Prisha learned it in private with David so they could "surprise us" in this exact moment of the rehearsal process. It's been the best-kept secret since the KFC chicken original recipe was leaked on Reddit last Christmas.

When we finish "Razzle Dazzle," David silently ushers us all in front of the mirrors to "watch our little leading ladies do their thing." Everyone waits with bated breath as Jane plays the intro to the song.

Now, I've seen Mum perform more times than I can remember, and certainly more times than I ever asked to—on stage in the ensemble, in the kitchen while she's loading the dishwasher, on the couch beside me, drowning out the TV— but this . . . this is different. It's like I'm no longer watching Rose Mitchell, wife of Roger, mother of Charlotte and Noah, wannabe Real Housewife of Ballarat. All of that is gone.

I watch with a strange mix of bewilderment and awe as this woman—this *stranger*—sings and dances alongside Prisha. Her movements are sharp but subtle, her singing voice bright and clear and powerful. Every lyric feels like a Pulitzer Prize-winning poem, every line and shape of her body its own work of art. But the thing that surprises me the most—the thing that transforms her almost completely—is her eyes. Her periwinkle blue eyes. Exactly the same as mine, but in this moment? They couldn't be more different. There's a glint there, an *edge*, that I have not seen in the seventeen years this woman has been my mother.

"The Rose Mitchell Sparkle," I say under my breath.

"What?" Chris whispers from beside me.

I shake my head, unable to take my eyes off her. "Nothing."

The church hall disappears as I watch the two women dance in their matching black leotards. Prisha is incredible, too, but Mum is honestly something else. When the song finishes, the cast erupts into rapturous applause—a standing ovation that swiftly brings me back into my body. I join them on my feet in a daze, overcome by a sudden inclination to take back every horrible, sarcastic thing I've ever said to Mum.

I try to catch her eye while they take their bows, but she's apparently too busy smiling at David and Pania and Prisha and Alex and the rest of her adoring fans to notice me. David immediately takes her aside when the final scene is done, and dismisses the rest of the cast.

"How'd you go?" Eli asks me as we're packing up our things.

"Uh—" I shove my jazz shoes into my bag "—it was all right, I guess. How about you? Your Fred Casely scene was awesome."

"Like we expected anything less," he says with a cute shrug.

A looming presence appears out of nowhere behind Eli. Rich brown skin. A sky-high black ponytail. A glare that could cut glass.

"Can I talk to Noah for a sec?" Prisha's smile is clearly only meant for Eli.

"Sure," he replies, meeting my gaze as if to check if it's okay that he leaves me in her clutches. "I gotta run, anyway. Don't want to miss the bus."

He kisses me softly on the lips and whispers, "See you soon, Noah Mitchell," in my ear before running out of the hall.

"Uh, hi?" I say to Prisha, who folds her arms across her chest and sinks into one hip.

"What was that?"

"I'm sorry, what was what?"

"Don't give me that, Noah. You were all over the place in that run-through. Don't think I didn't notice how distracted you were."

It's certainly not Prisha's job to keep track of how distracted I was or wasn't, but I don't have the gall to say that to her face. "Sorry," I reply. "I was just nervous."

"You almost ruined 'Roxie.' *Again*."

"It wasn't *that* bad." Which is true, compared to all the times I actually *did* drop her. "It was just a little slip-up."

"Nothing is a little *anything* to David. He notices *everything*.

And I need him to know that I am handling this role."

Sounds like Alex isn't the only one under pressure at the moment.

"You *are* handling it," I reply. "You're amazing. You're—"

"Flattery will get you nowhere with me," Prisha snaps. "I've known you way too long for that."

"Okay." I hold my hands up. "No compliments."

"Noah, this is my *life*. I don't know how I can make that any clearer. You are messing with my *career*. And I still have no fucking clue why you're even in this show and don't say it's just to please your mother—"

"It's a—"

"—because we both know that's not true, and I am damn well going to find out why."

"Prisha, please. Just—"

"No," she cuts in, raising a finger to silence me. "I don't want to hear it. Just get your shit together. If you make one more mistake that affects my performance during rehearsals—or so help me god, on *stage* in front of a thousand people—I *will* tell everyone what you did to my brother. Let's see how your precious boyfriend feels about you then."

"Prisha, that's not your secret to tell," I reply, keeping my voice low. "And you know your parents would kill you if you told everyone."

"Look, whatever." She flicks her wrists. "I honestly couldn't care less anymore. I'm not gonna let you ruin another Kandiyar's life."

With that, she stalks off across the room. Luana and Yvette squeal and pull her into a hug, presumably showering her with praise. I linger in the corner, stewing over what Prisha said, while Mum deals with the last of her fans.

I pull my phone out and send a quick text to Eli.

Okay, well, I didn't DIE, but Prisha did not seem to enjoy my performance. I think I'm gonna need some roller-rink rehears-als STAT.

His reply comes instantly. **You just wanna make out with me.** Smirking emoji.

"Are you good to go?" Mum asks, suddenly in front of me, her bag slung over the crook of her elbow.

I grab my things and follow her outside, feeling Prisha's eyes on my back as I leave.

"Well," Mum says, as we climb into the car, "that wasn't *too* bad, I don't think. David seemed happy with all my scenes, but he's obviously not giving us his proper notes till Tuesday, so who knows what he really thought. Pania had some lovely things to say to me, though, which is rare for her, especially whenever that wife of hers is in earshot."

Usually, I'd think Mum is just fishing for compliments, but she sounds genuinely worried she didn't do a good job in the run-through. Which is ridiculous, because—as much as it pains me to admit it—she was legitimately incredible.

I want to tell her, to say the words out loud, but . . . I don't know where to start. I honestly can't remember the last time either of us said anything *nice* to the other without some form of agenda.

"Mum . . ."

"Mmm?" she says, pulling out of the car park and onto the road.

You were incredible today.

I finally understand why you love this so much.

I'm sorry for being a snarky jerk all the time.

She glares across at me for a second, then shifts her gaze back to the road. "What is it?"

"Um . . ." I take a deep breath. "You know in that last song? The one with Prisha? It was—I mean, *you* were . . . and I don't know why I expected anything different, but today you—"

"Darling, just spit it out," she snaps. "What is it that you have a problem with now?"

Heat rises up my neck. "It's not—I don't—"

"*Please* tell me this isn't about David again? I already told you there's nothing going on. You need to let it go." She flicks her blinker like the gesture is a full stop on our conversation.

"N-No," I stammer, taken aback by the sudden change in atmosphere, "it's nothing like that, I—"

"Look," Mum cuts in again, "just leave it, whatever it is. I honestly don't have the patience for this right now. I am *completely* exhausted. You have no idea what it's like to play a role like Velma Kelly."

I shrink down into my seat.

"You just concentrate on your own show," she goes on. "The whole cast saw how you nearly dropped Prisha on her face today. Is that what she was talking to you about after the run?"

"Yes," I say, disdain bubbling up in my throat like tar—an all-too-familiar feeling. "But it's fine. We sorted it out."

"Darling, David can tell when someone isn't committed. We all can. And—I hate to say it—but that's *you.*"

I grit my teeth, keeping my eyes glued to the road in front of us.

"And just because you and Eli are together or whatever, it doesn't mean—"

"This has nothing to do with Eli," I protest, not for the first time. "And while we're on the subject, thanks for asking how our trip was. Thanks for saying a proper hello after not seeing me for two whole days. You almost completely ignored me."

"Darling," Mum warns, "I am not doing this. You know how important that run-through was for me."

"And what about how important this whole *weekend* was for *me*?"

"Yes, because it's always about *you*, isn't it, Noah."

"Oh, you have *got* to be kidding me."

"What is *that* supposed to mean?"

"Does it matter?" I reply, defaulting back to my standard sarcasm. "I thought you were 'not doing this.'"

"You're right," she says, her voice suddenly prim and pious. "I am not playing this game with you. And I'm not getting involved in whatever drama you're creating with Eli and Prisha and Alex and the rest of the cast. You're on your own."

I draw in a deep breath and ball my hands into fists, digging my nails into the skin of my palms.

"You know," she adds after a second, "I asked you to do this because I thought it might actually be *nice* for us to spend some time together before you finished school and left us all behind, but . . . *clearly* I was wrong."

It takes everything I have not to scream or punch the glovebox or throw myself out of the moving vehicle.

Rose Mitchell strikes again.

TWENTY-FIVE

I DON'T SAY A word to Mum all week. She basically ignores me, too, although probably no more than she has been lately anyway. I make it my mission to keep up my *Spire of Dusk* commitments, despite being a walking zombie from my grueling daily workouts with Alex, extra rehearsals with Eli, and an endless string of mid-year practice exams at school.

This whole "Online Best Friend/Real Life Boyfriend" thing is more exhausting than originally anticipated.

In *Chicago* rehearsals, it's like I'm walking on eggshells. Or thin ice. Or thin, icy eggshells. Prisha's eyes are on me at all times, like she's coiled and waiting to pounce, and Mum manages to be equal parts self-obsessed and condescending, which is a truly infuriating combination.

There are only two things that get me through the Tuesday and Thursday rehearsals:

1. Eli's green eyes.

2. The occasional "you got this" from Alex Di Mario, as if we're doing weights at the gym.

I do my best to avoid number 2 happening in front of number 1, because I can't risk Eli finding out about my workouts with Alex when it's clear he's already jealous of our weird little semi-friendship. It would be so much easier if I could just prove to Eli that Alex is nothing more to me than a surprisingly chill guy with whom I share an unexpected symbiotic relationship, but I know Eli won't understand. Not with his history with Alex.

When Mum knocks on my bedroom door on Saturday morning at 10:07 a.m., it still feels like the middle of the night. No matter how much sleep I get at the moment, I just can't seem to catch up.

"Noah," she says, inviting herself in and unceremoniously flicking the lights on.

I groan, shielding my eyes with my forearm. "*Mum.* What are you doing?"

"You need to get up. We have the cast barbecue today."

"The what?"

"The *Chicago* cast barbecue," she says, like I should definitely know what she's talking about. "I know David said it's not compulsory, but it definitely *is* compulsory."

That's popular-girl talk for, *If you don't come, no one will want to be friends with you.*

"You never told me about a barbecue," I argue, sitting up and rubbing my sleep-filled eyes.

She huffs. "I didn't think I had to. Everyone's been talking about it at rehearsals all week."

"Not to me."

"Well, you don't talk to anyone besides Eli, do you?"

It's way too early to start a fight. "Wait, so what time is this not-compulsory-but-definitely-compulsory thing?"

"It starts at twelve," Mum replies, skirting my bed to yank open the blinds. Sunlight pours in, blinding me. I honestly think I might be part vampire. Just a much less sexy variety than the ones on *Spire of Dusk*.

"But we obviously need to be fashionably late," Mum goes on, "so . . . we'll leave here at twelve-fifteen."

"Where's the party?"

"*Barbecue*. And it's at the Kandiyars' house."

The breath leaves my chest. "The Kandiyars' house?"

"What did I just say?" She makes her way to the door. "Pick a nice shirt to wear, will you? And some chinos. I don't want you turning up in a dirty T-shirt and jeans like you're on your way to some . . . computer game thing."

I ignore the unnecessary sass and say, "Mum, I can't go to the Kandiyars' house. You know that."

She whips around, one hand on the doorknob. "Noah. Get over it. All that . . . *stuff* with Tan happened years ago. This is an important cast function and a wonderful opportunity for me to solidify my position as a BMTS leading lady. I need my son there in full support of that."

"You're not running for Congress, it's—"

"No discussion. You're going."

She slams the door behind her before I can so much as think about putting up a proper fight.

The air outside the Kandiyars' house in the bushy-but-super-rich part of town smells of eucalyptus and roses, freshly mown grass and tangy barbecue smoke. If I wasn't so nervous that I could die, it would be quite a pleasant aroma.

When Mum knocks on the front door, I half expect Tan to greet us, before presumably telling me to fuck off and to never show my face here again. Instead—much to my relief, but only under these exact circumstances—it's Prisha, wearing a breezy floral dress, her jet-black hair draped over her shoulders in thick, gleaming curtains.

"Come in!" she says, smiling her heart-stopping smile. She waves Mum inside, before adding to me in a tight-lipped whisper, "You're only here because Rose Mitchell is your mother and don't you forget it."

"Trust me," I reply, "there's nowhere I'd rather be *less* than here."

It's been three years since I visited Tan's house, but not much seems to have changed. The walls have been painted a slightly different shade of off-white, the water feature in the garden has been upgraded, but it all *feels* exactly the same. I used to love coming here . . . .

I'd be lying if I said I hadn't tried to semi-regularly stalk my ex-best friend on social media since I last saw him in Year Nine but, given I've been blocked on all platforms, it's been fairly difficult. I occasionally see his avi—TandalfTheGr3y—pop up on various MMO leaderboards if I ever bother to log on. Okay, I *purposefully* log on to see if his name is on the leaderboards. But other than that, I don't know anything about his life anymore.

My afternoon at the cast barbecue consists primarily of:

1. Following Eli around like a lost little lamb.

2. Fake laughing at theatre jokes I don't understand.

3a. Feeling increasingly awkward as Mum gets increasingly inebriated.

3b. Trying not to notice every single time David touches her. (I know she already told me he's not harassing her, but would she really tell *me*, her underage son, if he was?)

4. Tuning out of inane conversations, anxiously scanning the crowd for Tan.

When Mum takes it upon herself to serenade the cast with an a cappella rendition of "Don't Rain on My Parade," I seek refuge in the bathroom. Approximately two minutes and forty-five seconds later, I make my way out through the kitchen—all marble and brushed black steel—where I'm waylaid by Mrs. Kandiyar by the French doors to the garden.

"Noah!" she says, arms outstretched. She's about half Prisha's height, but otherwise, they're almost identical. She's even wearing a floral dress like Prisha, only hers brushes the floor, rather than her thighs. "It's so nice to see you."

I plaster on a smile and hug her hello. "It's nice to see you, too." (By which I really mean, *I've been doing my best to avoid you all afternoon.*)

"It's been too long," she replies, shaking her head. "Too long."

The *last* time I was here, we were sitting around the oak dining table by the bay window—me, Tan, and all four of our parents—tears streaming down Mrs. Kandiyar's face as she begged Tan to explain the situation to her.

"Is he . . . I mean, is Tan here?" I ask. "I haven't seen him outside."

"He's in town with Simon and Dylan."

The relief is instant. There will be no horrifically awkward reunion today.

"But you should come back when he's home." She reaches down to take my hands in hers. "I think you two need to talk."

I bite my lip. "There's . . . We don't . . . He . . ."

"I know he still blames you for what happened," she says, her dark eyebrows knitting together. "But *I* know that you only did what you thought was right. And I think—no, I *know*—that Tanesh misses you very, very much."

I want to tell her to stop talking. That it's not going to help. That Tan's never going to forgive me. That I don't *deserve* his forgiveness. But I just stand there, letting her words wash over me.

"I know he has new friends at North," she goes on, "and he still sees Simon and Dylan outside of school, but—"

"Noah!" a voice calls from outside, saving me from Mrs. Kandiyar's heart-to-heart.

She turns towards the garden. "Hello, Elijah."

"Hi, Mrs. Kandiyar." He skips through the door and kisses me on the cheek, slipping his hand into mine. "Come outside," he says. "Keegan just started a debate about whether *CATS* counts as a real musical, and I need you on the affirmative side with me."

I laugh, not sure how much help I'll be arguing that particular point. "Okay."

"Come back soon, Noah," Mrs. Kandiyar calls out as Eli pulls me through the door and across the grass.

And I know she doesn't mean "come back soon" to the kitchen. She means "come back soon" into her son's life. Which is something I just can't do.

Eli drags me over to the stone fountain in the center of the garden, where Keegan and Chris are already mid-debate. Soon, Luana and Yvette saunter over to join us, followed by Alex Di Mario. He's wearing a white linen shirt, unbuttoned basically down to his navel, and tight, bone-colored chinos. In other words, he's walking porn.

"You two are a bit cute, aren't you," Yvette says to Eli and me, nodding at our linked hands. "We love a bit of a *showmance*."

"It's not a—"

But Luana cuts me off. "Let's see if it stands the test of time." She tips her head to one side. "Showmances rarely survive once the show's done. Right, Eli?"

Eli rolls his eyes. "Can you not?"

She shrugs and takes a sip from her flute of champagne. "Just saying."

"Is it official?" Yvette asks, and I feel my skin flash with heat. "I mean, are you like, *boyfriends?*"

"We're . . ." Eli says, glancing over at me with an impish grin, ". . . seeing what happens."

My stomach flips. What does that mean? *Seeing what happens?* Is Eli hedging his bets? Waiting for me to ruin everything? Waiting for Alex to come to his senses and take him back?

I return Eli's smile, even though I'm hardly smiling on the

inside. "Yeah," I reply. "We're just seeing what happens."

"Well, I think it's cute," Keegan says, a rare compliment. "Two massive nerds, madly in love."

Okay, maybe not *quite* a compliment.

"Excuse *me*," Eli protests, "I am *not* a nerd."

"Oh, please," Keegan replies, flicking his blond fringe off his face, "we all know how many hours you waste playing those pathetic *Lord of the Rings* computer games."

Eli scoffs. "*Firstly*, the games have nothing to do with *Lord of the Rings*, they're called RPGs, you total noob."

"Whatever, nerd."

"And *secondly*," Eli goes on, "don't be jealous just because I have varied interests. I can't help it that my entire life doesn't revolve around musical theatre."

Keegan raises one eyebrow. "Yeah, and it shows."

"What is *that* supposed to mean?"

"Noah," Keegan says, ignoring Eli and turning his smug gaze on me. "Please don't tell me you play boring straight-boy video games, too?"

"No," I lie. "They're . . . not really my thing. I usually just . . . read. Or study."

"Or work out," Chris adds, and my heart stutters in my chest.

"What?" Eli says with a chuckle.

"He's been working out with Alex," Chris carries on, completely oblivious to the fourteen-ton bus he's throwing me under right now.

All I can manage in reply is a disjointed, "I—uh—my—what?"

Alex, standing opposite me, cringes, just enough for me to notice.

"Luana said Noah's been working out with Alex before school," Chris elaborates for the group. "I mean, good for you. Maybe I should join you guys." He does what I think is supposed to be a bodybuilding pose and then laughs, but the air around the group is suddenly thicker than honey.

"What?" Eli repeats.

"My mum works out at Lakeside every morning before work," Luana explains. There's something in her hazel eyes that makes me think she knows exactly what she's doing. "She said she sees Alex and Noah there all the time. Getting all *sweaty* together."

"Maybe she's got the wrong guys," I say, which even I wouldn't believe. "How does she know it's us?"

Luana scrunches up her face, incredulous. "Uh, because she picks me up from rehearsals like three times a week? She's seen you both at the BMTS hall a zillion times."

Eli slips his hand free from mine. "Is this true?" His voice is only a whisper, but I'm sure everyone can still hear him.

"Oh my god, wait," Yvette says, her voice dripping with scandal. "Did Eli not *know?*"

"You're having secret workout sessions with Alex?" His voice is still low, but frighteningly calm. "After . . ." He stops, but I know he was going to say *after we kissed and I told you how much history there is between me and Alex and how self-conscious I feel around him?* His eyes are glistening with betrayal.

"I . . ." I don't know what to say. It's not like anything has been happening between Alex and me at the gym other than him showing me how to use the equipment and me trying not to vomit, but I know that's not what this would look like. "I mean, yeah, we've been working out, but—"

"It's just a few gym sessions," Alex says, sounding slightly less nonchalant than usual. "Who cares?"

"*I* care," Eli snaps at Alex. "And I didn't ask for your opinion."

"Eli, please," I say, trying to loop my fingers through his, but he yanks his hand away.

"I'm sorry," he says, "I gotta go."

He darts around the fountain, through the French doors, and into the kitchen.

I whip around to Luana. "What the hell was that?"

"It was Chris who let the cat out of the bag," she says with a pout. "And it's not *my* fault you're cheating on Eli."

"I'm not—"

"There's nothing going on," Alex says firmly. "Just because two gay guys go to the gym together, it doesn't mean they're having sex."

"No," Keegan says with a shrug, "but it doesn't mean one of them—" he cuts his eyes to me "—doesn't jerk off over the other one in the showers afterwards."

"Fuck you, Keegan," I say, storming off into the house after Eli.

"It was just a joke," he calls after me. "Relax."

By the time I make it into the kitchen, Eli's nowhere to be found.

"Eli?" I call out, heading down the hallway. "Eli, can we just talk?"

Just as I reach the front door, it swings open and a boy steps through, silhouetted by the afternoon sun.

"Thank g—" But I stop in my tracks.

"*Noah*?" Tan says as the door shuts behind him. His deep brown eyes bore into mine. "What are you doing here?"

He seems so much older. So much like his dad. His shoulders are broad now, his voice deep.

"I'm . . ." My mind is blank. "I'm . . ."

His brow crinkles.

"I'm in *Chicago*," I say quickly, forcing the words out. "With Prisha."

"I know," he replies. "But why are you *here*?"

"The barbecue. The cast barbecue."

"Prisha said she wasn't going to invite you."

I shrug, feeling like a little kid all of a sudden. "She had to, I guess."

Tan folds his arms across his muscled chest—the muscles are new, too—and glares at me. I can't tell if he's waiting for me to speak or leave or . . . I don't know, apologize?

"I . . . um . . ."

But what am I supposed to say? Sorry I ruined your life? Sorry I was a terrible friend? Sorry I got you expelled?

His heavy brow creases. "What?"

"Sorry, I just . . . need to find my mum."

And with that, I turn and make a beeline towards the back garden, a dull ache spreading through my chest.

I find Mum draped over a wicker outdoor armchair, talking with David, Pania, and Pania's wife, Beth.

"Mum," I say, hearing the urgency in my own voice.

She ignores me.

"*Mum*," I say again, louder this time.

"Darling," she drawls, "can't you see we're in the middle of something?"

"We need to go."

"No, we don't, we're just getting started." She holds up her flute of champagne in an imaginary toast.

"*I* need to go," I reply. "So, can we please just go?"

"Noah," she snaps, "I am not going. If *you* want to go, call your father. I am not a taxi service."

I stomp back across the garden, through the house, and out onto the front lawn. Thankfully, I don't run into Tan again on my way out.

I slide my phone from my chinos pocket and call Dad.

No answer.

He's probably in surgery. Or on the golf course. Either way, he won't be home for hours.

I stare down at my phone, wondering how else I can escape this hell hole.

I could steal Mum's keys and drive myself home . . . I've had my learner's permit for a year and a half, so it wouldn't be dangerous, though still technically illegal. I could call an Uber, but I doubt there'd be any drivers around out here in the bush, so I'd be waiting forever. Maybe I could—

"Noah," someone says from behind me, and I turn to see Alex, leaning on a veranda post, looking more like young Marlon Brando from *Streetcar* than ever. "Do you need a lift?"

TWENTY-SIX

???

From: MagePants69 <magepants69@gmail.com>

To: Arctic Fox <rcticf0x@outlook.com>

On: Sunday, 31 May at 10:23 a.m.

If the boy you liked was secretly working out at the gym with the ridiculously hot guy who slept with you and broke your heart and who is a better version of you in every way, and the boy you liked had been lying about it and covering it up for weeks and then you found out and he tried to tell you nothing was going on … would you believe him???

Yours,

M

The email comes through while I'm eating breakfast the morning after the cast barbecue, and what little appetite I woke up with instantly evaporates. I bury my head in my hands and let out a long groan.

Alex dropped me off at home last night—a total gentleman as always—and then I spent a couple of hours trying to get a hold of Eli, to no avail. There was still no sign of Mum when I eventually forced myself into bed at midnight. I somehow managed to get to sleep despite the cyclone inside my head, but now that I'm awake and dealing with reality again, I just want to go back to bed.

Dad left early for golf, or the hospital (it's always impossible to know which), and Mum is still asleep, so at least I'm alone to wallow in my self-pity. I stare out the kitchen window for a while, absently stirring my mushy cereal as I watch the trees in the backyard being whipped back and forth by the wind.

After a long while, my phone pings, and my heart leaps into my throat.

But it's only Charly.

Bub, guess what?! I'm coming home for Mum's 40th! Shocked emoji. **But it's a surprise so DO NOT TELL A SOUL!**

I reply with three party popper emojis.

Charly: **That's it? A few shitty party poppers? Noah, I haven't seen you for MONTHS . . .**

Sorry, I write, **I'm SUPER happy you're coming home and I obviously can't wait to see you but I have a problem we need to talk about first.**

Excuse me, she replies, **can we just be excited about my thing for ONE SECOND?**

Char, I'm serious. This is important . . .

Eye-roll emoji from Charly. **You're the worst. But fine.**

Okay, I start, **so you know that Reddit thing 'Am I the Asshole' where people ask the internet if they're the one who's being a dick in a particular situation or if it's the other person**

who is being unreasonable?

If this is about Mum, I am so not playing.

It's not about Mum, I reply. **That's a whole other thing for a whole other time. ANYWAY. I've been working out with the guy playing the lead role in Chicago for over a month now (just so I can build a bit of strength for the show SO DON'T MAKE A BIG DEAL ABOUT IT) but I didn't tell Eli, because they have history (and yes, before you ask, it's Sex History) and then Eli found out about the workouts and now he thinks I'm cheating on him at the gym every morning. SO . . . I know I probably should've told Eli about the gym-with-his-ex thing, but I'm also allowed to do whatever I want, right? And just because they have their own shit, it doesn't mean I should sacrifice MY needs entirely. Right? And storming out of a party and not answering my calls is just a tad dramatic. RIGHT? Or . . . and here's where I need your help . . . AM I THE ASSHOLE?**

A few seconds after I press "send" on my mini essay, my phone buzzes. I answer with a wary, "Hello?"

"You're not the asshole," Charly replies matter-of-factly. "But Eli is *also* not the asshole."

"Great. Because that's not at all confusing, Char."

"Look, bub," she says, and I know the exact face she'd be pulling in Sydney right now, "these things are always complicated, and like I said *last* time you had a crisis and begged me for help, people like to know where they stand. It's all about honesty. So, no, you absolutely shouldn't have lied to Eli about working out with this guy—who, by the way, I've seen photos of and I mean, *wow*—but you're right, you also should be allowed to be friends with whoever you want."

"Okay, and—"

"*But . . .*"

"But?"

"You *do* have to factor Eli's feelings into this, even if it doesn't seem fair. I mean, is it worth making him feel super uncomfortable so you can go to the gym with this guy, when you could easily just work out with someone else?"

I sigh into the phone. "So, what exactly is the moral of the story, then?"

"Moral of the story is: You need to be honest with Eli from now on. Completely honest. He won't trust you if he can tell you're hiding something."

Awesome. That's just perfect.

"And if you really want to keep working out with the sexy leading man," she goes on, "just be up-front with Eli about it and explain why it's so important to you."

"I think it would be easier to stop working out forevermore," I say. "It's not like it's turned me into an underwear model or anything, so what's the point."

"And *maybe* Eli overreacted," Charly adds, "but there is always a reason."

I look out at the trees. The wind seems to have died down a bit.

"Okay," I reply. "Got it. Thanks, Char."

"Great, now back to *me*," she says, her voice instantly full of pep. "On a scale of One to Wetting-Your-Pants-Like-When-Mum-and-Dad-Told-Us-We-Were-Going-to-Disney-World, how excited are you about seeing your big sister in three weeks?"

I snort. "Char, I was five when that happened. Let it go."

"Still happened, bub."

"Fine," I say, rolling my eyes even though she can't see it, "I am Wetting-My-Pants level excited to see my big sister in three weeks."

"Ohmygod," she says, like it's one word, "you should invite Eli to Mum's party!"

"It's a family dinner, not a party."

"Of *course*," Charly replies, with a tone I can't quite decipher. "*Dinner*."

"And that is *not* a good idea. Mum's definitely not a fan of the whole Eli situation. She thinks I'm going to cause some kind of apocalyptic cast drama."

"I'll ask her for you, then. When has she ever said no to me?"

Ahh, to be the perfect, popular, preferred child.

"Besides," Charly adds, "I'm only in town for a couple of days, and I *need* to meet this boy."

"Well," I say, pushing my bowl of soggy cereal across the table, "I'll probably need to make sure Eli's talking to me first, won't I?"

"Three weeks, bub. You got this."

Eli is super cold with me at rehearsal that afternoon. He doesn't ignore me completely—and he's not flat-out rude like Mum—but there are no hellos or hugs or kisses, no encouraging glances. We do make eye contact a few times, but he quickly averts his gaze, which is highly unusual for him, given he's basically the King of Eye Contact.

Alex avoids me, too, looking somewhat sheepish for the first time in history. I send him a text when I get home.

Hey, Alex. So, I'm sure you probably already guessed this, but I think it's best if I don't come to the gym with you for a while. I'm sorry it turned into such a big awkward thing. And thanks for all your help. I may still be a skeleton man, but it's not for your lack of trying haha.

His reply doesn't come through until after I've showered, had a mumbled conversation with Dad, and scoffed down my dinner in front of the TV.

All good, dude. I get it. Eli can be a bit dramatic, but he seems to really like you, so . . . I hope you boys sort it out. I'll see you at rehearsal. Thumbs-up emoji.

I head upstairs to my room, flick the lamp on, and sit on my bed, legs crossed. I open Eli's email to RcticF0x and stare down at it for a while, knowing I need to write back ASAP—he'd definitely be wondering why I haven't replied—but not knowing the right thing to say. Because this could be make or break.

There's one particular line in his email that hits me, the one where he so casually refers to Alex as a "better version of him in every way." Which, for starters, is completely not true. But the fact that he wrote it in an email to the person he trusts more than anyone makes me think that he's not just being dramatic, that he actually *believes* that, and that he probably assumes everyone else agrees—myself included.

What was it that Charly said this morning? That maybe Eli did overreact, but there must've been a reason? Well, I think I know the reason.

Re: ???

From: Arctic Fox <rcticf0x@outlook.com>

To: MagePants69 <magepants69@gmail.com>

On: Sunday, 31 May at 7:18 p.m.

Sorry for this hideously late reply. I've been out with my mum all day. (FUN)

Based on the above evidence, I'd say you should probably trust the boy on this one. It sounds like he didn't think he had a choice. And that he didn't realize that what he was doing was super shady. Which makes him a complete fool. But (and this is just an educated guess) a fool who is totally in love with you and would do anything to make you happy because you're categorically THE most awesome person on the planet and don't you forget it.

Yours,

RcticF0x

That last bit might have been a *bit* much, but what the hell. At least it's not a lie.

TWENTY-SEVEN

I DECIDE TO GIVE Eli some space for a few days. As Noah Mitchell, that is. I play *Spire of Dusk* with him every night as RcticF0x, even though it's more than a little demoralizing at the moment, given we *still* can't defeat that damn dragon. It's obvious that both of us are feeling the fatigue of being stuck in an endless loop of dying and respawning, but neither of us is willing to give in. It feels like both of us *need* a win right now.

MagePants69 eventually replied to RcticF0x's email, agreeing that he should probably forgive the Kind of Cute Boy, but that he needs some time to process the whole thing first. Which is fine. I just wish I could ask him whether 'some time' equates to hours or days or—god forbid—*weeks*. I just . . . I can't afford to mess up this apology.

Sunday afternoon's rehearsal takes me to the last place I imagined I'd be going on a non-Eli-related excursion: the Sunnyside Roller Rink.

"Wait," I say, when Mum pulls up out front. "We're not rehearsing here, are we?"

Mum clicks her tongue. "Do you *ever* pay attention when David talks?"

"I try my best not to."

She ignores me and proceeds to check her bright red lipstick in the rear-view mirror. "Today is our first rehearsal on the set."

Eli showed me the *Chicago* set a few weeks ago at Sunnyside. He couldn't find the light switch, though, so it just looked like the eerie silhouette of a half-built house. He said, "When we move into the theatre, they'll break the set into pieces and put it back together on stage, like a giant, house-sized jigsaw." Which seems like a lot of unnecessary effort to me.

The rest of the cast is bouncing off the warehouse walls when we walk into the vast, skylit room off the main Sunnyside corridor. I can't say that I share their excitement, though, since it turns out the *Chicago* set *is* just a half-built house—a few walls and platforms and doors, all made from the same plain timber. I think I must be missing something.

"Can't wait to see it when it's painted," Chris says from beside me. I turn to see him gawking at the set with stars in his eyes.

"What color are they painting it?"

"Black. *Chicago* sets are always black. It's iconic."

"That sounds equally as boring."

"You just have to add the pizzazz yourself," he laughs.

I scoff. "Yeah. Because I naturally *exude* pizzazz."

We run through the whole first act on the set, with Jane thumping out the accompaniment on an electric keyboard in the corner of the cavernous room. I keep glancing down at the floor, expecting to see the different-colored lines of tape that mark out the entrances and exits in the church hall, but there are actual doors to walk through now, proper steps to climb. It's incredibly confusing.

"I know it's a big adjustment," David says on our break between acts. We're all huddled on the set, drink bottles in hand. "But keep your wits about you and you'll be fine. This is why we bring you here for this rehearsal—so you're one step ahead when we hit the stage. The important thing is that you *use your surroundings.*"

A shiver runs down my spine.

"What did you just say?" The words are out of my mouth before I know what's happening.

David pauses, taken aback by the interruption. He turns to me with a strange look on his face, something like surprise mixed with curiosity, and a dash of reproach.

"Noah," Mum whispers, poking her head out from behind Prisha and Alex. "*Shoosh.*"

"No, no, it's fine, Rose," David says, giving her a wink, "it's good for people to clarify if they don't know what I mean. Not everyone is a seasoned professional like yourself. I *said*—" he turns back to me "—that it's important to use your surroundings. Make the environment work for you. It's just as much a part of this show as you are."

And holy fucking shit. He's right.

The second I get home, I send an email to MagePants69. I may not be able to figure out how to fix things with Eli in real life just yet, but I can certainly solve one epic problem today.

URGENT
From: Arctic Fox <rcticf0x@outlook.com>
To: MagePants69 <magepants69@gmail.com>
On: Sunday, 6 June at 6:24 p.m.

You need to meet me on Spire of Dusk IMMEDIATELY.
And I mean RIGHT NOW. Non-negotiable.

I know what we've been doing wrong. This whole
fucking time . . .

I know how to defeat Lightdrinker.

In the end, it's *painfully* easy. It's almost impossible to believe
we've been stuck at this roadblock for almost two whole months,
and all we had to do was *use our surroundings*.

RcticF0x <make sure you aim directly at the stalactite>

MagePants69 <dw i got this>

His fiery-haired Bard weaves her hands in front of her chest,
sparks dancing in the air around her, before launching a bolt of
azure lightning straight at the stone ceiling of Lightdrinker's Lair.
The dragon rears his head, maw open wide, ready to unleash his
trademark shadowflame upon my Warrior, but MagePants69's aim
is true. The razor-sharp onyx stalactite breaks away from the ceiling
with a loud *crack*, then plummets through the air and impales the
hulking creature straight through his thorny spine. Lightdrinker
cries out in pain, his long neck straining. He freezes for a second,
as if petrified, then falls to the gravelly floor with an almighty thud.
The walls around us shake. And then there's silence.

"Yes!" I shout, fist-pumping the air. Mr. Nibbles jumps off my bed and darts across the room in fright.

MagePants69 *<yessssssssssssssssssssssssssssssssssssss>*

RcticF0x *<FINALLY>*

MagePants69 *<how the hell did you figure that out, you beautiful fucking GENIUS>*

RcticF0x *<haha just came to me>*

MagePants69 *<well i could NOT BE HAPPIERRR>*

A wave of nerves spins my stomach. This is the moment I've been waiting for . . . .

I grab my phone from my desk and call Eli. While I wait for him to answer, another message pops up on my screen.

MagePants69 *<sorry to ruin the party, m'lord, but someone's calling me rn and i really should take this. meet you in the tav in 10?>*

I type my reply one-handed.

RcticF0x *<of course. see you soon, m'lady>*

"Hello?" Eli answers as my Warrior portals back to the Andar Valley town square.

"Hey."

Insert awkward pause.

"So," I say, eventually, "I know I should have done this sooner, and I probably should be doing it in person, but I just wanted to say that I'm sorry. Like, really, truly, wholeheartedly sorry." There's silence on the other end, so I add, "About the gym thing. Obviously."

"Okay," Eli replies flatly. "And?"

"And . . ."

I didn't prepare for an "and."

"And," I say slowly, "I should have told you. Right from the start."

"And?" Eli says again and I let out a silent sigh.

"And . . . the only reason I went behind your back with Alex is because he seemed like he genuinely wanted to help me and I thought—" *I thought you'd only want to be my boyfriend if I looked like him.* "I thought it was something I needed to do. And I didn't want to make you uncomfortable, so I hid it from you. But I see now that if I'd just *told* you, we could have figured something out together, because it was a decision that affected both of us, and it was selfish of me not to involve you. And I'm sorry."

There's another awkward silence, and then Eli says, "You're a fool."

"I am. Very much so."

"But, luckily for you, a *cute* fool. I accept your apology."

I bite back a smile, praying that Eli is smiling right now, too. "I'm going to make it up to you. I promise."

"Oh? *How?*"

"Well, many ways. Most of which are currently TBC and probably NSFW. But I've already stopped working out with Alex. Just so we're clear."

"Noah, you—"

"It's fine," I interrupt. "If it makes you uncomfortable, I don't want to do it."

"*Okay.*"

"And . . . I wanted to ask if you'd like to come to my mum's birthday thing? At our place? There will be tons of food and cake and we'll probably be allowed to have some wine—if you like wine, I actually hate wine, but—*anyway*, the dinner is after one of our Sunday rehearsals in a few weeks, so you'll be able to come straight home with us. It's just a little family thing. An intimate dinner. My sister will be down from Sydney, and she's desperate to meet you. You'll love her. She's like the Jekyll to Mum's Hyde."

"An intimate family dinner?" Eli says after a moment, trepidation in his voice. "You don't think I'd be intruding?"

"Not at all," I lie, picturing Mum's sneering face whenever Eli's name comes up in conversation. "It'll be totally fine. If it's okay with your mum, obviously. I don't want to get you in trouble. But . . . I'd really like you to be there."

Eli is quiet on the other end of the line, and I literally cross my fingers while I wait for his reply.

"I'd love to," he says finally.

I can't help but fist pump the air again.

Victory number two for the day. And this one feels even sweeter than slaying that damn dragon.

Eli and I fall back into our usual pattern relatively easily. He's still a bit withdrawn—or cautious or . . . *something*—when I first see him at rehearsal on Tuesday, but by the end of the clean-up call on "Razzle Dazzle," he's all smiles and cheeky glances again.

On top of this, our current mood on *Spire of Dusk* could only be described as "giddy delight." High Priestess Leora sends us back into Lightdrinker's Lair to retrieve and shatter the dragon's onyx heart, a key-shaped shard of which we then use to unlock the gates of the Citadel of Unholy Darkness, where Queran (everyone's

favorite shirtless vampire, who we're desperately trying to destroy)
lives with the rest of the sexy Vampires of the Vale.

TL;DR we're absolutely nailing it.

The morning before Mum's fortieth birthday, I'm woken by a
high-pitched squeal that can only mean one thing: Charly
is home.

"Wake uuup!" she says, plonking herself directly on top
of me.

"Hhhhnnnnn," I murmur. She knows that getting out of
bed is one of my least favorite activities. I glance at the clock
on my bedside table through one puffy eye. "Char, get off. It's
too early."

She pushes herself up and perches on the edge of my bed, her
bum right by my pillow and, by extension, my face.

"Bub, I've only got *two days* in Ballarat and we are going to
make the most of them! Starting now."

"Can we start in five minutes?" I mumble. "Or maybe five
hours?"

"When did you get so boring? Come on. Up!" She stands and
gently slaps me on the face a few times—which would annoy
me immensely if anyone other than my sister did it—then skips
over to the door. "Noah, seriously. Come on."

"Mmmmmmm. I'll be there soon."

"I made pancakes," she says in a singsong voice.

I bolt upright, like a zombie out of a grave. "Coming."

Mum and Dad are both out this morning, much to Charly's

annoyance ("Couldn't they have rescheduled their precious commitments just this *one* time?"), but she knows as well as I do that our parents are not the type of people to compromise on their extracurriculars. So, we sit together at the dining table and eat way too many pancakes, just the two of us, catching up on the last few months. It's actually kind of perfect.

Charly is her usual bubbly self, but there's something . . . different about her. She seems genuinely interested in politics and the environment and all these social justice issues that High School Charly wouldn't have given a damn about, especially if it got in the way of a good party. It's as if a few months at university has expanded her mind, her *awareness* of the world outside our little town.

This is Charly 2.0. And I have to say, I'm a little bit obsessed with her.

"Now," she says, finishing her cup of coffee, "tell me *everything* about Eli."

I feel myself blush. "There's not a lot to tell, really."

"Oh, *please*," she scoffs. "No detail is too small. I want to know *everything*. Age, star sign, address, school subjects, hobbies, eye color, favorite Pokémon or whatever it is you nerds fangirl about these days. And, obviously, how you met, when you plan to get married, and whether you'll be adopting or using a surrogate."

"I forgot you were like this." I laugh.

"What?" She lifts her eyebrows. "Nosy and annoying and the most wonderful person you've ever met?"

"Sure, let's go with that," I reply, still chuckling.

With Charly back, the house instantly feels like a home.

TWENTY-EIGHT

CHARLY COOKS A BREAKFAST feast for Mum and me the next morning. Bacon and eggs and homemade "birthday" hash browns. Dad left at dawn for the golf course, so it's just the three of us. Mum doesn't even seem to notice he's not there, probably because she's just so happy to have Charly home. Having said that, she still manages to disapprove of some of Charly's latest life choices, namely her eyebrow shape ("They're a bit bushy, don't you think?") and her new "Sydney wardrobe" ("Those kinds of jeans weren't flattering when they were invented in the '90s, honey, and they're certainly not flattering now."). Luckily, Charly seems to have a built-in force field that repels snide comments from Mum. Something I, unfortunately, did not develop.

"Honestly," Charly whispers to me while we're loading the dishwasher, "you'd think our father could skip eighteen holes of golf for his wife's fortieth birthday breakfast."

"You'd think."

"Please tell me he's got everything organized for the party?"

I snort. "Char, stop calling it a party. The four of us plus Eli having dinner does not qualify as a *party*."

She freezes, bent over the dishwasher, plate in hand. "*What?*"

"You told me to invite him."

"Not that." She puts the plate on the bench with a clang. "Are you seriously telling me Dad hasn't planned a proper surprise party?"

"Ummm . . ."

"Oh my fucking *god*! Noah—" she lowers her voice to a furious whisper "—it's her *fortieth* birthday. You think she'll be satisfied with a *family dinner?*"

I shrug. "Maybe?"

Charly groans and runs her fingers through her blonde hair. "I told Dad to plan something *big*. I would've done it myself but do you know how hard it is to plan a surprise party from interstate? *Ugh*, that man is *useless*."

That man. I know she's hardly Dad's biggest fan, but this is a new level of disdain.

"Maybe we—" I start, but Charly cuts me off.

"It's too late for a party now," she says, pulling a hair tie off her wrist and twisting it around a messy bun on top of her head. "Did Dad organize *anything?*"

"I'm . . . not sure."

She rolls her eyes. "I gotta go. Apparently, I have a family dinner to plan."

I play a quick hour of *Spire of Dusk* with MagePants69 before rehearsal. I feel guilty for not helping Charly organize Mum's last-minute birthday dinner, but there's not much I could achieve before rehearsal, and party planning isn't really in my wheelhouse.

Thankfully, Mum is showered with birthday love at rehearsal. It's as if the day has been officially declared "Rose Mitchell Appreciation Day." The church hall is decked out with colorful bunting and balloons and streamers, with a huge banner strung from the rafters that says *Happy Birthday to our Lovely Leading Lady*. It's so over-the-top that I physically cringe when I walk in. (Or maybe that's the guilt . . . .)

We sing "Happy Birthday" after our vocal warm-up, which is, without doubt, the most harmonious version of "Happy Birthday" that has ever been sung. I barely recognized the *real* melody, after having only heard a bunch of tone-deaf teenagers butchering the song at school when the more festive teachers force us to sing it for each other.

The cast even chipped in for a gift—a giant bouquet of flowers and a bottle of Veuve Clicquot.

"Thank you, thank you, thank you," Mum says to everyone at the end of the rehearsal, doing a little curtsy. Then she adds, in a Southern American accent, "Y'all sure know how to make a gal feel special."

I manage to contain my eye-roll, instead locking eyes with Eli across the room, who offers me a *give her a break, it's her birthday* smile.

Mum waltzes out of the building on cloud nine, with Eli and me in tow. She shows absolutely no signs of being anti-Eli as he climbs into the back seat of the car, which means Charly has already had a quiet word with her, or she's just too high on adulation to care.

When we arrive home, Mum heads immediately upstairs to shower and change. She pauses on the landing to call down, "Make sure you put on a shirt, Noah! And a jacket. The nice one. The navy-blue one."

I can hear Charly in the kitchen, so I take Eli straight through to meet her. She smiles and waves, then points at the phone pressed up against her ear, rolling her eyes.

"You said you were going to order a cake," she tells the person on the other end, who I'm assuming is *That Man*. "No, I didn't . . . I had to get a *Woolworths mud cake* because all the bakeries were already closed by the time I realized. You—I know, but—*Dad*, it's her fucking *fortieth* birth—Oh my god, Dad, people swear. Including your daughter. Get over it . . . No, you're totally missing the point . . . She would *not* have hated it just because you organized it. Just—Look, it's too late. Come home right now so we can try to salvage at least *some* part of this day."

She hangs up and lets out a groan. "Honestly, what is *wrong* with him?"

Eli lingers awkwardly behind my shoulder. "Charly," I say, "this is Eli."

Her expression changes instantly, as if she's only just realized there are two of us standing here. "*Hiiiiiiiiii.*" She dances over and kisses Eli on the cheek. "Hello. Welcome. I'm so sorry about—" she flaps her hands in the air "—all *that*. You'd think an award-winning neurosurgeon would be capable of planning a party for his own wife, but apparently not."

"Honestly, Char," I reply, "she said she didn't even want a party."

"Oh, Noah, *please*. This is our *mother* we're talking about. You think she actually meant that? That whole 'I'll be too tired from rehearsals' charade was just so she could act even more surprised when her intimate family dinner turned into a fully catered fortieth birthday garden party extravaganza."

"Rose is only forty?" Eli asks. "I mean, she looks super young, but forty is . . . She must have had you two when she was like—"

"Twenty-one," Charly replies, pointing to herself. "And Noah when she was twenty-two. Dad was very old-school."

"*Was?*" I add, with a wry chuckle.

Eli clears his throat. "Since I'm here," he says, clearly keen to change the subject, even though he's the one who brought it up, "how can I help? If you've got an apron, I can pretend to be a caterer?"

Charly studies his face for a moment. Her eyes flick from his to mine and back again. Then she announces, "I love you already." She loops her arm through Eli's and takes him into the dining room. "What are you like with floral arrangements?"

Dinner is intensely awkward. Like, curl-up-into-a-ball-under-the-table awkward. And Charly was right, Mum clearly thought the family dinner was just a cover for her *real* birthday celebration. Which, of course, does not exist.

The night is kind of like watching a car crash unfold in slow motion. At each step of the way during dinner—nibbles, wine, entrees, wine, mains, more wine—Mum's face lights up with anticipation, like *this* is the moment we're going to flip the secret switch and glitter is going to rain down from the ceiling and all her closest friends are going to jump out from trapdoors under the rugs. The doorbell even rings at one point, and she gleefully trots off to answer it, singing, "I wonder who *that* could be?", only to find a pair of Mormon missionaries wanting to give her a free bible and a pamphlet about the dangers of pre-marital sex. (At least they didn't come empty-handed.)

When she sits back down at the table, I try my hardest to not feel sorry for her. It's hard to explain, but it's as if she suddenly seems more human. Like she's no longer my overbearing, self-centred mother, or "Rose Mitchell, leading lady." She's just a forty-year-old woman whose family failed to plan anything special for her birthday.

Charly glares at me from across the table, and I give her a subtle, wide-eyed shrug. What was *I* supposed to do? No one told me there was meant to be some big, elaborate birthday surprise. I thought *Charly* was the surprise. And yes, I've been a little wrapped up in my own problems lately, but Mum also *is* one of my current problems, so . . . .

"That was delicious," Eli says to Charly, his plate of chicken tikka masala wiped clean.

"Well," she replies, with a pointed look at Dad, "we have the lovely people at Taste of India to thank for that."

"Indeed," Dad says, piling saffron rice onto his fork, obviously not wanting to start a public feud with Charly.

When we're all finished, Eli and I clear the plates, and Charly brings out the cake, which is probably only *just* big enough to feed all five of us. There's a silver plastic *40* stuck in the top, ringed with gold candles. I turn off the lights and we start a rousing—and completely off-key—rendition of "Happy Birthday."

Dad huffs. "Do we really have to do the singing thing?"

"Just *sing*," Charly hisses in between lines of the song.

We make it through, with Eli valiantly attempting to harmonize with our terrible singing voices, and Charly says, "Blow out the candles!"

Mum, whose smile is so fake it makes my teeth cringe, leans over to blow out the candles in one long puff, before sitting back down, wordlessly.

"Time to cut the cake!" Charly announces, handing Mum a knife like it's Merlin's sword. (Honestly, my sister's efforts to make this night exciting deserve a Golden Globe.)

Mum slices down the center of the cake.

"If it's dirty," Charly teases, "you have to kiss the nearest boy."

"Give it a rest, Charlotte," Dad says. "She's forty, not fourteen."

I pull at the collar of my shirt.

"But she could pass for twenty-five," Eli adds, his smile quickly fading.

Dad pushes his chair back from the table. "We're done here, right? I'm going to lie down."

We all watch him as he retreats to the lounge room. The sound of the distant TV fills our painful silence.

"You know what," Mum says, her lips twisted to the side, "I think I'm going to go upstairs and lie down, too."

"Mum," Charly starts, "we haven't—"

"It's fine." Mum dabs a hand to her forehead. "I'm not . . . I'm not feeling that well. It was a long day. Thank you for dinner."

As she disappears down the hallway, Charly drags her hands down her face. "What a fucking *nightmare. That* poor woman."

Part of me wants to remind Charly who she's talking about, but she's right. Even Rose Mitchell doesn't deserve a total shitshow of a night like tonight.

Charly sighs, defeated. "I'll clean up. You guys just go chill out. Maybe we can put on a movie later or something?"

"Sure," I say, taking Eli's hand and leading him to the stairs.

"I feel *awful* for your mum," he whispers.

"Me too," I reply, and I really do. "But she'll probably just pretend the night never happened, which means we can all erase it from our memories."

"Is . . . is your dad always like that?"

"Um . . ." I chew on my bottom lip. "I don't know. I guess?"

"It's almost as bad as me not having one at all."

I don't really know what to say to that, but we soon reach the landing and I push open the door to my bedroom. Eli bursts in and says, "Wait, *what?* You play *Spire of Dusk?*"

My eyes cut to my computer, which is currently displaying the login screen for the game.

Holy shit. No, no, *no.* I must have left it open when I rushed out of the house this morning before rehearsal. And not only that, the bright-yellow note detailing The Plan is still stuck to the corner of the monitor.

"Uhhh," I reply, which is officially the world's worst attempt at stalling. "No . . . I . . ."

I duck over to the desk, snatch the sticky-note from the screen and switch off the monitor. I crumple up The Plan—trying to look like I'm tidying and not hiding evidence—and shove it into the pocket of the navy-blue jacket Mum wanted me to wear tonight, currently slung over the headrest of my Ergolove Destroyer.

"Are you okay?" Eli asks, studying my face.

"Yeah, I'm fine," I reply, "I'm just . . . it's . . . uh . . . Charly."

"Huh?"

"It's my sister's. The game. Not the computer. Charly plays the game. She's a huge gamer. Secretly. No one knows."

"Your sister is a huge secret gamer? How has this never come up?"

"It's . . . a whole big thing." My palms are already dripping. "She doesn't want anyone to know about it because she thinks it'll ruin her reputation."

Eli furrows his brow. "That's . . ."

"Charly!" I call out, my heart thumping in my chest.

I hear footsteps on the stairs, then Charly pokes her head into my room.

"What's up, bub?"

I stare back at her, trying to telepathically communicate the fact that I desperately need her to just go along with this.

"*What?*" she says, her body still out in the hallway.

"I told you not to use my computer to play games."

She stares back at me blankly. "What games?"

I raise my eyebrows as high as humanly possible.

"Oh," she replies, gaze flicking to my computer. "*Those* games. Um . . . yeah. Sorry?"

"You know I don't like people coming into my room when I'm not here," I say, which hopefully doesn't make me sound like a creep in front of Eli, but I don't know what else to say.

"Yeah," Charly says with a slow nod, finally cottoning on, "I know. Sorry. I was just . . . *desperate* to play. You know me. Completely addicted to computer games."

"What class do you play?" Eli asks, sounding genuinely interested and not like he suspects I've lied to him *yet again*. "On *Spire of Dusk*."

"Uhhh . . ." Charly looks to me, eyes wide. "I play the . . . only one *worth* playing."

Eli laughs. "Oh, you're one of those Warrior snobs."

"Can't help it." She shrugs. "I love me some Warrior."

My sister wouldn't know the difference between a Warrior and a walrus. I need to get her out of here before she ruins this.

"Yes, well, bye," I say. "Just don't come in here without asking next time. Okay?"

"Okay," she replies, with a too-sweet smile. "Noah, can I just talk to you outside for a sec?"

"Right now?"

"Right now."

I follow her into the hall and close the door behind us.

"What the hell was that?" she whispers, dropping the grin.

"It's a very long story, and one I cannot get into while Eli is sitting in there on my bed."

Charly narrows her eyes. "I don't know what you're up to, bub, but you are going to tell me *everything* tomorrow. Every. Single. Thing."

"Fine," I say. "Just go away. Please."

"Honestly," she says, shaking her head. "I'm gone for like,

four months and this whole family loses its mind."

I shoo her down the hall and slip back into my room. I switch the monitor off and join Eli on the bed.

"I think I might need to play *Spire of Dusk* with your sister sometime," he says, planting a kiss on my lips. "I reckon she'd be *fierce*. Maybe *she* could convince you to join us."

Okay, this is officially getting too weird now.

TWENTY-NINE

I GET UP EARLY the next day so I can leave the house before Charly wakes up. I can't face the inevitable interrogation about Eli. Out of all the close calls, that one was by *far* the worst. I *knew* he was coming over. I *knew* we'd go to my bedroom. The stupidity is beyond comprehension. The one saving grace is that I had at least logged out of the game. If that screen had shown my avi, my screen name, even our current location in the game, The Plan—which is not so much a plan anymore but my *life*—would have been completely ruined.

I know what you're doing, Charly messages me as I walk into first period applied computing. **Just because I'm flying home in a few hours doesn't mean we're not talking about this. We do have phones, you know. And if I'm going to pretend to be some sort of computer game uber nerd, I at least need to know why. End of story.**

Another message comes through. **PS I'm just looking out for you, bub.** Kissing emoji.

And then another. **PPS please be nice to Mum for the rest of eternity. Dad slept on the couch last night and now she's not talking to him. We're lucky she's talking to us. So just . . . be nice, k?**

My reply is simple: **I will be as nice to her as she is to me.**

I spend the next couple of weeks avoiding Charly's calls. I also become adept at changing the conversation with Eli anytime he asks me about my "gamer girl" sister. He keeps begging me for her email address and her screen name so he can add her on *Spire of Dusk*, and it's not as if I can say, *Don't you already have a campaign you should be one hundred percent committed to?*, so I just keep telling him Charly is super hard to get hold of because of uni and work and I'm sure they'll get to play eventually.

Aside from stressing about Mum and Eli and Charly and *Spire of Dusk*, I *also* spend a lot of time catastrophizing a little thing called "Rehearsal Camp." When Eli first mentioned the camp a month or so ago, I legitimately thought he was joking.

"So, it's like band camp?" I laughed. "Like in that old movie with the girl and the flute and the apple pie?"

He just rolled his eyes.

Out of the whole *Chicago* process, nothing has instilled more terror in me than Rehearsal Camp. Which—surprise, surprise—is exactly what it says it is. A camp. For rehearsing. From what I can gather, we're all going to pile onto a charter bus, drive to a school camp facility in the middle of some paddock halfway to Melbourne, run the show for *two days straight*, and sleep in bunk beds built for children on the night in between.

Why on earth a bunch of *grown adults* think this is an

appealing idea, I will never know. But it's not like I have a choice in the matter.

On Friday night, an email comes through from MagePants69.

Shit! Sorry!

From: MagePants69 <magepants69@gmail.com>

To: Arctic Fox <rcticf0x@outlook.com>

On: Friday, 3 July at 6:49 p.m.

M'lord. I completely forgot to tell you that I'm going away for a couple of days. I won't be able to play SoD till Monday after school. DON'T HATE ME.

We'll show those slutty vamps who's boss upon my return. Promise.

Yours,

M

Re: Shit! Sorry!

From: Arctic Fox <rcticf0x@outlook.com>

To: MagePants69 <magepants69@gmail.com>

On: Friday, 3 July at 6:51 p.m.

You're officially off my Christmas list.

KIDDING. Enjoy whatever it is you're off to enjoy! I shall entertain myself while you're gone. (Not like that, get your mind out of the gutter.) (Okay, probably like that.)

BYEEEEEEE.

Yours,

RcticF0x

Not long after, Eli calls me to convince me about the joys of rehearsal camp.

"I swear, it's the actual *best*. Our *Rock of Ages* camp a couple of years ago was one of my all-time favorite weekends ever. Period."

"If I could go on a rehearsal camp with just *you*," I reply, "I would be a lot more excited."

"We wouldn't get much rehearsing done."

"My point exactly."

"Speaking of," he says, his voice melting like honey, "when do you think we might, uh . . . try again?"

"Try again, as in *sex*?"

No, Captain Obvious. Try again, as in scuba diving.

Eli chuckles. "I mean, I was trying to be subtle, but yeah. Sex."

I feel like I need to open a window in my bedroom all of a sudden. "Soon. Hopefully."

"Yeah. Hopefully."

We're both quiet for a second, and I start wondering if he ever had *phone sex* with Alex Di Mario and—

"I better go," I say. "I, um, want to get a good sleep before the big weekend."

"That's not a bad idea," Eli replies. "I'm pretty sure we only got a couple of hours of sleep last year. Way too much fun to be had. It was such a wild night."

My stomach twists at the thought. "I can only imagine."

"Sweet dreams, Noah."

"Sweet dreams, Eli."

I hang up the phone and place it gingerly on my bedside

table, knowing full well that I will *not* be having sweet dreams tonight. I'll be having nightmares about the last time I went on a school camp. In Year Nine. With Tan and Simon and Hawk. When everything turned to shit.

I sit with Eli on the bus to Perrivale Camp. We're in the back, surrounded by the rest of the younger cast members. The air is close and stale, and I'm pretty sure someone keeps farting, so it really does feel like we're off to school camp. Which makes me feel sick to my stomach.

When we arrive and alight onto the patchy brown grass, Pania reads out the cabin allocations. Predictably, I end up sharing with Eli, Alex, Keegan, Chris, and the three straight Barbarians—Shawn, Shaun, and Steve. Having to sleep in the same room as a bunch of guys (including four straight guys) gives me low-key anxiety, but at least Eli will be there. If I try hard enough, I might be able to block out all the testosterone and pretend he and I are back in our hotel room, just the two of us, snuggling on one of the single beds.

Actually, I probably shouldn't imagine that . . . .

The rehearsals themselves are fine. David takes us to a big recreation room sitting atop the hill above the cabins. It's our "home" for the next two days, he says. The rec room has polished timber floors—already marked up with our colored rehearsal tape—and massive floor-to-ceiling windows across one side. There are dart boards, a projector screen, a box of kids' toys, and a table tennis table pushed into one corner. We're looking out onto rolling hills and fields and trees, so the atmosphere is almost pleasant, as long as you ignore all the singing and dancing and being screamed at by David.

We run the whole show twice during the day, and do "working notes" with Pania and David in between. We only pause for lunch—a sausage sizzle coordinated by Mary and the rest of the BMTS wardrobe department—and dinner—a standard school camp meal featuring our choice of shepherd's pie, spaghetti bolognese, or ambiguous vegetarian stew.

After our night-time choreography clean-up session, David tells us we're allowed to stay up for supper (read: home-brand black tea and a pack of Family Assorted Arnott's biscuits) as long as we're in our cabins with lights out by midnight. I make sure I'm back in the cabin well before the rest of the boys so I can get changed without fear of having my bare ass towel-whipped by Shaun, Shawn, and Steve, and climb into my top bunk. Eli isn't far behind, and soon, the cabin is full and buzzing with a strange kind of boyish excitement. Maybe men never really grow up. Maybe we're destined to live our entire lives as our seventeen-year-old selves.

Now, there's a scary thought.

Steve, who is parading around in nothing but plaid boxer shorts, digs in his bag for a minute, then announces, "Party time!", pulling out a bottle of Jim Beam, brandishing it in the air like a trophy.

Suddenly, the walls of the cabin close in around me. I feel like I'm going to be sick.

"Dude!" Shawn says from his top bunk opposite mine. "Score."

"I was waiting for someone to bring out the grog," Shaun says from the bunk below Shawn.

Keegan scoffs. "Bourbon? Really? Honey, the gays only drink clear spirits."

"Speak for yourself," Eli scoffs. "I don't discriminate."

"There's a good boy," Steve says, passing Eli the bottle. He takes a swig and holds it up to me from his bottom bunk.

"I'm good," I reply, shaking my head.

Eli frowns, then passes the bottle back to Steve, who chugs at least four shots' worth of the amber liquid in one go.

Despite my best efforts, my mind travels straight back to Year Nine. I can still see the challenge in Tan's eyes. Hear the laughter filling the cabin. Feel my pulse racing.

I shake the memory away.

"Di Mario, you want some?" Steve says, holding the bottle out to Alex.

"Nah, I'm good," he replies, waving his hands in front of his face. "My voice is tired and I gotta sing all day tomorrow."

"Not the precious vocal cords," Keegan says in falsetto.

"Hey," Chris says, taking the bourbon from Steve, "if I had a voice like *that*, I'd be protecting it at all costs, too."

"Well, you don't," Keegan replies flatly, "so drink the hell up, bitch."

Chris laughs, takes a swig, and passes it back.

"You sure you don't want some, Mitchell?" Steve asks, shaking the bottle in my direction.

"Yeah," I say, my voice catching in my throat. "I'm good. Seriously."

Eli pokes his head out from under me, and mouths, *Are you okay?*

I nod, and he purses his lips.

"Just have some," Keegan says. "No one likes a party pooper."

"What are you, *five?*" Alex replies with a laugh. "If Noah doesn't want any, he doesn't have to have any."

Eli whips his head around to Alex. "What do *you* know about what Noah wants?"

Oh, please, no. Not now. *Please.*

But Alex just shrugs and lays his head on his pillow, refusing to take the bait.

Eli jumps out of bed and grabs the bottle from Steve. "Just have some," he says to me, smiling sweetly. "Try it. You might like it."

"I don't want to try it," I say, and suddenly I'm fourteen again. And it's not Eli, it's Tan. And it's . . .

Eli shakes the bottle. "Just a little bit."

"*No,*" I say, but it comes out as a shout. "Sorry—" I run my hands through my curls "—I just . . ."

But I need to get out of here. This is too much. I can't do this.

I hastily climb down the ladder, slip on a hoodie with my pajama pants, pull on my joggers, and head outside into the freezing cold, accidentally slamming the door. Eli will only be a second behind me, so I hurry along the path towards the recreation room, my breath fogging the air in front of my face.

A light catches my eye and I turn to see Mum standing outside one of the cabins in a dressing gown, the light from her phone illuminating the grass at her feet. I slip into the shadows of the cabin beside me.

Mum knocks on the door. It opens. She steps inside.

Eli whisper-shouts my name from somewhere in the darkness and I duck around the corner of the cabin.

I know he's desperate to find me, but I don't want to be found. I need to be alone.

I skirt the cabin, then head up the side of the hill towards the back of the recreation room. When I make it to the top, I walk around the back of the building, hoping to find an unlocked door somewhere so I can slip in and escape the cold. But when I reach the next corner, I hear a voice. A different voice.

"No, I *know*," Prisha says. She sounds like she's been crying. "But I thought this would give me another chance to prove myself."

I press my back against the cold brick wall of the rec room.

"Of course," she goes on, "but what choice did I have? . . . I can't afford to be picky . . . I *can't*. I was the only person in my class who *didn't* get an agent after showcase . . . I mean, I doubt a trip to Ballarat is on any of their to-do lists . . . I will, I just—In what version of my dreams did I end up living at home with my parents, playing Roxie Hart in an amateur production of *Chicago*, you know? . . . Yes, I know, but none of that matters if no one important gets to see me do it. The whole music theatre industry thinks I'm just some pathetic girl who tanked her showcase performance and . . . Okay. I'm sorry . . . I know . . . Yeah, I probably should go, too. It's freezing out here . . . Okay. Soon. Yes. Good night. Bye."

Tanked showcase performance? The only person in her class who didn't get an agent? What happened to the "very important project" coming up later in the year?

I hold my breath while I wait for Prisha to leave. After about a minute, I take a cautious step so I can peek around the corner, and a twig cracks beneath my foot, like I'm in some C-grade horror film.

"Hello?" Prisha says, definitely still there. "*Hello?*"

I freeze and scrunch up my face, resisting the urge to swear.

Prisha's face looms around the corner, the light from the rec room windows casting a hazy yellow glow over her pretty features. "What the *fuck?*" she snaps. "Did you follow me up here, you little creep?"

"No," I reply, shaking my head. "I was just . . . I needed some air."

She narrows her eyes and pulls her dressing-gown tighter over her chest with one hand. "Did you hear any of that?"

I nod. How do I keep getting myself into these situations?

"How much?" she asks.

"A lot more than I wanted to."

"Jesus." She rolls her eyes. "Well—" she holds her arms out wide "—now you know. Prisha Kandiyar, the washed-up musical theatre actress who came crawling back to Ballarat with her tail between her legs."

"You're not a washed-up anything, Prisha. You're—"

"Oh, *spare me*, Noah. I'm not here for a fucking pep talk. Least of all from *you*. But if you—" She goes to jab a finger towards me but stops herself, placing her hand on her collarbone instead. She turns her glare into a stiff smile. "I would greatly appreciate it if you kept this to yourself. I don't need the whole cast—the whole *town*—knowing my personal business. Especially not this. It's . . . mortifying."

"I know exactly what you mean," I reply, and she wrinkles her nose.

Prisha scoffs. "Don't try to make this about you, Noah."

"I'm not, I'm just—"

"You're what? Gonna use this against me? Kick a girl while she's down?"

Honestly, it hadn't even occurred to me, but . . . now that she mentions it . . . .

"No," I reply calmly, "but maybe we can come to some sort of agreement?"

"What *kind* of agreement?"

I shrug. "I think you know what I mean."

She runs her tongue along her front teeth. "I really don't like you, Noah."

"Let's be honest, Prish, I'm not your biggest fan, either."

"Just . . ." She glances over her shoulder. "Don't tell anyone. Please."

"I won't if you won't."

"Fine. It's a deal. Whatever." She turns and marches off down the path towards the cabins.

"Pleasure doing business with you," I call after her, and she gives me the finger over her shoulder without looking back.

Sunday at Perrivale Camp is almost exactly the same as Saturday, except that it's hailing all morning. Jane has to plug an external amplifier into her electric piano so we can hear the music above the sound of the golf ball–sized hailstones pelting against the tin roof of the rec room.

As soon as we finish our afternoon rehearsal session, we pile back onto the bus for the hour-and-a-bit drive back to Ballarat. I take a window seat at the front this time, and when Eli gets on, he pauses beside me, nodding to the empty space on the aisle.

"Is this seat taken?" he asks.

When I finally crept back into the boys' cabin at 4:00 a.m. last night, everyone was asleep. I'm fairly certain I heard Eli's blankets rustle as I climbed up the wooden ladder to the bunk above him, but if he woke up, he didn't say anything. Which was great, because I was way too tired to figure out what I could and couldn't say to him about why I freaked out.

And while I'm definitely still mad at him for the whole Trying-to-Assert-His-Dominance-Over-Alex-by-Using-Unnecessary-Peer-Pressure thing, it's also not fair to blame him entirely for my reaction last night. Not when it was my decision to keep him in the dark about what happened between me and Tan.

So, with a faint smile, I say, "No, the seat is not taken."

He sits, warily placing his hand on my leg. Like he's using the physical contact as some kind of litmus test of how angry I am. His touch is warm and tingly and lovely. I don't know if I could ever be truly angry with him.

When Prisha passes by our seats, she plasters on a grin and nods down at me. "Good work today, Mitchell."

Eli waits until she's seated in the back, then whispers, "What was *that*?"

"I have no idea," I say, even though I have every idea.

Eli spends most of the trip apologizing for last night, and I spend most of the trip telling him it's not a big deal and I'd rather not talk about it.

When our charter bus finally pulls into Ballarat Station, he says, "If you come to Sunnyside when I finish work tomorrow night, I will make it up to you. I promise."

"Aren't *I* still the one who's meant to be making it up to *you*?"

He laughs. "Probably. But, I mean, I can't even remember what that was for, so let's just say it's my turn now."

"Let's call it even, instead. You don't need to do anything. Honestly."

"Six o'clock tomorrow night?" he says with a smirk, completely ignoring my suggestion. "Sunnyside?"

I snort. "Six o'clock. Sunnyside."

THIRTY

"WHERE ARE YOU OFF to?" Mum asks on Monday afternoon as I pull open the front door. A gust of freezing cold air billows past me into the hallway. "Noah?"

I turn to see her standing in the hallway with her arms folded across her chest. She's wearing her turquoise designer pilates gear, so she either had pilates this afternoon, or she just wanted to *look* like she'd been to pilates when she went out for coffee.

"Shut the door," she adds, "it's freezing."

I gently close the door, not wanting to seem antagonistic. "I'm going to Sunnyside. Eli and I are going to revise all the choreography together."

"Is that necessary?" She lifts her eyebrows. "You almost looked like you knew what you were doing at Perrivale on the weekend."

That is legitimately the closest thing to a compliment Mum has ever given me.

"Well," I reply, "I'm still a long way from meeting David's unattainable standards and the show is like, two weeks away, so . . ."

She walks closer, her brow creased. "I know I've said this

before, darling—and I know you never listen to me anyway, so I don't know why I'm even bothering—but . . . please be careful with Eli."

"For your sake or mine?"

"For everyone's."

My blood instantly starts to boil, but then Charly's voice pops into my head saying, *Please be nice to Mum*, and I take a deep breath.

"Thank you for your concern," I reply, trying my best not to sound sarcastic, "but I don't need to be careful. I know all about Eli and Alex. It's fine. I'm fine."

"So—" she cocks her head to one side "—he told you about how he got drunk at last year's closing night party and ended up screaming at Alex in front of everyone? How he accidentally outed himself to the whole cast?"

Uh, *no*, he did not tell me that. And neither did MagePants69.

"Of course," I reply. "He tells me everything. And we're not going to ruin your precious show, so relax."

"I'm just . . ." Mum sighs. "I do *try* to be helpful, sometimes, darling. I am your mother, you know."

Like I could forget.

"I don't need your help," I say, failing to keep a lid on my frustration. "Especially not with Eli, so can you just . . . let it go?"

A flicker of hurt flashes behind her blue eyes. Honestly, if she keeps this up, I'm going to have to start seeing her as an actual person with real feelings, and I don't think I have the mental capacity for that right now.

"Alex said you had a little meltdown at camp," she says, which throws me for a second. I didn't realize Alex was talking to Mum about me behind my back. "In the boys' cabin. That wouldn't be because of—"

"Mum, we're not doing this," I cut in. "And I have to go. Eli is waiting for me."

"How are you getting there? Do you need a lift?"

"I'll get an Uber, it's fine."

"When will you be home?"

"I don't know."

She opens her mouth to reply, but I swing the door open and step outside before she gets the chance.

When the Uber drops me off at Sunnyside, Eli is leaning against the wrought-iron fence, already waiting. He's in black jeans, the green sweater he was wearing the day I met him, and a navy-blue snow jacket. It's about minus six million degrees today, so I'm equally as rugged up, with a big woolly scarf looped around my neck.

He waves me over and I jog across the road, rubbing my hands together.

"Hey," he says, pulling me into a hug. "Let's get out of the cold. This is torture."

"You didn't have to wait outside," I reply. "And sorry I'm late. Mum was . . . you know what, don't worry."

"Is everything okay?"

I try to imagine him yelling at Alex in front of the whole cast, making some big humiliating scene, but I just can't picture it. It's so . . . *un-Eli.*

I don't know why Mum would lie, but—actually, scratch that. I know exactly why she would lie: to get her own way. It certainly wouldn't be the first time.

"Yeah," I reply, forcing all thoughts of Rose Mitchell and cast parties out of my mind, "everything's fine."

"Good." He smirks. "Come with me. There's . . . something I want to show you."

He walks me over to the enormous chimney that stands outside the front of Sunnyside Mill, gesturing to the wooden door set into the red bricks. "After you."

"I'm sorry, what?"

"Go inside. It's much warmer in there. Trust me."

I look down, and see that the big brass padlock is gone. I push the door open and let out a silent gasp. The interior of the chimney—which looks much more spacious from the inside—has been converted into a comfy, cozy oasis. The hole at the top must be completely blocked off, because it would be pitch black in here if it weren't for the warm glow cast by several sets of battery-powered fairy lights strung up around the walls. The floor is covered with colorful, slightly tattered Turkish rugs, with multicolored cushions and blankets strewn all over the place. There's a little wooden shelf stacked with books against one wall—well, I guess the whole *room* is one wall, given it's round—and a big green beanbag opposite it. The brass padlock is sitting on top of an upside-down terracotta pot by the entrance.

Eli shuts the door behind him and takes off his coat. I do the same, hanging my jacket and scarf on a wooden hat stand beside the door.

It's surprisingly hot in here. Eli must notice my confusion

because he points out a small, glowing box beside the shelf. "Propane heater. Mum and I use it when we go camping."

My stomach flips, a fiery image from three years ago flickering in my mind.

"Is that . . ." I swallow, ". . . safe?"

He shrugs. "Can't burn a brick chimney down."

"The same doesn't apply to human flesh, unfortunately."

"The heater is fine," he laughs. "We use it in our tent, so it's more than safe in here. I promise. Sit."

He motions in the general direction of the floor and I take a seat on a pile of lumpy cushions. Eli sits opposite me, legs crossed, his knees almost touching mine.

"This is incredible," I say, gazing up past the fairy lights into the inky blackness above. "It's like . . . the ultimate secret cubbyhouse."

"'Secret' being the key word," Eli replies. "My boss has no idea this place exists. I don't think he even knows there's a key to the padlock. And if he does, he definitely doesn't know *I* have it." He casts his eyes around the chimney, a look of pride mixed with a soft kind of sadness on his face. "I set it up last year. It came in handy when everything went down with Alex and—" He scrunches up his nose. "Sorry, I didn't mean to bring him up."

"It's fine."

"I know. But, I mean, I haven't even told you about any of that yet."

"No," I reply, though RcticF0x knows parts of the story, "you haven't. But you don't have to, if you don't want to."

"There's not really that much to tell." He takes in a deep breath. "We started hanging out during *Oklahoma!* rehearsals last year. Everything was super cute. Alex had been out for a while, but I hadn't told anyone I was gay yet—except for my gaymer bestie—so there was a bit of an interesting dynamic between us." He grimaces. "This is too weird, isn't it?"

"It's not weird," I say. "If it's not weird for you?"

"I should have told you ages ago. I'm sure my reactions to everything Alex-related would've made a hell of a lot more sense if I had."

I shrug.

After a brief moment of quiet, he goes on. "So, we were hanging out a lot, and things kept . . . progressing, and we eventually slept together. Right in the middle of our performance week at Her Majesty's. I immediately asked him to be my boyfriend, which seemed like a perfectly reasonable request to me, but he was like, 'I don't wanna be tied down' or whatever, and then totally ghosted me. Which is not easy to do when you're in the same show, let me tell you. It was almost like a comedy routine. And it made everything super awkward on stage. I even missed a couple of cues because my head was so *not* in the building. I got in a ton of trouble from the director—our old one, who was even stricter than David, if you can believe it—and he basically obliterated me in front of the whole cast after one of our matinees. And then, if all that wasn't mortifying enough, there was an . . . *incident* at the closing night party."

Wait. Mum was telling the truth? She couldn't have been actually *looking out for me*, could she?

"An incident?"

"Not my finest moment," Eli replies, shaking his head at the memory. "I'd had way too much to drink—I'd only just started drinking, so it didn't take much—and I had a fight with Alex in the bathroom and then screamed at him in front of like, the entire cast. As if we were on one of those daytime TV shows my nan watches. But the worst part—aside from looking like a rage monster in front of everyone—was that I was so drunk that I didn't realize I was literally outing myself to the whole cast. So then it became this huge thing where I had to personally message everyone to apologize for ruining the party and to ask if they could keep my sexuality to themselves because I hadn't told my mum or my school friends, and I wasn't ready to come out, and blah blah blah, it was horrendous and my life was an absolute mess for months."

I always thought MagePants69 told me *everything*, but he never mentioned any of this. Was he too ashamed? Did he think I'd judge him? That I wouldn't want to hang out online with him anymore?

"Wow," I say quietly. "That's . . . a lot."

"Yeah," Eli replies with a grimace. "Sorry. I just wanted to be completely honest with you. I've wanted to tell you for so long. And, like I said, it probably would've made things a lot easier if I'd told you the truth from the start."

I feel myself cringe so hard internally that I'm worried my whole body is going to flip itself inside out. "Thank you for telling me. I . . . really appreciate your honesty."

"So, *anyway*," he says with a shy smile, "when all *that* was going down, I spent a hell of a lot of time in here. My secret little nook. It's where I come whenever I need to escape. I've added bits and pieces over time—the bookshelf, the beanbag. The heater is my latest winter accessory."

"Do you come here often?"

Eli chuckles.

"Sorry," I say, "I did *not* mean that to sound like a cheesy pick-up line. I meant, do you . . . do you feel like you *need* to escape the world often?"

He contemplates that for a moment, then shrugs one shoulder. "I think everyone needs to escape sometimes, don't they?"

Let's face it, if I had a private hidey-hole like this, I'd probably move in permanently.

"When I'm in here," Eli goes on, "it's like the rest of the world doesn't even exist."

I let out a long breath, looking around the circular brick room, then return my gaze to Eli.

"Which is *why* I wanted to bring you here," he says, sliding closer so that our knees are touching. "When we're together, all I ever want is to be properly *together*. Just us, you know? But there's so much out there—" he gestures to the door "—that complicates things. People, pressure, the past. And I don't want any of that to get in the way of what we have."

"But all that stuff will still exist when we leave here," I say as he places both hands on my thighs. "The people and the pressure and the past."

"I know." He nods slowly. "But at least we can have this moment together before we face the world."

Then he leans in and kisses me softly on the lips.

"Noah," he says, and I can see that his cheeks are flushed, even in the dim glow of the fairy lights. "Can I ask you something?"

I swallow. "Of course."

"Do you want to be my boyfriend?"

My heart does a backflip, swapping places with my stomach for a second, before returning to where it belongs.

MagePants69 just asked me to be his boyfriend. It happened. It actually *happened*.

"Yes, Eli," I reply, unable to stop myself from grinning like a fool. "I would love nothing more than to be your boyfriend."

He kisses me again. As I kiss him back, he leans in further and further until I'm lying down on the nest of cushions. Slowly, he lowers himself on top of me, our lips not parting for a single second. He presses his hips into mine, running one hand through my hair. I slip my arms around his back and pull him closer, relishing the feeling of his body weighing down on mine, the hardness and heat between us. Soon, jumpers are removed, zips are undone, and hands are roaming freely. It feels even better than it did in the hotel room, if that's even possible. There's something about the warmth of the chimney, the closeness of the air, the gentle glow of the fairy lights, that makes the whole thing feel even more intimate, even more electric.

We spend a long time—minutes, hours, days—gently exploring each other's bodies, finding all the parts that make each other melt, until Eli finally whispers, "Do you want to try again?"

I nod.

"You have to say it," he replies, eyes twinkling.

My pulse is pounding in my chest and my ears and my crotch. "I want to have sex with you."

"I want to have sex with you, too," he replies, before reaching over to the shelf and pulling out a box of condoms from behind a book. He rips one off the roll and holds it out to me. "Here."

"You're sure?"

"I'm sure," he replies. "I'm ready to go."

I take the condom from him and unwrap it with a smile.

"What are you smiling at?"

"Nothing," I say, carefully putting it on. "I'm just not nervous this time. At all."

Because *this* time, there's no pressure for it to be perfect, no awkward slip-ups on my behalf, no thoughts of Bards or Not-Exes ruining the moment. Here, inside the chimney, with my beautiful *boyfriend* . . .

We're the only people in the world.

THIRTY-ONE

NOAH MITCHELL. ANSWER YOUR FUCKING PHONE. I WILL NOT BE GHOSTED BY MY OWN BROTHER. (But seriously, please call me back, I'm worried about you, bub) xxx

I'm standing at my locker on Tuesday morning when I get Charly's message. I reply straightaway, mainly because I don't want her to fly down from Sydney and storm the school, demanding information as to my whereabouts.

Hey . . . I reply, but before I can type anything else, another message comes through.

HEY? Seriously, Noah. HEY?! REALLY???

Okay, chill, I reply. **I'm sorry I've been incommunicado, I've just had a lot going on.**

Finding more people to help cover up the web of lies you've spun?

Either she's joking or she knows me way too well.

It's not easy being an underground crime overlord, I write, figuring sarcasm will raise fewer alarm bells. **But I do have news . . . I have a boyfriend.**

EXCUSE ME?! Love-heart-eyes emoji. **Eli is your boyfriend? OFFICIALLY???**

Correct. And there's something else.

Go on . . .

My thumb lingers over the send button, and then, **We had sex.**

YOU HAD WHAT NOW?

I can't help but laugh.

I send back a monkey-covering-its-mouth emoji, which I figure is self-explanatory.

By the way, Charly writes, **I see what you're doing here. Distracting me with wonderful news when I'm trying to be mad at you, but I'm SO happy for you and Eli! You need to tell me EVERYTHING when I see you in two weeks for Opening Night. Including why I'm pretending to be the queen of online gaming. OKAY?**

Okay, I reply. **I promise. For now, let's just rejoice in the fact that someone liked me enough to want to be my boyfriend.**

Bub. Why do you do that? You're a total catch.

Char, I'm the fish you throw straight back into the ocean.

"Morning, Snitchell," a boy says from beside me. Hawk. I lock my phone and shove it into my blazer pocket.

"What do you want, Dylan?"

"'Dylan?'" He sneers. "No one's called me that for years."

"I don't use my mortal enemies' nicknames."

"Good one." His eyes flick to my locker and back to me. Something is going on, but I don't know what it is. "Have a great day, *Noah*." He walks off down the corridor, making a point of bumping into me as he leaves.

I glance over my shoulder to make sure Simon isn't waiting to pants me (or something equally as childish and humiliating) but there's no one there. I turn back to my locker just as Maddison Whitely (Right-Wing Barbie) sidles up to hers. She gives me a disdainful smile before spinning her combination lock. I do the same, the intricate motion ingrained in my muscle memory. When I slip off the lock and open the metal door, my eyes go wide and my hand flies to my mouth to stifle a gasp.

Because there, in the back corner of my locker, staring straight back at me, is the very last thing I ever expected to find …

Cabbage O'Reilly.

I swing the door shut with a clang but it's too late.

"Was that Mr. Conley's statue thing?" Maddison asks.

"What? No." I frantically shake my head.

"Oh my god, it *was*. Open your locker."

"No."

"Open it."

"*No.*"

Maddison turns to the busy corridor, students floating past, and shouts, "Noah stole Conley's leprechaun! Someone get a teacher!"

The floor tilts and I place a hand on my locker to stop myself from falling.

How did they do this? How long have Hawk and Simon been planning to put Cabbage O'Reilly in my locker? *When* did they do it? This morning? Yesterday? What the hell is going on?

I glance at Maddison, and one look at the triumphant expression on her face is enough to confirm her involvement. But how did she—

Wait . . . that day before media studies last term . . . we were both at our lockers . . . and she was watching me . . . and she had her *phone out* . . . .

Oh, for fuck's sake.

"You *filmed* my locker combination?"

She just pouts and shrugs one shoulder.

"What is all this about?" someone hisses from behind us, the voice instantly recognizable. The Daughter of Medusa. Of *all* the teachers who could have possibly been nearest to the Year Twelve lockers in this moment, it *had* to be her, didn't it?

"Noah is the one who stole Mr. Conley's statue," Maddison repeats for Mrs. Jamison's benefit. Her self-righteousness is nauseating. "I just saw it in his locker."

Mrs. Jamison turns her petrifying glare on me. "Is this true, Mr. Mitchell?"

Over her shoulder, I see that Hawk and Simon have come to gloat from a safe distance down the hall.

"No," I reply. "I—"

"Open your locker."

"I can't."

"And why is *that*, Mr. Mitchell?"

"Because . . ."

But you know what, enough is enough. I don't care what Hawk and Simon do to me anymore. Maybe I deserve it and maybe I don't, but I can't spend my whole life throwing myself under the bus to avoid their attacks when they're clearly never going to stop.

"Because Cabbage O'Reilly is in there," I say. "But I did *not* steal him from Mr. Conley's desk. It was Dylan Hawkins and

Simon Zhuang." I point an accusatory finger over Mrs. Jamison's shoulder at the boys, who plaster baffled expressions on their faces. "It's *always* them."

"Open. Your. Locker," Mrs. Jamison orders, without so much as a glance at the boys.

I grit my teeth and open the door, reaching in to pull out the porcelain leprechaun. It really is the ugliest thing I've ever seen.

"Here." I hand it to Mrs. Jamison, and the students gathered around us let out a collective gasp. "But I *swear* I didn't take it."

"Then how, pray tell, did it end up in your locker? Your *locked* locker?"

"Because Maddis—"

She holds up her hand. "I don't want to hear it. Come with me, Noah."

An *oooh* wafts through the huddle of students.

"You two as well." She beckons to Hawk and Simon.

"But, miss—" Hawk starts.

"Save it, Mr. Hawkins," she snaps. "My office. The three of you. *Now.*"

"Suspended?" Mum growls when I traipse through the front door two hours earlier than usual. The school must have already called her.

I sling my bag off onto the floor in the middle of the hallway. "Yep."

"Even though you told Mrs. What's-her-name it wasn't you?"

"Yep."

"Darling, that doesn't make any sense." She follows me into the kitchen. "Did Dylan and Simon get suspended, too?"

"No, they did not." I plonk myself down at one of the wooden stools at the breakfast bar. "They got a warning. Apparently, my word means nothing, and I have no evidence that proves it was them."

Once again, the truth has utterly failed me.

"But," I go on, "Mrs. Jamison said they'd been 'implicated' in my misdemeanours too many times to let them off scot-free. So, they got a metaphorical slap on the wrist and were told to stay out of trouble."

"Have those boys been . . . I mean, have they been *targeting* you or something?"

I shrug an, *I guess you could say that.*

"How long has this been going on?" Mum's voice is kind of shrill. "Did you not think you could tell me?"

"Mum," I say flatly, "what would've ever led you to believe that I would come to *you* with my problems?"

She flinches at my words. "I don't know what's going on with you, Noah, and I don't . . . but if people are hurting you, you need to *tell me.*"

"No one is *hurting* me, Mum. It's fine."

She stares at me for a long moment, like she's trying to decode my brain. Then she throws her hands in the air and says, "Well, your father is going to be furious."

"That'd be an improvement on not acknowledging that I exist."

"*Noah,*" she warns.

"I thought you'd be *happy.* I'll be able to give your precious show one hundred percent of my focus now."

"Darling, this is *not* the time to be snarky."

"Then what do you want me to do?" I say, my voice rising. "I'm just trying to find a positive in the situation. Isn't that what you learn at yoga?"

Mum presses her fingers to her eyes. "Noah, I cannot deal with this right now. The next two weeks are—"

"*Too important*," I cut in. "Yes, I'm aware."

"Good, because they should be important to you, too."

"You don't get to tell me what's important."

She takes a slow breath, lifting her palms to her chest, then pressing them calmly towards the floor as she exhales. "These are two of the biggest weeks of my life, Noah, and I refuse to let anything throw me off course. Including you. So . . . this is what we're going to do. We are going to pretend that none of this ever happened. And then *after* closing night, we'll deal with—" she slaps on a smile "—whatever this is. Okay?"

"Of *course*," I reply, pushing off my stool and heading for the stairs. "Because everything is always about you. Even when it's about me, it's *still* about you."

"Darling," she calls from the kitchen, "that is *not* fair."

"Yeah, well, life's not fair, Rose. Get used to it."

Mum is true to her word. She doesn't mention me getting suspended *once* in the two weeks that follow. I can tell Dad is furious about my suspension, but his desire to keep things civil with Mum after the Great Birthday Party Debacle clearly outweighs his need to reprimand his son.

We bump into Her Majesty's—which is ridiculous stage people talk for "moving the set into the theatre and putting our costumes in the dressing-rooms"—do two full days of tech rehearsals, a "sitzprobe" with the orchestra, then three dress rehearsals. In all that time, Mum barely even looks at me.

My dressing-room allocation is the same as my cabin allocation at Perrivale, except for Alex, who has his own principal dressing-room with a gold star on the door. Keegan seems weirdly territorial about his bench space, but Shaun, Shawn, and Steve are very chill about the whole thing, lounging around in their cheap Bonds jocks, talking about football or cricket or some other boring ball sport. Chris just jokes around, as usual, making fun of himself. Part of me really wants to tell him to stop doing that, but I'm way too awkward to have that conversation.

Weirdly, after spending a few days in the dressing-room, I notice that some of my self-consciousness seems to have disappeared. Not all of it, but definitely some. I guess all the locker room hangs with Alex were good for something, even if the workouts themselves didn't seem to achieve much.

The only downside of being at the theatre all the time is that Eli and I don't get to hang out, just the two of us. We also don't have any time to play *Spire of Dusk*, which he was very apologetic about via email to RcticF0x, who was very understanding in reply. I do enjoy sharing a dressing-room with him, though. Which obviously has *nothing* to do with the fact that he looks incredibly hot in his *Chicago* costumes. (I didn't realize I had a thing for guys in 1920s wrestling suits until I saw Eli in his "Razzle Dazzle" outfit, which is . . . I mean . . . I think another trip to the Sunnyside chimney is in order. STAT.)

Being backstage takes a lot of getting used to, because a) it's always dark, b) the wings—which are divided by long "legs" of heavy black fabric—all look the same and I never know where I'm supposed to enter and exit, and c) David said we're not allowed to so much as whisper when we're side-stage, so I have to play charades every time I want to ask where something is.

When Mum and Prisha step out onto the stage in their wigs and costumes and makeup, I barely recognize them. Mum, with a jet-black bob, blood-red lips, and smoky eyes. Prisha, wearing a honey-blonde wig and a 1920s silk nightie. They're both walking differently, holding themselves differently. Even their facial expressions seem like they belong to other people. It's like the superficial transformation has changed them at a cellular level.

I have to admit, being on stage *is* kind of fun. Scary and disorientating and overwhelming . . . but also fun. Staring out into the empty auditorium—eight hundred and ninety turquoise velvet seats; two balconies propped up by thin, Corinthian-style columns; an enormous wooden dome with gilded embellishments set into the lofty ceiling—the whole thing suddenly feels *very* real.

Then I wake up one frosty Saturday morning, and the thing we've been working towards since March is finally upon us. The nerves hit me like an electric shock. It's as if the countless rehearsals, the endless notes sessions, all that extra time spent with Eli at Sunnyside, my grueling workouts with Alex, the two whole *days* at Perrivale Camp, the never-ending technical rehearsals, the orchestra calls, the dress runs on stage—the entire lead-up to this very moment . . . It's like it never even happened.

I let out a groan and pull my doona over my head, wishing I'd talked myself out of this four months ago.

But there's no turning back now.

This is it.

It's Opening Night.

THIRTY-TWO

THE HOUSE IS BUZZING with nervous energy. I've never seen Mum so physically flustered in my entire life, and she's not even playing it up for dramatic effect. I can tell. She really is this stressed.

Charly arrives from Sydney around 11:00 a.m. and immediately starts pressing me for information about what's going on with Eli. "You're hiding something from him," she says, tailgating me into my bedroom. "Does it have something to do with you getting suspended?"

"No," I reply. "And I don't know what you're talking about."

"Did you really steal Conley's leprechaun?"

"What would I want with an ugly little leprechaun?"

"You tell me, bub. You tell me."

I eventually manage to get her off my case by telling her I'm so nervous that I might vomit at any second, and if there's one thing about Charly that hasn't changed since she left home, it's her paralyzing fear of vomit.

Dad disappears around noon, I'm guessing to the golf course.

Honestly, he may as well just move into the clubhouse and save himself the fifteen-minute commute every day. Mum seems glad to have him out of her hair though, and anything that helps reduce the tension in the house is definitely for the best. For all our sakes.

Charly makes us lunch, but Mum can't stomach it. At around 3:00 p.m., she tells us she's heading to the theatre. She says she wants to be there nice and early so she can "focus" and "get in the zone." I wouldn't know how to get in the zone if I tried. I don't think I'd even know which zone to get in.

"Chookas," Charly sings, dancing down the hall to kiss Mum on the cheek. ("Chookas" is apparently what theatre people say instead of "Good Luck," which is actually considered *bad* luck, which makes zero sense to me, as usual.) "You'll be *amazing*."

"Thanks, Char," Mum replies, half out the front door.

"See you there," I call out from the kitchen.

Mum pokes her head up over Charly's shoulder. "Don't you *dare* be late, Noah."

"I thought we were always supposed to be fashionably late?"

Mum ignores me, gives Charly an anxious squeeze, and heads off down the path to her car.

When I get to the theatre two hours later, my dressing-room is empty. I slide my backpack off my shoulders and notice a small envelope on my desk, propped up against a mason jar filled with periwinkle blue flowers.

Seriously, why is my boyfriend so adorable?

I smile and glance over my shoulder, expecting to see Eli lurking in the corridor, waiting for me to open his card, but there's no one there. He must be up in the green room already.

I tear the envelope open and pull out a square card that reads *Best of Luck* in loopy, gilded lettering. But when I open the card, I see that it's not from Eli at all.

Noah,
Chookas for your first ever Opening Night!
I know this has been a bit of a challenge,
and I know I haven't exactly made it easy for you,
but I really am glad you decided to join the cast.
Thank you for doing this for me.
CHOOKAS! Break a leg! (Have fun.)
Love Mum xoxo

I stare down at the card, trying to figure out if I feel like crying or laughing or something else entirely. I place it on my desk beside the flowers, then find myself walking upstairs to the principal characters' dressing-rooms, as if I'm in some kind of lucid dream.

I knock on Mum's door and push it open. "Mum?"

Her bag is on the bench, her make-up all laid out neatly on a bright blue hand towel, but the room is empty.

I turn and make my way down the hall to Alex's dressing-room, where I find him doing push-ups, wearing nothing but black exercise shorts.

"Alex?" I say, but he must not be able to hear me over whatever he's listening to in his headphones. "*Alex.*"

He looks up, mid-push-up, then springs to his feet. He takes out one earbud and says, "You're here early."

"Yeah, well, I didn't want to face the wrath of Rose Mitchell if I was late, and I didn't want to risk getting stuck in Ballarat's nonexistent traffic, so . . . here I am."

"You can chill here if you want," he says, before dropping into an effortless burpee.

"I was looking for Mum, actually. Have you seen her?"

Alex jumps up from the floor. "Stage?" He drops back down.

"Maybe. I'll go look." I awkwardly watch him do a couple more burpees—it's quite hard not to stare when this boy is shirtless—then say, "Chookas for tonight, Alex."

"Thanks, dude," he replies, pausing when he next jumps up to his feet. "You too."

"Are you . . . feeling okay?"

"Yep."

"Are you nervous?"

He places his hands on his hips. "Dude, when have I ever *not* been nervous?"

I chuckle, and he sucks in a deep breath, running his hands through his hair.

"Do you want to talk it out?" I ask.

"I think I'll be all right," he replies. "It's just . . . on top of already wanting to shit my pants because of the seven pages of notes David gave me after the last dress rehearsal, my agent decided to come up from Melbourne to watch the show tonight. I'm kinda feeling the pressure from all angles, you know?"

"You'll be amazing," I say with a smile. "Just be yourself."

"That's the exact opposite of what I need to do," he laughs.

"But thanks, anyway. Have fun out there."

"You too." I turn to go, but then pause. "Hey, um, thanks for . . . everything. I really did enjoy hanging out while it lasted."

"You too, dude." He claps his palms together. "Now, let's kick this show in the dick."

My eyes widen. "I'm sorry, what?"

"You've never heard that expression?" He chuckles, then adds with a shrug, "Must be a theatre thing."

I scoff. "You're all so weird."

"Get used it," he says. "You're one of us now."

And it's strange, because there's a part of me—a tiny part, hidden somewhere deep, *deep* down—that is very happy to hear him say that.

Being on stage in front of almost a thousand people feels different than what I imagined. Very different. I thought it would be like that moment in class when the teacher calls on you to solve an equation for "x," when you've been daydreaming about *Spire of Dusk* for the past twenty minutes, and you don't even know which of the twelve equations on the whiteboard she's asking you to solve. Just with fifty times as many people watching.

But it's more like riding a rickety old roller coaster—fun (if you ignore the nausea), and exhilarating, but with a slight risk of death, serious injury, and/or humiliation. It's a feeling that leaves you thrilled and giddy, and just a tiny bit wobbly in the legs.

At the end of "We Both Reached for the Gun," the audience

erupts into rapturous applause, and, for a split second that feels like a lifetime, I'm suddenly sitting in a front-row seat in the stalls, gazing straight up at myself on stage. The *Chicago* me is dressed as a 1920s reporter, wearing a plaid vest and high-waisted brown pants, holding a pencil and a pad of paper high above his head. He's drenched with sweat. Red in the face. His chest is heaving, his eyes alight with a strange mixture of relief and ecstasy. I watch as the boy holds his final pose, waiting for the applause to die down, and think to myself: *He actually likes doing this. He enjoys it. He might not completely understand it, and he might not be very good at it . . . but he* likes *it. And he might not rule out the idea of ever doing it again.*

Then the scene-change music starts and I snap back into my body, staring out at the auditorium.

Miraculously, I make it through the entirety of my first public performance without a) injuring myself, b) injuring someone else (namely Prisha), or c) making a complete fool out of myself in any of the hypothetical scenarios I mentally prepared for.

When we arrive at "Nowadays," Velma and Roxie's big finale, I conceal myself in the shadows of the downstage OP wing—how's *that* for stage terminology—to watch Mum dance.

I didn't end up finding her before the show. She didn't come to our cast warm-up on stage either, and the closer it got to curtain, the more terrified I was of going to look for her. The last thing I wanted was for her to think I was about to start a fight (which, granted, would be on-brand for me) and then blame me for making her lose her focus on stage, consequently ruining her entire life.

Halfway through the song, something brushes my back, and I have to clap a hand over my mouth to stop myself from screaming in fright. I whip around to see Eli standing in the semi-darkness behind me, stifling a chuckle. The blue light from the stage hangs shadows from the angles of his face and turns his red hair a silvery grey.

I open my eyes as wide as possible, as if to say *You scared me!* and he does a cute *sorry not sorry* shrug. He takes my hand in his and we turn to watch Mum and Prisha light up the stage.

A moment later, Alex—in a brown three-piece suit and fedora—slips into the wing behind us, his eyes glued to the stage. For a second, I think things are about to get horrifically awkward, but then Alex leans over and whispers to us, "Rose is absolutely smashing it tonight."

"She sure is," Eli replies, still gazing out across the stage.

And I may not know much about theatre, but it doesn't take a *New York Times* critic to see that Mum really is amazing out there. She's incandescent. She's electric. She's . . .

"She's incredible," I say, and Eli gives my hand a little squeeze.

"So are you," he replies, before turning to Alex. "You killed it tonight, Di Mario."

"Thanks." Alex smiles, his eyes flicking from Eli to me. "Congrats, boys." At first, I think he means congrats on our new relationship, which makes me feel hot in the face, but then he says, "Great show. Both of you."

Eli wraps one arm around my waist and pulls me close.

"We made it," Alex adds, letting out a quiet sigh of relief.

Eli kisses me softly on the cheek. "We sure did."

THIRTY-THREE

AS SOON AS WE take our bows, I grab my phone and head to Mum's dressing-room to wait for her. I still haven't figured out exactly what I'm going to say—I've never been great at conversations like this—but it'll be something along the lines of, *You were mind-blowingly incredible tonight and I'm sorry for being a terrible son and I promise I will try harder to support you and I really do love you, too, even though I am the absolute* worst *at showing it.*

While I sit in the armchair in the corner of her room, a message comes through from Charly: **BUB! WTF?! You were so great out there!**

That's a gross exaggeration, I reply. **But . . . I didn't split my pants in front of a thousand people, so that's a huge win, as far as I'm concerned.**

You're coming across the road to the party, right? Charly writes, followed by a string of alcohol-related emojis.

I'm seventeen, Char. It'll be a lemon, lime and bitters for me. But, yes, I'll meet you there soon.

Dad had to leave at interval, she replies, **(emergency brain thing) but I'm heading over now. Can't wait to squeeze you!**

No public displays of sisterly affection, please. Vomit emoji.

Whatever, bub. I'm proud of you.

After about ten minutes, Prisha walks past Mum's door and says, "What are you doing?"

"Waiting for Mum."

"She's got a meet and greet in the foyer." Prisha sounds more than a little jealous that *she* doesn't have a meet and greet in the foyer. "David just took her out through the auditorium."

"Oh," I say. "That's okay. I can wait."

"Pretty sure she's gonna be a while. But . . . suit yourself."

She walks off down the narrow corridor between the dressing-rooms. Before I can tell myself not to, I jump up from the chair and poke my head out the door.

"Prisha?"

She stops, turning around on the spot as she slips off her honey-blonde wig. Her long black hair is concealed underneath a tan stocking cap, pinned down with enough bobby pins to sink a ship. "What?"

I force a smile, pushing aside our less than pleasant history. "Well done tonight. You . . . you were fantastic. And I'm not just saying that."

"Thank you for not dropping me on my head."

"Anytime," I reply, and she bites back a smile before disappearing down the hall and into her dressing-room.

I plonk myself back down in the somewhat uncomfortable armchair and wait another ten minutes, scrolling through *Spire of Dusk* subreddits on my phone. When there's still no sign of

Mum, I make my way down to my dressing-room, deciding I'll have to save my speech of atonement for later. When I walk into the room, Eli is sitting at his station in a white T-shirt, emerald-green chinos, and white sneakers, with a string of pearls around his neck. He looks like a red-haired Harry Styles.

"You," I say, leaning down to kiss his marshmallow lips, "look incredibly hot."

He raises an eyebrow. "*You* look like you're still in costume."

"I was trying to find Mum." I unbutton my sequinned finale shirt and slip it off.

"And I *would* look hot," Eli adds, "if I wasn't wearing half an outfit."

"What do you mean?"

"Apparently, I thought it would be a great idea *not* to pack my jacket." He draws his lips into a straight line. "Which also means I'm going to freeze to death on my way to the pub."

"Take mine," I say, reaching over to grab my navy-blue jacket from its hanger on the end of the costume rack.

Eli takes the jacket and holds it up in front of his chest. "It doesn't really . . . *go*."

I scoff. "Okay, fashion police. Just wear it so you don't get hypothermia on the walk over."

"But then *you'll* get hypothermia?"

"I'll be fine," I lie. "You can give it back to me when I get there."

"You're not coming now?"

"I really need to find Mum. Meet you there in ten?"

"I can wait."

"It's okay," I say. "I don't want you to miss out on the canapés. You've been talking about those arancini for weeks."

Eli nods. "That's because those arancini are life-changing. They fill them with—"

"Just go," I say with a laugh. "I'll see you soon."

"Great job tonight," he says with an earnest grin, before planting a loud kiss on my cheek and ducking out the door.

I finish getting changed into my "party outfit," which is tan chinos, a white shirt, and my navy-blue jacket—minus the jacket, obviously—and rub some product into my still-sweaty curls. I take a quick look at myself in the mirror (you know what, I could definitely look worse) and jog back upstairs to Mum's dressing-room. When I arrive, the door is closed, which means she's finally back. I knock once. No reply. I lean my ear to the door and hear muffled voices.

"Mum?" I say, with another knock, a little louder this time.

Still no reply.

I warily turn the handle and push the door open, just enough for me to peer into the dressing-room with one eye closed, in case Mum is getting changed. But before I can close the door again, it's too late . . . .

The air in my lungs turns to lead. My face burns, red hot.

My hands drop to my sides and the door swings open to reveal a half-naked Rose Mitchell propped up on her dressing-room table. Her carefully laid out makeup strewn all over the floor. Our esteemed director standing there with his suit pants crumpled around his ankles. His hips driving into hers.

I feel like I'm going to vomit, but I can't move. I want to scream at them to stop, but my voice is nonexistent.

Mum's head snaps towards me and her eyes fill with animalistic terror.

"Noah!" she chokes out, too breathless to speak properly.

David stops thrusting and yanks his pants up to cover his junk.

"This isn't—" he starts, but we all know *exactly* what this is.

I stare at Mum, still unable to move or make a sound.

"Noah," she says again, grabbing a frilly dressing-gown and holding it over her bare chest. "I—"

But I turn on my heel and sprint down the corridor before she can finish. I barrel downstairs, past my dressing-room, through the stage door, and out into the night. I rest my hands on my knees, sucking in lungfuls of freezing July air until the wave of nausea dissipates, then set off at a jog around the block to the pub.

When I arrive outside the double wooden doors across the road from the theatre, I rub my eyes with my fists, trying to erase the image of David's bare ass clenching and unclenching as he—

Stop.

And the sounds of my mother—

Stop.

I shake my head, knuckles still pressed to my eyes.

I take a calming breath that isn't calming in the slightest and push open the door to the pub. I scan the room for Charly, but I can't see her. I pull out my phone and type a hasty, **Where are you? Need to talk.**

"Great job tonight," someone says from beside me and I turn to see a beautiful boy with neat black hair standing arm in arm with a wrinkled old woman, presumably his grandma.

"Uh, thanks," I reply, my eyes desperately searching the crowd behind them for my sister.

"Bellissima," the lady adds, grinning brightly. "We *loved* the show."

I force a smile and turn away. Jane offers me a meek smile from the other end of the bar and I manage a lifeless wave in reply. She points to the back corner of the pub, and my eyes find Eli, talking to Alex, Keegan, Prisha and—my heart clenches— Tan. As if this moment could get any worse.

I walk over, with absolutely no idea what I'm going to do when I get there. I don't want anyone to know what I just saw— *ever*—but I need to tell someone or I'm going to explode.

I need to tell Eli. And I need him to tell me everything is going to be okay.

"Here he is," Keegan says, as I reach the group. "Our little debutante!"

I feel like I'm underwater, or stuck behind some kind of veil. This doesn't feel real.

Eli, still wearing my jacket, takes a sip of beer.

"Noah smashed it tonight." Alex claps me on the shoulder.

"Yes," Prisha says, "and we're all very surprised."

Keegan laughs into his glass of wine, and I just stand there, frozen, my pulse pounding so hard my vision shakes with each beat of my heart.

"I'll be honest," Tan says to me, "I was expecting a total train wreck, but you weren't actually half bad."

"Eli," I say quietly, trying to meet his eye. He doesn't look up from his beer.

Something isn't right.

I glance over at Prisha, another wave of nausea flooding my body.

Did she tell Eli about me and Tan? Did *Tan* tell him?

"I need another drink," Keegan says, heading for the bar.

I glance over my shoulder to see if Charly has appeared (she hasn't) then turn back to the group.

"Eli," I say again, my voice strangled and weak, "I need to talk to you. Please."

Finally, he looks up, his expression painfully blank. Without a single word, he turns and walks away, placing his half-full glass on the corner of the bar and heading straight for the door.

"What's his problem?" Alex says, but I don't have time to reply.

I dart across the sticky carpet, hot on Eli's heels. I grab his hand and he whips around to face me.

"Fuck you, Noah," he whisper-shouts, tears in his eyes.

"Eli, what's—"

"No," he snaps. "I don't want to hear it."

He wrestles my jacket off, balls it up and throws it at my chest.

"Maybe check the pockets next time," he says, before storming out onto the street.

I hastily fish around in the jacket until my hand finds a ball of scrunched-up paper. I pull it out, feeling the walls close in around me.

It's the jacket I was supposed to wear to Mum's birthday dinner. The one that was slung over my gaming chair when I took Eli up to my bedroom. Where I shoved the balled-up sticky-note so he wouldn't see it.

I unfurl the yellow paper and stare down at The Plan, tears blurring my vision.

No . . .

I dart for the door and—of course—at that *exact* moment, Mum bursts through in a flowing red dress, her blonde hair tied up into a neat bun. Thank god she had time to do her hair while my whole world was falling apart.

She dashes over to me and grips me by both shoulders.

"Darling, you and I need to talk," she says quietly. Calmly. "I don't think—"

"I have nothing to say to you," I reply, my voice rising.

She winces, holding a finger to her freshly painted, glossy pink lips. "Just let me explain," she whispers. "It's . . . complicated."

"What could possibly be complicated about my mother screwing the director of her son's first musical behind her husband's back?"

"Noah, please," she hisses, "keep your voice down. This is an *adult* problem, and you—"

"Don't understand? Seriously? It seems pretty simple to me, Mum. It seems like you slept with the director so he'd give you the lead role in the show. I mean, how desperate can you possibly be?"

"Just—"

"*No,*" I shout, and a few people turn to look over their shoulders at us. "I'm leaving."

"Please stay, darling." Her face is flushed bright red, her eyes glassy, her lips trembling. "You're making a scene. I need you to—"

"I don't *care* what you need. This is about *me.*" I stab my finger to my chest. "*Me.* Not you. And I am *leaving.*"

I wrest myself from her grip, and push past her to the door.

"Darling—"

I whip around, flames erupting inside my chest. "For fuck's sake, stop calling me *darling*!"

She lets out a feeble whimper and I slam the door in her face.

THIRTY-FOUR

I CAN'T SEE ELI on the street.

I duck into the dark alley beside the pub and call him. No answer.

I message him eight times in a row—

I'm sorry.

Eli, come back.

I'm sorry, can we talk?

Please let me explain.

I'm so sorry. I'm such a jerk.

Eli, please just answer your phone.

Eli, I want to explain. I'm so sorry. You have no idea.

Please, Eli. Talk to me. I know I fucked up. I'm sorry. Shit.

—but he doesn't reply.

I call him five more times. No answer.

I even email him from my RcticF0x email address, which is probably a bit of a kick in the pants at this point, but I don't know what else to do and I need him to know how sorry I am.

I can't stay here, because Mum will be out any second to explain why she's decided to ruin our family, so I dart around the corner onto the main street and call an Uber. I almost put in Eli's address—he wouldn't have the heart to send me away if I turned up at his place—but then remember his mum has the power to throw me in jail, so a midnight visit is probably a terrible idea.

My phone pings as the Uber pulls away from the curb with me in the back seat.

Charly: **Bub, are you still here? Mum's acting super weird.**

On my way home, I write back. **Where the hell were you?**

My friends from school were down the street at this super cute new wine bar. I just went to say a quick hello. Why'd you leave? You feeling okay?

Ask our mother.

There's no way I can deal with all *that* right now. Not when Eli is ignoring me, and our relationship just publicly imploded and my life is in literal pieces.

When I get home, Dad's still out. Either his surgery was a long one, or he's ended up at the clubhouse, drinking with his golfing buddies instead of joining us at the party. He can't stand Mum's theatre friends, which suddenly makes a hell of a lot of sense.

Either way, I'm glad he's not here. Because what the hell would I say to him if he was?

I shut myself in my room and slide my chest of drawers up against the door. I know Mum will try to ambush me with some form of "woe is me, I'm poor Rose Mitchell" act when she gets home, and there's no way I can physically tolerate that tonight.

I pace around the room, my mind in a frenzy. I can't think straight. My pulse is still racing. My nerves are shot.

Eli hates me.

Mum is having an affair.

"Fuck!" I shout to no one. How the hell am I supposed to deal with this?

I wrestle myself out of my uncomfortable opening night clothes and toss them in a pile on the floor. I pull on some boxers and a T-shirt and climb into bed, where I proceed to call Eli approximately every three minutes for two hours. In between calls, I message him a constant stream of apologies. In between messages, I try not to picture Mum and David half naked in her dressing-room, or the look on Eli's face when he stormed out of the pub.

In between all of that, I cry.

And cry.

And swear.

And cry.

Until I somehow fall asleep.

"Noah," Mum says through the door the next morning. I've been ignoring her attempts at communication for over an hour, so I don't know why she thinks I'll respond now. "Open the door."

I pull the covers over my head. My phone starts vibrating on the bedside table and I flip the doona off my face to glance at the screen: *Mum.*

"Answer the phone!" she yells from the hallway. "We need to talk."

I decline the call and type out a message, my thumbs hammering the screen.

I'm never talking to you again. And I quit the show. Oh, and fuck you.

There's a brief moment of silence while Mum reads my message, and then she starts thumping on the door.

"Open the damn door, Noah. And don't you dare speak to me like that. You're not quitting anything."

Another voice says, "Mum, what the hell? It's eight-thirty."

"Charlotte, tell your brother to open the door."

"Charly," I yell back, "tell Mum to tell you what she did last night."

"She already knows," Mum says. "Let me in."

I message Charly straight away: **WTF Char. You know??**

She told me last night, Charly replies. **On the way home from the pub. I know it's a lot to process, bub, but it's more complicated than you think. Just let her in. Talk to her.** Love-heart emoji.

I glare down at the screen, incredulous. **Fuck. That.**

There's some mumbling from the hallway, and then a loud bang as the door jerks ajar, the chest of drawers sliding across the carpet just enough for Mum to slip through into my room.

"Go away," I say, pulling the doona back over my head. Mum sits on the end of my bed and places a gentle hand on my foot. I jerk it away under the covers. "Don't touch me."

"Noah, please. We need to talk." She sounds exhausted.

"Isn't *Dad* the one you should be talking to right now?"

"He's at the golf course."

I don't reply.

Mum lets out a heavy sigh. "I'm sorry you had to find out like this, Noah. It must have been . . . I mean, no one needs to see their parents doing that. Especially not with other people."

I flip the doona off my face, feeling waves of white-hot anger washing over me. "This is not a *joke*, Mum."

"Do I look like I'm joking?" she asks, and no, she doesn't. She looks drained. Depressed. Broken.

"Whatever." I go to pull the covers back over my head but Mum pulls them away.

"Darl—" She stops herself. "*Noah*. We need to talk about this."

"What is there to say, Mum? I thought David was *harassing* you. This whole time. I was legitimately worried about your safety and you were having a fucking *affair*. Have you even *told* Dad?"

Mum purses her lips. "Not yet."

"Then we have *nothing* to talk about."

"Look," she says quietly, "I know this makes no sense to you now, but one day you will understand how things like this happen. How people . . . how someone can make you feel like you're—"

"Mum, I am not sitting here while you try to defend yourself. You screwed up. This is your fault. It's your job to fix it."

"That's not . . ." She picks at her manicured nails. "It's not that simple."

"I don't care," I snap. "Leave me alone. I already have enough to deal with."

She pats my foot and stands up, straightening her dressing gown. "I'll let you sleep, then. We can talk about it before we go to the theatre for tonight's show."

I can't help but scoff. "Mum, I'm serious. I *quit*. I'm not doing *Chicago* anymore."

Her eyes go wide. "You can't just *quit*, Noah. Everyone is relying on you. You're—"

"Yeah, and I was relying on *you* to be a good mother and a faithful wife, and look how that turned out."

She bites her lip and glances out the window, her blue eyes filling with tears, before she slips out into the hallway.

Within seconds, Charly is in my room, taking Mum's place at the end of my bed.

"Bub, please just let her talk to you," she urges. "You don't—"

"How can you defend her?" I ask, scrambling out of bed and pulling on some clothes. "Did you know about this?"

"Of course not," she replies. "But, I mean, I'm also not surprised."

I shake my head at her, infuriated by her indifference.

"I need to get the hell out of here," I say, slipping on a jumper and grabbing a pair of sneakers. "I cannot handle this. Not on top of everything else that's going on."

"What do you mean?" Charly's brow creases. "Did something else happen last night? With Eli? Is that why he wasn't at the party either?"

"Yes, Char. Something else happened. With Eli. And I need to fix it. So, please excuse me if I leave our car crash of a mother to deal with her own problems for once, while I go and sort out mine."

"I have to leave for the airport in like, two hours," she says. "Can't you just stay and we'll figure this out? We need to talk to Mum."

"I'm not talking to *that woman* until she tells Dad what she's done."

"Bub, seriously, just—"

"No!" I shout, snatching my CHGS backpack off the floor. "I need to do this."

Charly stands up, watching as I shove clothes into the bag. "Why are you packing?"

"Because I'm leaving. I can't be in this house right now."

"Then . . . I'll come with you. Until I have to get the train."

"I don't need your help, Char. I can handle this myself."

"Can you?" She folds her arms. "Because it seems like you've handled the whole thing with Eli pretty fucking terribly so far."

Her words are like daggers. Mainly because she couldn't be more right.

"Screw you, Char." I grab a beanie and shove it onto my head like it's an exclamation mark. I zip up my backpack and storm downstairs, straight through the front door, and out into the frosty July air.

I don't go to the theatre that night. I know I'm letting everyone down. I know I'm probably making things incredibly difficult for them.

But I don't care.

My phone buzzes all afternoon while I walk aimlessly around the shops in town. I check every time to see if it's Eli, but it never is. I don't bother reading any of the messages. I know what they'll all say.

You're ruining the show.

You're so selfish.

You're an awful person.

You don't deserve Eli, anyway.

When it gets to 6:00 p.m.—the time I'm supposed to be at the theatre—my phone practically explodes with messages and calls.

Mum, Charly, Alex, Pania, Keegan, Chris. Numbers I don't even have saved in my phone.

Everyone but Eli.

A message comes through from Prisha, and this—for some reason, out of the millions of messages I've received today—is the one I decide to open.

Noah Mitchell, get your ass to the theatre RIGHT NOW or I will tell every soul in this building EXACTLY what you did to my brother. See if Eli forgives you after that.

My reply is simple: **Tell them whatever you want. I don't care anymore.**

I hit send, turn my phone off, and keep walking.

I know I can't go home, but I don't know where else to go. It's moments like this when I wish I still had friends. In the end, I walk up to the top end of the main street, towards St. Tom's and the other private schools, and check myself into a boutique hotel using Dad's credit card.

I wonder if he knows about Mum yet . . . .

I turn my phone on, ignore the barrage of notifications, and send him a message.

Hey. I'm staying at a friend's place tonight. I'll get myself to school tomorrow. I also type, **I hope you're okay,** but then delete it. As soon as I send the message, I turn my phone off again and flop back onto the bed.

Did I really think the truth would never come out?

Did Mum think the same about her and David?

Am I just as bad as her for lying to Eli all this time?

Am I *worse*?

Maybe Tan and Hawk and Simon were right to cut me out of their lives. Maybe I *deserve* to be alone. Maybe Eli will be better off without me.

"*Fuck!*" I beat my fists on the bed.

I had a *boyfriend*. The boyfriend I've wanted since the second I spoke to MagePants69 online over a year and a half ago. And he liked me. By some absurd stroke of luck, he actually *liked* me.

Skinny, pimply, nerdy, awkward, snarky, no-friends *me*.

And I ruined it. I ruined everything.

THIRTY-
FIVE

WHEN I WAKE UP the next morning at dawn—can you still call it "waking up" if you didn't actually sleep?—I turn on my phone to check if Eli has called or messaged or emailed overnight, even though I'm certain he wouldn't have. The second the home screen lights up, a call comes through from Alex.

I stare down at the phone, waiting for him to hang up, but he doesn't. It just keeps on ringing.

"What the . . ." I wait a moment longer, then take a deep breath and press accept. "Alex?"

"Meet me out the front of Lakeside Fitness at seven-thirty," he says.

"What? I'm . . ." I glance over at my school backpack, trying to remember if I even packed any gym clothes.

"Just come," he urges. "Please."

"Alex . . . I can't."

He's obviously planning to talk me into *un*-quitting the show, and I don't think I could handle even the slightest amount of confrontation before my first day back at school since my Cabbagegate suspension.

Alex must somehow read my mind from across town, because he says, "It's just a workout. I promise," and hangs up.

I check out of the hotel and walk straight to Lakeside Fitness. It's only a few blocks but it's dangerously close to home, so my heart beats a frantic rhythm the whole way there. I can't tell what I'm more nervous about—going back to school, running into Mum or Dad, seeing Alex, or never seeing Eli ever again. The more I think about the current state of my existence, the more I want to throw up all over the footpath.

When I arrive at the gym, Alex is waiting out front.

"You came," he says, with a stiff wave.

"So it seems," I reply, mirroring the gesture.

"It's been a while since we've done a workout. You reckon you'll survive?"

"I guess we'll soon find out."

Alex takes me through one of his standard back and biceps workouts—which is a complete struggle after not doing any exercise other than the show for over a month—and doesn't say a word about *Chicago*. Not one. He barely says anything at all.

After the workout, we head into the locker room, and he says, "We should do this again."

"Yeah," I reply, still suspicious. "Maybe."

We start to undress in silence, and I brace myself for the moment when he brings up the show. But it never comes. We shower, put on our school uniforms and leave the gym, and still nothing. Alex hugs me goodbye and starts walking off towards

St. Peter's—which is the opposite direction of CHGS—and I can't bear the sequinned elephant in the room a second longer.

"I'm sorry!" I call out.

He stops. Turns around. Doesn't say anything.

"I know I'm an asshole for quitting the show," I say, throwing my hands in the air. "I know that. It's just . . . there's this thing with my mum. And with Eli. Everything is completely fucked up and I'm sorry and . . . I don't know. The thought of being at the theatre with both of them . . ." I bite my lip to stop myself from crying.

Alex still doesn't reply, but he starts walking back along the sandy gravel path towards me, his expression as nonchalant as ever.

"I know I'm being selfish," I say. "I know I'm probably ruining the show for everyone. But I just—" I wipe a stray tear from my cheek "—I can't come back."

"Look," Alex says calmly, right in front of me now, "I don't know exactly what's going on with Eli, but I heard what happened with your mum, and—"

"Aren't you at least going to yell at me for quitting?" I glare back at him. "Try to guilt me into coming back? Or . . . or is everyone *glad* I quit?"

Alex furrows his brow. "What?"

"Prisha told everyone what happened with her brother, didn't she? And now no one wants me to come back to the show? I fucking *knew* this would happen."

"Dude, I have literally no idea what you're talking about." He shakes his head. "Why would anyone *not* want you to come back? Did you not read any of your messages yesterday?"

"I . . ." I place my hand on my pants pocket, feeling my phone through the grey fabric. "No."

Alex turns to go. "I'm sorry, but I need to run. I'm gonna be late."

"Wait, what do you—"

"Read the messages!" he calls out over his shoulder as he jogs off down the path and across the road. Within seconds, he disappears behind the perimeter hedge of one of the lakeside mansions that line the opposite side of the road.

I slip my phone out of my pocket and click into my messages. I scroll down to the first text from yesterday afternoon, which came through at 2:33 p.m.

Alex: **Dude, Rose said you're not doing the show tonight? Are you okay?**

The next one is from Charly: **Bub, I'm so sorry. I didn't mean to get sassy. Please call me so we can talk this through. I love you.**

Then Mum: **Noah, please answer your phone. I'm worried about you.**

Alex: **Noah, call me back. I just want to help.**

Keegan: **Um, so I heard what happened. Are you okay, babe? That fucking sucks.**

Chris: **Hey Noah. If you need someone to talk to, I'm here, okay?**

Alex again: **Eli said you guys broke up?? Fuck, dude. I'm so sorry. Are you okay?**

(Unknown): **Noah, it's Luana. I know we're not exactly besties, but Keegan told me what happened with your mum and it fucking sucks and if you need to vent to someone who** knows what it feels like, let me know, yeah?

Pania: **Don't worry about the show, Noah. We'll figure it out. You do what you need to do.**

(Unknown): **Mate, I'm sorry about you and Eli. You guys are bloody great together. And I can lift Prisha on my own, so don't stress. Steve.**

Alex: **Dude, are you okay?**

Alex: **Let me know if you need anything, all right?**

Alex: **Noah. Call me. Please.**

The messages go on and on and on. I read them with tears streaming down my face. Every single text is someone else asking if I'm okay. No one blames me for ruining anything. No one says I'm a horrible person. They're all just checking in. As if—

I take in a breath and look up to the cloudy, grey sky. A wave of emotion crashes down on me.

As if they're my friends.

THIRTY-SIX

MONDAY MORNING APPLIED COMPUTING has never been more awkward. I'm met with a wall of whispers when I walk into the lab, every single person staring at me out of the corner of their eye. Even though no one could irrefutably *prove* it was me who stole Cabbage O'Reilly, the general CHGS consensus is that it was one hundred percent my crime, and I did *not* do the time. I'm pretty sure if you did a poll with the students, the over-whelming response would've been "expel Noah Snitchell."

Hawk and Simon scowl as I take my seat in the row in front of them, but I know they won't do anything to me here. I'm sure they're planning something big—the biggest yet—but whatever it is, it won't go down at school. Not when they're finally on Mrs. Jamison's radar.

It's Conley, though, who is the most awkward about my return. He can barely even look at me. Every time I glance over at his desk, he places a gentle hand on Cabbage O'Reilly's porcelain head, like he's worried I'm going to jump up, nab his precious little ornament, and do a runner.

But the thing is, when your boyfriend broke up with you because he thinks you're a dirty liar (which you *are*) and you just found out your mum is having an extramarital affair, the very least of your problems is an alleged crime involving a teacher's *leprechaun*.

We don't have a show on Monday night, and I already checked out of the hotel, so I'm not sure where to go. I contemplate messaging Alex to ask if I can come over, but I don't think I could handle having to talk about what happened, and I only packed one spare pair of underwear. Which leaves me with only one option . . .

I have to go home.

By the time I get there—after doing an aimless lap of Lake Wendouree while contemplating my family's crumbling existence—it's almost 5:00 p.m. The sky is already turning pink.

I open the front door and call out a tentative, "Hello?" but no one replies. The lights are all off.

I walk into the kitchen, and there's Mum, hunched over the marble breakfast bar, her hand loosely gripping a glass of white wine. I drop my bag onto the tiles and her head jerks up.

"Oh," she says, clearly coming out of some kind of daydream, "you scared me."

I suddenly feel like a visitor in my own home. Should I sit? Should I stand? Should I walk straight back out the door?

"Are you okay?" Mum asks, placing her glass on the marble bench top. "I've been worried."

"About me? Or about the show?"

She purses her lips and says nothing for a long while.

Finally, she motions to the breakfast bar and says, "Sit."

"I'm fine." I fold my arms.

She takes a sip of wine. "Your father . . ." She pauses, draining her wineglass. "Your father is staying at a hotel for a while."

The air around me seems to grow colder.

"Okay," I reply. "Is he . . . coming back?"

Mum gets up and pours herself another glass of wine by the sink.

"I don't know."

"What do you mean you don't know?"

She slowly turns around, her eyes glistening. "I . . . I asked him for a divorce this morning."

Time stops for a second, like someone took a photo of this scene and I'm staring down at the image. Like I'm flicking through a family album and saying to myself, *Remember this? This was the exact moment when your family fell apart.*

"Oh," is all I can say as tears build behind my eyes.

Mum sucks in a shaky breath, looking like she desperately wants to collapse into someone's arms. Probably David's. The image is enough to turn my stomach to molten lead.

This is all her fault.

I turn to walk away and Mum says, "Noah, please just sit with me?"

But I can't fix this for her. For any of us.

After school on Tuesday, I take shelter from the incessant rain in a cafe around the corner from CHGS. I sit there, drinking cup after cup of tea, trying to figure out if I've made the right decision.

At some point during tea number four, some kids around my age burst into the cafe, laughing and shaking raindrops from their hair. One of them—a handsome white boy with too-perfect posture—offers me a polite smile on his way to a table in the back corner. Another guy—a buff East Asian guy who could give Alex Di Mario a serious run for his money in the "strutting" department—takes a seat next to his friend, putting an arm around him and planting a lingering kiss on his cheek. Okay, *more* than friends, then. The two girls—one short and curvy and wearing a bright pink hijab, the other tall and blonde and remarkably like an Elf from *Spire of Dusk*—sit opposite the boys, still giggling uncontrollably. They're like a walking advertisement for Best Friends™.

I watch them out of the corner of my eye, a dull hollowness spreading through my chest. Perfect Posture catches my eye and smiles again, and I hastily turn back to my tea.

I drain the last few drops from my cup and head back out into the rain.

I don't want to be late for the show.

My return to *Chicago* is two things:

1. Kind of nice.

The cast is overtly warm and welcoming, and I don't even think they were instructed to act that way. Even Prisha is civil. It turns out that—for all her threats—she didn't end up telling anyone my little secret (my *other* little secret). Plus, now that the show is open and David's job is technically done here, he's disappeared back down to Melbourne, which means I don't have to see his face every day and be reminded of The Thing I Will Never Think of Again. Mum is clearly devastated that he's not around anymore—I try my best to ignore this fact—but at least the lack of David seems to be providing a small amount of distraction from the dissolution of her twenty-year marriage.

And 2. Incredibly painful.

Eli moves into a different dressing-room, and he won't even look at me—on stage or off. My first night back, I stand side stage while the girls are doing "Cell Block Tango" and I can't help but feel like they're singing about me. *I* had it coming. I had it coming *all along* and I did nothing to stop it.

I know I deserve the silent treatment from Eli. I do.

But that doesn't mean it doesn't hurt like hell.

From Tuesday night's performance onwards, I stop trying to contact him. No calls, no messages, no emails. He's made it very clear that he wants nothing to do with me, so I need to respect that. (For now.) I just wish Mum would do the same for me. She keeps trying to talk to me at home and at the theatre, but I can't. I won't.

I don't have anything to say.

I log onto *Spire of Dusk* on Thursday after school, hoping in vain that Eli might have logged on too, but there's no sign of the Half-Elf Bard.

Our dynamic duo is finally done for.

I decide to carry on with our campaign alone. It's not easy fighting solo through quests that are built for two or more players, but my Warrior is stronger than ever, and playing the game at least gives me something to do, aside from stressing about Eli. Of course, *Spire of Dusk* is a constant reminder of just how much I screwed everything up, but . . . I feel like finishing our campaign will, I don't know . . . not *fix* things, but . . . If I can defeat Queran and the Vampires of the Vale, I will have done at least *something* right this year, and all our hard work won't have been for nothing.

I also decide to start going to the gym with Alex again. Now that I don't have to hide it from anyone, I look forward to our workouts more than most things in my day. I'm obviously never going to look like Alex—and there's a tiny part of me that's starting to believe that's actually *okay*—but working out just feels good. You turn up, do the exercises, and go. It's predictable. It's easy. Well, not *physically* easy, it's physically horrendous. But it's so nice to feel completely in control of one thing when the rest of your life is in fucking shambles.

Before I know it, we've arrived at our final performance of *Chicago*. Months of work—literal blood, sweat, and tears—and after two short weeks of shows, we're done.

It's almost unfathomable.

Chicago has become such a big part of my day-to-day existence—which I never thought I'd say about some old musical from the 1970s—and I almost can't imagine my life without it.

When we take our final bow, a weird hollowness fills my chest. It's a strange sadness, a dull ache that feels a little like longing, but with a bitter twinge of something I can't quite put my finger on. Regret? Loss? I can't tell if what I'm feeling has to do with the show itself, or the cast, or the fact that Eli will be gone from my life, once and for all, as soon as the curtain falls.

(You know what, it's probably that last one.)

And then there's the closing night party.

THIRTY-
SEVEN

THE PARTY DOESN'T START till after bump out, which is where we get all of our shit *out* of the theatre.

I catch a lift to Beth's and Pania's house with Steve and the other straight guys. I will do anything to avoid Mum's attempts at reconciliation, including sitting in a dual-cab ute with three guys talking about AFL and roof cladding.

When we arrive, the party is already in full swing. I expected more of a "wine and cheese and listening to old Broadway vinyls" kind of situation, but this is a legitimate party. Everyone is laughing and drinking and dancing. Everyone is just so . . . happy.

My first order of business is to get a drink. If I'm going to finally talk to Eli—which I wholeheartedly plan to do tonight— I'm going to need some loosening up. It's probably a terrible coping strategy, but you know what? I don't care. When you've gone from sitting alone in your bedroom playing computer games every night, to attending the cast party of a musical— that you *performed in*—in four very short months, you get to cut yourself a bit of slack.

I grab a can of beer and find Keegan and Chris in the lounge room, arguing about something musical related, as usual.

"Jennifer's version is good, but it's not the best," Keegan says.

"Oh, please," Chris replies, swishing his can of bourbon and cola a little too spiritedly and sloshing a bit onto the couch. "Whoops."

"I'm *serious*," Keegan presses. "It's Nicole, hands down. No one can out-sing that bitch. Pussycat Dolls for life."

"Whatever, you're ju—"

"Guys," I interrupt. "Sorry, I'm sure this conversation is incredibly important—"

"Uh, vital."

"—but have you seen Eli? I, um . . . need to talk to him."

"Oooh," Keegan says. "Is this the big, cinematic apology moment?"

Chris laughs.

"Something like that," I reply.

"He was here when we arrived," Keegan says with a shrug.

"Haven't seen him for a while, though," Chris adds. "But while you're here—who sings the best version of 'Memory' from *CATS*? You can be our deciding vote."

"Is that the song with the tap-dancing cockroaches?"

Keegan purses his lips. "No, no, no, honey. That's—don't even bother. Bye, girl."

He shoos me away, and I head out the back door onto the deck. There are paper lanterns strung from the balustrade, casting a faint glow over the unruly garden beyond. Sitting at a wooden outdoor table by herself is Prisha. She turns when she hears me slide the door closed.

"I just needed some air for a second," she says. "Everyone is already so drunk."

I hold up my can of beer. "Not me. Yet." I wrap my arms around my chest. "It's freezing out here."

Prisha shrugs. "How's your mum?"

"Right now?"

She rolls her eyes. "No, smart-ass. I mean how is she about your dad. About the . . ."

"Divorce?" I'm almost used to the "D" word now, which is hardly something I ever anticipated. "I don't know. I think she's more upset about David going to back to Melbourne, to be honest."

"I'm sorry," Prisha says. "For what it's worth."

"Thanks." I take a sip of beer. It's bitter and bubbly and not that nice. Maybe I should've tried the vodka. "And, um . . . thanks for not telling anyone about Tan."

"I mean, you probably won't believe me," she replies, "but it was Tan who convinced me to keep it to myself."

"What?" I feel my brow scrunch. "Why?"

She shakes her head. "Who knows. And thank *you* for not spilling the beans about me, either."

"Well, there were barely any beans to spill."

"Except that I'm a total music theatre failure?"

"You're not a failure," I reply, and I really do mean it.

"Funny you should say that," Prisha says, one eyebrow arched. "Alex's agent came to the show on opening night, and she offered to represent me."

"What?" I gasp. "Prisha, that's amazing."

"I know," she laughs. "She missed my awful showcase

performance because she was overseas—thank *god*—and she said she would be 'thrilled' to represent me. I'm moving to Melbourne next week to start auditioning for shows."

"Holy shit," I say, feeling like I should hug her or high-five her or something. "That's nuts, Prisha. And so soon!"

"It's a little stressful, but . . ." She looks up at the cloudless night sky, dotted with stars. "It's like, so weird how things just work out sometimes, isn't it?"

My thoughts return to Eli and my stomach clenches.

"Have you seen Eli?" I ask.

"I'm pretty sure he left," Prisha replies, looking towards the house. "Maybe twenty minutes ago?"

Disappointment spills down my spine in a cold trickle. "Oh. Right. Do you know where he went?"

She shakes her head. "Sorry."

But then it comes to me, like a spark in the night.

I know *exactly* where Eli would be.

"Well, congrats on the agent and Melbourne and everything," I say, already heading to the sliding door. "I'm happy for you. Really."

"Thanks," Prisha calls out. "I hope you sort your shit out, too. Really."

I offer her a brief smile and slip back into the house.

I make my way to the kitchen, toss my barely touched can of beer in the bin and march around the house until I find Mum, standing in the hallway talking to Pania and Sierra.

"Mum," I say, and she turns to me, stunned. Which I guess is warranted, given I haven't spoken to her in days.

"Noah?"

"I need you to drive me somewhere," I say.

She frowns. "Is everything okay?"

"It will be. I just . . . Can you please take me?"

"Right now? I'm—" She glances at the other women and back to me, and I brace myself for a big fat N-O. But then she blinks away a thought and says, "Yes. Okay."

She follows me out to the car and climbs into the driver's seat, turns the ignition, and pulls out of the driveway.

"Wait," she says. "Noah, where are we going?"

I buckle my seatbelt, and turn to face the road.

"We're going to get my boyfriend back."

THIRTY-EIGHT

I KNOCK THREE TIMES on the wooden door to the chimney out the front of the Sunnyside Mill.

"Eli?" I ask of the door, but there's no reply.

I glance around the curved, red-brick wall at Mum's car. She has the lights on inside, and I can see her concerned expression from here. She said she was happy to wait in the car while I did what I needed to do, and for Rose Mitchell to miss her own closing night party for her son's sake . . . well, let's just say there's a first time for everything.

I knock again, harder this time.

A voice from behind the door says, "Go away. You don't exist right now."

"What?" I frown at the weathered wood. "Eli, just—"

But then I remember. *When I'm in here, it's like the rest of the world doesn't even exist.*

"Eli, I do exist," I say. "Even though you don't want me to. Just . . . let me in. Please."

I stare at the door expectantly, but it still doesn't open. I lean my forehead against the scratchy wood, looking down at the wrought iron door handle. Only now does it hit me that, with the padlock *inside* the chimney, I could easily turn the handle and open the door myself. Unless Eli has barricaded himself in, *Les Miserables* style, which is a strong possibility. Either way, I have no doubt that invading his private space in a moment like this would be the final nail in our relationship's proverbial coffin.

So I wait.

I'm shivering now, the midnight cold piercing straight through my T-shirt and flimsy jacket. (No, not *that* jacket.) I want to bang on the door and beg Eli to let me into the warmth of the chimney . . . .

But I don't.

I wait.

And I wait . . . .

Something icy touches the bare skin of my neck and sends a shiver down my spine, like I've been shot with a frost arrow on *Spire of Dusk*. I look up to the night sky and almost laugh.

You have *got* to be kidding me.

It's *snowing*.

I hold out my hand to catch a couple of the floating flakes and watch them melt on my palm. It only snows in Ballarat once every couple of years—actually, I think I was in Year Eight the last time it snowed—so *of course* the heavens have decided to blanket the city with ice at the exact moment I'm shut outside the Sunnyside Mill trying to win back the love of my life.

I knock one more time and say, "Um, I don't want to be dramatic or anything, but it's kind of, uh . . . snowing out here."

The door immediately creaks open, just a tiny bit. I can only see one of Eli's emerald eyes through the crack, but I can tell he's been crying.

"Hi," I say as gently as I can manage through my chattering teeth.

He opens the door and a breath of warm air escapes the chimney. "Come in," he says, glancing up at the falling snow. "But only because I don't want to be held responsible for you freezing to death."

I step into the fuzzy heat of the chimney. Eli closes the door behind us and reaches over to turn off the bluetooth speaker that's balancing on a pile of books on the wooden shelf.

"Happy closing night," I offer, but Eli just folds his arms and stares back at me. "Can we talk?"

"I don't know what there is to talk about," he replies, lowering himself onto the floor.

I follow his lead, making sure to leave a suitable buffer of colored cushions between us, even though my body is longing to be close to him.

"You don't have to say anything," I start, crossing my legs. "It's . . . I just wanted to apologize."

Eli lifts his eyebrows, his face otherwise impassive.

"I am so, *so* sorry for lying to you. And I don't expect you to forgive me—ever—but I thought you at least deserved to know the whole story."

"I'm not interested in your justifications."

"I'm not trying to justify anything," I reply, already wishing this was easier. Simpler. "The last time we were here, you told me *everything*. You told me the whole truth, and you deserve to hear the same from me. Regardless of what you think of me when I'm done."

Eli twists his mouth to one side, his eyebrows furrowed. "If you must."

"Don't, um—"I wipe the tip of my nose, which is still dripping from the cold "—don't feel like you need to say anything. I'll talk and you can listen. Okay?"

"Fine." Eli clasps his hands in his lap. There's a defiance in his eyes that makes me feel like he doesn't really want to hear what I have to say, but I'm grateful he's letting me talk to him at all. That he allowed me into his secret nook in the first place, when he owes me literally nothing.

"So . . ." I crack my knuckles. "I don't have any friends. I mean, I *didn't* have any friends. Before I joined the cast. And I promise this is not some big attempt to make you feel sorry for me, I'm just . . . I need you to know everything."

Eli shrugs.

"Up until halfway through Year Nine," I say, "I was best friends with Prisha's brother, Tanesh. Tan. Him and me and these two other guys from school—Simon and Hawk—were inseparable. They were the ones who introduced me to gaming, a million years ago. We played everything together—PC, Xbox, PlayStation, old Gameboys Tan's dad found in their garage—every spare hour of every day. Until they cut me out of their lives completely." I glance over at the fairy lights, finding it hard to look Eli in the eye. "Barely anyone knows what happened between me and Tan and the boys. It's really only us, our families, and our vice principal from CHGS, but . . ." I can already feel the swell of emotions inside my chest. "Okay, so . . . in Year Nine, we went on this school camp down in Wilson's Promontory. I was sharing a cabin with Tan and Hawk and Simon, which was obviously perfect. The whole *thing* was perfect until . . ."

Eli narrows his eyes, and I can tell he's thinking back to that night in our cabin at *Chicago* rehearsal camp.

"The boys had been . . . *experimenting* for a few months," I go on, already hating that I have to say all of this out loud. "Not sexually," I add, seeing the look on Eli's face. "I mean with . . . things. Alcohol, mainly. Cigarettes. Vapes. Hawk's cousin's Ritalin. They were already fifteen but I was still fourteen—not that it really matters—and I was even more of a nerd back then than I am now. I'd never broken a single rule. And I just . . ."

I wipe my clammy palms on my jeans to give myself a moment to breathe.

"That night after lights out, the boys turned on their phone torches, and Simon pulled this glass bottle out of his backpack. He held it up to the rafters like it was the Holy Grail or baby Simba or something, and told us it was this homemade bourbon that a friend of a friend of his makes in his basement, and that it was almost *seventy percent* alcohol."

I expect Eli to react to that part, but he doesn't, so I just keep going.

"They all took turns doing shots straight out of the bottle, trying to act all chill and macho—even though they couldn't stop coughing because they'd basically swallowed lava—and I was just sitting there on my bottom bunk, watching. Thinking I was probably about to die of alcohol poisoning, because I'd barely had a sip of *regular* alcohol at this point, let alone some weirdo's double-strength basement bourbon. But . . . I didn't want to look like a complete loser in front of the boys, so when it was my turn, I took this massive swig, *choked*, and spat it out all over my sheets. Which they thought was the funniest thing that'd ever happened. And *then*, as if drinking alcohol on school camp wasn't already bad enough, Tan went to his bag and pulled out a *joint* and one of those old-school zippo lighters—you know those metal ones with the flip-top that they always use in action films and—"

"I'm familiar," Eli cuts in, and I get the feeling I need to move this along.

I clear my throat. "I had no idea where a Year Nine would've even gotten weed, but rich kids have a way of getting whatever they want, and Tan and Prisha are the richest people I know, and . . . Anyway, Tan decided *I* should be the one to try the weed first. Probably because I'd made it very clear that I thought the whole thing was incredibly irresponsible. So, he shoved the joint into my hand, held the lighter out in front of my face—already lit—and stood there waiting for me. Like it was some kind of challenge. A test."

I take a quick breath and keep going, before I can convince myself not to.

"I told the boys that we didn't know what the hell we were doing. That we were only *kids*, that we were going to get in massive trouble, that someone might get hurt . . . but they wouldn't listen. They thought it was hilarious. They kept calling me a loser and a pussy and told me I was overreacting and I started crying and I felt sick and Tan kept shoving the flame closer and closer to my face and I just—"

I stop for a second as the feeling of being in that cabin floods my body. The adrenaline. The nausea. The chilling dread.

"I lost it," I say, guilt joining the awful mix of emotions swirling in my stomach. "I knocked the lighter out of Tan's hand and he dropped it on my bed, right where I'd spat out the bourbon."

Eli stares back at me in the dim glow of the fairy lights, his neutral expression starting to crack.

"There was this *whoosh*—" I make a little explosion in the air with my hands "—and the whole bed was on fire. I guess the alcohol and the cotton sheets . . . it was honestly like a fireball in *Spire of Dusk*."

"Fuck," Eli says under his breath, then, "sorry. I didn't mean to say that out loud."

"It's all right," I say with a weak smile. "So . . . anyway, it was a legitimate miracle that none of us got hurt, aside from a few singed eyebrows. The teachers called our parents to tell them we were okay, and none of them seemed super keen about driving five hours in the middle of the night to check for themselves, so we just went back to bed. In a different cabin, obviously, because the other one was in no state for a slumber party."

"And did the—" Eli starts, but then holds his hands up. "Sorry, I'll let you tell the story."

I swallow and go on. "The next morning, our vice principal showed up to question us about the fire. Tan told us to say that a spark from one of our phone chargers must have set the sheets alight while we were sleeping, but I knew Mrs. Jamison wouldn't buy that. By the time it was my turn to be interrogated—lucky last—I still had no idea what I was going to say. But then our PE teacher burst into the room and handed Mrs. Jamison a ziplock bag with Tan's metal lighter inside—a bit melted, but *clearly* still a lighter—and I knew it was all over."

Eli lets out a slow breath, and even though this is the *very* last thing I ever wanted to tell him, it's too late to stop now.

"And so . . . I panicked," I say, shaking my head. "I knew that if none of us fessed up, we'd *all* be expelled. Guaranteed. And that was *not* an option for me. But there was no way the boys would ever own up to drinking and doing drugs on school camp and burning a fucking cabin down, so . . . I told Mrs. Jamison the truth. The whole truth. Every single detail."

"And she believed you?"

"Why wouldn't she?" I reply. "I was Noah Mitchell—I'd never done anything wrong in my entire life. And then when Mrs. Jamison questioned Tan for a *second* time, he threw himself under the bus. He told Mrs. Jamison that the whole thing was his fault. That it was *his* alcohol. *His* weed. That the rest of us hadn't even *touched* it. I don't know why he felt the need to protect Simon and Hawk—or *me*, for that matter—but . . . I guess that's where we were different. I don't—" My voice cracks, and I blink back tears. "I've never forgiven myself for what happened on that camp. For what I did."

"What do you—"

"Don't you see?" I say, my voice rising. "*I* was the one who spilt the bourbon. *I* was the one who made Tan drop the lighter. *I* was the one who ratted out my best friends and let Tan take the fall. The whole thing is my—"

"*Noah*," Eli interrupts. "That fire was not your fault. Tan bringing drugs to camp and pressuring you to do things you didn't want to do was *not* your fault. None of it was. You have to know that, right?"

I cast my eyes down to my lap. "What I *know* is that if I'd just kept my mouth shut, I wouldn't have lost my only friends in the world."

We're quiet for a moment and I feel a flutter of nerves in my chest. This conversation is far from over yet.

"Tan got kicked out of school," I go on, "and had to transfer to North, because St. Tom's and the Catholic schools don't accept expelled students. Then CHGS swept the whole thing under the rug. There were no police involved, no fines, no . . . I mean, if Tan had already been a student at North when we went on that camp, he would've been in a hell of a lot more trouble, that's for sure."

Eli purses his lips.

"The only part that *wasn't* kept quiet," I add, "was that it was *my* fault Tan got expelled. No one at school knew what happened inside that cabin—we were expressly forbidden from talking about it—but everyone blamed me anyway. Hawk and Simon started calling me 'Noah Snitchell,' and made it their mission to turn my life into a living hell. Which they were doing a pretty good job of until . . ."

Eli leans forward, just a little. "Until what?"

I take in a deep breath. "Until I met you."

THIRTY-NINE

ELI LOOKS AWAY. TAKES in a long breath.

Eventually, he turns back and says, "Why did you never tell me all this? You could have told me."

"I couldn't," I reply, too loudly, and he inches back on his cushion. "I couldn't tell you. I couldn't tell anyone. I lost *everything* because of what happened on that camp. My friends. My—"

"That doesn't mean—"

"And aside from the fact that I wasn't actually *allowed* to tell you, I didn't *want* to. Do you really think you would've wanted to hang out with me if you'd known the whole truth, right from the start? That I stabbed my best friend in the back to save myself?"

Eli just stares back at me.

"The point I'm trying to make," I say, hoping he doesn't stop me again, "is that I was lonely. *Alone.* I had my family, obviously, but you've met my mother. And my dad's never paid me much attention, and Charly was always busy with school and her friends and then she left. So, when Tan and the boys cut me out of their lives, it was literally down to me and my computer.

That's when I changed my screen name to RcticF0x. Because—"

"Because they're solitary creatures," Eli says. "I know, I googled it."

I meet his eyes for a moment, then drop my gaze to my lap.

"From the *second* you and I started playing that old sci-fi game with—"

"*Solscape*," he offers automatically.

"*Solscape*." I can't help but smile. "From the second I 'met' you . . . I fell in love with you. And I swear I'm not trying to be cheesy or dramatic, and I'm not just saying that so you'll forgive me. It's true. I've been completely and irrationally in love with you for a year and a half. And the fact that I could never do anything about it was . . . excruciating. I knew your mum had her rules—which I totally understand now, given her job and everything, but . . ."

Eli lowers his gaze and fidgets with his thumbnail.

"But I just couldn't shake the feeling. Every time we played *Spire of Dusk*, all I wanted was to see your face. To have you in the room beside me. It was unbearable. I needed more. I needed . . . I don't know, a real connection?" I groan at myself. "God, I sound like some thirty-year-old loser on an online dating app."

He looks up, but doesn't laugh.

"And then one night," I say, my mind spinning backwards in time, "you accidentally let it slip that you were in *Chicago*, and—"

"What?" he snaps. "I did not. I'm always super careful about that stuff."

I shrug. "Maybe you were tired or distracted or . . . I don't know, but it happened. You didn't spell it out, exactly, but you said, 'Rehearsal was great tonight.' And Mum had *just* gotten home from *Chicago* rehearsal, so it wasn't hard to put two and two together."

"It could have been a rehearsal for anything," Eli argues. "The fucking Ballarat Madrigal Choir."

"But it *wasn't*," I reply. "And the craziest part was, Mum had already asked me to do the show with her. She said they needed extra boys and begged me to join the cast, so . . . I decided it was fate and said yes."

Eli shakes his head. "Can we hurry up and get to the bit where you lied straight to my face for four months?"

My stomach turns.

"Once I met you," I say, feeling hot shame flood my cheeks, "I knew there was no way you'd like me back. You were so chill and confident and beautiful and I'm . . . the complete opposite of all those things."

He looks like he wants to say something but he doesn't.

"So, I decided that maybe RcticF0x could help me out for a little while. Just until I was certain you liked me back, and then I'd tell you the truth and everything would be okay. But . . . I got in too deep. I started second-guessing everything, worrying that I'd lose you *and* MagePants69 if I told you the truth. And Prisha was threatening to tell everyone what I did to Tan, and I found out your mum could literally put me in jail if she wanted to—"

"That's not how it works."

"—and *then* you dropped the Alex Di Mario bomb. How could I possibly compete with *that*? I mean, come *on*. What person in their right mind would go from Alex Di Mario to *me*?"

I run my hands through my curls. "Why do you think I started going to the gym with him?"

Eli scoffs. "That's—"

"But you have to understand, the last thing I ever wanted to do was hurt you. I just . . . I convinced myself that I could keep living this double life. That Noah Mitchell and RcticF0x could give you everything you ever wanted and you'd never have to know the truth. And for a while, it worked. I just had to be careful. There were a couple of times when I almost screwed everything up, but—"

"The arctic fox on your lock screen," Eli cuts in. "It wasn't a dog. And you don't have any cousins in Alaska."

I shake my head, hearing how ridiculous that actually sounds.

"And in the hotel room," he adds, "when you said that thing about how I didn't think sex was a big deal. I hadn't said that to *you*, I'd said it to RcticF0x."

The brick walls of the chimney close in on me.

"And when I saw *Spire of Dusk* open on *your* fucking computer in *your* fucking bedroom and you somehow convinced me it was your *sister* who was playing." His eyes are glistening with tears now, his brow creased. "I mean, how stupid could I possibly be? Were you just like, 'Fuck, this idiot will believe literally *anything* I tell him.'"

"No," I protest. "Of course not. I felt *horrible* for lying to you, but—"

"Not horrible enough to stop?"

I stare back at him, my heart pounding in my chest. I feel sick.

"I thought that if I could . . . if you'd . . ." I pause to take a steadying breath. "I thought that if I could get you to fall in love with me, everything would work out. That if we made it that far—"

"I'd be so in love with you that I couldn't possibly be angry at you for lying?" He lifts his eyebrows. "Have I remembered that correctly? From your little sticky note?"

"Eli, I *know* I was wrong. I *know* that what I wrote on that note was the most ludicrous plan in the history of the universe, but I . . . I loved you—I *love* you—and I was just so scared that you wouldn't love me back."

For a long, painful moment, neither of us says anything. Eli stares up into the shadows at the top of the chimney, taking slow, deep breaths. I stare at *him*, trying to think of something else I can say that will make him forgive me.

Finally, I say again, "I love you, Eli."

"No," he snaps, dropping his gaze to meet mine. "You don't get to say that. You don't get to lie to someone for months because you think you're not, what, pretty enough or cool enough to be with them? That you don't look enough like Alex Di Mario? Do you seriously think I only liked him because of his muscles? How shallow do you think I am?"

"That's not—"

"This was just a *game* to you, Noah." He's almost shouting now. "You think I didn't want to meet you, too? You think I didn't *dream* about bumping into you on the street and swapping numbers and going on a date and falling in love and eventually finding out we'd been gaming together for years? It would've been like something out of a *movie*. Of *course* I liked you, Noah. I fucking *loved* you."

Loved. Past tense.

I bite down on my tongue to stop the tears but it's too late.

"But I knew I could never meet you," he says, quieter now, "so I settled for the awesome thing we had online. Nothing made me as happy as logging onto *Spire of Dusk* and chatting to you in the Tav. *Nothing*. And if that was all it could ever be, so be it. My mum's rules were perfectly clear. And I wasn't going to risk losing my computer and my phone and my freedom for the rest of eternity to meet someone who might not be anything like the RcticF0x I knew online. It was too risky. It was never going to happen."

"But I *made* it happen," I say. "If that's really what you wanted, you should be thanking me right now."

"Thanking you for *catfishing* me? Are you fucking kidding me?"

"I wasn't catfi—"

"That's the literal definition of what you did, Noah. You *catfished* me."

I blink back at him. "Well . . . maybe technically . . . but . . . no one got hurt."

"But they *could* have." His green eyes flare with rage. "I could have. *You* could have. What if I was actually some creepy forty-year-old man, and I told you to meet me here at Sunnyside—alone—and you turned up and something horrible happened to you?"

"But that didn't happen, Eli," I reply, trying to keep my voice from shaking.

"But it *could* have," he stresses. "You *know* why my mum made those rules. It's not just her trying to assert her authority over her only child, it's because the world is *not a nice place*, Noah. There are people out there—" he gestures wildly to the door "—who will hurt you. People who will do horrible things to you. People who will lie to you, and manipulate you, and take advantage of you when you don't know any better. People who will ask you to send them nude photos of yourself and then post them online for the whole world to see. People who'll—"

He stops, shaking his head up at the void above us.

"Wait," I say, a chill trickling down my spine despite the warmth of the chimney. "The kid from Ballarat. The one who . . . with your mum and the police in Melbourne. It was . . . it was *you?*"

"What?" He snaps his gaze back to me, scrunching up his nose. "*No.* That's not—"

"Sorry, I—"

"Why would you—"

"I just thought . . . because you—"

"Oh, fuck's sake, Noah!" His voice echoes around the chimney. "Is that what it would take for you to see how messed up this is? For me to be the victim of some awful online crime? Would you *then* realize how truly fucked up your little plan was?"

"I didn't mean to put you in any danger, I—"

"Thought you were helping me?"

"Yes."

"By manipulating me."

"*No,* I . . . I know it was reckless, but—"

"Do you?" His eyes are wide. "Because you didn't seem to care too much about my safety until thirty seconds ago when you thought some pervert had plastered naked photos of me all over the internet."

There's silence for a long moment while we let the dust of our words settle.

"Look." Eli sighs. "When your mum's bedtime stories of choice are all about criminals and the messed-up things they've done, you learn pretty quickly not to trust people." His green eyes meet mine, and I see nothing there but disappointment. "But I trusted you, Noah. For whatever reason, I really trusted you."

My hope drains straight through the floor. "And I broke that trust. In so many ways."

"I really like you," he says. "But I can't be your boyfriend. Not now. Not with . . . everything."

I stare down at my lap, a lump building in my throat. "I know. I don't . . . I shouldn't have come here tonight. I just . . . I am so, *so* sorry, Eli."

He bites his lip and offers me a sad smile. "I know."

My eyes blur with tears and I let my head drop into my hands. But I can't do this here.

"I should—" I clear my throat, wiping my eyes. "I should go."

I push myself up to my feet, and Eli does the same.

"Will you be okay getting ho—"

"I'll be fine." I head for the door but Eli's voice stops me in my tracks.

"*Noah*," he says, and I turn back around. "That stuff that happened to you? The shit that went down on that camp? You need to stop blaming yourself for your friends' stupid mistakes."

My heart aches—literally, physically *aches*—to reach out and touch him, squeeze him, kiss his marshmallow lips. But all I can do is walk straight out the door into the snow.

RcticF0x.

Alone again.

FORTY

WHEN I WAKE UP on Sunday morning, Mum is already out. I make myself some scrambled eggs, shower, and walk straight to the bus stop. Thirty-five minutes—and a whole lot of anxious overthinking—later, I alight on the side of the road and walk another fifteen minutes to Tan's house in the bush. My shoes crunch along the gravel path to the Kandiyars' front door, the smell of eucalyptus and roses wafting by on the breeze.

I knock on the door and wait.

Now that I'm standing here, I'm not sure if I can do this.

But I need to. Eli was right.

When the door finally swings open, I'm greeted by Tan's mum's smiling face.

"Noah!" she sings. "What a surprise. It's so lovely to see you!"

"Hi, Mrs. Kandiyar," I reply sheepishly.

"Prisha is still sleeping, if you're looking for her?"

"No, I, um . . . is Tanesh home?"

"He is," she says with a warm grin, ushering me into the vast entryway. (If she knew why I was here, I'm not sure she'd be smiling.) "Go on upstairs. He's in the games room with Simon and Dylan."

As much as the thought of being in the same room as all three of them terrifies me beyond belief, I was counting on the fact that they'd be here together. Sundays at the Kandiyars' have always been a thing.

"Thanks," I reply. "Do you mind if I join them up there?"

Mrs. Kandiyar smiles and pats me on the arm. "Of course not. Go, go."

I climb the floating staircase to the first floor. I slow my breathing as I approach the upstairs lounge room, where the boys will be slouched on couches, snacking, and playing whatever the latest first-person shooter is on Tan's PlayStation.

I walk into the room and plant myself firmly in front of the TV. The guys all gawk at me as if this is some sort of glitch in reality.

"What the fuck?" Hawk says with a scowl.

Simon drops his controller into his lap. "You just got me killed, asshole."

Tan just stares up at me.

"I'm . . ." I clear my throat. "I wanted to tell you that this is over. Whatever it is you're trying to achieve—whatever you've been trying to achieve for the past *three years*—it's done. The pranks, the teasing, making me feel like total shit for no reason . . . it all stops now."

The three boys are silent.

"I know that what happened on that camp was shitty," I go on. "Worse than shitty. It was . . . and I'm sorry—" I lock eyes with Tan, whose brown cheeks have darkened with a deep blush "—that you got kicked out of CHGS. I really am. But that was *not* my fault. All I did was tell the truth." I crack my knuckles. "I don't care what you think about me, or what . . . *unspoken rules* you think I broke back then, but I do *not* deserve to be punished for the rest of my life because *you* all screwed up." I swallow the lump in my throat. I cannot cry in front of these boys right now. "I've . . . told a lot of lies lately. Lies that have backfired beyond belief. And I convinced myself it was okay because the last time I told the whole truth . . . *this* happened. But I'm done. No more lies. No more bullshit. Say what you want about me, but I will *not* apologize for being honest. Ever again."

I walk over to the door, turning back to the boys when I reach the threshold.

"It stops now," I say, feeling like I've dropped an invisible microphone on the plush carpet of Tan's upstairs lounge room. "All of it."

By the time I get home, it's after midday. I walk into the house feeling taller somehow. Stronger.

Free.

I find Mum in the lounge room, sitting on the couch, talking on the phone. She smiles up at me and mouths, "One second."

I perch on the arm of the couch opposite her as she says her goodbyes, hangs up, and places her phone facedown on the coffee table.

Rose Mitchell making her son a priority is a new thing she's trying. As of about twelve hours ago.

"Who was that?" I ask.

"It was . . ." She purses her lips. "David."

"Oh," I reply, shifting my weight on the arm of the couch. "And—" I can't believe I'm about to ask this question "—how is he?"

Mum tips her head to one side. "He's fine. He's . . . coming up to Ballarat next week for a meeting, and I said I'd—I mean, if it's okay—I said I'd meet him for coffee."

I attempt an *I'm totally cool with my freshly separated mum going on a coffee date with the man who broke up her marriage* nod, and Mum forces a smile in return.

We sit there quietly for a minute, and then, before I can stop myself, I say, "Do you not love Dad anymore?"

Mum shifts her gaze to the window behind me. Eventually, she takes a breath and turns back.

"Can we be honest with each other?" she asks.

"I guess." I shrug. "Yeah."

She smiles another sad smile. "I don't think I've loved your dad for a very long time."

Her words are like scalpels, carving out tiny pieces of my heart.

"But," she adds, "I don't want you to think it means we don't love you and Charly. Because we do. *I* do. Love you. I hope you know that."

I nod. "I know."

"In hindsight, this has been a long time coming," Mum admits. "And I clearly shouldn't have let it get to this point. I should have ended things years ago and not put us all in this ridiculous position."

"So why didn't you? End things?"

Mum draws her lips into a line, her eyes glassy. "I was scared."

"Of what?"

She scoffs. "Well, I mean, how does someone start over at my age? And who'd want anyone as—" she shakes her head, looking for the right word "—*difficult* as me?"

This is by far the most genuine interaction I've ever had with Mum. The most candid. The most . . . *real*. I have this strange urge to reach out and touch her hand. But I don't.

"Sorry," she says. "I'm supposed to be the one comforting *you*. I'm a terrible mother."

"You're not a terrible mother. You're ..."

She lifts an eyebrow. "I thought we were being honest?"

I can't help but laugh. It's dry and sharp. But it's sincere.

"Did I ever tell you what I wanted to be when I was your age?" Mum asks.

"No," I reply, and I can safely say that I've never thought about Mum's teenage ambitions. I just assumed she'd already gotten what she wanted: the husband with the fancy job, the mansion on the lake, the shiny car, the two kids (even though one of them is a total loser).

"I wanted to be a dancer," she says. "I wanted to do musicals. Professionally. I wanted to study theatre like Prisha did."

"Really?"

"Oh, yeah." Life flickers back into her face. "I was going to be a *star*." She lets out a wry chuckle. "Weren't we all."

"But . . . you didn't go to uni."

"No." She looks out the window again. "When I met your father, I fell in love harder than you would believe. I was only eighteen, and he was older. Halfway through med school. He was charming, and charismatic, and funny, and—"

"Wait," I interrupt, "you're still talking about *Dad*, right?"

"It's true," she says. "Honestly. He was everything I'd ever wanted. So . . ."

"So . . .?"

"*So*, when I had to choose between moving across the country to study theatre and staying here to be with your dad, I . . ."

"You chose him."

Mum nods. "And then, before I knew it, I had Charly. I was only twenty-one. It would be like Charly getting pregnant in, what, a year and a bit? And dropping out of uni so she could move home to raise the baby. I mean, can you *imagine* Charly with a baby?"

My sister may have come a long way since she left school, but the thought of her with a *baby* is . . .

"I was only a kid myself," Mum goes on, her eyes glazing over. "And suddenly there was this tiny person who needed me, every hour of every day. I barely had time to shower, let alone follow my Broadway dreams." She scoffs. "And your father . . . well, he's fairly old-school, as you know. He was overjoyed about the baby, and he adored her, but *he* wasn't the one trying to get her to sleep when she was crying bloody murder. He wasn't feeding her or changing her or lying awake all night because he was convinced she was going to stop breathing in her cot." She shakes the memory away and looks to me. "And then *you* came along a year later. And, then I had *two* babies. When, really . . . I don't even know if I'd wanted the first one."

Okay, I think this might be getting a little *too* honest.

Mum must notice the hurt flash across my face, because she slides across the couch and places her hand on mine.

"I'm sorry," she says gently. Almost maternally. "I don't mean that I don't want you *now*. But I wasn't ready for kids back then. Not even close. There was so much I wanted to do. So many things I wanted to see, to . . . achieve. Just for me."

I know it's not my fault that I exist, but I tell her I'm sorry, anyway.

She stares at me for a moment, searching for something in my eyes. "Charly was always so easy for me to understand," she says. "I was so much like her at school. Popular. Easygoing. Smart enough to get okay grades but not so smart that it caused me any problems. But you . . ." She draws her lips into a thin line. "You've always been a puzzle that I couldn't solve. Even when you were a baby. I could never figure out what you wanted from me. When Charly cried, I knew whether she was hungry or tired or needed a new nappy, but no matter what I did with you—no matter how much time I spent trying to figure you out—I just couldn't get it right. You were a complete mystery to me. And . . . I don't think much has changed."

Her eyes are glistening with tears now. Mine are, too.

"No matter what I do," Mum says, "I can't get anything right with you, Noah. We're too different, I think. You and I. You're so smart, so complex, so . . ." She shrugs, a weak laugh escaping her. "See? I don't even know how to explain you, let alone *understand* you."

I quickly wipe my eyes and say, "You don't need to be able to explain me, Mum. Or understand me."

"But I should be able to. I'm your *mother*."

"Well," I offer, "if it makes you feel any better, I don't understand you, either."

She smiles, her hand still on top of mine. "I'm sorry about your dad. About David. About how you found out." She cringes at her own words. "I know this is going to be rough on all of us. And I'm sorry for lying to you and Charly. I'm sorry for—my god—so many things. Too many things. Seventeen *years'* worth of things."

"I'm sorry for seventeen years' worth of things, too, Mum."

"Your father—" she starts, then lets out a sudden sob, burying her head in her hands. She takes a few breaths and then looks up, running her pinky fingers beneath her eyes. "I lost sight of who I was when I was with him, you know? I kept giving him tiny pieces of myself, one little sacrifice after another, until I . . . I lost myself. The *real* me, I mean. The original Rose Howard. Not the awful version you all know now."

"Mum, you're not—"

"Let me finish," she says. "I am so, *so* sorry, Noah. And I don't expect you to forgive me straightaway—for anything, least of all this thing with your father—but I *will* be better. I promise. I know this will sound awful, and I probably shouldn't be *this* honest, but I already feel more like myself. Because someone . . . because David *saw* me. He—" She lets out another sob, which soon turns into a full-on, shoulder-shaking cry.

We sit there like that—Mum bawling with her head in her hands, me sitting helplessly beside her—for a long, long time.

"Mum," I say eventually, and she looks up, her cheeks red and blotchy and slick with tears. "You were incredible in *Chicago*. I've been meaning to tell you for ages, but I . . . I didn't know how. Eli and Alex and I all watched you from the wings on opening night, and . . ." My eyes fill with tears again and I'm not even sure why. "You're *phenomenal*. Honestly. I was so proud to see you on that stage and . . . I know we don't see eye to eye most of the time . . . but I do see you. And maybe Dad doesn't, but I do. I see you."

Tears spill from Mum's eyes and she stands up, taking me in her arms. It's the first time we've hugged since . . . God, I don't even know when.

"Do you know what's amazing?" she asks, and I shake my head against her shoulder, my tears wicked away by the fabric of her blouse. "That you turned out the way you did, even with a mother like me."

I pull away just enough to look at her.

"I guess I must be naturally awesome," I reply with a snotty chuckle.

Mum smiles. "You know what," she says, her periwinkle blue eyes—exactly the same as mine—sparkling down at me. "I think you might be right."

FORTY-ONE

THE HORDE OF VAMPIRES closes in on my Warrior.

"*Shit,*" I say out loud, since there's no one I can message it to in the game.

Queran—the ripped and brooding leader of the Vampires of the Vale—launches a ball of shadow-flame straight at my Warrior. I dodge, and his fireball ends up taking out a bunch of vamps, instead.

"You shall pay!" he shrieks, his evil laugh echoing in my headphones.

Until this very second, I've managed reasonably well in the game by myself. But this battle is a wonderful reminder why *Spire of Dusk* is not designed to be a single-player game. But that's my only option now. I'm doomed to be a single player for the rest of my life.

But I *will* finish this game.

I have to finish it.

"Noah?" Mum calls from the hallway and I hit pause.

I swivel around in my Ergolove Destroyer. "Yeah?"

"I'm off to yoga," she says, poking her head through my door, "but I'll be back in time for dinner. Do you want to order us some Thai?"

"Sure. The usual?"

"Perfect." She disappears. A second later, her head pops back into the doorway. "Did Eli . . .?"

"Reply?" I shake my head. "Nope."

She sighs. "Give it some time. He'll reply."

"Have fun at yoga," I say pointedly.

She takes the hint and trots off down the hall. "See you soon!"

It's been a month since the closing night of *Chicago*, and things at home are . . . weird. But also kind of nice. It's just Mum and me in the house now. And Mr. Nibbles, but he's not much for conversation. Dad is letting Mum keep the house in the divorce, which I thought was incredibly generous until I found out he'd already bought himself a new house that—surprise, surprise—backs directly onto the golf course.

He's nothing if not predictable.

I had lunch with him the weekend after closing night, which was awkward to the point of being almost comedic. The conversation was stilted and robotic and I could tell he was supremely uncomfortable talking to me about anything to do with Mum, their marriage, their impending divorce, or anything that remotely involved his or my feelings. And I know it was *Mum* who had an affair for months, not him, but I still would've liked to hear the words "I'm sorry" come out of his mouth. Sorry for not being present enough, sorry for not putting as much time and energy into his wife and kids as he did his job and his golf game.

I'm definitely not saying I'm okay with what Mum did, but . . . who am I to judge, after everything I did to Eli. And she was right: I *don't* understand what she's been going through. Hopefully, I never do. But I do know what it's like to feel alone. When Mum felt that way, she started sleeping with another consenting adult behind her husband's back. When *I* felt alone, I decided to go undercover in an amateur musical in order to meet my secret crush and force him to love me.

Objectively speaking, which one of those situations is more ridiculous?

(Don't answer that.)

In the four weeks since closing night, a total of *seven* people have spoken to me at school. Some of them, on more than one occasion. Now, I'm not saying I'm anywhere near having *friends* at CHGS—because who wants to make a new friend when there's only two months of classes left?—but someone asking what books you're borrowing while you're waiting in line at the library makes a surprising difference to your day. Especially when you've spent the past three years being either ignored or ridiculed for no reason.

I also received a *very* unexpected message the week after *Chicago* closed. When I saw the notification pop up, I legitimately almost had a panic attack. It took me *two days* to open the message, but when I finally did . . .

Hey, Noah, Tan wrote. **Prisha told me about your mum and your boyfriend and everything. Sorry, mate. And I'm sorry about Hawk and Simon and all their shit. I should have told**

them to stop ages ago. I should have done a lot of things. But . . . whatever. I hope you're doing okay.

My reply was pretty simple: **Thanks, Tan. I hope you're doing okay, too.**

Maybe I should've written more. Maybe I will one day. But not today.

And then there's Alex. I've been going to the gym with him three times a week, so I guess you could officially call us "gym buddies." The most unlikely gym buddies on the planet, but still . . . it's pretty cool. I did ask him if he wanted to give *Spire of Dusk* a go, but he politely declined. I believe his exact words were, "Dude, I'm not really into all that medieval fairy stuff," which is an entirely inaccurate description of the game, but, you know, choose your battles.

My phone buzzes on my bed and I lean over to grab it, having to push Mr. Nibbles aside to find it.

Charly: **Did Eli reply?**

No, I write back. Apparently, it's the question on all of our minds. **He's not going to reply.**

Hang in there, bub. Stranger things have happened. One time, I legitimately vomited all over a guy on our first date (bad sashimi) and I thought he'd never be able to look at me again. And let me tell you, he much more than LOOKED at me on our second date.

I wrinkle my nose. **Gross, Char.**

See you next week, she replies. **Can't wait to squeeze you.**

You too. Love-heart emoji.

I scroll through my messages and stare down at the last thing I sent Eli, which was from exactly one week ago:

I miss you.

I don't know why I sent it. I know there's no chance of us getting back together, I just . . . I missed him. I *miss* him. So much. More than I thought it was possible to miss anyone. But I guess, when you screw up—really, truly screw up—you just have to live with the consequences.

I lock my phone and toss it back onto the bed. Mr. Nibbles hisses at me.

"Sorry, Nibsy," I say, before turning back to *Spire of Dusk*.

I hit un-pause, then click my mouse frantically, slicing off my enemies' heads, one after another. There's a sudden break in their advances, and I launch my Warrior through the air towards Queran. He lifts his arms to cast a spell, and it's the exact opportunity I need. My Warrior's axe swings down through the air, cleaving the vampire's body clean in two.

"Holy shit!" I throw my hands in the air.

I did it. I actually freaking did it.

I'm too stunned to lower my arms as the screen flashes with golden light, and High Priestess Leora appears where Queran stood only moments ago.

"You have slain the leader of the Vampires of the Vale," she says, her voice like the ringing of a bell. *"And for that, the Lightseekers will be forever grateful."*

"Yeah, you'd wanna be," I say to my screen, finally dropping my hands to my lap.

"But your power is too great," she goes on, and I feel my brow crease. *"We cannot risk losing the peace you have restored in the Three Kingdoms."*

"I'm sorry, what?"

"Everything in life hangs in a delicate balance, and something that once bolstered peace can be the very next thing to destroy it. Your existence is now a danger to the Light, and to us all."

She raises her hands in front of her chest, her many talismans glowing yellow. I double click on the ground on the other side of the screen to make my Warrior leap out of the way, but the interface is locked.

"We are truly sorry if you feel deceived," Leora says, *"but we thank you for your assistance."*

She hurls a golden ball of shimmering light at my Warrior, and I watch helplessly as it slams straight into his chest.

The screen flashes blood red.

YOU HAVE BEEN SLAIN

"No!" I cry out, dropping my head into my hands. "No, no, no."

I made it to the end. I slew the vampires—hordes and hordes of vampires, including a fucking vampiric *dragon*. I did exactly what I was told. And that wannabe Galadriel played me like a harp.

I let out a pained groan.

Karma sure is a poetic little bitch, sometimes.

The red screen fades to black and then, after a moment, my Warrior respawns in the Lažov's Keep town square.

And my heart stops dead.

Because standing beside the fountain at the center of the square is an avatar I know all too well . . .

The fiery-haired Bard.

My eyes flick to the top left of the monitor.

Players in session:

1. RcticF0x

2. MagePants69

I squint up at the screen. "What the . . .?"

I must have somehow missed the *<player joining>* message in the midst of all my vampire slaying . . . .

MagePants69 <hey stranger>

My stomach flips.

RcticF0x <um . . . hi?>

MagePants69 <did you just die?>

I sit up straighter in my chair and rub my eyes. Is this actually happening?

RcticF0x <leora killed me. turns out she's a dirty double-crosser>

MagePants69 <damn you fake cate blanchett>

There's silence—no messages, I mean—for a moment, and I reach over to check my phone. Eli still hasn't replied.

MagePants69 <you wanna go to the tav?>

This has to be a dream, right? Or I literally died when my Warrior died and I'm currently in the afterlife?

MagePants69 <???>

RcticF0x <sorry. yeah. if you want>

MagePants69 <i want>

By the time our avatars have taken their seats by the fire in the Tav, my stomach has curled itself into a ball and climbed up into my throat, and my heart has decided this is a good time to test some fresh new beats.

"*So, where are we, exactly?*" MagePants69's Bard asks. Her sweet, computerized voice is music to my ears.

"*Lažov's Keep,*" my Warrior replies.

"As in, the Lažov's Keep from Lažov's Keep II: Spire of Dusk?"

I type the command for \</laugh> and my Warrior lets out a brash guffaw. *"Correct."*

The Bard takes a sip of her ale, and my fingers hover over the keys. I'm not sure what's going on here, and I don't want to get my hopes up, but . . . I have to ask.

"Did you get my message?"

"I did," the Half-Elf replies.

"And?"

She flips her braid over her shoulder. *"Well, I'm here, aren't I?"*

Warmth swells in my chest as I suck in a breath through my nose.

It's not an *I miss you, too,* but it's definitely not nothing.

"But just so we're clear," the Bard goes on, *"I'm not here for Noah Mitchell. I'm here exclusively for RcticF0x. I'm here to finish what we started."*

Her words dispel some of the fuzziness in my chest. I lean back in my chair and crack my knuckles.

It's not even remotely how I hoped this conversation would play out, but . . . *"Okay."*

"That's it?" she says. *"Okay?"*

"As Noah Mitchell who wants more than anything to atone for the way he treated Eli Callaghan? No, that's not it. But right now? As RcticF0x? Yeah, that's all."

The Bard raises her orange eyebrows. *"Good."*

I can't believe I'm actually sitting here in the Tav with MagePants69. It feels so normal. So *nice.*

I blink away my tears.

pose.

"Actually," I say eventually, *"I have a better idea . . ."*

I wait for a moment, my fingers held lightly on the keys. Am I really about to say this?

"How would you feel about starting over?"

The Bard's eyes go wide. *"Sorry, I just hallucinated for a second, I thought you said 'starting over.' "*

"*Think about it,*" my Warrior says, leaning forward across the table in the Tav. "*A fresh campaign. RcticF0x and MagePants69, back to level one. Where it all began.*"

"*Uh,*" MagePants69 replies, "*have you lost your mind? We're literally almost across the finish line.*"

I type the command for </shrug> and my Warrior lifts his hulking shoulders. "*I think it's our only option.*"

I move my cursor to the top right of the screen and click on the little cog icon, taking us both into the game settings. I tap *CAMPAIGN SETTINGS* and drag the cursor to the bottom of the drop-down menu, where it says *NEW CAMPAIGN.*

"*Wait!*" Eli's Bard says, holding up her hand like a stop sign. I've never seen that command before. "*This is ludicrous. We've put so much time and energy into this campaign.*"

"*I know,*" my Warrior says with a nod. "*But we got this far once, we can do it again. But differently. Better.*"

I sit and wait for MagePants69 to reply.

Time slows. My pulse races.

"*Noah,*" the Bard says. Hearing her say my name—my real name—makes my eyes prick with tears again. "*Are we really doing this?*"

I type my reply before I can talk myself out of it.

"*You can trust me, m'lady.*"

I click my mouse emphatically and the interface goes black. Seconds later, three words appear in glowing, gilded letters in the middle of the screen:

STARTING NEW CAMPAIGN

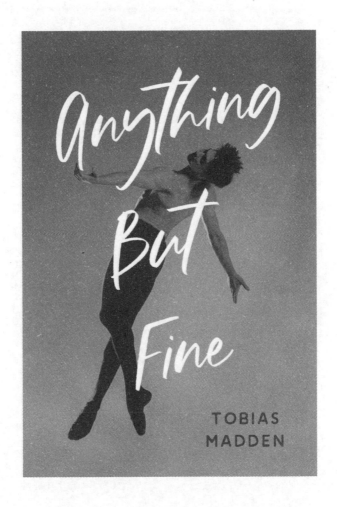

ACKNOWLEDGMENTS

EVERYONE SAYS THAT YOUR "sophomore" novel is difficult to write, and it turns out they weren't wrong! There are so many people who helped bring Noah's story to life, so I'd like to thank some of them here.

My brilliant literary agent, Claire Friedman, who always has my back, at every step of the way.

The team at Penguin Teen Australia, including but not limited to (as Noah would say) my incomparable publisher, Zoe Walton; my wonderful editor, Mary Verney; my publicist extraordinaire, Tina Gumnior; my marketing guru, Laura Hutchinson; Tijana Aronson; Abby Wilson; and everyone else who played a part—big or small—in the production and distribution of this book!

My stellar US publishing team—Tamara Grasty, Lauren Cepero, Lizzy Mason, and everyone else at Page Street YA. You're all amazing!

Reece Carter, for not only being a wonderful first reader but for the constant writerly chats (aka venting); Prashanti Middling, whose words of wisdom—both before I started writing the manuscript and again when it was complete—were essential in creating these characters and their world; the wonderful community of readers on Instagram and Twitter who have supported and encouraged me on this long and winding journey, and spruiked my books to everyone they know; all the incredible booksellers, librarians, and teachers in Australia and New Zealand who have helped my stories find the people they're meant to find (mid-pandemic, which was no small task!); my former team at Bloomsbury Australia, who were (and still are) endlessly encouraging; and Ash Collins, for being the absolute best for the last 18 years.

I'd like to give an extra-special shout-out to the Ballarat Light Opera Company and Ballarat Lyric Theatre, who gave this budding young theatre nerd a home, all those years ago, and showed me where a life on stage could take me. I don't think I truly understood myself until I started performing, and the casts, crews, and creative teams of *Oliver* (2001), *Half a Sixpence* (2002), and *Chicago* (2004)—all led by the inimitable Fred Fargher—will forever have a place in my heart.

A huge thank you to the Assettas and the Maddens. I honestly could not ask for a better family, and your support means more than you'll ever know. To my big brother, Judd, who introduced me to the world of PC gaming (and then hogged the computer all day and night). To my dad, Peter, who was the complete opposite of Noah's dad, aside from his profound love of golf. To my mum, Vicki, who definitely was not the inspiration for Overbearing Rose, and who is the best mother anyone could ever ask for. To Ollie, my darling boy, who has finally learned that when daddy is at his desk, it's time for snoozing on the couch.

And to my beautiful, perfect husband, Daniel. What started out as a "showmance" during our Australian tour of *CATS* is now the marriage of my dreams. I couldn't imagine doing any of this—any of life—without you and your love. Thank you. I love you.

ABOUT
THE AUTHOR

Originally from Ballarat, Tobias worked for ten years as a dancer, touring Australia and New Zealand with musicals such as *Mary Poppins*, *CATS*, *Singin' in the Rain*, and *Guys and Dolls*. He now lives in Sydney with his husband, Daniel, and their Cavoodle, Ollie. Tobias's debut novel, *Anything But Fine*, was shortlisted for Book of the Year for Older Children in the 2022 Australian Book Industry Awards. In 2019, Tobias edited and published *Underdog: #LoveOzYA Short Stories*, which featured his first published work, "Variation." He also co-wrote the cabaret show *Siblingship*, which played to sold-out audiences around Australia. Tobias is a passionate member of the #LoveOzYA and LGBTQ+ communities, and he currently works part-time in theatre marketing.